PRAISE FOR *UNITY*

"Imagine *Neuromancer* and *Lilith's Brood* conceived a baby while listening to My Chemical Romance and then that baby was adopted by *Ghost in the Shell* and *Blue Submarine no. 6*. The baby's name is *Unity*."
—Meredith Russo, author of *If I Were Your Girl*

"Breakneck pacing, non-stop action, and delightfully-damaged characters combine with some of the most intricate and clever worldbuilding I've seen in ages to make this an incredibly memorable debut."
—Sam J. Miller, author of *The Art of Starving*

"*Unity* is a wild firefight of a novel. But amidst the vivid dystopian worldbuilding—the undersea metropolises and scorched badlands—and all the breakneck action is something deeper, a philosophically and emotionally resonant exploration of what it means to carry multiplicities of ourselves, our myriad shades of being. Elly Bangs is a writer of both kaleidoscopic imagination and deep literary empathy, a cyberpunk star in the making."
—Omar El Akkad, author of *American War*

★"A dystopian science fiction novel about what it means to be human, and what it takes to retain and reclaim one's humanity."
—*Foreword*, starred review

"*Unity* is a killer debut by a thrilling new writer. Trust me, you're all going to be hearing a lot about Elly Bangs and this gleaming and gritty world she's created. And cyberpunk fans? Put down the game controller and read this now. This is the real stuff."
—Daryl Gregory, author of *We Are All Completely Fine* and *Spoonbenders*

UNITY
ELLY BANGS

TACHYON
SAN FRANCISCO

Unity
Copyright © 2021 by Elly Bangs

Interior and cover design by Elizabeth Story

Tachyon Publications LLC
1459 18th Street #139
San Francisco, CA 94107
415.285.5615
www.tachyonpublications.com
tachyon@tachyonpublications.com

Series editor: Jacob Weisman
Editor: Jaymee Goh

Print ISBN: 978-1-61696-342-2
Digital ISBN: 978-1-61696-343-9

Printed in the United States by Versa Press, Inc.

First Edition: 2021
9 8 7 6 5 4 3 2 1

For N.

PART I:
UNDERWORLD

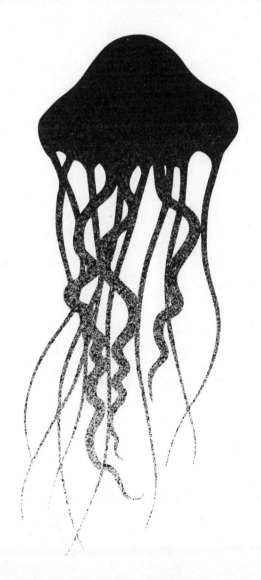

I

This is the first thing I remember when I begin to cohere in unity: a woman standing at a railing, peering down into the vats at the final bottom of Bloom City—and a man in a cramped air transport lavatory, watching his reflection in the scuffed plastic mirror point a wave pistol at its own head.

Across ten thousand kilometers of distance I remember both these scenes, simultaneous with each other: how the beat of the compressors throbbed in her bones; how the power cell hummed and exhaled ozone when he primed the weapon to fire; how every nerve in her last remaining body drew taut as she braced herself to fall; how his reflection gazed back so stoically as to seem already dead, but his pulse was only quickening as he lay his finger on the trigger.

Just as he braced to fire, the woman swung her legs over the railing and leaned forward so that it was only one hand, then one finger, holding her back from the drop. She knew the machinery would leave no trace: in minutes, her body would be minced and spread thin across the ocean floor, unified with the trash and tailings. Meanwhile, the man imagined that whoever found his corpse would never grasp the irony: that after every narrowly dodged killing shot of every battle of every war, it would be his own weapon that finally did him in.

These two people were equally convinced of their own insignificance. Each could name only one person who might miss them. Neither knew then what I'm startled to realize now: that if he had pushed, or if she had let go, nothing would be left of the world today but a uniform ocean of lifeless quicksilver, the ghosts of billions dead, and the single lonely intellect of my lost sibling. Nothing else would have survived the last war.

I used to believe I could never have any one beginning, but in the eerie symmetry of that moment, I know I've found it. This is where all the threads of my memory start—because the story of these two people is my story too. Because the events of the past five days will forever define the person I'm becoming.

Because whatever else it is, and however hopeless it may seem to me as it all weaves itself, scene by scene, into the fabric of my being—

This is the story of how I survived.

How we'll all survive.

DANAE

We lay still, clutching each other in the muggy heat of my three-by-three meter coffin apartment, waiting to see if the world would end: Naoto and I, our complicated friendship transformed by the pressure into a desperate kind of love for as long as it took the news to come in that doomsday had been called off again. Epak and Norpak were pulling back their subs and drones to their respective corners of the Pacific, settling back into their stalemate. They were standing down their nanoweapon stockpiles—and in that first deep breath, my whole cluttered mind snapped into a focus as clear and sharp as broken glass: for five years now I'd been rotting in exile, here in the sweltering submarine underbelly of Bloom City. Nothing up on dry land—not the strife and desolation, not the Keepers, not even my own guilt—scared me more than the prospect of trying to make it through a sixth.

So we cleaned ourselves up as best we could. Then we went to meet the mercenary who I hoped would get me out of that claustrophobic city, shepherd me across a thousand kilometers of wasteland, and carry what little was left of me home.

"On second thought, maybe I should go alone," I whispered to Naoto on the elevator up to the lower habitat level. "The favor I called in to arrange this meeting isn't worth much. There's a very strong possibility it's a trap."

He was still tying back his unkempt black hair. "If it's a trap, you might need someone to get you out." He gave me a long look. "Are you sure you're up to this?"

"I have to be."

"You don't look well."

I rolled up the sleeve of my coveralls and stabbed a single-use Pascalex injector into my arm, and he did the same; even this short ascent would take us from four atmospheres down to three. I answered, "You've never seen me well."

His eyes were bloodshot from more than the pressure change when he met mine, and my skin burned with a fresh wave of guilt: that he'd spent the whole time we'd known each other watching me slowly fall apart; that we'd likely never see each other again after tomorrow; and that I knew, however well he hid it, how much more he wanted from me than I had to give. In some other world, we could have been simply in love. Maybe we could have been one person. In this universe I was too broken for the former and too damned for the latter.

The doors reeled open, and we tugged our hoods up and put our heads down to walk: past the Medusas guarding the elevator with machetes; on into the shoulder-to-shoulder foot traffic chattering to itself about the ceasefire; past one of Naoto's own murals, wherein waves of blue seawater morphed symbolically into yellow-gold fusion energy; onward into the perpetual aquapolitan dusk, thick with moisture and holographic light, to the booth in the smoke bar my contact had named.

I froze when I saw the man who sat there waiting for us.

"What is it?" Naoto asked, reading my face. "Danae? Do you know him?"

"No, it's—"

"What?"

I shook my head. Working for Medusa Clan, I'd met any number of people who made a career of violence and death. Most of them, like Duke, put more work into the spectacle of their brutality than the brutality itself: they wore necklaces of human molars, swelled their muscles with carcinogenic gene therapies, tattooed their faces and pierced their bones. Waiting there in the glowing smoke was a man who did everything he could to put up a clean façade, but the violence still shone through it. The scars on his scalp couldn't all be combed over. The skin graft around his eye and cheek was seamlessly bonded, but it reflected the wrong shade of brown under the harsh bluish lights here. I shuddered with the instinctive knowledge that the sight of him had been other people's last—but what had stopped me in my tracks, what Naoto struggled to read in my expression, wasn't fear. It was an eerie certainty that I had seen this man before.

I had. But I would be very far from Bloom City by the time I realized which eyes I had seen him through.

"Seats taken?" I shouted over the din, and the mercenary affected casual disinterest. The video panes all blasted dissonant Medusan anthems and told us the news in five languages at once; this was the closest thing to privacy that could be had in Bloom City. Naoto pulled up a chair at my side, facing backward to watch the crowd.

"You think this truce with Norpak will hold?" the mercenary mused, never making eye contact.

"I do. I hope so. I . . . I've been hoping things would calm down enough for me to take a little vacation."

I tried to keep a straight face. As if Medusa Clan ever let its tech servants leave the city on a whim. As if they wouldn't break both my legs for talking about it.

"Getting some fresh air?" His real question was clear: *Going to the surface, or another aquapolis?*

I'd spent enough time in the underworld to learn how to transact in the common language of thinly-veiled code, but until now I'd only played this game with techs and fixers and toecutters of the lowest order, and never for stakes this high. I enunciated carefully, "Yes. Somewhere good and dry." *Inland.* "Where I can take my mind off my work. Where my boss won't be able to reach me."

The mercenary took a contemplative pull from a hookah that rattled in the throbbing noise: knowing now that Medusa Clan considered me its property. Knowing what he'd be getting himself into if he helped me escape. He said only, "Sounds nice."

In the corner of my eye, Naoto gave me a subtle nod to signal that the leg-breakers didn't appear to be coming for us yet. So far so good.

"It's too bad that even with a ceasefire, security will stay tight for a while," the mercenary said. "Long waits. Invasive luggage searches." Translation: *will you be smuggling anything besides yourself?*

"I travel light," I replied. "All I need is a good travel guide. The kind that can take me far off the beaten path. Keep me out of harm's way."

He took in another mouthful of smoke. "Smart. Especially if you end up in a seat with no extra legroom." Likely translation: *will you be content to make your unsanctioned exit in the usual way, i.e. stuffed inside a deuterium drum and clenching an O2 cannister between your knees?*

"Yes."

"Anything you want to steer clear of, besides . . . work?"

There was no code for my answer. How could I explain the Keepers, here and now? My pause drew out dangerously long before I swallowed and said "Evangelists."

His eyes never left the video panes, but I could sense his attention like a faint, chilly wind. Finally he said "I was thinking of taking a trip myself. What's a good getaway this time of year?"

"Oh, I . . . I couldn't say."

"There must be some specific sights worth seeing."

I worried about refusing to tell him where I was going, but I worried a lot more about the next detail: "I have tickets to a show. The problem is . . . it's at dusk on the equinox. Only three days from now."

The mercenary didn't respond.

I cleared my throat and continued. "Which means I'll need to be on my way by tomorrow night, I think, at the latest. No matter what, I absolutely have to reach my destination within three days. After that there's no point in going at all."

He nodded, but I sensed something wrong. His icy composure waned for a moment.

"What do you think? Do you think I can make it there by show-time?"

"Yes. Tomorrow. That's probably a good time."

I couldn't help the suspicion that a mere twenty-four hours was too long a wait for him, but it went against all the sense I had about a negotiation like this. And why hadn't he brought up his price? I was afraid to wonder what could be going on now behind all those fine scars. I shared a forced smile with Naoto and carefully ventured, "A vacation can be expensive these days."

The mercenary sighed. "Can be."

"I've put away some money for it. I want to use it all. However long it'll last."

"How much?"

"Nineteen thousand Epak squid. It's all I have with me, but if it's not enough, I'll have more once I get there. Wealthy family."

He shook his head. "It should be enough."

I tried not to look stunned; I'd braced for him to ask for at least fifty thousand more upon arrival. I swallowed hard and said, "I should go pack, then. But . . . are you still thinking about traveling too? Maybe we'll run into each other along the way."

"It's a small world."

I never saw him put it there, but I noticed a paper napkin on the table in front of me, folded in half, indented with writing. I shoved it into my pocket.

"Let's go already," Naoto told me through a forced smile.

I took one last look at the mercenary to stare at something hanging from a string around his neck. Fine, twisted metal, glittering through the shadows we left him in.

We kept our heads down the whole way back to the elevators. My mind raced to think I'd actually gotten away with it: bought myself a trip out of this sweltering hole in the ocean without the Medusas knowing.

As if on cue, I felt the hand close around my shoulder.

He loomed over me, his face a mask of tattoos, two silver rings punched through his jaw: a Medusan lieutenant. One of Duke's own men. He held his shard in my face to ask, "Who is this?"

Naoto hung back, watching in horror. My heart seemed to stop. I forced myself to look, certain I was doomed—but the image in the glass wasn't the mercenary. It wasn't anyone I'd ever seen. Pale, bald, with a blue corporate tattoo on his right cheekbone.

"I said, who is this man?"

"I don't know," I said, sincerely. "No idea."

The lieutenant studied me. "He's been asking for you. Five times this week. He keeps coming around the elevators, wanting into the barracks module. Won't identify himself."

In the crowd behind him, Naoto visibly braced himself and reached for something in his pocket. I managed to furtively glare at him and shake my head.

The Medusa added, "If this man comes around again, who knows what will happen to him."

"Who knows," I agreed, and managed to hold myself upright until the elevator doors closed, leaving Naoto and me blessedly alone.

"What the hell was that?" he asked. "Were we made?"

"I don't think so." I opened the now sweat-stained napkin note with a shaking hand. Inside was a shard address, a bank account number, and the words *1800 HRS, AIRLOCK 38*. I sighed with mixed relief and said, "I think this might actually work. What about your scans in the bar? Did you get a clear read on our merc?"

He plugged his shard into the scanner clipped to his belt. Holographic light danced through the glass in his palm.

"Crystal," he said, but his eyes narrowed.

"What is it?"

"There's a beast of a wave rifle tucked under that baggy coat of his, plenty of electromag armor and energy storage in the lining, knives, odds and ends, but . . . he has no cybernetics. None at all. Not even an aim-assist."

"Are you sure? Nothing? Could he have tricked the scanner?"

"There's no tech in that man's body. That's for certain. The question is, are you sure he's a real mercenary? We don't know this isn't part of some twisted long con to bust the emigrant network for the Medusas. I've never heard of a mercenary without at least an aim-assist."

"No," I said, feeling over my memory of him. "He's a mercenary. I'm sure of that much." That shiver of vague recognition passed through me again. I looked hard at Naoto and asked, "But what's your gut feeling? Can I trust him?"

He hesitated. After a moment, he frowned and shook his head, and we stood in a tense and awkward silence while the pressure around us slowly, steadily mounted.

The inside of the elevator doors was stenciled with the Medusas' icon: a stylized jellyfish with tentacles symmetrically splayed, poised to sting. The Clan's namesake was an old symbol of survival. The more poisoned and anoxic the oceans had become, the more the jellies had thrived; a hundred years since the last wild shark had cast its bones to the lightless bottom, the medusa was the only apex predator left in nature. I traced the sharp lines of red and purple, taking them in, trying to believe I'd be free of that venomous embrace after tomorrow—and then the doors slid open to admit us back into the barracks module.

I started to step out, but Naoto touched my shoulder to ask, "How are you holding up, Danae?"

I was a sweating, shuddering mess. I dreaded to worry him even more than I already had, but I had no one else to tell and it was too much to keep to myself.

"There are a lot of ways I could die between here and Redhill," I said.

He showed me his best forced smirk. "You said you're what, ten thousand years old?"

"Twelve," I whispered.

He snorted a laugh. "So that makes you the most mature, world-wise human being I've ever met by a factor of, what, two hundred? You must have faced death many times. I'd have thought you'd be yawning at it by now."

He was trying to comfort me, but I couldn't help but cringe and tell him, "I never had to think about death when I was whole. I always had other bodies. If anything, I'm *less* adapted to mortality than you are."

"Right." He winced at himself. He hesitated and said, "So maybe I can't know what it's like for you. I'm no one and you're everyone. I was just trying to say . . . that if anyone can get through this, I know you will."

I cupped his cheek. "You aren't nobody. And I'm going to miss you more than words can say."

He reached out and wiped the tears from my face. I knew how much he wanted to tell me to stay here with him, but he was better than that. He knew I had to go—and I felt the warmth of all his misplaced admiration spreading through my chest like liquor: him loving me not as what I was, but as what I had been, could've been, yearned to be. I'd forgotten just how badly I needed that.

I grabbed the collar of his coat and pulled us together and kissed him violently, and he clutched at my back and moaned—and we all but helplessly slid down the elevator's metal walls and collapsed into its corner, faces greased with sweat and tears and saliva, heart-broken and desperate for touch. The doors reeled shut.

Home.

God help me, I was going home.

ALEXEI

I didn't know what about me had broken in Antarka, but I went about fixing it the only way I knew how: I went looking for a job.

That was all I needed to be well again, I thought—the exercise of my skills in the pursuit of their mastery. The Major taught us that the only true happiness is what a knife feels when it cuts well. So I stumbled through the cramped halls of plastic and rust, to the dim space behind the upper plankton pumps, where Stitches still loitered in the stink and noise, doling out the work no one else wanted. It was just like old times: as if I were still the new kid who'd never taken a breath of pressurized air before; who'd descended into Bloom City with nothing but a borrowed rifle and the readiness to trade other people's lives for a weekly wage. Just like back then, I took the first job he offered me: what turned out to be smuggling one haggard and high-strung thirty-something woman out of Medusan indenture and up onto land.

Somewhere good and dry, she'd said. *Where my boss won't be able to reach me.* If there was any such place—assuming her boss was the same as mine. I checked the time and dimly remembered Empress Dahlia was expecting me. She'd killed men for lesser slights than missing an appointment with her, but there was nothing I wanted less right now than to be lavished with her approval.

This new job was far out of my element—I was a destroyer, not a protector—but I had expected to feel at least a little better once

I committed to the task. I thought all the noise in my head would quiet down; the alien white-heat that had lodged in the center of my chest since Antarka would finally cool. Neither happened. Nothing changed.

I tried to concentrate on the money instead. If not the paltry sum this new job would pay, then all the squid Medusa Clan was steadily funneling into my accounts for the work I'd just completed. More than enough to retire, if I wanted—but there was no solace in that thought either. On my way out of the bar, I tipped the staff a thousand-squid bill, just to see how it felt. I felt nothing.

My feet dragged under me as I passed one of the habitat level's few windows. Dim lights trailed away into the murky brine, and I caught myself thinking compulsively about finding my way to an airlock and welcoming the black Pacific into my lungs—but my blurry reflection in the black mirror looked too much like the Major, and I knew what he would say if he could see me. I could hear his voice, dripping with disdain: *Any weapon must be kept in proper repair. The mind is no different, Alexei.* His ghost had never left me. It wouldn't allow me to simply kill myself.

So I slid into the frayed seat of an autopharmacy booth and closed the plastic door behind me. Before it finally, mercifully slid its needle into my vein, the machine asked me where my troubles began. I didn't know how to answer. I wondered if the algorithm asked everyone the same absurd question before dispensing the anti-depressants and anti-agoraphobia and anti-suicidal-ideation drugs that likely kept all of Bloom City on its feet. In 2159 AD, who on this Earth could remember the moment their troubles began? No one remembers being born.

My shard rang in my pocket again as I stumbled back into the crowd and let it carry me. It was Kat calling again. I imagined her in her self-contained pod somewhere in the ocean, in her nest of holograms and cables and interfaces, knowing something was terribly wrong with me, but not what—and until I knew myself, I couldn't find the will to answer her. I could only keep walking and try to give the drugs time to work.

"Stop," barked a voice from behind me. "Pay the toll."

I looked up to find the crowds gone, replaced by two boys no more than fifteen, brandishing sharpened rebar. Their armbands told me they were new recruits into Medusa Clan. It took me a look around to understand I'd been walking a long time in my daze; I'd unthinkingly stumbled into the blacklight district.

"Pay the toll!" the kids shouted, louder, in case I was hard of hearing; the pressure changes ruptured a lot of eardrums in this town. "Empty your pockets! That shiny necklace thing. Give it. Now!"

"I can't," I heard myself mutter. "It . . . means too much to me."

"Pay the toll! Last warning!"

I could all but see the gears turning in their minds. They'd only planned to intimidate me, but it wasn't working—and now that they were close enough to see the rifle hanging under my coat, they'd realized their own dilemma: if they took even one step backward, I'd be too far away to stab, but I might still shoot. They could only retain control of the situation now by going in for the kill.

I watched them work it out. Watched them brace themselves to lunge. Saw, in my mind's eye, the rusty metal popping through the flimsy material of my electromagnetic armor and sliding wetly out the other side of me, and in that image, so suddenly—

I exhaled. My mind stilled. The fire in my chest dimmed. For the first time since Antarka, I was at peace.

"Little polyps," said a third voice, melodic and resonant, stopping the kids in their tracks and banishing my moment of clarity. Rebar clattered to the ground. Duke, second-in-command of all Medusa Clan, asked, "Who's this you're bothering?"

The recruits stood frozen at attention, shivering in the humid heat.

"Who?" Duke barked. The horrid leather of his jacket creaked audibly with his every step closer. He stomped his boot on the steel floor, making them jump.

"Don't know."

"You don't know," Duke echoed. "You stalked without knowing the prey. He could be dear to the Clan, for all you know. A beloved friend to Dahlia herself. You don't even know you're face to face with the most efficient human killing machine in your Empress's entire arsenal, do you? You're lucky I was here to save you."

He wrapped one oversized, gene-hacked hand around the back of each of the kids' necks and squeezed, lifting them onto their toes like kittens. Then he tossed them down the corridor to his underlings, muttering, "Cage. Four days." He turned back to me, squeezed my shoulder in his huge palm, and said, "Alexei, Alexei. You were due in Dahlia's keep over an hour ago. It's not like you to miss such an invitation. When surveillance picked you up, I thought I'd better come find you myself. See if you had your head on straight."

He crackled his knuckles, loud as a snapping spine.

"I'm fine," I said.

"You're superb, is what you are. Antarka was your finest work yet." He smacked me hard on the back and started walking me forcefully back down the corridor.

"Oh," I heard myself say.

"But I know that look. Something in here—" he stabbed a thick finger into my ribs above my heart— "is giving you pain all of a sudden, isn't it? As if you were a little child again. It happens to even to the strong, now and then. Lucky for you I know every cure there is, and you've come to the right part of town to receive treatment. Remind me: you swing both ways, don't you?"

"Not tonight," I said, outside of myself.

He squeezed me tighter and made some hand-signs to one of his underlings as we approached the plastic flap at the door of the love hotel. "Cheer up, Alexei! Thanks to you, Norpak has no first-strike capability. There is to be no war, you understand? No Gray Day. Not one city will be reduced to nanobot pudding tonight, and in the morning you'll wake up and realize forty-six lives is such a small price to pay for one good move in this game."

I managed to meet his eyes. "Is that true? Is this peace real?"

He lowered his voice to say, "There was never going to be a war. The nanoweapons race, the brinksmanship, it's all the game we play to keep the other side in check. Dahlia's great *Pax Epak*."

"Then what was it all for?"

But his boots were already pounding away down the corridor behind me, his human-leather jacket changing color in the passing ultraviolet. His underling was parting the plastic flap for me, pointing my way into the red smoky light beyond, and her orders were written in the look she gave me: until Duke told her otherwise, I was not allowed to be alone. Not to piss. Not to sleep.

My shard rang in my pocket, and this time I was too dazed not to answer.

For a long moment there was no sound but Kat's ragged breath, scrambled into uneven bursts of static.

I skipped our usual catchphrases. "I'm sorry."

"I didn't know if you were hurt," she shouted. "One moment everything was fine, mission nearly complete. Then you were out of contact. All feeds dead. You've never done that to me before. You cannot fucking do that to me, Lex."

I said nothing. The Medusan woman's cold, patient gaze never left me. Music throbbed through the wall from the rooms beyond.

"Something happened to you in Antarka, didn't it?" Kat asked me.

The memory stung me when I blinked. The afterimages were still burned into the insides of my eyelids. I shuddered deeply, and before I could stop myself the words had already left my mouth, "I think . . . I saw God."

She laughed nervously. "Uh. Please be fucking kidding me."

"I saw it. How it looked through me. It knew everything. What I've done, all my crimes. It—"

"That's absurd. Tell me exactly what you saw."

An eyeball. A vast, unblinking eye in the sky.

I shook my head and said, "You must have known someday you'd have to forget about me and go on with your own life. You had to know that."

Her breath went silent on the other side.

"Never," she said.

Duke's underling watched and waited—ready to pin me to the metal floor if I tried to leave, if I reached for a weapon to hurt myself, if I declined the treatment that had been prescribed.

"I have to go," I said. "I'll call back with details on a new job."

Kat's voice was incredulous. "Already? What is it? . . . Lex? Hello?"

I don't know why my hand moved automatically for the thing hanging from my neck. It was the only good luck charm I'd ever carried: a short length of copper wire, once bent into the crude shape of a person but now only a twisted barb—and I finally knew, remembering the glint of those two rebar spikes aimed at my heart, and peering now through that yonic entryway at the salt-greased bodies on display in the smoky red light ahead, exactly what I needed: none of the things I had spent my life up until then pursuing. Not mastery. Not money. Not sex.

All I needed now was the job that would finally kill me.

I

I remember the calm on that last night in Bloom City. We had no warning of the bloodshed to come. Fifty thousand refinery workers and plankton farmers and Medusan soldiers danced and drank themselves to exhaustion, then crawled into the darkest and driest corridors in sight and faded out one by one. By four a.m. the chatter in the habitat level had died down, and then there was only the ceaseless and ever-present thrum of the refineries, gulping down seawater and letting out a slow but steady flow of deuterium: that liquid gold that made the great oceanic city-states so rich, providing an endless supply of ammunition to the wars that had ravaged dry land for a hundred years.

That night found Alexei Standard staring up at the ceiling of his room in the love hotel. His host lay motionless next to him, her closed eyelids dusted with dim pink light, but he had no doubt she was awake and keeping up her vigil. His electromagnetic armor and coat hung on the wall, but he'd set his wave rifle in arm's reach and pointed it pre-emptively at the door: an old habit that clung to life harder than he did himself. Tomorrow he would leave this place and head for the strife-ridden hinterland—and in that thought, for the first time in three solid days, he felt the promise of sleep begin to tug at the edges of his mind.

On a deeper tier of the city, Danae stared over the ridgeline of Naoto's body at the mural he had begun to paint on her wall, letting it sink in that she'd never see it finished—that tomorrow she would either die, or live to stand under the real sky again. She wanted to believe in the latter, to hold that image in her mind and cherish it, but in the long hours of that night there was nowhere left to hide from the deeper fear: there was no home for her to go back to. Not really. Even if she made it out of this prison city and all the way back to Redhill—even if she found the rest of herself again—she would still be condemned to the isolation of a single, fragile body. She would still never be forgiven. She would still be a murderer.

At that moment, a pale man with a blue corporate tattoo on his cheek crept alone among the habitat level's shuttered fronts and sleeping bodies and passed, again, the elevators down to the Medusan barracks module. Without thinking he gritted his teeth, so hard he could hear a molar begin to crack. It had taken him more than sixty years to find Danae—to stand here and know the two of them were separated now by only a single elevator and a few sealed doors—but he'd spent weeks trying and failing to cross that last distance, and he had no more patience. There was no privacy in this place. He could never get anyone alone long enough to put on their flesh, and without that he couldn't become anyone who the Medusas would ever allow into their protected keep. The only solution he could imagine was to flush his target out into the open, where he might reach her. So he took a deep breath and braced himself for what was coming. He considered the heavy briefcase in his hand—not the one he had become so accustomed to carrying for seventy-two years now, but this new one he so loathed, packed with far cruder devices. He took his shard from his pocket and typed a message to the other two of himself: *Stand by. Will detonate in ten minutes.*

Something else was awake in Bloom City that night. In a chamber made up to look like an ordinary storage tank, set apart from the habitat sections, there was a machine that never slept: Medusa Clan's prized molecular assembler, a throbbing mass of solid-state machinery in a reinforced vacuum chamber. Its end product was pumped invisibly through a nanoscopic tubule and injected into a hollow sphere the size of a human heart. When the sphere was full, a robotic arm gently transferred it into the next warhead on the line, there to wait for its fateful commands. Anyone looking inside the nanoweapon core would only have seen what looked like oil, black and viscous, with a dull metallic luster; unidentifiable by sight as a mass of a billion tiny mechanisms, each the size of a blood cell. They were simple machines, identical, and with a single function: to make copies of themselves out of any matter they touched. Even the people who operated the assemblers, who walked among the rows of loaded warheads and took inventory, couldn't fathom what they themselves had made—because it's one thing to know in factual terms, and something else to truly understand: to hold such an object in your hands and grasp that it encloses a hunger deep enough to eat the whole world.

ALEXEI

On the edge of elusive sleep, I remembered it, vivid as a hologram: a night, sixteen years ago, when a room full of children felt the concrete around them shudder.

Like a dozen times before, like they'd been taught to, they leaped from their bunks, skittered on bare feet over the cold floor, and collected around the sturdiness of the walls and corners of the room. None spoke. All eyes were glued to the hairline cracks in the ceiling, all ears listening for the muffled blasts. Guessing at the distance. Among those fifty-odd orphans, two stayed close. They let their gazes down from the ceiling and peered at each other in the near-perfect dark. They held hands and leaned in close to whisper.

"I love you," said the girl, twelve years old, into the boy's ear.

"I love you too," whispered the boy, ten.

"Matron said I'm too young to know what that means. Loving and being in love. But I *do* know. I care about you. More than anyone or anything else." Her grip on his hand tightened. "Do you feel that way about me?"

He studied the freckles in her pale skin. "Yes."

She kissed the side of his face as another shockwave sounded, closer and louder than those before. More concrete dusted the floor.

"People out there want to kill us. What would you do if someone tried to kill me?" Before he could answer, she said, "If someone tried to hurt you, I would kill him. I will do anything to protect you. No matter what."

"I would kill him too. If someone tried to hurt you."

"They say it's hard to make yourself do it. Even the soldiers who are out there. It's hard even for them."

"I don't care. I would do it."

Another loud blast shuddered through the walls, followed by the low rattle of bomblets and the whistles of flechettes. The boy only stared into her unblinking eyes.

"What if I die anyway? Sometimes you can't protect someone. You do all you can and they still die."

The boy said nothing.

"If I died, all I would want is for you to still be alive. If there are ghosts, if I was one, I would still want you to stay alive."

"That's all I would want, too—for you."

"Then if you died, I would stay alive," she said. "No matter what. Because I'd know it would be what you wanted more than anything."

"Yes."

"I want to make a promise with you. Promise me that if I die first, you'll stay alive."

"And if I die, you have to stay alive too."

"I promise," she said.

"We promise each other," he said.

Their hands held more tightly as the rumbling blasts grew fainter.

"I love you, Eryn," said the boy.

In response, the girl handed him something she'd made out of loose wire. A crude stick-figure of a human being, its edges glinting in the darkness. "So you never forget me or our promise. I love you, Alexei."

Nightmare leaked into the memory. I was standing in that room as an adult. I was stepping between the steel bunks, and all the children were screaming. My heels hit the ground with the resonance of distant bombs, and that twelve-year-old girl and ten-year-old boy were staring at me, backing away into the corner, wide-eyed. They were in the ironsights of my wave rifle. I tried to put it down, but I couldn't. The sights settled on Eryn's face, and my finger was on the trigger, pulling.

I bolted upright with the sound of the shot ringing in my ears, but the room was silent. The music had been shut off and the ducts all held their breath. No matter how long I listened, I could detect no other sound in the muggy, sour-smelling darkness.

The woman who'd been watching me was gone.

My shard rang suddenly, making me jump again. I let out a sigh and answered, my fingers so sweaty on the holographic glass that they barely registered.

"Dahlia Lem is dead," Kat's digitally scrambled voice said.

It took a moment for the information to process. I made sure I was awake. I stifled my urge to ask her to repeat herself.

"How do you know?" I asked.

"You think I wouldn't be watching Bloom like a hawk with the hell you're putting me through?" she shouted. "Medusa Clan's whole network just lit up with e-warfare, like a Christmas tree doused in napalm. I don't know what's happening, but if I were you, I would give serious thought to getting the fuck out of Dodge, and pronto."

"Kat, what happened?"

"I'm still finding out. Half the keep module is flooded, but as for whether it was a torpedo strike or a bomb or an accident? I'm working on it. Mainly I'm working on finding you an escape route. And forget about getting out the way you came in. Trust me. You don't even want to know—"

"Wait." Something was happening outside. Shouting, then a waver shriek I knew I hadn't imagined.

"What was that? Lex?"

"Recontact in twenty." I hung up. I darted into the corner behind the door and rushed to strap my armor back on without ever taking one hand off my rifle. I tried to remember the layout of the surrounding corridors, think of the best positions to take, gauge the distance and direction of the feet pounding on the metal floor out there—but when my weapon was primed and ready against my chest, I couldn't steady my hands to aim it. The same panic I'd felt on the ice fields of Antarka kept creeping in. Everywhere I looked, the eyeball's ethereal gaze was there in the signal-static darkness in the corners of the room. Footsteps halted just outside. A red-light shadow played slowly across the translucent plastic walls, enlarging and distorting as it approached the door, each strobe flash mutating the silhouette into the next in an endless series of my victims. The door slid open. The overhead light clicked on, and a gun snapped out toward my head.

It was one of the proprietors. I lowered and disarmed my weapon in a hurry. After a twitchy moment she did the same, swearing under her breath and holstering the tiny pistol somewhere in the folds of her ornate red silk robe.

"You," she said. "You can't wave that thing around in here."

"Sorry." I wiped the sweat off my face and struggled to control my breath. "I heard a shot—"

"A customer needed to be convinced to leave. You need to leave too. Real bad news. It's not personal. It really isn't. I like you okay, Standard, but you're not one of us, and we have to seal this place up, and we only have enough canned air in here for the workers—"

"I understand."

She led me to the brothel's big armored hatch and shoved me gently through. She watched me through the gap as it closed, her painted and sparkling eyes full of apology, and I knew there was nothing I could say to convince her I needed none. No matter how much safer it was behind that door, the last thing I wanted right now was to be locked up airtight in the middle of this city.

The bolts screeched shut. Distant shouts echoed between the narrow walls, and the smell of fire was already wafting on the recycled air. My shard rang in my pocket. "My dear Alexei Standard." Duke's holographic image grinned up at me through the glass. Red emergency lighting glittered on his jaw rings like monstrously curved teeth. "I take it you've heard the big news."

"Norpak broke the ceasefire?" I asked. "Already?"

"No, surprisingly. It seems a lone wolf scored a lucky hit against some corroded seals with an improvised explosive. We don't know the who or the why yet, but I doubt it was Norpak. Those ninjas take far too much pride in their work to resort to such sloppy methodologies." He had to raise his voice over a background din of shouted orders, boots pounding on metal floors, waver fire. I heard someone read out new casualty estimates.

I had followed the corridor to another sealed hatch. Three corpses were splayed out under the flickering lights, all Medusas. Wisps of smoke rose and perfumed the air with burning plastic and cooked flesh. "If the ceasefire is still in place," I asked, "what is this?"

"It's an election! We are all casting our votes now to choose Dahlia's successor."

I averted my eyes from the dead and said, "I can't be part of this."

Duke guffawed. "You don't get a vote, chum. Not that it matters. The situation is well in hand. What's left of the keep is mine already, as will be the rest of Bloom shortly—and where Bloom goes, all of Epak follows."

"Then why call—?"

"Because it would be a shame if you died in this petty little squabble, that's why. I'm sending you the keys to all the safe rooms in that sector of the city. Sit tight, Alexei. When the dust settles, you'll work for me."

I shook my head. "I need a way out of the city."

He ignored me. "The Clan will have lost some of its best talent in the shakeup, and there'll be no shortage of work. I've had my eye on you for years, Alexei. I've seen what you're capable of. I need those talents at my disposal. I need the very sharpest knife in Dahlia's old drawer."

I choked out the words "I should go."

He only chuckled and leaned tighter into the camera. "You wouldn't go against a decree straight from your new Emperor."

Before I could respond, a series of metallic thuds sounded—on both my side of the call and Duke's, I realized. He held his hand up to silence everyone. For a moment everything was still—but when the sound came again, I felt the vibration in my guts, the ripple of seismic violence in the plates under my feet. The pipes all began to scream.

"Section 40," someone yelled to Duke. "The emergency seals aren't working. It's sabotage. We're locked out!"

"God damnit, you said we had nodespace under control!"

"We did!"

"High ground! Everybody move!"

The call cut off.

I turned to a sudden uproar: a few other locked-out people had managed to pry open a sealed door to a stairwell. I watched panic carry them upward, but I didn't follow. Everyone in Bloom would be rushing to higher ground now, because there was only one way to read the signs.

One of Duke's rivals was trying to sink the city.

DANAE

The boom rang through the metal substructure and resonated tangibly in the pit of my stomach, but then there was nothing. I sat up and silenced my breath. I listened for an eternal minute, but no more sounds came—and this deep in the city, everything was always clanking and hissing and flexing under the pressure. It could have been a random airlock failure, the ping of a misdirected active sonar, ordinary metal fatigue. When I lay back down, Naoto's eyes were open, two pools of reflected holographic light in the black.

His fingers softly traced the length of my forearm, stopping at the place where the bones had knitted a few degrees crooked. I'd had to treat it myself when I first came here: I couldn't trust any Medusan doctor to keep my secret, if some casual medical scan were to reveal what was woven into my nervous system.

"I never noticed that before," Naoto whispered. "How'd you break it?"

The answer to that question was the last thing on earth I wanted to remember. I sighed and asked, "Can't sleep?"

His silhouette nodded. "I've been thinking about the surface. I keep trying to imagine that much empty space. What's it like?"

I glanced around at the tight plastic walls. "It's different."

He chuckled. "All those lifetimes of experience, and that's all you can say about it? It's 'different?'" He propped himself up on his elbow and said "Tell me something. Tell me a story. Since this is our last day together. Since neither of us can sleep."

"What about?"

Lost in thought, he scratched the fine hairs running down the middle of his belly. "Tell me about one of the times you saved humanity. Tell me again about Blood Rain."

I winced. "That's a horrific story. Why would you want to hear that?"

"Yesterday I thought Epak and Norpak were finally going to annihilate each other, and all of us with them. Today I have to say goodbye to you. I'm a giant knot of stress in the shape of a man. A horrific story is exactly what I need to get me through it. Because . . . in the end, you won, right? You cured it. You survived."

"Did I?" I whispered, maybe too quietly for him to hear.

When I didn't say more, he continued, "Okay then, something else. Lighter-hearted. Tell me about your first life."

I stared. "Which one do you mean by first, exactly? You mean this body before unity, or the first person who ever unified, or—?"

"Chronologically. I know, I know, twelve thousand years old. I meant your oldest life. What's your earliest birthday?"

I stared into the darkness for a long time before answering. "September 12, 1998."

I could feel him listening intently. "What was your first memory?"

I sighed. "A video screen. It was a huge, heavy box. Low-rez, two-dimensional. Cathode-ray tubes."

I breathed slowly and let the memory move through me. I didn't want to admit it to Naoto, but it was calming. Maybe it was what I needed, too—to take shelter in a deeper corner of my mind.

"It showed a city at night," I continued, "with small lights stretching flat out to the horizon. Lamps glinting along a river or a canal. Then there were missile blasts. Clouds of fire, mushrooming up and disappearing quickly. March, 2003. That's my first memory." I clarified, "Chronologically."

Naoto nodded. "That was the nuclear war?"

"No. That was decades later. It was—" Another sound rang out through the night, but this time we didn't just hear it. The vibration was tangible in the walls around us, followed immediately by an audible creak of metal fatigue through the substructure.

He scrambled out of bed and crawled through the low space to call up the video pane; I stayed frozen. A jumble of text burned into focus, everything throbbing red with urgency, garbled with fear. The stinging light traced Naoto's hunched, nude outline as he read.

"Explosions," he said, but I had to read it for myself. "Near the keep. Conflicting reports. Dahlia—" He swallowed visibly. He didn't need to say it. Whatever had happened, whoever had started it, it meant civil war.

I only managed to pull my coveralls halfway up my torso. My hands were shaking too much to work the zipper. My bags were packed at the foot of the bed, but I could only stare at them.

"That's it, then." He responded the last way I would have expected: he laughed, loudly. Then he took a deep breath and gathered his clothes. "I guess the decision's been made for me. We have to make our run for the surface right now. Immediately."

I barely heard a word he was saying, least of all the 'we.' "No. This changes everything. I didn't plan for this. There's no way out now."

"There's always a way out."

"This isn't the job I hired the mercenary to do, and even if I could reach him—"

"Then forget him. It was a huge risk to trust him anyway. This could be our best shot, Danae. We don't need anyone to smuggle us anymore. We don't have to worry about being seen. The Clan will be much too busy tearing itself apart to worry about a couple of runaways."

I was still only marginally processing anything he said. My mind was fixated on the pressure. The ocean squeezing the module around us like a can in a fist was as much an engineering challenge as it was a wicked blessing for Medusa clan: we were all captives of the dissolved gasses in our own bodies. As long as I stayed down here at four atmospheres, those gasses remained harmless—but if I tried to leave too quickly, they would boil blood, burst arteries, necrotize bone. To work for Medusa Clan and live under its protection was as much a medical condition as a social one.

"There's nothing to do but bolt the door and wait this out—" I started, but I choked on my own words. I'd never make it to Redhill before the equinox now. I cut Naoto off to say, "Look. At worst, Medusas are already slaughtering each other in every corridor in Bloom. At best, the city's under full lockdown. Any modules that aren't flooded will be inaccessible. The elevators won't work. Even the fucking *doors* won't work!"

He put his hands softly on my shoulders. "Not without an emergency root override."

"Sure, if I had—"

I flinched when he dug the roughshod circuit out of his pocket. "It only opens the maintenance areas, but that includes the main elevator shafts, even under lockdown. I'm kind of surprised you never made your own, given your skills. Given all the system access you had, working for the Clan."

"I didn't, because they'd flay me alive if they ever found out. They'd flay you alive."

He caught the edge in my voice. "All the more reason for us *both* to get the hell out of here."

It was only then that I finally processed that he was speaking in the plural. I shook my head frantically. "No. No! Absolutely not! You can't come with me. I can't have you endangering yourself for me."

"It's not just for you, okay? I'm a muralist! A muralist who's spent his whole miserable life in a city with no natural light and no wall bigger than two by six meters. This is not the first time I've thought of leaving. It's all I've been able to think about for weeks now."

I knew he was telling the truth, but it still confounded me. "You never told me that."

"Because I knew you'd worry too much to let me come with you, no matter what I said. And yes, I admit it: I've been scared shitless of going to the surface. I wasn't sure I had the guts." He gestured to the warning lights and glitchy scenes of carnage dancing across the pane behind him. "So much for that!"

"But where will you go? How will you live? Life is hard on the surface—and if you do this, you'll be an outlaw. The Medusas will put a price on your head. There's no coming back from this."

He held my shoulder. "It's my risk to take."

"You certainly can't follow me to Redhill. It's within the borders of the Confederacy. Far too risky."

He flinched slightly and hurried to say, "Of course. I'll just go with you to the edge of the Econ Zone. Deal?"

I closed my eyes and let the adrenaline wash through me. I synchronized my breathing to his. I ran through every mind trick I'd ever learned to dissipate a panic attack. When I looked at my hands again, they held solid. I zipped up my coveralls and grabbed my bag—and just I started to tell Naoto to stay, Dahlia Lem's image flashed across the pane.

I'd been so naïve and so crazed with fear the night I'd first come to this city, offering myself in exchange for her protection. For five years I'd done whatever she asked: fixing and breaking things in nodespace, intelligence, counter-intelligence, small acts of sabotage and theft. I'd made myself an accessory to all her atrocities, all for the sake of putting that many more walls, armed guards, and meters of ocean depth between myself and the Keepers.

Now she was dead. The most dangerous single human being in all of Epak, if not the whole world beyond, killed in an instant by a blast of pressurized water through a single broken seal.

"You're right," I said. "Let's go."

ALEXEI

The higher the pressure, the greater the need for meditative calm. The Major had drilled this principle into me, into all of us, never knowing how literally his philosophy would be tested—that seven years after his death, his last surviving protégé would huddle in a deserted Bloom City love hotel under a ceiling weighted with thirty meters of ocean, while the walls on every side of him held back three hundred thousand people in the process converting themselves into a single panicking riot.

I controlled my breath. My task was set out before me: I had to get out of this place. There was no room in my mind for anything else.

I called Kat. "Are you with me?"

"Till the bitter end," she answered. "Did you ever read Dante's *Inferno*?"

"No."

"How about *Huckleberry Finn*?"

"No."

"Seriously? Lex, honey. As soon as you get out of this bind, I'm putting a whole reading list on your shard."

"The point."

"The point is, the only way out of hell is out through the bottom. I found an empty construction sub docked way down on the lower refinery level. It's all screwed up with electronic warfare, but I think I can crack it by the time you get there."

"The lower refinery level." My lungs ached, thinking about it. "The pressure down there must be two atmospheres higher than what I'm breathing now, and I don't have any Pascalex on me."

Kat's voice through the scrambler was taut with nervous energy. "You're in for some pain one way or another. For what it's worth, the sub is supposed to have a deluxe deepwater trauma kit on board, complete with drugs and automated diagnostic equipment. Assuming nobody jacked it."

I nodded and started walking. "It'll have to do. How do I get around the lockdown?"

"All the elevators have been recalled to their top floors. The shafts are all empty. If you can get into one of them, it should take you straight down. But the doors are pressure-sealed so you'll need a little something."

I was already pressing the gray putty along the seam of the door. I stuck in the detonator leads and jogged down the corridor as far as it ran. In that confined and airtight space the explosion still made my ears pop, and the whole substructure around me rang like a gong. Through the wrenched-open elevator doors an intense wind howled, underlaid by the sound of metal debris clattering to the bottom.

"Still kicking?" Kat asked through the bud in my ear.

"The night is young," I said as I squeezed through.

"I'm watching you. Keep the line open."

In the sliver of light from the corridor, I made out a set of recessed pipes, secured with clamps at regular intervals. I found that if I held the pipe tightly enough, I could brace my feet against the wall and get just enough traction to climb very awkwardly down. I went to it. Within a few meters it was pitch black.

"There's another pressure-sealed door at the bottom of all this, right?" I heard my voice echo into infinity. "If I use another explosive charge in a confined space, it'll pop my head like caviar."

"I'm . . . looking into it," she answered, not very reassuringly.

I started to feel water running over my hands on the pipe, and I could hear the trickling echo in the space. With every step down, the flow increased. I told myself that it was too warm to be ocean water, but the thought only reminded me that by now I was probably in the express segment of the shaft, starting down into the interval between one module and the next. In this place the pressure of the deep was only arm's length away in any direction, only barely restrained, and atmospheres higher than the air I was breathing.

Under the trickling and the whispers of air there were other sounds: distant crackling thuds, punctuated by bursts of inhuman wailing. Torpedo detonations. Sonar sweeps.

I pressed the bud into my ear. "Kat, are you hearing this?"

"Nothing to worry about." Her garbled voice paused. "Probably. Hopefully. At this point, Duke's rivals must know their only real shot at the throne is to drown the whole city with Duke inside it, but his side has nearly all the combat subs. They've managed to intercept all the incoming torpedoes. So far."

"Won't they target the construction pod?"

"Focus, Lex. One foot in front of the other. Just like Dante."

I hadn't read the *Inferno*, but I knew what it was about. I wondered if that hell had a part just like this. I considered the notion that the only way out of a dark place is to push all the way through. I wished I could believe it.

Maybe I'll just stay down here, I thought. Maybe this is where I belong. Far from that sky and its inhuman gaze. But just as I thought this, a soft glow dusted the shaft around me.

"Oh holy fuck," Kat's voice gasped.

I looked up instinctively to see a bright red star flicker at the top of the shaft. The thunder of the torpedo strike was followed by the low and rising sound of burning wreckage on its way down—presumably with an immense mass of water coming directly behind it.

"Let go!" the shard was shouting in my ear. "Go! Plug your ears and jump! Jump now!"

"What happens at the bottom?"

"Trust me, Alexei!"

I looked down into the void.

So this is how it ends, I thought, and dropped.

Hell ceased to be quiet or smooth. The lightless walls came howling straight at me. I covered my head and braced for oblivion—but eerie light flashed over my eyelids, followed by a wave of air that slammed into me with bruising force. I felt it lifting me on a screaming pillow of upwelling pressure, until I dropped out the now-open floor of the shaft and splashed down into a roiling vat of heavy water.

The rush of air had slowed me down just enough to keep the water from shattering my bones on impact, and I managed to reach the ladder and climb out just before the elevator wreckage exploded down after me on a roaring white column of sea.

My ears kept ringing as I shook myself off, and my face was full of salt. Looming machinery came into focus as my vision cleared: pumps; storage tanks enclosed in mountains of pipe; everything lit in glaring orange lines of light. The industrial cavern of the deuterium-tritium refinery level.

"Still kicking?" Kat asked.

I could only cough and spit, but that was all the answer Kat needed.

"Some of Bloom City's elevator shafts double as part of the 'Catastrophic Breach Alternative Shunt System,' or C-BASS." She was reading from a manual. She chuckled. "That's a clever acronym, don't you think?"

"Construction pod."

"On your left, fifty meters. Virgil's got you."

DANAE

Not many people knew how to access the narrow ducts that ran between modules and stayed open even when all the hatches were sealed. Fewer still knew about the points where it was just wide enough for two human beings and their backpacks to squeeze between Bloom City's substructure and its outer shell. Thankfully, Naoto was one of those few, and what he didn't know, I did. Now we crawled through those hidden spaces by the light of our headlamps, soaked in an uneven rain of frigid salt water, stopping and holding our breaths whenever we heard shouting or screaming or the clattering of feet through the walls. I only prayed the material was thick enough to stop a stray waver shot from within. Whenever it quieted down again, we grabbed the next beam and kept climbing.

"Are you sure this is normal?" I asked, waving my hand through a column of falling water. "It's not coming through a breach?"

"There are always small leaks in the outer shell." Naoto barely raised his voice above the sound of the water. "The pumps at the bottom catch it. Wait—do you hear that?"

I held still and listened. The sound was distant, buried under the dripping, the creaking metal, and the muffled wailing of alarms: a faint droning buzz, but it didn't sound mechanical. It ebbed and flowed very slightly.

"How much farther to that hatch?" I asked, scooping saltwater out of my eyes.

"It can't be more than ten more meters up. But, uh . . ." He paused guiltily. "Once we get it open, we'll have to sprint across about twenty meters of the main habitat level to get to the other hatch."

"What other hatch?"

My headlamp traced the edges of his apologetic glance. "The one that actually gets us to the elevator shafts and out of the city."

I swore under my breath and pulled nervously on my backpack straps. Of all the places to have to leave the protection of these crawlspaces, there was nowhere I less wanted to be than the open space of the habitat, but there was nothing to do now but keep climbing.

We'd felt and heard the seismic thuds of underwater explosions since leaving the barracks module, but so far they'd been mercifully distant. If one of those torpedoes flew true, there'd be nowhere less safe than where we were now.

The disconcerting buzz grew louder as we climbed. As we neared the hatch, it was almost deafening. In hindsight, it felt terrible to have wondered whether it was a hissing pipe or a machine; for all my lifetimes of knowledge and experience, I had never imagined, much less heard directly, the sound of a thousand doomed people screaming at the same time. I couldn't guess how many more were still trying to force their way into the habitat from other parts of the city.

I could only look for a moment before ducking back into the crawlspace and slamming the hatch behind me, but the images stained my vision: the terrified masses, packed almost too tightly to breathe, fighting to stay upright against the fire-hose surge of frigid ocean from the doors to the elevator dock. The whole space was layered with smoke and the stench of sea salt and burning plastic.

Naoto ducked away from the hatch and wiped water out of his eyes. "Fuck. Fuck!"

"Is there a way around? What's up there if we keep climbing?"

He shook his head rapidly. "Nothing. I've memorized all the schematics. Oh God. A torpedo must have hit the main surface shafts. The emergency seals must be destroyed, which means the ladder wells will be flooded too. We're fucked."

I stared back down into the lightless crawlspace. "Then it's over." My mind was empty. Numb. "We'll just have to go back. Wait for another chance."

"We can't."

I glanced down into the red-lit shadows below us, trying to read him. "You think the way back is flooded too?"

"No, I mean it's—" He rubbed his face and blew sea out of his nose. "I know, okay?"

"Know what?"

"I'm sorry, I shouldn't have done it—" His voice kept choking. He might have been crying, but it was hard to tell through all the water falling over us. "When I couldn't find you the night before last, I hacked your pane. I read your unsent drafts. Your suicide note."

I shuddered and turned away, hugging the ladder rungs, sheltering my face under my arm.

"I know you won't survive another year waiting for the equinox," he yelled over the roar. "I know nothing I can do for you will make it bearable. You have to get out of Bloom. And for my own sake, I need you to."

"Naoto . . ."

He seemed to steel himself. "Call him. Call the damned merce-nary."

I hesitated. "But what if you were right about him?"

"Then at least we'll be out of the pan and into the fire."

I took the shard from my pocket and tried to keep the water off long enough to dial. We cupped the holographic glass between our heads to hear it.

I couldn't believe it when the mercenary answered. His voice was chillingly calm. He just asked, "Are you still going through with the vacation we discussed?"

"Yes," I stammered. "Bringing a plus-one, just for the first leg of the trip."

"Understood. Where are you?"

I swallowed hard and said, "We're in the outer shell of the main habitat."

"Isn't it flooded?"

"It will be soon. But where . . . where are *you*?"

"Outside."

It took a moment to know what he meant. I managed to open the hatch and avert my gaze from the drowning masses long enough to scan the slit windows set along the ceiling. A white light hung out-side, drifting along the howling perimeter, peering in at the carnage. Perversely angelic.

I shut the hatch to snuff out the screams. "You're in that sub? How did you get—?"

"No time to explain that."

Naoto and I exchanged nervous looks, and I knew what we were both thinking. Even now, it felt dangerous to trust him.

"Do you have any canned air?" the voice from my shard asked impatiently. "Any kind of breathing apparatus?"

I took a mental inventory. I glanced at Naoto, but he shook his head. I asked, "Your sub doesn't have an airlock?"

"It's just a construction pod. The cockpit hatch can't re-seal itself under water. I only have one idea."

"Tell us."

"You're under about thirty-five meters of ocean right now. If you can get outside, you can grab on to the cargo cage of this pod, and I can surface at full speed."

I was speechless for a moment. "How long will it take to reach the top?"

"Forty to fifty seconds. It's your best chance of making it on just the air in your lungs, and the cage might hold you if you lose consciousness. Once we surface, we'll need to get you both into the cockpit and re-pressurize it before hypothermia and decompression sickness can take effect."

"Oh God."

"It might be safer to stay in Bloom and enlist another contractor at another time. These aren't ideal conditions for leaving the city."

I met Naoto's eyes and said, "No. We have to leave now. No matter what. How do we get outside?"

"If you can find a point where pressure inside the city is equal to the water outside, I'll cut a hole in the outer shell. Once it's equalized, you can swim out." It was all coming together in my head as he said it. We were already in the right place. "Do you agree?"

"Yes. We'll do it."

Naoto grabbed my shoulder. Visibly bracing himself.

The chillingly calm voice said, "Where am I going?"

I handed Naoto the shard and he reluctantly answered, "Look for the second 'O' in 'Bloom' where it's painted on the outside of the habitat. Pry open the outermost layer—not the substructure. We're there. We're ready."

"Precise. On my way."

"Wait," I said, taking the shard back. "What should we call you?"

A pause. "My name is Standard."

"I'm Danae. My plus-one is Naoto." I acknowledged the look Naoto shot me for that and added, "I just thought . . . we're about to put our lives in your hands. We should at least know each other's names."

"Understood."

The line died, leaving us alone again. We held each other's salt-water-streaked faces, and I tried to shut out the screams coming through the wall to tell him, "You can still turn back. Stay in Bloom. Even with this mess, it's safer here than the places I have to travel through."

"If the whole city doesn't drown!"

"We'll be lucky to survive this ascent. Just tell me you're not doing this for my sake—that it's not about protecting me or staying close to me. Whatever you think, I'm not worth it."

He held me in a tight, shivering hug. "It's my decision, and I've made it."

He'd dodged my real question, but there was a more pressing issue. I pulled back and gripped Naoto's arms hard to say, "If you're coming, you need to promise me something. If something happens to me—if I'm incapacitated, but not dead, and the Medusas are close to capturing us—" I steeled myself. I enunciated clearly: "If that happens, you have to kill me."

Naoto blinked hard. "Excuse me?"

"I can't let them have what's in me," I said. "If I . . . If I'm dead, it will take care of itself. Until then, in the wrong hands, it's a danger to everyone. To the whole world. We can't let them find out about it, and we absolutely can't let them take me alive."

He was staring at me in utter shock.

I shook him hard. "I don't need you to understand. I just need you to make me this one damned promise. If you want to come with me, that's my price. Take it or leave it, but choose now."

He nodded—barely, then fully. "Okay."

"Say it."

"I promise."

From below we heard the wrench of metal and a new roar of water. The ocean there at the bottom of the red-lit metal space was as black as it was frigid at first—but then it all ignited with that white headlight, tracing the outline of the rip in the outer hull, just wide enough for us to crawl through.

"Hyperventilate now," I told him, cinching the straps on my backpack as tight as they would go. "It'll help you hold your breath. And remember to exhale as you rise. The air in our lungs is going to expand to four times its current volume as we ascend—"

"I know, I know." I watched his lungs heave. I read the fear in the creases in his face.

"On the count of three. One, two—"

"I love you!"

"Three!"

The shocking cold hit me like electrocution before I went totally numb. The sharp edges of the peeled-open hull bit our hands as we pulled ourselves out into the pod's blinding headlights, onto the cargo cage spreading open for us like jaws.

The sub's engines began to roar the moment Naoto and I managed to grab it. The vibrations hammered on our guts, all sound amplified by the water. We lay flat against the bars (narrow enough to hurt, but set wide enough apart that we could easily slip through if we were careless) and the water began to rush at our faces, prying at our lips and nostrils, pressing us down in an unbearable gravity. Naoto clamped one arm around the cage and tried to cover his nose and mouth with his free hand. I could only turn my head enough to look up into the sub's spherical cockpit and see the mercenary perched there, faceless, a demonic silhouette against the lights of the controls. I looked back, counting down the markings on the outer wall as we rose.

Past the top of the habitat, lines of orange flood lamps peaked like a dawn, shining through an upward waterfall of glittering bubbles rising from the breached elevator shafts. It was then I saw them, just visible in the bright murk: the huge, toothed doors of the emergency seals. The control box. The blinking light.

The realization hit me harder than the ocean. The seals hadn't been breached; they'd never closed in the first place. Like half of Bloom City's subsystems, they must have been hacked amid the infighting, and that control box held the one and only physical override.

I didn't think. I turned my body and let the weight of the water rip me down between the bars of the cargo cage, then swam with all the force I could squeeze from my cold-shocked muscles. The straps of my backpack ripped and fell away into the abyss.

I didn't know if I'd make it before I drowned, but I tried. The roar of the pod's engines faded behind me and the antigravity of the air in my lungs gave way to an intense downward suction as I approached the vortex of water surging down into the habitat. By the time I reached the box it took all my strength to cling to it.

I had just enough oxygen left in my bloodstream to do it. I pulled the cover off and twisted the knob inside. I looked down.

Nothing happened. There was no groan of machinery, no flashing lights. The seals at the bottom of the blown-open elevator shaft were still wide open.

I felt strangely calm. I had passed the point of panic. There was nothing to do now but let the ocean into my lungs. Five years of running from Asher Valley were at their end. When the headlamps started to glow on the metal wall in front of me, I thought it was the first glimmer of the light at the end of death's tunnel—and when I turned to see the sub driving toward me through the light-stained water, a mess of serrated claws and roaring thrusters, my last thought was that it had come to drag me down to the other place. Then I was gone.

ALEXEI

I wrenched the hatch closed against the blast of morning light, and the bubble cockpit hissed and creaked ominously as it strained to re-pressurize itself and stop our blood boiling long enough for the drugs to kick in. My two new clients were sea-soaked ragdolls draped over the reclined seats, leaving just enough room for me to crawl awkwardly over them.

"Is she okay?" Naoto groaned, repeatedly. He could barely form the words, between the shock of the ascent and the chemicals I was feeding into his arm.

"I'm trying to ascertain that."

Under these circumstances, I could think of several reasons why Danae was still unconscious. I had to hope it was simple oxygen deprivation and not a concussion or embolism or stroke or something else I couldn't treat. My vision was blurry. My aching hands kept spilling the contents of the trauma kit over my clients' limp bodies, but I finally managed to dig out the Medusan field medic scanner and unfold it around Danae's head and neck.

At the last second I held back from hitting the power button. I didn't have time to tinker with the scanner to make sure it wasn't networked. If it was, there was a risk it would transmit personally identifying information back to the Medusas. Maybe enough for them to find us here.

"Is she okay?" Naoto croaked, more insistently.

I had no choice. I flipped the switch and watched the screen flare to life.

"She's—" I started, but when the image cohered, I had no words. I could only stare and wait for it to make sense.

"She's what?" Naoto demanded.

The overlay began to print out warnings like *anatomical variation exceeds diagnostic parameters* and *anomalous neuroelectric activity* and *cybernetics not recognized*, but these were all crude, euphemistic terms for what I was seeing.

The many-spined, crystalline thing that branched throughout the inside of Danae's head and down into her spine did not look like cybernetics. It didn't look like any technology I had ever seen, but neither was it remotely biological.

"I said is she okay?" Naoto grabbed at the sleeve of my coat and pulled hard.

I blinked slowly. "I don't know."

The scanner began to flash with frantic warnings: *Unidentified nanoweapon. Quarantine immediately.* Alarm noise filled the cockpit—abruptly silenced by Naoto's hands snatching the scanner off Danae's head and ripping out the power cell.

He glared at me—drugged, half-dead from the ascent, pushing himself upright on shivering arms, yet visibly bristling with threat response to ask, "What did you see?"

However weak he was, I saw him bracing to attack me if I gave the wrong answer—but I had no answer at all. I had no words to describe or even categorize it.

Danae groaned and stirred. "Naoto?"

He was so visibly relieved that he nearly seemed to forget me. He sank back against the wall of the bubble and stroked her hair. "I'm here," he said. "We made it. We're at the surface."

I sank back against the dashboard. With my last moments of full lucidity, I set the autopilot to take us to the shore and hopefully off anyone's sonar. Waves of light played across bubble around us, eerily serene, and I let myself start to fade into the haze of Pascalex and narcotics.

When I opened my eyes again, four hours had passed, and we were all still alive. The sub bobbed gently just below the water's surface, in sight of the rocky floor, half-hidden now in a thickening field of debris that had floated up from the fighting below and washed toward the shore. Between the decompression cycle and the drugs, soon we'd be able to open the hatch without succumbing to the pressure change. Until then we were stuck here together, three bodies crammed into this plastic and metal womb, wreathed in multicolored strata of pollution.

We had been laying in a pile all that time, continually coughing or trying pointlessly to twist into less painful positions. Now that my vision had cleared, I gave them each a look over, as much to check for further injuries as to try to get a better sense of them than I had in the bar. Naoto was in his mid-twenties, Danae a bit older. He had an angular and stubbled face, with a few frayed braids hanging over a neglected undercut; she had deep brown skin and short-clipped hair, and her sea-soaked Epak coveralls draped over a body somewhat hollowed-out by some combination of stress and starvation.

"How do you both feel?" I asked.

"Alive," Danae answered.

The image of the artificial structure inside her head flashed through my mind's eye whenever she spoke.

"Barely," Naoto croaked in agreement. He'd taken the shock harder.

Danae was gritting her teeth and nursing her forearm.

"Are you injured?" I asked.

She shook her head. "It's nothing. An old break. Hurts with the pressure change."

"If you need something for the pain—"

"You should have left me," she interrupted. "When I swam for the emergency seal, you should have kept going. I didn't mean to endanger Naoto like that."

Naoto rolled his eyes exhaustedly.

"Moving forward," I said, "you'll need to be more explicit with parameters like that."

She covered her face in her hands and groaned. "I'm sorry. It was beyond reckless of me. I just . . . had to do something. I thought I could save all those people. And for what. They're all dead anyway."

"Some," I said. "Not all."

"What do you mean?"

"I saw what you were trying to do. I jammed the seals shut with the sub arms before we surfaced. It should have bought them some time to evacuate."

She pushed herself half-upright, propping herself up with a hand on my chest to meet my eyes. A very strange feeling moved through me. We couldn't have met before, but my déjà vu was almost dizzying. She braced her head against the wall of the bubble and wriggled her arm free, and it took me a moment to recognize the offer of a handshake.

"Thank you for helping us, Standard."

I was slow to respond. No client had ever tried to shake my hand. The awkwardness of pressing our bodies together in this space was a simple survival necessity, but this voluntary contact was something else. I stuffed down my discomfort and shook her hand briefly.

She paused in thought. "Is that your last name?"

I nodded.

"What's your first?"

The console somewhere beneath us mercifully chose that time to declare that the pressure had equalized. Ignoring the bright pain in my joints and the groans of the two people beneath me, I leaned up and pushed the hatch open. The air felt shockingly cold and clean on my face. My hands were shriveled and clammy in my gloves as I hauled myself up and out.

I called back down, "We should move quickly, before what's happening in Bloom spreads any farther. Assuming you still intend to travel inland."

"Yes," Danae murmured. "Inland." She avoided my eyes to stare at the rifle at my side with a look of sickened fascination—as if she thought she could read its history, count its killing shots. She squinted at the initials carved into the cedar grip: M.S. I hung it over my shoulder and reached a hand down to help her up.

Naoto kept his eyes fixed in mine. He looked like he couldn't decide whether I was his savior or his enemy.

"What's your destination?" I asked.

Danae heaved herself up over the lip of the hatch. I was only half surprised to hear her respond, "I can't tell you that. Not now. I'll say more once we're out of Epak's sphere of influence."

"You hired me as a guide and as a guard. I can't be effective in either role if I don't know your destination. I also need to know more about the threats you anticipate, besides Medusa Clan. I didn't understand your comment earlier about 'evangelists.'"

"Some people want me dead," she said. "Me and . . . anyone like me."

"Like you in what way?"

Naoto shot me a warning glare as he handed his backpack up to me. Something big and square-edged jutted through the fabric. Danae only rubbed the salt out of her eyes and stared away into the surf.

The way they both kept blinking at all that white sky and flat water, looking so shell-shocked, made me wonder how long it had been since either of them had seen the surface. Maybe they never had. Maybe that was why I couldn't wring any straight answers out of them.

"I'm not trying to be invasive, but I will be useless to you unless you give me more information." That was what really scared me, I realized. Right now I could stand the thought of death much better than the thought of uselessness.

"So ask," Danae muttered.

I wanted to ask whether the object embedded in her cerebrum was, as the scanner had indicated, a nanoweapon that could spread and begin to eat us all from the inside out at any moment. Instead I settled for, "The people you say want you dead. How well-equipped are they? How can I recognize them? What sort of methods will they use? Do they have some way of tracking you?"

"I'm sorry," she finally said. "I wish I could tell you more. It's . . . it's hard for me to talk about. They're a radical religious sect. They're nomadic wastelanders, but unusually resourceful and determined for that. They will use any method: guns, sabotage, suicide bombs. They don't care about collateral damage. They're also fond of torture and ritual execution and may try to take me alive to that end. They could be anyone, anywhere. The last time I saw them, five years ago, they vowed that they would stop at nothing to exterminate me."

'Exterminate' struck me as a strange verb for the murder of a single person, but I asked the more pressing question: "If you haven't encountered them in five years, are you sure they're still hunting you? I would think nomadic wastelanders would have moved on by now."

She shook her head. "I'm not sure of anything."

"Do they have a name?"

She looked at me briefly. "Keepers. They call themselves the Keepers."

I climbed back down into the cockpit to grab the last of the medkit supplies, but I stopped. Milky waves sloshed along the bubble around me, and I could only sit and try to get it through my head that if I'd been looking for a worthy death, this was the last job I should have taken. I wasn't headed for any front lines. I was an armed babysitter, guarding against the specter of an enemy that might not even be there anymore.

The escape from Bloom had given me exactly what I needed for as long as it had lasted. I'd been able to forget about Antarka, focus on the present, fix my mind completely on all the analytical and technical details of escape and survival. I'd been at peace for the exact length of my dead drop in elevator shaft, but now it was all seeping back, faster the safer I felt. My trigger finger twitched.

Desertion, the Major's voice echoed in my head. *Of the most unforgivable kind.*

"You're right," Danae called down, shaking me from my thoughts. "We should go."

I held my waver above my head as we stumbled for the shore in the neck-high sloshing tide. We clambered up the sand and rocks and arrived, newly shivering and dripping with the foamy spume of Bloom's industry, to empty the water from our boots. The old buildings here had all been ground down to their foundations by the storms and quakes and the sea.

"Hard to breathe up here," Naoto wheezed.

"Your lungs might need a couple of weeks to adjust," Danae told him apologetically. "It's not just the pressure change. You're also getting over a thousand parts per million of carbon dioxide in every breath now."

When we reached the road, my clients and I started in opposite directions. We looked back at each other through a tendril of wafting smoke.

"It should be less than two klicks from here to Bloom's land port," I said. "There might still be trains running."

Danae shifted uneasily. "A train. I'd expected we'd travel by cargo truck. We'll be much harder to track that way."

She was right. All my tactical sense told me to follow her lead away from the city, anonymously bribe a long-hauler with a meter or two of empty space between crates, but that would take time. I said, "A train will put distance between us and Bloom a lot faster. Under the circumstances, and given your time constraints, that's my suggestion."

She gave me a half-hearted nod, and the three of us started down the shattered highway. Thirty wordless minutes later we were scrambling up and over the barricades of rubble that ringed Bloom City's lone remote foothold on dry land: a small, dirty port serving the aquapolis' offshore elevators and algae fields.

There was almost no security left in the passenger terminal. I suspected most of the guards had been called to fight over more strategically important locations, and in their absence the wastelander tent city had pushed over a section of fence and spilled into the waiting area. It was a hollow victory: the ferries would only be carrying passengers to shore once the main elevators were repaired. Refugees fleeing death under the waves would merge with those running from the Holy Western Confederacy or the pure environmental brutality of surface life, but we had some time before that particular riot kindled. The remaining Medusas were high-strung and trigger-happy, but easily avoided and not especially concerned with checking our identities.

Still, the hairs on my neck kept standing up. Something was

watching us. I kept looking over my shoulder, but there was never anyone there.

We passed a group of people who had stopped, all cupping their eyes against the sun to gape upward and murmur among themselves:

"Tell me I'm not the only one who just saw that."

"I saw it."

"What? Ain't nothing."

"It's gone now, but it was there. I saw it too."

"Like it was invisible, but the sun lit up its edges."

"Yeah."

"Fuck's sake, what was it?"

"It was a . . ." The spectator hesitated. "Had to have been a sundog. Some kind of an optical illusion."

My pulse quickened and my feet stopped under me. My spit tasted metallic when I dared to look back and follow the lines of their pointing fingers up into the hot, empty sky.

"A giant fuckin' eyeball," someone muttered. "That's what it looked like to me."

My clients had stopped. They were taking their cues from my body language and bracing themselves to run. I shook my head and pushed myself forward.

I struggled to keep up at least an appearance of vigilance as we headed for the train platforms, scanning the crowd for possible threats—but whenever I resisted the urge to look upward, my attention wandered back to the clusters of aquapolitans who had somehow made it out of the city without the main elevators, all of them showing the effects of unsafe decompression. Mottled skin. Shaking hands and stumbling motion. Occasional tears of blood. Any sub pilots with the right mix of greed and guts would be ferrying people up from the depths now—taking their passengers for all they were worth, decompressing them in a hurry, maybe not even giving them Pascalex before letting them out into the terminal to sicken and collapse. I wondered how many had simply tried to swim.

In the corners of my vision, their bruised and bloodless faces transformed. They were all there: the forty-six dead in Antarka.

The adults.

The children.

"Standard?" Danae called, and I blinked, and they were gone. When I caught up, she looked out over the crowd and leaned in to whisper, "I just overheard that the trains are mostly empty and unstaffed, but Duke ordered them all to depart. Whether that's to bring in reinforcements or just to keep Bloom locked down, I don't know. We might still have time to get on the train to Crossroads Station. What do you think?"

"About what?" My voice sounded almost drunk. I was crumbling much faster than I'd expected.

"Do you think it's safe?"

I took a last look around. The crowd was a blur. "There's no one here. Let's go."

We paid our bribes and climbed onto the train as the levitation was humming noisily to life. I picked out an empty compartment and Danae heaved herself inside and sank onto the thin couch. I muttered something about settling in while I kept watch outside, but Naoto followed me into the corridor and slid the door shut behind him.

"I asked you a question, but you didn't answer," he told me quietly. He stood close with one hand obviously grasping something in the pocket of his coat. "Tell me what you saw on that medical scanner."

"You're my clients," I answered emotionlessly. "I saw . . . whatever you want me to have seen."

"What do you *think* you saw?"

If my silence wasn't good enough, I didn't know what he wanted from me. I enunciated carefully. "The scanner identified it as a nanoweapon. Is that accurate?"

"It's the opposite of a weapon," he said.

What was the opposite of a weapon? I shook my head and said, "If it isn't dangerous, it isn't my business."

He stared into me, close enough for me to count the burst capillaries in his sclerae—deciding whether he believed a word I said. Estimating how hard it was safe to push me.

"Danae knows the surface a lot better than I do," he told me. "Better than anyone alive. If she says we need someone to guard us up here, I believe her. Just remember you're not the only one guarding her. Or her secrets."

I nodded.

He locked the door behind him, and I was finally alone again, standing in the narrow corridor and staring out between the bars on the window, useless.

I wondered if any car on this train had a bar. A drug dealer. Anything. The Major's voice was ringing in my ears, telling me it was reckless and irresponsible to leave my clients there undefended, let alone to do it for the sole purpose of getting high, but the pressure still building in my chest told me I'd never survive this ride sober. I walked.

The door at the end of the car slid open just as I reached it. A small woman with woven black hair stood there, wide-eyed, hands stuffed into her pockets, blocking my way. I stepped to the side to give her room to slide by me, and she took it—but as I stepped into the rattling vestibule between the cars, a shiver of reflex made me glance over my shoulder. The next reflex threw me onto the metal floor just in time for the shot to pass invisibly a few centimeters above my head and carve a spitting, smoking hole into the plastic wall.

My rifle was in my hands and primed to fire before I noticed myself do it. I crouched beside the door as it slid automatically shut. I'd seen her taking cover just outside my clients' compartment, a wave pistol in each hand. There would be no delay to take advantage of since she could fire one pistol while the other primed—and my armor was next to useless, since she'd be aiming for my head at such close quarters. One way or another I had to act quickly. All she needed was one hard kick to the flimsy lock to gain access to my unarmed clients.

I palmed the switch on the door and heard it slide open. I assumed a firing stance and turned the corner, and in a blink her head was directly between my sights: I'd caught her in a dive for better cover. I had every advantage, and my finger was on the trigger, and I was pulling—I was trying so hard to pull it—

I couldn't.

She fired her first shot with less than seven meters between us and missed. I felt the heat reflect off the metal wall and briefly set fire to the hair above my ear, but she was still centered in my sights and my finger was still on the trigger, and I was still straining every fiber of my body to pull it, still hooking my finger into an aching claw to depress that insignificant piece of metal—

She fired the other wave pistol. I heard the fizzling pop of cooking flesh before I registered the splash of ragged, electromagnetic fire where she'd hit me. The pain blossomed over my ribs and stabbed like a burning shank down into my lung.

Every nerve of my body was still twitching with electric fear. I wasn't afraid of her, or death. I was afraid of the sky just outside these metal walls—afraid it was watching—and in the grip of that impossible fear, it was as if I could feel every blood cell corkscrewing through my every twisted artery, all of them straining to deliver the half kilogram of force to tell the wave rifle to impart the burst of high-frequency microwave radiation that would incinerate my enemy's brain from the inside out—just as it had those forty-six times in Antarka only days ago, as it had hundreds of other times before that—

But they couldn't. I couldn't.

I couldn't kill.

My enemy crouched there half hidden behind a cargo rack, waiting those three eternal seconds for her wave pistols to prime again. Enough time. I rapidly ejected my waver's power cell, flipped the clip down to bridge the connections, and rolled it down the floor to her feet.

It exploded in a rain of sparks and burning chemicals, and a single arc of plasma danced briefly and brilliantly through the corridor before expending itself. The electromagnetic pulse made the whole train shudder briefly.

Her guns clattered to the floor under the flickering overhead lights, and she let out one drawn-out cry as the darkness washed over both of us.

DANAE

"So I guess this is it," I was telling Naoto, wrapping him tight in my arms and smelling the ocean salt in his hair. "Once we get to Crossroads, that's goodbye, isn't it?"

He stiffened in my grip. "There's something you need to know about Standard."

"What?"

The first waver shriek from just outside cut him off mid-word. We stared at each other for only a second before he ran to press himself flat against the wall by the door, bracing to fight whoever came through it, fumbling for something in his pocket.

I was less composed. I didn't know where I was until my back hit the wall, and it was all I could do to hold myself upright against the sill of the slit window. In that sharp sound, in my head, I was right back in Asher Valley, living and dying through it all over again: the smell of my own burning flesh, the screams from my own throats, the rising chorus of waver fire, the lack of an exit.

"It's them," I gasped. "They've found me."

Get down! Naoto mouthed. He waved frantically for me to hide, but I couldn't move.

"They've found me."

Two more shots sounded in fast succession. I clamped my hands

over my mouth to swallow the scream, already seeing ghost images
of twenty Keepers in makeshift armor bursting through that door
to shoot me down or hack me to pieces—but instead there was a
loud snap and two irregular thuds, punctuated by a blood-curdling
groan. The lights flickered and there was a feeling on the air that
made my skin crawl. Ionization. Burnt chemical odors wafted in
under the door.

The silence drew out. Hot adrenaline splashed through my chest
when a voice outside yelled, "Clear." It was Standard. "Open the door.
Hurry."

Naoto grudgingly obeyed once I gave him a nod. We both gaped
at what waited on the other side: our bodyguard, dragging a half-
conscious woman by her armpits into the compartment and sealing
the door behind him. She couldn't be more than sixteen years old.
She was in some kind of shock. Her legs and torso struggled against
our grip, but her arms were too racked by spasms to offer much
resistance.

"What the hell happened?" Naoto asked.

"She must have followed us from the terminal," Standard said. He
ejected the power cells from her pistols one by one and set them on
the cot without ever taking his eyes off our captive. "I've secured all
the doors to this car as a precaution."

Naoto knelt to pat her down. He looked up at me to ask, "Is she
one of them? One of your Keepers?"

I was still too shocked to form words—but the more I looked at
her, the more I knew it was the last thing in the world she could be.
I'd forgotten to tell Standard one crucial detail: the Keepers would
never allow a woman to handle a weapon. She had none of a Medusa's markings, either.

Yet there she was: living proof that someone wanted us dead—
and if not the Clan or the Keepers, then who?

"Tell us who hired you," Standard said. His voice was eerily calm.
"Names, objectives, parameters."

The assassin only glared up at us and gritted her teeth against whatever pain had disabled her arms. I couldn't see how she'd been injured; she had no visible wounds or waver burns.

"What if she was just trying to rob us?" Naoto said. "This could be random."

Standard shook his head. "Someone hired her."

"How do you know?"

He never took his eyes off her to tell us, "I recognize her type. An underworld teenager who romanticizes mercenary labor but has limited to no experience of it."

Our captive glared viciously up at him.

"How do you know that?" I asked.

"She has aim-assists in both arms," he sighed. "And the aim of someone who's never fired at a living human target before."

Our captive broke her silence to shout, "You don't know shit about me."

Naoto carefully pulled up her sleeve to inspect her hand and forearm. A network of geometrically branched lines was drawn in blood blisters and dark traces beneath the skin. All those hair-thin electrodes, designed to automatically fine-tune her muscle response for machine-like shooting accuracy, had violently shorted out at once.

"Fuck," the captive hissed, squeezing her eyes shut against the sight of her own wounds. "My arms. The fuck did you do to my arms?"

It was only then that I noticed the pain creasing Standard's own face. He stepped back against the wall, wincing and gritting his teeth to stretch his arms back to carefully remove his coat. One by one, he unfastened the interlocking pieces of his thin, matte-black armor.

"Are you hurt?" I asked.

"It's nothing." He cautiously inspected a dark circle on his chest, just above the bottom of his ribcage. It took me too long to recognize what I was seeing: blood and blackened skin showing faintly through the material of his undershirt.

I gaped. "You're *shot*?"

"I said it's nothing." He peeled the fabric away from the blister. "It was a low-energy shot. The plates absorbed most of it."

When he pulled the shirt off, his naked torso held me in sick awe. His skin bore dozens of marks from other waver burns like this one: circles and ovals of various sizes; some old and fully scarred, others still healing in uneven shades of pink. These were complemented by a constellation of other old injuries: thick and ragged lacerations indenting the muscle of his left shoulder; at least two clusters of healed-over shrapnel wounds; blotchy, discolored patches rising above his hip, etched by some chemical or bio-agent or nanoweapon. I tried and failed to look away as he attended to this newest addition, callously picking away the crisp dermis before applying a self-adhesive patch. Naoto and I shared a glance that asked, more clearly than words:

Who in the hell was this man I'd hired to guard me? Just who was Standard? I'd stumbled into that smoke bar praying for a cheap but marginally competent hired gun who wouldn't instantly betray me to the Medusas, and instead I'd unknowingly come away with a hardened veteran of multiple wars, a genius of violence. I hadn't decided yet whether that was better or worse.

I still couldn't stop staring at the dull gleam of the bent-up wire necklace.

He restored the shirt, the armor, and the coat, and that was that. When I looked back, I caught a twinge of despair in the eyes of our would-be assassin: not for her failure or her capture or her injuries, I realized, so much as her perverse envy for the record of violence etched into Standard's cruel body.

"I'll ask you again," Standard told our captive. "Who hired you? What were your objectives? How many others are there?"

"Others?" I echoed.

The young woman's strained voice barely rose above the thrum of the magnetic fields under our feet. "You know I'm not telling you shit. A merc doesn't give away her employers or her comrades."

Standard was unfazed. He picked through the pile of her belongings until he found her shard. With a few keystrokes he interfaced it with his own, then made a call. "Are you with me, Kat?"

A scrambled voice creaked out of his shard to answer, "To the bitter end."

"Our party has its first guest. Find out who invited her."

"On it."

Standard hung up. "My associate is tracing her recent activity in nodespace. Some information about her employer or her objectives might still be cached in her shard."

"How long will that take?" Naoto said.

Standard shook his head.

Our attacker was only looking at me now.

For five years I'd lived in fear of what the Keepers would do to me if they ever caught me, but at least that fear was known and familiar. This was somehow worse: standing here with my would-be killer, knowing nearly nothing about who had sent her or why—and every second we did nothing, the train carried us inexorably closer to Crossroads Station.

"If she's working with a group, they must know we're on this train," I said. "They could be setting up an ambush for us at the end of the line. Right? Isn't that likely?"

Standard lowered his eyes. "It's what I would do."

"We need to get off this train," I said. "Right now."

"We're already moving at a hundred KPH."

"Let's not act without thinking," Naoto said. "This is all speculation. We don't know anything for sure."

I forced myself to turn and give our captive a long look. "You're right," I said. "We need to know exactly what we're dealing with. By any means necessary."

Naoto hesitated to ask. "You mean . . . torture?" He looked at Standard—who seemed to shudder and look away in response. It wasn't the chilling composure I had expected from a mercenary.

"Torture doesn't work," I answered. "It's never been a remotely effective method of retrieving information. Even the Medusas know that. But I . . . I have other options."

Naoto flinched. "You can't. Can you?"

Standard gave me a questioning look, but did not ask.

"Wait outside," I told him. "Keep watch." When he was gone, I turned to Naoto and whispered, "I can brush the surface of her memories without internalizing them. One-way link."

"Is that . . . ?" He trailed off, but I could fill in the blanks. Wise? Safe? Ethical? In each case the answer was the same.

"Not at all," I said, flexing my fingers. "It's unforgivable."

It never would have occurred to me to do something like this, when I'd been whole. The person I had been back then would have been incapable of such a hideous crime. If it were only my own life at stake now, even the person I had devolved into since then might have simply accepted the risk of walking into a trap at Crossroads Station. But Naoto's life was something else. It was too high a price to pay for my principles.

He touched my arm as if to stop me.

"What . . . what are you going to do?" the young assassin stammered.

"She might still tell us," Naoto said.

"She might lie," I said. "This is the only way to be sure."

"Wait," the assassin said.

I crouched down on the thrumming floor. I cleared my mind and focused on my breath. It had been so long since I'd sent a thought-command to my unifier that for a moment I was afraid I wouldn't remember how—but I pressed my palm to the assassin's forehead. I closed my eyes and willed.

The pain of all those shorted cybernetics was the first thing I felt in the moment I became her. It was in my hands and arms and the back of my neck, so razor-sharp and white-hot that it almost shattered our connection the moment it cohered—but I focused, compartmentalized, endured. I moved deeper. I reached into her writhing morass of intrusive thought and involuntary recollection. I tried to touch only the memories I needed.

There. I'm in the corridor of the second-to-last car, racked with adrenaline, shooting at the woman's bodyguard. I miss. Fucking shit, what's wrong with me? Why can't I shoot straight? I just need to shoot the bastard like I shot Grenley. It's not different. It shouldn't feel any fucking different. Finally I hit him. I hit him in the chest. But he's not dead. Fuck me, he's still there. I'm holding the trigger down, but the guns are still charging. Everything is fucked. But why isn't he returning fire with that huge motherfucking wave rifle of his? What the fuck could he be thinking?

(*What* had *Standard been thinking?* I wondered, in the corner of myself that was still Danae. *Why not just fire?*)

For a split second, I lost my focus. The internal burns weighing her arms down surged with fresh pain, and her memory blinked. Now I was in a dim room, naked, bound by different restraints. Naked with Grenley, the creature that bought me at the age of ten, that hacking old imp with the infinite appetite for young flesh, the debts owed to the wrong people, the smug and fatherly self-assurance that none of his little girls would ever have the guts to earn their own freedom by hard-boiling his perverted brain.

(*No. Not this.* I cringed with two bodies at once. I felt two different jaws ache from clenching. I banished the memory. I focused again.)

(*Focus.*)

There. I kept to the sidelines of the station and memorized the image in the shard. The image the client had sent. A woman, thirty-one years of age, 1.7 meters tall, African descent, bony; names include Danae, Ruth, Sybil. This was going to be my breakthrough job. I was going to make a name for myself, move down into Bloom proper once the smoke cleared, work for the Clan. No more hunger pangs. I wasn't going to fuck this up. I staked out the station for hours—and just my luck, there she was. With a guy, Japanese or Korean looking, sour-faced. A second man was with them. I could tell I didn't want to fuck with that guy even before I saw the wave rifle peeking out from under his coat like he didn't care who saw it. I'd have to take care of him to get to her. So I watched them. Followed them carefully onto the train.

(*Focus.*)

Rewind further. The call had come in at midnight ten hours before. The face in my shard had said: one woman, taken alive, alone, by any means necessary. Fifty thousand squid, payable upon delivery. Fuck me, I'd thought, what a fucking fortune. I'd said yes. For a second I wondered who my new employer was, who the target was. It didn't matter, but I kept wondering anyway. There was just something odd about him. His voice sounded so old, somehow. Older than a voice ever ought to be coming from a face that young. Just an ordinary Epak face, thick, bald-headed, with a blue logo stamped on his right cheek. Something about him was definitely off, but what did it matter? I'd finally found myself a job. I grabbed my guns and suited up.

(*Freeze here. Focus.*)

The man with a blue facial tattoo.

I returned to my own mind enough to remember where I'd seen that face: in the shard of the elevator guard on the night I'd hired Standard. The Medusan lieutenant said that man had been looking for me. Whatever our attacker had found so instinctively off-putting about him tugged at something in my own memory, but I couldn't name it.

That was it. There was nothing else to know.

Except that he had said my name was Sybil—that name, out of all of them. I hadn't used it in decades; there was no way the Medusas could know to call me that. Even the Keepers couldn't.

Who on Earth could still know me by that name?

Serena's body jerked when I took my hand off her head. All the defiant strength in her eyes was gone, replaced by a pure bewilderment that faded by degrees into an even purer fear, and I slumped onto the floor, finally seeing her for what she was: just an angry kid whose aspirations to violence were only for want of any other kind.

I wanted to apologize, but I was afraid it would only make it all worse. I pressed my palm against her forehead one more time just to will her into a few hours of dreamless sleep. I wished I could do the same for myself.

Naoto stood back, looking stricken. I motioned at the door, and he opened it and brought Standard back into the compartment.

"Her name is Serena," I said, when I found the breath to speak. "She acted alone. She hasn't told anyone else we boarded this train. She knows nothing about her client other than the address he called from, which you'll find as the most recent incoming call in her shard's log. The unlock code is 2-9-1-0-6." I swallowed hard. "Her only orders were to get me alone and take me alive. You two would've been collateral damage."

I knew they were both staring at me, but I refused to meet their eyes. Standard was good enough to not ask for any explanations. Serena kept breathing—and looking down her internally-burned arm and the persistent mis-healed crookedness in mine, I knew exactly what I'd become.

Naoto picked up her pistols and started to put them in his backpack.

"Don't," I groaned. "Leave them for her. They're all she has. When she wakes up, she'll need something to pawn to get medical attention."

Standard regarded me cautiously and said, "You aren't worried she'll come after you again?"

I looked back at Serena's sleeping form one more time and felt a withering wave of regret. "No I am not," I said. I climbed onto the cot and pulled the curtain closed behind me.

"Danae—" Naoto started.

"No more trains," I said. And I lay there in silence for the rest of the ride to Crossroads Station.

PART II: NAMELESS

I

Alexei didn't understand what he'd seen through the hairline gap in the door. From his perspective, Danae had simply put her hand on the assassin's forehead, a silent minute had passed, and then she'd called him back into the room, suddenly knowing everything. Just as suddenly, Alexei knew less than ever about his clients—but his mind was clearing now, his heart falling back into a rhythm.

He had exactly what he needed now. He'd squandered his first chance to die, but he could rest assured there would be more, because he knew now that Danae was no ordinary tech servant on the run from Medusa Clan. She had secrets—maybe the largest and deepest secrets he had ever been close to—and where there were secrets like that, death always followed.

Danae lay still on the cot, face to the wall. Naoto stayed close, every so often whispering useless consolations. He told her she'd acted in self-defense. She ignored every word, until he had nothing left but to sit and stare out through the slit window. He'd never seen a sky that was farther away than the paint on the rusty crossbeams of Bloom City's main habitat, and his lungs had never tasted un-pressurized air; he'd followed Danae into another world altogether, knowing he could never go back. He needed someone to be there with him in that moment, and I regret so much—all the more for what lay ahead—that he had no one.

Far behind them, Bloom City was finally beginning to dry. Though no part of me was there to see it, the years I spent in those claustrophobic spaces make the scenes all too vivid in my imagination: how the seals were being repaired, flooded compartments drained, corridors sprayed clean of blood. Duke must have strolled victorious among his competitors—some bound and kneeling, others already dead—all flanking a path of crimson carpet that still squished with saltwater under his boots. He stood before the half-smashed remains of the throne he had coveted all his life and paused to savor a single touch of gilded, waterlogged wood under his fingertips—but just as he was about to sit, an urgent clang of running footsteps turned his attention to an underling offering him a data pane. At first he couldn't understand why anyone would bother him with something so random: nothing but a fragmented emergency transmission from a portable medical scanner in a beached construction pod. But he looked closer. For all the glory he'd hung on the moment he finally sat on the Medusan Throne, he was barely aware of its ruined leather as he sank down. All his awareness was fixed instead on the many-spined thing in the center of a nameless woman's brain, drawn in pale holographic light.

This is a story about people without names—some who lost their names, others who'd never had them. Serena had no family. Duke needed nothing but his title. Alexei's last name was borrowed from a man who was not his blood. Danae had hundreds of names buried underneath that simple alias, but there was none that she could call herself anymore.

While the train hummed onward into the scorched lands once called California, another nameless person sat cross-legged on a softly rocking corrugated steel floor somewhere on the ocean, enclosed in her nest of colored wire and glowing holographic panes. She'd learned the value of anonymity the hard way once. Since then, it had been her policy to use a different pseudonym for every transaction, with only enough of a common thread between names that she could still build a reputation. To one of her clients she was Vera Cruz, to another Jo Burg; to the only living person who had ever really known her, she was Kat Mandu.

Barely diverting her attention from the half-dozen other streams of data flowing liquidly across her vision, she called him again.

"Are you with me," Alexei answered. She could hear the rasp of pain in his voice.

"Are you okay?" she asked.

"The plates caught it."

Her cringe was audible in her voice. "God damnit, Lex."

"I'm fine."

"Uh-huh. You're fine like I'm a sun-tanned extrovert."

"I have a favor to ask," he said. "I need to know whether anyone might be developing nanobots for . . . medical, or cybernetic applications. Like Gray, but able to safely reside within a human body. Leaks, rumors, anything you can find."

Kat snorted. "I can ask around, but I can tell you right now the answer is no. Nanobots are about as friendly to living tissue as sulfuric acid. All they're good for is turning people and things into glittery pudding. Why?"

"But in theory—"

"In theory, lots of things. Programming nanobots to do much of anything at all besides eat and multiply is decades out. Teaching them to play nice with human flesh, long-term? You're looking at centuries."

He sighed. "Never mind, then. See if you can find out anything about a group called the Keepers. Variations on that name, especially with religious connotations. Anything you can learn."

Kat sighed and rubbed her eyes. "I'm on it. And in reference to the *last* favor you asked me for, your party guest isn't on any VIP list. Name's Serena. Classic back-alley fare. No link to Medusa Clan. As far as I can tell, the guy who hired her either didn't know what the hell he was doing or didn't have the right connections to hire someone better." She studied the face in the video log she'd pulled from Serena's shard: those jowls, that blue corporate tattoo. "He looks like somebody's frumpy uncle, not some kind of underworld power player."

"You found him? Who is he?"

Kat needed a moment to put her thoughts in order before she could answer. The information strewn around her pod was making her head spin. "Buckle up for this one, Lex. Until recently he was a fourth-tier logistical stooge for the Glass Corporation, high in the running for the most boring man on Earth. No connections to anything, no interesting communications, avowed pacifist, hadn't left the company housing block in years. Then about a month ago, out of the blue, he cleaned out all his own bank accounts and went missing. His data trail ends there without a trace. It doesn't pick up again until yesterday . . . when suddenly he appears in a bunch of Medusan surveillance scans, planting a half-dozen improvised explosive devices near Dahlia's keep."

Alexei's voice in her ear was uncharacteristically disheveled. "He . . . say that again?"

"That's right," Kat said. "That 'lone wolf' Duke told you about— the guy the Medusas think assassinated the Empress of fucking Epak—is the exact same guy who hired a bargain-bin assassin to kill you and abduct your client. That, or somebody is trying extremely hard to make us *think* that's what happened. I don't know which idea makes less sense to me."

The whole thing was even more surreal now that she'd heard herself say it. She slapped her hands to her forehead and yelled, "Precisely what the fuck have you gotten yourself into, Lex? Who are you guarding?"

There was something ominous about his hesitation before he responded, "That's the question, isn't it."

This is a story about the nameless—and there is one more nameless person I'm condemned to remember. He was back in the passenger terminal of Bloom City's land port, slumping against the refugee fence: a heavyset bald man with a blue corporate tattoo on his right cheek.

I would give anything to forget him completely, but I can't. Not just because of everything that happened, or the role he played in it. I remember Luther, and the thing he had become, because even now some small part of him is part of me too. It hurts me to know it always will be.

BORROWER

This is it, I thought to myself, again and again. I felt my blood-caked lips chanting these words like a mantra. *This is it, this is it, this is it.* Anyone nearby in the crowd must have thought I'd gone mad. My eardrums had both burst; I could only feel my voice, not hear it. Even before my hasty decompression, I'd been too close to the last bomb when it went off. I stabbed a second injector of Pascalex into the inside of my forearm and felt the warmth of the shot move through me. It was a fatal overdose, but it would take time to kill this flesh, and the flesh was dying anyway. Better to squeeze as much functionality out of it as I could.

I was in an ecstasy of fear: I was going to face real death. This wasn't something I'd prepared for. How can a person prepare to surrender his immortality? I had incorporated the measured possibility of my death into the plan—I was only the gamma copy, after all—but it was something else to face the reality.

But it was worth it. I had done it. *This was it.* My plans so achingly long in the making were rapidly coming to fruition. For one fleeting moment I had even seen her through the crowd. After seventy-two years, I had seen my own beloved Sybil with my own eyes. That alone was nearly worth the price.

I picked the shard out of my coat pocket. I had to spit on it and wipe it off thoroughly before I'd removed enough red crust that it would respond to my touch commands.

Accomplished, I typed. *She's on the surface. On the train. Number 892 to Crossroads Station.*

While I waited for a response, I applied pressure to the wound in my abdomen. I inspected its severity. The knife that Medusa man had stabbed me with before I'd knocked him out had been at least ten centimeters long; I suspected he'd perforated one of my kidneys. I should have been in agony, but I was as numb as ever, or I couldn't feel pain in the conventional sense. In all the time I'd been having this problem, I had never gotten used to it. The sensory dissociation was still so unsettling.

Nearly failed, I typed. *Did not expect so much infighting. Medusa factions tried to destroy city. I thought she was dead. Despaired. But then I saw her.*

My body writhed against the fence as I typed that again for emphasis: *Saw her.*

Why haven't you followed her? was the response from the alpha copy.

I responded, *Flesh immobilized by wounds. Will not survive.*

Another wave of refugees fleeing Bloom City shuffled past the spot where I huddled. Some only glanced down at my wrecked flesh. Some stopped long enough to grimace at the pool of blood gathering beneath me. Most of them simply stumbled on, tracking it along under their shoes.

And the bounty hunters? asked the beta copy.

Four confirmed employed. Only one made it aboard train. Outcome uncertain. Do not suggest employing more. Unacceptably careless. Do it ourselves.

We cannot risk damage to her flesh, beta agreed.

I saw her, I typed again. *I saw her myself.*

The other two copies ignored my words again—and I knew exactly what they were thinking and feeling while that delay stretched

out. I knew perfectly well how much they envied me. It was para-
doxical—how can one envy oneself?—and yet I knew how I would
have burned with envy had one of them told me he had seen her. If
all went well, one of them would be the one to speak to her. To touch
her. To do so much more than merely touch her.

I knew I would gladly sacrifice myself many times over for the
sake of that moment. I would willingly submit to far more than two
real deaths if I could know for certain that my third and final self
would be the one to reach her.

This is it, I felt my throat chanting again.

Find her, I commanded the other two. *At any cost.*

We will, the alpha copy responded. *Any cost.*

Nothing can be permitted to stop us, the beta typed. *Everything
depends on it.*

Everything, alpha agreed.

Everything, I echoed.

I am moving to intercept the train, said the beta.

On my way to Crossroads from Camp Fresno, said the alpha. *ETA
six hours.*

Nothing more I can do, I typed. *Dying. Good luck.*

Another one of the Medusa men was standing over me. He was
shouting something, but I couldn't hear him. I knew what was happening: he knew I'd bombed the keep, and he wanted to know why.
He would want to take me alive, but it was too late for that.

More Medusa men and women came shoving through the crowd.
Eventually they brought a stretcher and lifted me onto it. They
stabbed a new needle into the same vein that had just accepted the
lethal dose of Pascalex and began to feed me synthetic blood.

"I am so sorry," I found myself saying to them, sincerely. I couldn't
hear my own voice, but I felt my way through the words as best I
could. I turned my head toward the passing crowds of refugees and
repeated, "I'm sorry to all of you."

The plan required all this strife. There had been no other way to
call Sybil forth. Still, I found myself itching to tell them that this

was not me. What I had done was not in my nature, I yearned to say aloud. I had never been a killer or a destroyer, only a borrower.

Already my vision was blurring. The Medusas would not be saving this flesh. No one would.

But as I died, I felt a great swell of hope. The plan was in motion. One of the other copies would finish what I had succeeded in starting. One of them would find her.

The chase had just begun.

ALEXEI

Whatever Danae had done had taken a heavy toll on her, though I could only guess whether the damage was mainly psychological, or physical, or something else. Naoto and I could barely get her off the train once we reached Crossroads Station. She stared past us with a blank, withered expression and only seemed to register a fraction of anything said to her. We gently lifted her off the cot and stood her up, and from there Naoto was able to walk her along, down the makeshift station's rusty steps and on into the relative anonymity of the crowds. I put on my goggles and tugged my scarf over my nose, as much to guard against the blowing sand as to hide my cringing; with every step I took, the waver burn at the bottom of my ribs provided a drumbeat of pain to remind me of my newfound inability to kill.

A scuffed media pane projected Duke's glowering visage out over the crowd; he'd already cemented his power and taken the throne. I was astonished he'd crushed all his competition so quickly. We all were.

"Your meds," Naoto kept saying. "Danae? Did you pack your meds?"

She gave a barely visible nod.

"Where are they?" he asked.

She squinted up at the naked sky and mouthed the word, "Backpack."

"The backpack you lost in the ascent?"

She nodded again.

I kept my eyes on the crowd and leaned in closer to Naoto to ask, "Do you know her destination, or is she the only one capable of discussing it and planning the route?"

The look on his face answered for him. He sighed and confided, "She just needs something to break the downward spiral, and I know what she usually takes. Find us an autopharmacy booth and I'll do the rest."

"There are no autopharmacies on the surface," I said. "There's probably a drug dealer in the market. What does she normally take?"

He stared at me long and hard, sizing me up. He leaned in close to say, "Look, I know the plan was only for me to tag along this far, but I can't leave until I know she's okay. Until she's functioning again, and safely on her way the hell out of this place. Just point me to a dealer. I'll handle it."

I nodded. His distrust was palpable, but I didn't mind it; I was a monster, after all. I was also thankful for his help, even if it gave me a second body to guard.

"No autopharmacies?" he echoed to himself, incredulously. "How does anyone live up here?"

It was all too clear now that he'd been a lifelong aquapolitan until today. He stared in disbelief at almost everything: the tents and yurts and crude shade structures melted together from hundred-year-old plastic trash, brand names still legible; the formations of trailers nestled among the walls of half-destroyed buildings; the clots of human beings whose skins were all pockmarked and leathery from the harsh environment.

"What do they do when storm season comes?" he asked Danae. "Pack up the entire town and move it out of the way?"

Danae only stared ahead. Her cold sweat attracted a thickening layer of dust, forming a mask.

"Essentially," I answered for her. "Those that can afford the energy expense usually try to migrate out of the path of the worst weather. Others may try to ride it out, if they can afford three months of provisions."

"What do they do if they can't afford either?"

"Perish," Danae murmured.

The market was a two-tiered labyrinth of stalls and narrow corridors. I took comfort in its cluttered design: lines of sight would be short here, hiding places numerous, crowds too dense to run through. Plankton burgers were frying on sheets of hot black metal. Hiding in their warm and pungent steam, burying our voices under the noise of the bustle, we were as safe here as we could be.

I pointed out a vendor stall with the white stripes that customarily signified dealers and dispensaries on dry land, and Naoto motioned for us to wait while he muscled through the crowd to negotiate the purchase. It took him a while. When he returned, he had an unmarked, single-use injector full of a milky, sky-blue fluid.

"I'm sorry it's not what you usually use," Naoto told Danae, his hands curling softly around her shoulders. "I can barely understand the accent up here, honestly, but they said it would help. It's the strongest mood stabilizer they had."

She turned sluggishly toward the wall for a semblance of privacy. She rolled up the sleeve of her coveralls, put the needle in her vein, and squeezed the bubble.

Naoto shot me a harsh look. "You could have warned me they don't even take cash up here. I had to barter a silver ring for that one injector."

Something was wrong. We were still well within Epak's Greater Economic Zone; this close to the coast, Medusa Clan enforced an informal requirement for everyone to transact in squid. The vendor wouldn't risk the severed fingers, unless—

"He cheated me, didn't he," Naoto said, reading my face.

I looked up from the headlines scrolling across my shard. "Yes, but we have bigger problems. The global market is in free fall. Squid will be functionally worthless on land for now."

"Since when?"

"Since Medusa Clan began to redeploy its forces for war with Norpak. Just now."

Naoto blinked hard and steadied himself against a canopy beam. "Fuck. It's revenge for Dahlia. Duke's going to drag the entire Pacific into full-scale war just to get revenge?"

I said nothing, but I couldn't make sense of what was happening. Even setting aside what Duke had told me, if Norpak had really orchestrated the bombing of Bloom with the blue-tattoo man as their agent, they would have gone on the offensive immediately afterward; a decapitation strike is pointless unless followed up by a rapid and massive attack. Instead it was Duke who had broken the ceasefire.

Naoto was visibly wilting with Gray Day fear, and I suspected my own effectiveness would start to degrade if I let myself think much more about it. I had to focus on our present and practical concerns. I had to keep my clients focused.

"We should barter for some basic provisions, and get you both into much less conspicuous clothes," I said, forcing my voice smooth against the pain in my chest. "Trade anything else you can both spare for metal money that might still have exchange value here. Then Danae and I need to move on from Crossroads as quickly as we can. The resumption of hostilities is only going to further complicate long-distance travel. As it is, she'll need something valuable to barter for onward transport. Any ideas?"

Naoto looked askance and nodded. "I have something."

"What is it?"

"Let me worry about that. For now, let's just—"

Danae cut him off with a gasp. She blinked and shuddered. Blood rushed back into her face. She passed him a wide-eyed glance to say, "That was no mood stabilizer."

"Are you okay?" Naoto asked.

"I don't know what I just put in myself." She stifled a sharp laugh. "But I think it's working."

Naoto rubbed his face nervously.

"I suggest we move on from Crossroads as soon as we can," I said. "We need a destination."

"Oh." She stared up at the harsh bright sky peeking between the plastic threads of the canopy. "Redhill? It's . . . east. Due east of here."

I tried to hold her attention. "How far east?"

"Arizona."

The name sounded strange in my ears.

She smiled drunkenly at me. "Yeah?"

"Nothing." I cleared my throat. "Just that—it's not called that any-more."

"But you know where Arizona used to be, don't you?"

I exchanged a glance with Naoto. "Yes, but that's a very large area. Can you be any more specific?"

"Not until we get closer. When we know it's safer. I have to protect myself. Not me, but *the* me. The self. Can't let anyone find out where *me* is." She snorted.

I gave up trying to parse any of that. "We can probably arrange transport via cargo truck to Camp Phoenix. Is that close to where you're going?"

"Perfect."

I could have tried to press her for more sensical detail, but it was enough to know our next step. For my purposes, I supposed it didn't matter exactly where in the former American state of Arizona she wanted to go; one way or another, we were headed deep into the Holy Western Confederacy. If I still wanted to die, I'd find ample opportunities there.

Danae's mood lightened as we moved deeper into the market. Between their existing clothes and most of Naoto's belongings, we managed to barter for decent provisions (a box of dried algae cakes, 500 grams of surprisingly good mealworm jerky, three gallons of grade-C reclaimed water), and clothes to disguise the two of them as common wastelanders (dirty plastic shirts, hooded military coats with a dozen patched rips, some ill-fitting boots with cracked soles). Whatever drug she'd taken was at least keeping her far from catatonic—but it was clear she wasn't entirely there with us, either.

We passed a pawn broker's stall advertising second-hand firearms. She stopped to gawk at the wall of weaponry, festooned with flashing lights. She turned around and clutched at Naoto and I, at the shoulders of our coats, grinning almost maniacally.

"Do you have any idea how *long* it took people to make fusion power work right?" she demanded. "Thousands upon thousands of scientists, all around the world, for 120 years."

Naoto pulled her in closer to him. "Easy, easy. Not so loud."

"Don't you get it?" she slurred. She slammed her fist on his chest. "It was supposed to save us all. The whole Earth would have limitless, carbon-free energy from seawater. No more oil wars. No need to fight over anything anymore! And instead of that, we got wave rifles: the most energy-intensive murder weapon ever invented. A hundred kilojoules packed into every shot."

"It's okay," he said. "It's going to be okay, just breathe."

The pawn broker himself was staring at me—at my rifle, I realized, exposed by Danae's tugs on the breast of my coat. I hid it again, too late. He whistled through his teeth and called out, "Now whose corpse did you pry that thing from?"

I wanted to hurry on, but my clients were still standing there whispering to each other, oblivious.

"Zaytsev SL-10," the broker pressed. "Only one army I know of ever issued that weapon." He flipped a succession of lenses back and forth over his eyes to squint at me, and then a grin flickered over his cracked lips. "You're the genuine article, aren't you? I don't believe it. An honest-to-God soldier of the Free Republic."

I muttered back, "No such place."

"Everything okay?" Naoto asked over his shoulder; my clients had finally started walking again. I nodded and followed, but the pawn broker's gaze burned a hole in my back all the way down the line.

The next thing that snagged Danae's attention and refused to let go was in a salvage shop: an old American Imperial flag in a cracked glass frame, all but bleached to white threads by the unfiltered ultraviolet of the terrestrial sun.

"Sometimes it seems like memory is in the world, in the ground, the dust," she said—to me, I thought. "In the ruins. Not in my head at all. As if our engrams are only organs for perceiving the ambient memory around us. Do you ever think that?"

I couldn't tell if it was a rhetorical question. I waited for something salient to our tactical situation. She just kept browsing distractedly among the ancient relics.

"How are you feeling?" Naoto asked. "Danae?"

She ignored him. "We'd been living under the threat of nuclear war for a century when it finally happened. We, I mean . . . humankind, I guess. We'd always believed that would be it for us, if it ever came to that. The end of the world. Extinction.

"I saw it myself. I saw five megatons erase Boston. It wasn't like in the movies; it was silent. So much light, but it was all perfectly quiet, like a sunrise. It took so long for the sound to reach me where I was. It must've only been two minutes, but it was endless. When it came . . . it was the last sound I ever heard. It made me deaf."

The more I listened, the less I understood. The war she was talking about had happened 110 years ago. I could only assume she was speaking in some kind of metaphor, but I couldn't parse it.

"But you survived," Naoto murmured.

She responded, "Yes. Most people survived. Five hundred million dead worldwide, twice that injured, but the rest of us were still there. No one had expected that. No one planned for it. We were living out a future we'd never believed in, and something . . . changed, in humanity, then. Something broke." She was staring into a case at a rusty combat knife on the moth-eaten velvet. She smiled. Tears dripped down her cheeks and splattered on the glass, but her voice was steady. "Something broke in all of us. In the heart of the world. I've been trying to fix it ever since. I haven't been able to."

Naoto leaned in close to her and said, "What about Blood Rain? What about Cruithne? You've saved the world twice already, remember?"

"Damage control," she responded. "It's never more than damage control. Even when I was whole, that was the most I could do."

I couldn't resist listening, but I didn't believe I would ever understand what she'd just said.

Naoto took her hand. "Come on. We still need to find a ride out of here."

The more I studied Danae, the stranger I felt. I should have been paying attention to everyone else but her; should have kept busy identifying firing positions, tracking each face in the crowd in the corner of my eye, staying vigilant for other killers like me. Instead I watched the way she fixated on one relic or another—and for fleeting moments, there was something eerily familiar about her.

She stopped suddenly. Her body stiffened. Her gaze focused on the exit, or the street beyond, full of dust and searing light.

"They're here," she said. "The Keepers."

I braced myself. Instinctively I grabbed both of my clients and pulled them down behind the curtain of a vacant stall.

"Where?" Naoto hissed. "Where did you see them? Danae? Hello?"

She blinked and looked at us like she didn't understand why we were so tense. Her eyes were dilated, almost freakishly. "I don't mean I actually *see* them. I mean, the Keepers have a post here. A mission. In Crossroads Station."

"You could have mentioned this earlier," I said.

"Well, I'm not exactly in my right mind," she said dismissively. "Am I paranoid? Or am I paranoid that I'm paranoid? Para-para-paranoia." She started to lean out of the curtain.

Naoto pulled her back. "Damnit, we have to run!"

"No," she said. Her expression abruptly hardened. "Five years now I've cowered in fear of them. Hiding in Bloom. Letting fear eat me alive. I need to know, and there's only one way to find out. We have an opportunity. We have a man with a gun." She looked up at me. "I want you to go look. It's in the church just down that street. Go . . . do reconnaissance. That's something people like you do, isn't it?"

I started to reject her idea.

A calm came over me. I'd squandered my first chance to die, back on the train. Now I was being given a second.

"That seems like a bad idea," Naoto told her.

"No," I interrupted. "It's smart. You two . . . stay here. If I don't return in five minutes, you should assume I'm not coming back."

Naoto gaped at me. Danae nodded.

"Wait," she said. "What are you going to do if you find them?"

A nervous pause passed between us.

"Reconnaissance," I said.

Without another word I slid back through the curtain. I cleared my mind, slid my goggles back over my eyes, and walked out into the burning light.

Only a hundred meters ahead, I saw it. The shadow of a cross loomed, ebbing and flowing through waves of smoke and dust as I approached. Now I could make out the front of the building clearly enough to note the ideal sniper positions on the roof, the small windows above the double doors. The entry was a perfect kill zone. I turned off my armor and brandished my wave rifle as visibly as I could, so that anyone in that building would see it—so they wouldn't wait to find out who I was before they opened fire.

For a few steps, I closed my eyes and just breathed. I had a thought that it was good to die on the steps of a church. It wasn't suicide. It wasn't the Major's version of cowardice. I was turning myself in for my crimes.

I felt the concrete steps under my feet and stopped.

Nothing moved but the sand on the wind.

I opened my eyes. Through a break in the dust the windows stared down on me, empty as a skull's sockets.

I went inside and had a look around. The interior was unusually intact: one of those unusually overbuilt or just lucky land structures that had survived multiple storm seasons. What made no sense was that it had clearly been abandoned for years, but there was no trash inside, no bedrolls, no graffiti, no fires. It was the perfect place to take shelter, surrounded by refugees in desperate need, but no one had sheltered here for a long time.

As I was about to leave, I saw something on the floor by the entrance, covered in dust. I lifted it and shook it off, and it fell apart in my hands, but what was left of the black and gold cloth banner still legibly read: WE ARE THE KEEPERS OF THE

They existed. They'd been here. Whoever or whatever they were.

I put away my rifle and stepped back outside. A young woman was standing erect in the middle of the street, staring hard at me, her face hidden under her goggles and shemagh.

I waved and shouted over the wind howling through the ruins, "Hey, do you know what happened here? ¿Que pasó aquí? Nani ga okotta?"

She said something then, but the wind carried her voice away.

"What did you say?" I yelled.

She repeated herself once and then broke into a run and disappeared amid the dust. All I'd been able to make out was the word 'cursed.'

There was still a shake in my hands when I returned to the market. I composed myself as well as I could and told my clients what I'd found. Danae knitted her brow and bit nervously at her knuckles.

"That's all wrong," she said. "No. That can't be right. They wouldn't leave. They knew I was in Bloom. They made me their mission. They said I was an abomination, and they'd hunt me to the edges of the Earth."

Naoto held her, and she clung to him. Her fingers dug in to his arms hard enough to bruise.

"We know someone is hunting you," I said. "Whether it's these

'Keepers' or another entity, our objective is the same. We need to get to the truck depot and try to negotiate transport to Phoenix."

"Yes," Naoto said. "Please. Let's just keep moving."

"Yeah," she said—but we only made it a few steps farther toward the depot before she stopped.

She was staring in delight at the last vendor stall at the edge of the market. Looking in, I saw a dozen small, translucent pieces of shimmering light, contained in glass. The holograms varied in size from a palm to a head. Each one was made up of a different set of shapes and colors, each in a different pattern of liquid motion. A small man with dark skin and silver hair sat cross-legged in the center of it all.

"We should hurry," Naoto whispered.

"These are all emotions, aren't they?" Danae asked the sitting man. "Specific mental and emotional states, synesthetically represented as abstract visuals. Right? I've heard about this kind of lightwork."

The sitting man nodded.

She focused on a yellow-golden one, full of angular shapes that looked like shattered pieces of bronze glass. The holographic light oscillated in ten-second waves, flaring and slowly dying out into static. She raised her eyebrows and said "This one is . . . oh, well that's too obvious. Orgasm. Male."

The sitting man raised an eyebrow and nodded, evidently impressed.

Naoto sighed nervously.

"Give me a tougher one," Danae said.

The vendor indicated another hologram. This one was made up of soft, warm colors, but as it turned, it revealed inward-facing needles of shimmering purple, dropping abruptly into sharp and turbulent black. It shuddered constantly.

She stared intently at it for a moment and said, "Melancholy, but . . . no, no. Pretending to be happy. While . . . secretly mourning the dead."

The sitting man grinned. "Unthoughtful laughter in the presence of an unrequited love."

"Oh, of course. Yes! I can see it now."

"We don't have much time before sunset," Naoto whispered, tugging the shoulder of her coat. She swatted his hand away without shifting her gaze from the ragged gallery of dancing light.

"You understand my art intuitively," the sitting man said, in strained English. "You truly get it! I've never seen that. Most people who see my art do not get it at all."

"It's wondrous!"

"I want you to see something." He went along, tapping each of the holograms to extinguish them until the stall was dark. He took a stack of five scuffed panes and set them up in a line, and they sprung to life in sequence, filling the space with a single panoramic mass of blood-red light. From any distance it was completely amorphous, but every small segment of that drifting red vapor concealed crisp features: dripping rivulets of yellow fire, humanoid figures in motion (I couldn't tell whether they were dancing or panicking), what almost looked like tiny stairwells of rough-hewn stone.

"Goodness," Danae sighed in childlike awe. "What is this?"

"My great opus," said the sitting man. "I have been working on this one for sixteen years. This one is not for sale. I cannot finish it. Can never get it right."

"But what is it?"

"If I lived a thousand years, I'd still not have enough time to finish it."

"But what *is* it?"

The artist sighed. "It's not possible to speak it. To try would only do violence to the entire truth of it. Understand? If I could put it into words, I wouldn't need to put it into light. Light is my only language for it."

She broke her gaze with the mass of color. She looked at him, studying his eyes. She leaned over the table to speak giddily into his ear. "What if you didn't need a language at all?"

He squinted. "What do you mean?"

She indicated the glowing morass and said, "This all has some meaning for you. Something you need to share, right? Words aren't good enough, so you use holographic light art instead, but you can't escape the same fundamental problems. Meaning is always lost on its way between you and your audience. First it gets corrupted when you try to translate what's inside you into something outside of you, and then it's corrupted again when the viewers try to translate it back into something inside of themselves.

"I'm saying, what if there were no translation? No medium, no middleman? You could have a thought, a feeling, and you could share it with someone else. No loss or misunderstanding. No noise."

The sitting man scratched his chin and stared into space in deep thought. Finally he opened his mouth and said, simply, "No."

"No? What do you mean 'no?'"

He looked into his luminous clouds and said, "Hypothetically, there would be no need for any of this. No need for art of any kind. There would be no art at all."

"But—"

"This is the work of my life," he said solemnly. "It is everything I am."

For a moment Danae stood chewing her knuckle in frustrated thought. Then she turned and walked on toward the truck depot—and I looked back to realize that she and Naoto had suddenly reversed roles: he was still back there, staring pensively at the field of holographic light. Finally he ran to catch up and leaned in to ask her, "Hold on. Is that true? Danae?"

"Is what true?" she sang, carefree again.

He looked over his shoulders and whispered almost too low for me to hear, "Is it true that unified people have no art?"

She didn't seem to register his question. She just marched on into the dust, whistling random notes and chuckling at the sound on her own lips. She glanced at the members of a local gang and said, "One giant negative-sum game. That's all that's left of this land. Violence for sale in thirty different flavors. Taking what little is left from somebody else and clinging to it until somebody else comes to take it from you. But I remember how it was before. I remember."

Naoto took a long look back before he followed us on into the dust.

DANAE

The world around me was spinning and glowing like an old carnival ride. I should have known better than to dose myself with an unlabeled injector full of what I now guessed had been an excessive amount of an impure reproduction of some military behavioral drug. Naoto should have known better than to buy it—but I could only admit, even through the saccharine haze, that I wouldn't have made it this far without it.

"Cursed," I heard myself say. "It doesn't make sense. It's weird. Very weird."

Standard was utterly stoic, as ever.

"The Keepers, you mean?" Naoto asked. "What do you think happened to them?"

"Sailors always used to be the world's most superstitious people," I said.

He squinted. "I don't understand what that has to do with—"

"The sea used to be the great unknown!" I explained, impatiently. It was so frustrating he couldn't simply hear my thoughts. One more of a million things that would have been infinitely easier now, if only I were whole.

"Okay," Naoto said.

"Ships would sail off and never return," I continued. "No one would ever learn why. Probably just sunk by storms, but it was left to the imagination, so inevitably it was all attributed to sea monsters and angels and whatnot. Now it's all reversed: the oceans are all lit up with nodes and cities and cable and sonar, and dry land is the great unknown. Communication is spotty and whole encampments get wiped off the map without warning every storm season. Ergo, wastelanders have become the world's most superstitious people. They have the madness of looking for a reason in everything."

Naoto scratched his head. "So you're saying . . . it doesn't necessarily mean anything, that the locals say the Keeper mission is cursed."

I chewed on my fingers in thought. "That doesn't sound right either, does it."

A feeling of uncomfortable cold fire tingled in my lips, fingers, and toes. I was still conscious of all the things that should have been tearing me apart—the trauma of escaping Bloom; the atrocity I'd committed by invading Serena's mind; my concern for Naoto's safety; my fear of the Keepers and the Medusas and whoever else was hunting me—but the drug drowned them all in an unfocused, bubbling euphoria. I was incapable of fear or regret and rendered perversely in love with everything around me: the blowing dust, the murderous sunlight, the ragged and blistered wastelanders surviving despite it all. This was a drug for young new recruits into atrocity-prone armies and brutal gangs; any teenager could ride this milky, sky-blue high through all the natural horror of a first kill, effortlessly bypassing that most basic instinct to never take a life.

I loved Naoto. I reached for that love in myself and focused hard on it; it was the only thing I knew I'd still feel once the drug wore off. I watched him stumble along in his ill-fitting second-hand clothes, increasingly frizzy braids swinging on the sandy wind, wincing hard and filling his lungs with air he must have found so shockingly thin and dry. I stopped him to ask:

"Are you really going to be okay out here?"

He pursed his lips. "I'll have to be."

"But just look at all this shit," I slurred. I motioned around at things in sight: the enormous sky; a three-legged dog; a distant outhouse;

a tall man in a ridiculous hat made of 150-year-old milk jugs, who frowned at us and hid his face under the wide, floppy brim.

"Come on," Naoto said, pulling me onward again. "We just need to talk to the truck depot chief and get you a ride to Phoenix."

"With what?" I asked. "I don't have anything left to barter."

He stiffened a little. "I'll take care of it."

"There's something not right about the way you said that."

He didn't respond. I quickly lost my train of thought again.

Something strange happened as we passed through the center of the encampment. There were a lot of refugees here from the farther hinterlands: sick, wounded, dying, malnourished, swaddled in whatever random materials they could pluck from the wind. I'd expected them—but not the dozen-odd men in black and white uniforms that had gathered there with them, conspicuously silent. At the front of the group, a little girl stood and sang.

This time it was Standard who stopped to stare.

"Who are they?" he muttered, weirdly distant.

"Deserters," Naoto said. "From the Confederacy."

"I didn't know there were any," I said. "They really fled all this way rather than participate in the genocides?"

Naoto nodded. "I overheard something about them. They refused their orders. Now they're as much fugitives as all their would-be victims."

The deserters were joined by women and children I surmised were their families. Their heads were lowered as if in prayer, or shame. They still wore their uniforms, but the shoulders were all frayed where they'd sawed the patches and insignia off.

"She's . . ." Standard trailed off. He was staring at the singing girl. He looked hypnotized. He muttered almost too quietly to hear, "What is that song?"

"You don't know it?" I smiled. "You've really never heard 'Amazing Grace' before?"

He shook his head slowly.

"It's about repentance, redemption, that kind of thing," I said. "A slave ship captain wrote it after he had a divine experience that filled him with remorse, in the middle of a storm he thought would sink him. It didn't used to be sung in a minor key, though. That's recent. It used to sound happy."

I snorted a mean laugh to myself and resisted a drug-addled urge to blurt out what I was thinking: there was no such thing as redemption. Not really. What I'd said was true, except that the ship captain had gone on trading in enslaved human beings for years after he wrote it. He'd been repenting his use of swear words, not his direct participation in one of the most heinous crimes in all human history. On my better days, I could think a song transcends its author's intent, that it belongs to the generations that sing it after him— but today I was running for my life in the first hours of a new world war, and even high as I was, I couldn't spare the energy.

. . . But these deserters. I kept staring at them: at the blisters on their lips; the gray dust worn deep into the black of their uniforms; the litany of scarred and still-healing injuries that seemed to count off the thousands of kilometers they'd walked. To think of them crossing half the continent on foot, side by side with the people they had been ordered to enslave and kill.

That's how humanity gets you, I thought: the bait and switch. The tiny flickers of sublime beauty it throws in, just to deny you even the little peace of mind you'd have if you could only dismiss them all as monsters.

It still meant something to Standard, that song. It was in the way he clasped the wire-thing hanging from his neck like a charm; how he struggled to turn his back on the girl and walk on, looking like he'd seen a ghost.

Whose ghost? I found myself wondering. One of his victims?

And why did he seem so familiar?

I wondered what his real name was, behind that one utilitarian word.

Naoto squeezed my hand to direct my attention. The truck depot waited dead ahead of us: a clot of vehicles surrounding a jumble of stacked trailers and freight containers, strung with tarps and lights to form a makeshift loading dock.

"What are you planning to barter with?" Standard asked.

Naoto gave him a cold look and started for the door to the central structure. "I told you. I'll handle it."

Standard stopped him with a tap on the shoulder. "A word of warning. In mobile encampments like this one, the chief of the local truck depot is often something akin to a local monarch. They control who and what can move during a storm season. They draw a lot of social clout from that."

"They tend to be petty, authoritarian assholes," I translated for Naoto.

Standard frowned. "I only meant . . . they're used to being treated with deference."

"Be quiet and let me do this," Naoto said, knocking on the door, bristling with nervous energy. "Both of you. Not a word."

I leaned in to him and whispered, "I know way more than you do about wastelanders. Why don't you let me do the talking?"

"Because you're high as a cloud."

I wanted to disagree, but he had a point. "Then why don't we have Standard do it?"

"Because we can't trust him."

I glanced back at Standard. He'd heard, but he just stood there stoically. "Why not?" I asked.

The door opened before he could answer, and a boy in coveralls led us up a spiral of stairs to the trailer at the top of the stack. Inside it was shockingly clean. The walls were lined with lavish cabinets full of liquor and trinkets, the floor covered in fine rugs, everything gleaming with yellowed sunlight through a crystal window. The depot chief sat at a scuffed desk made of real wood, attended by two armed assistants. He was a grizzled-looking man with coiffed salt-and-pepper hair.

Naoto composed himself, stepped forward, and said "We need one-way transport to Camp Phoenix."

The chief put on a knowing smirk the moment he heard Naoto's voice. He motioned for us all to sit down, and we did—but his armed attendants remained standing. They primed their pistols.

"So, uh," Naoto swallowed visibly and strained to ignore the weapons. "I'm told you're the man to speak to about that."

The depot chief took an ornate bottle of clear alcohol from a shelf by his desk and studied the label. "Your funky outfits almost had me fooled for a second. No. I think you'd better stay right here. I've got a room you can call home until the Medusas arrive."

Naoto's body went rigid in his chair. "What?"

I tried to soak up the chemically induced levity flowing through my veins, but I felt my whole body twitch. Standard took one good look around the room, but I could only assume he concluded, as I did, that if we tried anything here we'd be dead before we could stand up.

"Tough break, friends." The chief poured himself three fingers and swirled it around the glass before sipping. "Orders just came in a few minutes ago. I'm to look out for a pair of Bloomers trying to leave the Econ Zone. If I come across any such persons, I'm to hold them until they can be personally inspected by a Clan envoy." He looked straight at me to add, "It's odd. This isn't the first time they've leaned on us to catch their runaways, but they've never leaned quite so damn hard before. I think they're looking for somebody specific. Someone they want very badly."

I repressed a perverse urge to laugh. I was sure we were fucked: I could barely speak straight; Standard and all his lethal skills were no help; and we were as far out of Naoto's depth, figuratively and literally, as we could possibly be. Back in Bloom he'd never more than skirted the edges of the underworld, let alone been threatened with certain torture and death. I watched him in the corner of my eye, expecting him to snap at any second—but instead he slouched in the chair and smirked.

"And you must love the Clan," he said, coolly. "I bet you love taking orders from them, doing their dirty work."

The chief sneered. "It's not worth my risk to disobey."

"We'll make it worth the risk."

The chief leaned back and sipped doubtfully. "That'll take an awful lot of worth."

The guards put their fingers on their triggers when Naoto swung his backpack down and opened it, but the chief flapped a hand to make them stand down. Naoto lifted out the thing I'd seen jabbing into his backpack all this time: a huge brick of silvery metal, stamped with bar codes and sealed in a thick plastic blister full of oil.

"Lithium-6," Naoto said. "Four kilos. Ninety-eight percent enriched."

The depot chief's eyes visibly sparkled with avarice for a split second before he could force a poker face, and I was so sure we had him that I had to cover my mouth to stifle a laugh—but I was wrong. He took another long sip and studiously avoided the brick with his eyes, and his voice was as smooth and cold as ice when he responded. "I don't know what that's supposed to mean to me."

My smile turned into a wide-eyed grimace under my palm as I realized how massively Naoto's gambit had just raised the stakes for everyone in the room. Black-market trading in reactor-grade lithium was a much higher crime than merely aiding and abetting an escaped tech servant. The Medusas would do a lot worse than kill the depot chief if they caught him making this deal.

"We didn't come here to play games," Naoto growled, undaunted, understanding none of this. "We don't have time. We're only offering you this deal because we're in a hurry. This brick was worth ten thousand squid this morning. It's worth fifty times that now."

The chief shook his head. "I don't know anything about lithium. Whatever you think you're offering—"

"Look." Naoto rubbed the bridge of his nose in annoyance while I gripped the edge of my chair in fear: he seemed to think the depot chief was feigning ignorance to mess with him personally, not to shield himself from lethal liability. I tapped Naoto's shoulder and tried to shush him, but he leaned away and went on telling what the chief already knew:

"Look. Four kilos of lithium-6 makes two kilos of tritium—and unlike the ready-made tritium Epak sells you, this brick will never decay. It's enough fusion fuel to keep this place mobile for years." Or enough waver ammunition to equip a small army. "You can hoard. Invest. That investment will pay off nicely if, say, some infrastructure gets wrecked in the war, and fusion fuel isn't so easy to come by anymore."

The chief glanced at his own men, probably hoping they wouldn't turn him in themselves. Finally he threw up his hands exasperatedly and said, "Oh, well. In that case, why don't I just take it off your hands."

"What?"

"Robbing a few Bloom City fishfuckers won't exactly tarnish my reputation around here."

Naoto was still for a moment. Then his motion was so lightning-quick that I couldn't track it: whipping a single-shot wave pistol out of his pocket and pressing it directly into the plastic blister around the silvery metal brick. He glanced down the barrels of the guns suddenly pointed at his head, one after another, and then back at the depot chief.

Then he did the last thing I would have expected: he laughed.

"Ever seen lithium metal burn?" Naoto asked. "Beautiful, explosive, ruby-red flames, hotter than a waver strike. Sparks everywhere. Toxic smoke. And nearly impossible to put out, once it catches."

The chief stood up slowly, the creak of his old wooden chair filling the silence. He swallowed the last of his drink and set the glass down carefully. The two men stared at each other for a long moment that my spinning head drew out into eternity.

"One-way to Phoenix?" the chief finally said.

"Nothing more," Naoto said. "Nothing less."

The chief shrugged and motioned for us to get up. He came around the desk. Without warning he threw an arm around Naoto's neck and pulled him in close.

"I admit it, I'm a sucker for somebody who knows how to use the stick and the carrot at the same time," he said. "You've got some sand, kid, and brains to match. Fatty, delicious, Bloom-city brains that I'd sure like to fry up and have for supper, if I ever see you again. How does that sound to you?"

Naoto didn't move. "Fine."

"Don't get seen anywhere near my depot, any of you. Put your heads down, cover your soft little faces, and go out to the south watchtower. I'll send the next outgoing truck around to pick you up. Twenty minutes."

I stared at Naoto in shock, but he wouldn't meet my eyes. On our way out I grabbed his hand, and he gripped back tight enough to hurt. In that touch, I could feel his entire body shaking with adrenaline under the curtain of his too-big coat. I could feel how marginally he was holding himself together.

I ripped open his backpack and looked inside. There was nothing left there but our paltry stores of food and water, and I realized with a start that that brick had been the last of his earthly possessions.

"What did you just do?" I demanded. My blood was surging fast enough now to start to wash the drug out of my system; all my negative emotions paraded back into my awareness, one by one, beginning with shock. "Where the hell did you ever get your hands on four kilos of enriched lithium?"

"It's a long story, but in short—"

Shock gave way to fear. "You were supposed to stay here in Crossroads. That was our plan."

"But it was the only way to get you out—"

Fear gave way to anger. "You were supposed to look out for yourself. You were supposed to *be okay*. You could have traded that brick for a whole new life, but now you're dead broke and the depot chief will kill you if you don't leave town!"

"I know, damnit!" he yelled. "Tell me, really. What the fuck was the alternative? Were you planning to *walk* to Redhill?"

Anger finally lapsed into guilt. "You did it for me. You gave away everything you had left, because of me. I forced you to help me."

Naoto covered his face in his hands and groaned. He looked back and forth between Standard and I and said, "Look. It's a long, long drive to Camp Phoenix. We'll have plenty of time to talk about everything—but for now, can we just get from one side of this awful little town to the other and catch our ride without any more terrible things happening to us?"

As if on cue, the scrape of Standard's feet through the sand fell silent behind us. When I turned, I thought I saw him looking at his shard before quickly pocketing it. His brows furrowed under his goggles.

"Something wrong?" I asked.

He hesitated. "I'm sorry. I need to apply another treatment to the burn, and I'd prefer to do it privately this time. I'll make it quick."

I hoped my doubt wasn't too visible as I nodded.

We'd reached the unmanned south watchtower. Standard started up the skeletal stairs, visibly straining against the pain of his burn. The sandy wind howled through the rusty crossbeams.

"We have to leave him while we can," Naoto whispered in my ear. "Or dispose of him. We can't trust him."

I shook my head. "We need protection. We've already been attacked once, and the wasteland only gets worse from here."

Naoto gripped my shoulder. "Listen to me. Whoever he's working for, it isn't us. He said it himself: squid are worthless. That means *the squid you paid him* are worthless."

"Out here, yes, but maybe back in Epak—"

He cut me off. "There's more. After we surfaced, while you were still unconscious, he ran a cranial scan on you. It happened so fast, I couldn't stop him before. . . ." He was a quivering mess. "Before he saw your unifier implant."

Adrenaline punched me in the chest. I watched Standard hobble up the last flight of steps. I asked Naoto through clenched teeth, "Why didn't you tell me sooner?"

"I tried, damnit! But after what you made me promise in Bloom, I . . . I couldn't. . . ."

He'd been too afraid to tell me—afraid I'd kill myself pre-emptively to keep the Medusas from getting their hands on the tech in my body.

"Okay, okay," I hissed. I paced the dusty ground once.

He was pleading with me through his tears. "Please just tell me you're not going to hurt yourself. Please tell me you won't—"

I wanted to be angry, but the sheer terror in his voice made me realize just how cruel I'd been in asking for that promise.

"No," I said. "I won't. Fuck. Just let me think."

I grabbed one of the watchtower's beams and put my weight on it; the whole structure was too rickety to let us sneak up the stairs. Standard stepped inside the drafty cabin at the top, out of our sight. I told Naoto, "Tell me you still have that scanner hooked to your belt."

We rushed to set it up with shaking hands—sharing the pair of earbuds, each putting one interfaced contact lens into our dominant eye, then running a signal-interception program I'd written myself. Holographic light began to cohere in my vision; voices cut through the static in my ear.

"I knew it," I said. "He's calling someone." But I froze solid when the image fully resolved.

It was Duke.

"—loud and clear," he said. "Wise of you to return my call. Remove your coverings. I do not trust a man whose face I cannot see." He grinned. "Not even you, my dear Alexei."

I swallowed hard at what I saw: the throne Duke sat on was still waterlogged from Dahlia's death, but he'd already drilled new rank-rings into his jaw, and his scalp was raw from its latest tattoo: a sawtooth pattern in golden ink, forming a viciously stylized crown.

I stared at Naoto in fear through the superimposed image, further realizing that the man we'd hired was no mere bodyguard. He worked for Duke. He worked *directly* for Duke. Naoto primed his wave pistol and braced to run; I could barely move.

"Please be quick," Standard answered, peeling off his goggles and scarf. "I'm not in a secure location."

"Relax, Alexei. I bring you good news. Epak is again united, under me. We have only to complete the formality of a few public executions, and then we may devote ourselves fully to our revenge on Norpak for Dahlia's death. But first—"

"What?" Alexei interrupted. "But I thought you said . . . you said Norpak had nothing to do with the assassination. You said there would never be any Gray Day. That it was all a game."

Duke tipped his head back to glower harder down his nose. His jaw rings glittered fiercely, and for a split second I was sure I saw pieces of a human nose in the shoulder of his jacket. His voice was dripping with paternal condescension to say, "The masses believe Dahlia was assassinated by Norpak. If we do not retaliate, we demean ourselves before the entire world. Don't be so squeamish. This war will be over very shortly. Our Gray weapons are far more advanced than theirs. Meanwhile, at last, I have a job for you. Maybe your most important job yet."

Attached images scrolled across the contact lens my eye, and my heart all but stopped.

"The woman calls herself Danae," Duke said. "A tech servant. Clan property. Bloom surveillance has identified her accomplice as one Kusanagi Naoto, a civilian. We've tracked them as far as Crossroads Station, and we're currently interrogating a woman who had some contact with them there. I'll have more details for you soon, but we believe they're headed into the open wasteland."

"I'm sorry," Standard began. "I can't—"

"Sure you can. I know you have clever ways of finding people, Alexei. Someone works nodespace for you. Use those resources. Return them both to me, intact. Pay is five million squid—inflation-adjusted, metal equivalent, whatever you like."

Five *million*. I wilted in Naoto's grasp. He was tugging on my arm, pulling me down to duck with him behind a pile of sandbags at the tower's foot.

But Standard's image on the other side of the call didn't turn back, didn't brandish his wave rifle, didn't make any move to obey

Duke's new orders. He only stared pensively at his feet, seeming to resign himself.

"I can't—" he began.

But Duke ignored him and said, "You must be wondering why." He leaned forward on his throne almost giddily. He looked around to confirm he was alone before continuing. "You must guard this information with your life, but we received some telemetry from a stolen medical scanner. This woman is carrying a cerebral implant more advanced than anything our techs have ever seen. We need it. Now, I know what you're thinking, but her head alone may not be enough. We don't know how far the device extends into her body, and my techs want to see how it works in living tissue."

"No," Standard said. The word fell like a bomb.

Duke stared uncomprehendingly. "No, what?"

"They're my clients. I won't betray them."

I stifled a yelp.

Duke leaned slowly forward in his throne, and his gruesome jacket creaked with the movement. "You mean . . . you know where she is. She's there with you right now."

"Yes."

"Tell me exactly where you are, Alexei."

Standard shook his head. "No."

"I am commanding you to tell me where you are."

"I can't do that."

Duke's eyelids peeled back. The harsh overhead light and the interfaced contact lens combined to make his sclera burn like neon. His jaw rings glittered in the shadow of his scalp like a row of monstrously curved teeth.

"We will find you," he said. "I will never forget this betrayal."

"I know."

"I will personally scrape the flesh from your bones, Alexei. The prolonged agony of your public vivisection will be my magnum opus. The spectacle will be etched into every optic nerve in Epak, broadcast on every pane, exhibited to every child. They'll tell the story of it for a thousand years to come."

Standard's image nodded solemnly. "I accept."

"You don't—!" Duke bellowed, but his image froze. Standard had hung up on him.

I huddled there behind our cover, speechless and shivering as Standard's boots clanged back down the stairs. Naoto jumped to his feet and trained his wave pistol on the mercenary's head, but his hands were shaking so furiously that I doubted he could shoot straight.

"Why did you do that?" I shouted. "Why are you helping us? I barely paid you anything. If you were working for the Keepers, I believe you'd already have me burning at the stake. Even *they* couldn't pay you a fraction of what Duke just offered."

The mercenary looked past the gun quaking in Naoto's hand—past both of us, as if we weren't even there—and for an instant I thought I saw through a break in his icy calm, to an exhaustion so long held and bone-deep that I felt a surreal ache of sympathy for him.

"Why are you helping us?" I repeated.

Alexei Standard replied simply, "Because I told you I would."

He winced in pain as he descended the last steps and hobbled past us, a few steps out into the sterile plane. The weapon gradually sank down in Naoto's still-shaking grip, and a distant whine of motors and plume of dust announced the arrival of our ride. We shared a long, shell-shocked look, but then there was nothing to do but climb up into the hulking cargo compartment and look for a place to sit between the stacks and barrels; whether we trusted Alexei or not, it was either that or stay in Crossroads.

Just as the rear hatch was groaning shut, an odd intuition cut through the whirlwind of my thoughts. I looked back.

A stranger stood there by the tower, half-shadowed in the waves of blowing sand. With his head nodded down against the sun, he stared out from under his brows, straight at me. His face was unfamiliar, but his smile— that smile—

The hatch shut and locked between us.

"What is it?" Naoto asked me as the motors whirred. "Danae? What's wrong?"

It couldn't have been Luther. The drug, the stress, the physical toll of all this travel—any one of those could have caused me to see someone who wasn't there.

Luther had died a long time ago. I had to believe that.

I must have only imagined that stranger's mouth forming one voiceless word before the hatch closed:

Sybil.

BORROWER

Sybil.

I had seen her, and for the first time in seventy-two years, she had seen me too. For that single, shining moment of mutual recognition, all was right with the world.

Then the truck's hatch swung shut and locked, and my smile faded at the sight of it pulling away into the wastes—and I panicked. This should have been it. If only my damned alpha copy had been here, we could have overpowered the two men traveling with her, and I would have her already. Years of toil and planning would have come to fruition, and I would finally have in hand the solution to all my problems. But instead I was standing here, alone and impotent, watching her recede into the distance on a trail of billowing dust.

This should have been it. This should have been it!

I punched the tower. I hit it over and over again, throwing the whole force of my body into it, screaming at the top of my lungs into the hazy distance past the encampment's edge. I ground the sand between my teeth and cast my curses to the sky.

Then I composed myself and went to work.

I went back to the truck depot and asked to speak to the chief. One of his guards ushered me into his office alone.

"What is it, Rutger?" the chief asked, draining his daily bottle. "I'm closing up after one hell of a day."

"A truck pulled away from the south gate just a moment ago," I said. My mind was still racing from my encounter with Sybil, and I couldn't spare the focus to affect Rutger's usual speaking style. "Can you tell me its destination?"

The chief looked up distrustfully from his desk and reached down to slide a drawer shut, hiding something metallic from my sight. "Why would you want to know that?"

"It's a personal matter," I said.

"There was no truck at the south gate," he told me. "Understand? You didn't see any truck pull away from there."

The depot chief was an old man, by my standards. Frail. I imagined his liver swimming in a puddle of alcohol, the rotgut aftertaste in his spit, and I very much dreaded the thought of having to put on his flesh—but I would, if it was what it took to get access to his data pane. I had one last card to play before resorting to that.

"You can trust me," I said. "How long have we known each other?" I passed him all the hard money I carried, without subtlety.

He gave me a cautious look but started to take the metal from my palm. Suddenly he drew back, wincing. "Sweet Jesus."

I looked down at my mangled hand and pursed my lips apologetically. There was much more blood than I'd realized, dripping and pooling across the fine leather surface of his desk; probably I'd left a trail all the way from my tantrum at the watchtower.

"Pardon me," I said.

"Good God, Rutger. Those fingers are torn half off at the knuckle."

"So they are," I said. I reached behind my back to discreetly squeeze the bones back into place as far as they would go, pausing between wet snapping noises to say, "Please, sir. I need that destination."

"East to Phoenix, via Greenglass," he answered in a horrified daze. "Get yourself a damn medkit, will you?"

"Are there any other trucks going that way?"

He craned his neck to stare past me, at the blood I was dripping on his fine carpet. "Tomorrow morning at oh-eight-hundred, but they're—"

"I need to get there as soon as possible," I interrupted. "Can I pay extra to arrange an earlier passage? Money is no object."

"I can't. All my wheels are already on the road. Aren't you in some kind of pain? Are you sure you don't need a bandage or—?"

"May I buy a truck?"

He blinked slowly. "Come again?"

"I want to buy a truck that can take me to Phoenix. Name any price. Squid, metal, barter. Anything."

He stood there flabbergasted for a while before finally answering, "I'm sorry, but I . . . There's just nothing here with that kind of cell capacity. The next truck that can make that haul comes in tomorrow morning around eight."

I sighed and ruled out hijacking.

"Thank you," I said. "I'll be back then."

On my way out I stopped into the bathroom trailer, where I hunched over the sink and worked to scrub my hand clean and wrap it up in my handkerchief. I paused to pick out a loose bit of meat that would only become infected. Whatever pain I felt was just a low hum in the back of my awareness, but I kept my head down to shield myself from the mirror. The closeness of my reflection tugged at me with all the gravity of a black hole. One glance and I'd be lost in self-hypnosis for who knew how long.

The alpha copy was waiting for me on the street outside the depot. He was wearing the flesh of a wealthy man, complete with suit and tie. His vessel's resources had been instrumental in funding the search for Sybil.

The briefcase—my so-familiar briefcase—hung from his hand.

"You're late," I told him.

"And you failed," he said. "Why?"

"She's accompanied by two armed men. If you had been here as we planned, we would have her. She would be ours right now. Do you understand that?"

He glared; of course he understood. He grabbed my hand by the wrist to hold it up for his inspection, as if it was his own—which it was, in a sense. "You're injured. You've damaged your flesh."

"It was an accident. I was . . . frustrated. It's irrelevant. Tomorrow we can follow them by truck."

"Is there no faster option? Nothing at all?"

"I've exhausted every alternative."

We were glaring at each other, the alpha copy and me. How I hated this. I hated that there were two of us. It was a necessary evil: given the absolute necessity of my finding Sybil and the complexity of my pursuit, I had needed to increase my reach. One sacrificial copy to incite chaos in Bloom City and track her to the surface, then two copies to ensure I could follow her after that. That was the plan.

"I hate this," said the alpha copy. "I hate that there are two of us. I wish it weren't necessary—"

"I know. Secure your own accommodations. Rest and gather supplies. Meet me here at dawn and we'll proceed from there. Do you agree?"

It was a rhetorical question. Of course we agreed. Without another word, I turned away.

"Where are you going?"

"Home," I said.

As I walked, I had to stop myself from grinding my teeth to bits again. I realized what would have to come next. In all this excitement, I had forgotten the life I'd been leading before today. With some effort, now, I reprised the role: adopting Rutger's mannerisms, settling back into his gait.

"You're late," his wife (already I was thinking of her as that) said to me when I arrived. "I called work. They said you went out on your lunch break and never came back. What happened?"

"I'm sorry, babe." I adjusted my accent and cadence. I returned her hug, bending slightly to accommodate her pregnant belly. "Shit luck. I took a schematic out on my break to look over, and some kid, twelve years old tops, ripped it out of my hands and took off. Probably thinking to sell the tablet."

"That's awful! Did you get it back?"

"Yeah, I tracked him down, convinced him he couldn't sell it for crud. No harm done. Hurt my hand hopping a fence, but it's okay. Just a wild goose chase and some lost work."

"Thank goodness you're okay. I was worried."

"No harm done."

As we ate dinner—and later, as we fornicated—I was preoccupied. Things would have to be put in order. Arrangements would have to be made to cover my exit. I'd need to assemble a new identity, forge new documents, find a new name, bury my trail. It was nothing I hadn't done a hundred times before, but never in such a hurry—and even if my assumption of Rutger's life had always been part of my plan to find Sybil, I had worked so hard make that life my own. It was a shame to cast his flesh off so prematurely.

"Are you awake?" Rutger's wife asked me as we lay in the darkness.

I nodded with my eyes closed and laid my hand on her belly, the way I knew she expected me to.

"Can I ask you something?"

"'Course," I answered.

"Well," she said, uncertainly, shifting her weight between the sheets. "Are you okay?"

"Sure I am. Why?"

"I don't know how to say this."

"Well then, babe, say it anyway."

"I can't really . . . explain it. But there's this weird . . . feeling, I get from you sometimes. Just this weird feeling."

I swallowed and listened carefully. "Oh yeah?"

"It was a few weeks ago. It was the day they found your friend— Charlie?—in a coma. Suddenly I got this weird . . . vibe, from you. I was afraid to say anything about it. I didn't know how to explain it. Like something about you was . . . different. Strange."

I swallowed involuntarily. "I was just upset about Charlie."

"Somehow I felt like it was something deeper than that. I'm sorry. I know this all sounds . . . so. . . ."

"No, go on."

"Well, after a while I stopped getting that feeling about you, so I figured it was nothing. But . . . today, when you came home, it was back again."

I held still and did not speak.

"I'm sure it's nothing," she sighed. "Don't mind me. I'm just being hormonal."

"Probably."

I watched, anxiously, the slow rise and fall of her breasts under the moonlight-traced sheets.

"I love you so much, Rutger," she whispered to me.

Only when I knew she was asleep did I go back to work on the details.

ALEXEI

Oversized armored cargo trucks like this one wandered the entire continental wasteland wherever the dim promise of profit called to them, following no real schedule or defined route; there was no safer place for us now than out here, passing the last fringes of Medusan influence. Once the truck reached Greenglass Mountain to refuel for the final leg of the journey to Phoenix, we'd be entering the deep wasteland, where banditry was much more common. At this rate we wouldn't get that far until noon tomorrow.

I opted to give my clients some space to themselves in the cargo compartment while I kept watch from the small canopy-covered nest on the roof, not only because it made tactical sense. I could only assume they'd overheard my entire call with Duke, and now needed some time to decide whether to trust me or shoot me. Meanwhile, I stared out across the landscape as the sun set through the multi-colored layers of dust and distant pollution. The stars shone more brilliantly as we crawled farther from the coast, and the moon was a sliver of a crescent. Tomorrow it would be new.

I should have been thinking about Duke's plans to skin me alive, or Naoto's pistol, or Danae's mysterious implant, but all I could think about was the girl in the market. I knew better than to let myself believe it, but she had looked to me exactly like the child in my dream on the night we left Bloom: she had looked just like Eryn, as Eryn had appeared, what, sixteen years ago now? And for just a moment, she had turned, and it was as if my clients and the thousands of people around us had all faded out—as if she had been singing that mournful, haunting song directly to me.

I knew Eryn was gone. She must have died a decade or more ago. Just another nameless unit of collateral damage in the war. Still, I'd been seeing her in crowds ever since we'd left Bloom, and my attention kept drifting back to her gift to me, still hanging from my neck.

I clasped it in my palm and wondered what she would think of me, if she could see me now. I wondered if she'd still hold me to our promise.

I did as I always did in moments of pensive insomnia, in transit from one certain death to the next. I called Kat.

"Are you with me?" I asked.

"Till the bitter end. How about you? Still kicking?" Even through the vocal scrambler, I could hear the sleep-deprivation in her voice, only partially masked.

"The night is young," I muttered.

"Yeah, so. On that note, exactly what the fuck were you thinking?" She didn't sound accusatory so much as astonished.

"You mean . . . Duke."

"Yes. I was watching your call with Duke. You know, Duke? Supreme ruler of the world's most violent governing syndicate. Duke, who wears a jacket made of leather made of the skin of anyone he ever found just a little bit annoying. Duke, who you told to get bent and then *hung up on!*"

I swallowed. "I couldn't betray my clients."

"If that would have offended your precious honor too much, you could have, I don't know, *politely declined* to mention that his targets just happened to also be your clients."

"He would've found out. Sooner or later."

"Tell me straight, Alexei." Her voice caught momentarily. "You want him to kill you. Is that what this is? Some kind of suicide mission?"

I owed her the truth, or the closest approximation I could put into words.

"Danger," I sighed. "I just need danger. It's the drug keeping me alive. As long as I have it, I can think clearly, I can function. I can think about things besides Antarka. It's when things start to get safe. That's when I. . . ." I trailed off.

"Normally I would say you can handle a little danger," she said after a while. "But if you keep upping your dosage like this, eventually you won't be able to find a strong enough next hit. So what happens then?"

I filled my lungs with the dry air. The landscape was so empty, and in that moment I felt blissfully empty within it. I had everything I needed—and when this was all over, Duke would be there to give me the death I deserved.

"I just . . . have to finish this job," I said.

Kat went silent. Even her breath.

"How are you?" I asked.

"Oh, I'm just peachy. Thank you for asking."

I was afraid I'd lost her, but after a moment I heard her chewing on something, maybe noodles, and I couldn't resist chuckling at myself: at how it startled me to think of Kat eating. I'd only seen her in person once—and likely never would again, even if I survived this job—but I'd grown so used to her electronic voice in my ear that it was easy to forget she had a body, somewhere out there. That was probably how she preferred it.

She slurped broth and continued, "I'm curious, that's what I am. There's something freaky going on here. I need to get to the bottom of it. I see things in nodespace, I recognize patterns, it's what I do. There's an extremely odd pattern emerging."

"What kind of pattern?"

"There are these reports. An admiral in the Norpak Defense Forces said he was getting some weird feelings while alone in his quarters. Like he was being watched. So he fired a shot across the room at random—he must have been drunk as a skunk—and hit something invisible, hovering in the air. He said was only there for a moment, then gone."

I swallowed hard. "What was it?"

"He said it looked like a huge, levitating eyeball."

My heart stilled for a moment. I shuddered. I couldn't speak.

"So they relieved him of duty, naturally," Kat continued. "Figures they wouldn't want someone like that holding the big red button. What they don't know is, his was just one of several eerily similar reports from all over the world, completely unrelated. Sightings of hovering, semi-invisible eyeballs, stretching back a couple months. You can't even make this shit up."

An invisible eye.

I hadn't lost my mind in Antarka. I was certain of that now—and in that certainty, I realized how much comfort I'd taken in the notion that I might simply be insane.

My mind fell into a fever of thought, and I couldn't tell Kat any of it. Maybe the horrifying cosmic truth had been there all along, buried in the common threads between all the mutually murderous denominations of all the wasteland religions I'd always dismissed out of hand: maybe the world was really approaching its apocalyptic end. We were approaching the end of time—and there was something already there, waiting for us. It was watching.

Omniscience was just a word, I thought. It was one thing to know

104 - ELLY BANGS

its meaning in the abstract, and another to imagine what form it would take—what monstrous eyes would be needed to stare into our souls and judge our every thought and action—what it would do to a person, simply to be seen by such eyes.

Let alone to stare back.

"God," I whispered.

"I know, right?" Kat said. "It's pretty wild. And then there's the code thingy."

I took a deep breath and tried to compose myself. "Code thingy?"

"I don't know what to call it. I only saw it for a second, but I *know* it wasn't just the sleep dep. I was trying to dig up some useful information on your clients. I had some interesting leads, too, but they dead-end in a place called Asher Valley—and then my deck started acting a little weird, so I checked some config files. There was foreign code there. I couldn't even say what *language*. Syntax like I'd never seen. It should've been pure glitch, but I could see it working! Spying. Recording everything I did and transmitting it back somewhere. And then, fwoosh. Gone without a trace, like I'd hallucinated it."

"Someone hacked you," I said.

"You don't get it. Nobody hacks like this. The defenses I keep up can't be gotten through without me at least *knowing* about it. Not by anyone. If it was really a program of some kind, it was orders of magnitude beyond anything I can do. It shouldn't be possible. At least . . . not by humans."

We shared an awkward silence.

She chewed and slurped again and said, "So I'm thinking . . . honestly? I know it's supposed to be impossible, but my money's on fully sentient artificial intelligence. Either that or aliens from outer space. I can't think of any third hypothesis." She raised her voice suddenly. "And will you lay off this 'God' bullshit already? Even God doesn't write weird assembly code on the fly! Look, I know what I saw. No human being could have written it. Besides that, I only know one other thing about it."

I sighed and tried to focus. "What?"

"By the skin of my teeth, I was able to roughly geolocate where the data packets were being sent. It's somewhere in the former state of—"

"Arizona," I interrupted.

She paused. "Precisely how the fuck did you know I was going to say that?"

"Lucky guess."

"Bullshit!" she yelled. "Tell me!"

I looked down across the cargo compartment's metal roof, wondering at my clients inside. "All I can tell you is that there's something at work here that I don't understand. Danae, she's . . . There's something unusual about her."

"No shit." She chewed and slurped. "How about that thing in her head. Give me your best guess. What do you think it is?"

When I closed my eyes, I saw Danae putting her palm on Serena's head. "I think it's some kind of telepathy device. A machine-moderated mind-to-mind interface."

Kat snorted. "Under any other circumstances, I'd say you're off your rocker. If that kind of tech existed, it would make the best cutting-edge cybernetics on the market look like medieval trepanning. But, then, I guess the same goes for my code thingy."

I rubbed my eyes. "What about the Keepers? Did you find any leads on them?"

Kat paused. "Get ready for the weirdest news of an already weird night. I was able to dig up some mentions of a group calling itself *The Third Holy Church of the Kept Promise*, or 'the Keepers' for short. Your run-of-the-mill, wasteland-style, militantly misogynistic religious zealots, with a heavy dose of body-as-temple extremism thrown in for shits and giggles. Their founder published a manifesto saying that piercings and hair dye are mortal sins against God-given flesh, so you can imagine what they thought of medicine, cybernetics, gender transition, body mods, birth control, whatever. They had maybe ten thousand devout followers in North America at one time."

"Past tense?"

Kat's chopsticks clicked. "Therein lies the weirdness: they disappeared. Every last one of them. All on the same day. And I don't
mean they just went missing, or wandered off into the wasteland, or
drank poison together. I mean, according to the lore, they all literally evaporated into thin air. Sometimes right in front of people's
eyes. There's even a video. Want to see it?"

The image in my shard was of a young man on a dusty wasteland
street somewhere. He looked over his shoulder and heard or saw
something outside the frame. He turned toward whoever was shooting the video and ran at them in panic, and part of a shout escaped
his larynx before he blinked out of existence in mid-step. The clip
looped ad infinitum.

"I mean, come on," Kat said. "If you're going through all the trouble to fabricate a myth like this, at least shell out for some decent
special effects. Flashy lights, bendy distortion, a whooshing sound,
something."

I watched the disappearance again. I slowed it down and zoomed
in, a cold feeling seeping into my guts. "You mean . . . you think this
is a hoax."

"Of course it's a fucking hoax." She chuckled. "People don't just
get raptured. The unwashed hinterlands turn out a lot of weird folk-
lore."

Frame by frame, I could see it more clearly: the way the nothingness swallowed him by degrees, back to front, so that for a microsecond only his outstretched fingers remained in the empty air—and
then nothing. I thought of the empty church in Crossroads Station.
The young woman who'd watched me come out, then run. I shivered
at the memory of the word 'cursed.'

"Thank you, Kat," I sighed. "For all of this."

There was a pause before she responded. "Don't mention it." Even
through the vocal scrambler, I thought she sounded touched, and
my heart sank; I couldn't remember whether I'd ever thanked her for
anything before.

"Where are you?" I asked.

She chuckled. "You know I can't say that. Not even over a well-encrypted line. Not even to you." She slurped more noodles. "I'm in nodespace, that's where I am, and where I belong. The body is just an extraneous liability to store in a cargo container and feed and wash and keep anybody from killing. I don't know how you stand it out there in meatspace. I could never do it."

I wish I could see you, I thought, but only said, "I hope you're not still in the 'Paks. That's all I meant. I hope you're somewhere far from the war."

She sighed into her microphone. "Where would I go? I need a strong nodespace connection. For that I need a city. All the big cities are in the Pacific." She paused. "And if the shit really hits the fan, I don't think anywhere will be far from the war."

For a long while, we just listened to each other breathe through the static.

"Hey, want to watch a movie with me?" she asked. "I dug up some more pre-collapse American cinema. Some weird old cult hits in their classic two dimensions. *Big Trouble in Little China*. Ever heard of it?"

I could hear the hopefulness in her voice even through the scrambler, but I sighed and said, "The last working satellite's probably about to set."

"I could send you the file. We couldn't banter, but at least you could watch it on your shard and know I'm watching it too. If you want to."

"I . . . I should try to sleep. It's a long way to Greenglass."

"Remember I'm watching you," she said. "Remember you're not alone. Never. You got that, big guy?"

I held on to her words for a moment. "Kat . . ." I started to answer, but the shard beeped. The satellite had set, leaving me alone again between the wasteland and the endless black sky.

DANAE

With the residual smells of the ocean rising from our skins and per-
fuming the tight and dimly lit compartment, it was as if we were
right back in Bloom City. I had to focus hard on the whir of the motors, the way my teeth rattled in their sockets on the rocky terrain,
just to reassure myself that the last twenty-four hours hadn't been a
dream. I looked over at Naoto, slumped against twenty cases of algae
cakes, eyelids drooping, and realized what a comfort this claustrophobic space must have been to him. I reached out and clasped his
hand tightly—but when he looked up, he must have seen my dread.

"What's on your mind?" he asked groggily.

I studied him for a while before answering. "You're still in love
with me," I said. "Aren't you?"

He took a deep breath and nodded.

I said, "I'm worried you need things from me that I can't give
you. That our feelings are asymmetrical in a way that hurts you. I've
always had that worry."

He rubbed his eyes. "My feelings are my own responsibility. Not
yours."

I bit my knuckle pensively and stared at the slit window in the
rear hatch of the compartment, but there was nothing out there but
stars, jittering with the road.

"I've been a lot of people," I said. "I've been many women who
knew men who needed more from them than they could give. There
was one in particular. Since we reached the surface, I can't stop
thinking about him."

Naoto listened uneasily. "Who was he?"

"His name was Luther. He was a genius. I envied and admired
him very deeply, and it made me insensitive to his flaws. I didn't realize how intense his feelings for me were, or how poorly he was man-
aging them. We were going to unify, him and I, but then everything
. . . went wrong. It's been seventy years. He must have died a long

time ago, and I've lived so much since then, but it still keeps me up, some nights. I think he always will." I looked hard at Naoto. "We can't repeat that, any version of that, you and I."

He frowned. "You're saying I remind you of him."

I shook my head. "No. You remind me of me, not seeing his obvious flaws," I said. "Tell me why you made that awful deal."

He let out a ragged sigh. "I told you. It was the only way to get you a ride to Phoenix. I had no earthly way of knowing the chief was going to kick me out of Crossroads under penalty of—" He grimaced. "*Brain eating*, for fuck's sake."

"Maybe," I said. "But you still went in knowing you'd be giving up a small fortune. I'm not asking why you wanted to help me. I'm asking why you were willing to screw yourself over so completely to do it."

Naoto was silent for a while, hands draped over his knees, staring at nothing. My lives had given me a wealth of experience in reading people. Usually it was of limited benefit—the same nonverbal cues could mean something totally different from one person or context to the next—but in certain rare moments, it bordered on a kind of telepathy. Naoto's defenses were all stripped down, and I could read him like a book. I saw him weighing different lies, then different ways to sugarcoat the truth. I saw him give up.

"I thought I could stand the thought of stopping and settling in Crossroads, but when we got there, I couldn't," he said. "The truth is . . . I need to go to Redhill with you."

"Why?"

"Because I want to unify with you."

He studied my reaction with naked and shivering anxiety. "You're shocked, right? Just like when I told you I wanted to leave Bloom. Just like when I first confessed I was in love."

"No." A dozen different emotions clashed in my chest, but shock wasn't one of them. I sighed sadly and said, "I've always known, on some level. I still wish you'd told me sooner." I hesitated to add, "Why didn't you?"

He took a long time to work up the nerve to answer. "Like you said: you worry about me. I can't help the way I feel, but that's the last thing I want—to pressure you into anything, let alone *unity*. You have enough to worry about." He shrugged. "Loving you means I need you to feel safe with me. I need that a lot more than I need to burden you with all my innermost desires."

"I do feel safe with you," I whispered. "And I can't tell you how rare that is for me. I think . . . I wouldn't have lasted this long, if we hadn't met."

Our hands met and held in the gap between us. For a few minutes we just sat there, wordlessly sharing that touch.

He forced some levity into his voice to add, "Besides which, you'll have to forgive me for having no idea how the hell to broach *that* subject. I don't know the etiquette for proposing gestalt consciousness with someone. And do you have any idea how intimidating you are?"

I took my hands back. I winced and shook my head. "I'm nothing. You need to understand that. I'm a shell of what I used to be."

"A shell," he echoed. "A shell who's fluent in fifty languages, with three hundred years of combined training in a dozen different martial arts, who can play every instrument and understands science the entire rest of the world hasn't even—"

I cut him off. "I get it, but none of that matters. It doesn't make me any less irreparably broken."

He wanted to tell me I wasn't, but he kept it to himself. The truck bounced over some rough ground.

"When we get to Redhill," I said, "I'll vouch for you. You can unify with the rest of me, if you want to. You have so much to offer. More than you know."

A smile flickered across his lips, but his brows furrowed. "I don't understand. You're saying I can unify with the rest of you . . . but not *you?*"

I swallowed down the hard lump in my throat and shook my head. "No. Never with me."

He turned away, trying to hide the hurt, and failing. "Let me just say this once, so I won't spend the rest of my life worrying I was too timid to say it clearly. I want to unify with you. Not some other version of you. *You.* But if you don't want that with me, I . . . I have to respect that."

"It's not about what I want," I cried. "You have no idea how much I've *wanted* to, but we can't. I can't. I can never unify again. Not with anyone."

"Why not?"

I was crumbling. The wheels hit another rough patch in the road and threw us together between the jostling crates, and before I could stop myself, I balled the edges of his coat in my fists and sobbed, suffocating on the answer, but needing to say it.

"Because I'm a murderer," I said into his chest. "I killed a man five years ago, in a place called Asher Valley. I knew him. I gutted him with his own knife. I watched the life go out of his eyes."

Naoto's arms tightened around me. His hand held the back of my head.

"No one who takes a life may ever unify," I said. "That's the one rule. If you unify with me, you'd be a murderer too. It would infect you."

I had never told anyone. In the sixty years of chronological time for which I'd been whole, I had never needed to confess anything to anyone; I'd never needed to verbally process trauma. In all my lives I couldn't remember ever feeling more naked than I did then, clinging to him in the heat of that rumbling metal box.

He was silent for a long time. I was grateful for that. I was glad the roar of the truck's motors was loud enough to keep our mercenary on the roof from hearing me cry.

"I thought you were going back to reunify with the rest of you," Naoto said. "I thought that was whole the point of all this."

I shook my head slowly. "I lost myself in Bloom City. I lost my mind. I couldn't think. I only knew I had to get out of there or die— and I thought if I could just make it back to Redhill, at least I'd be with them again, my other selves. They can pass whatever judgment they want on me. I deserve it. I just needed to see the rest of me one more time." I gripped him tighter and met his eyes again. "But if you want to unify, that changes everything. That gives me a reason to go on. The first real reason I've had in five years."

He studied me—not fully understanding, but listening.

"I'm sorry for what I made you promise yesterday," I said. "Forget it. It was unbelievably cruel of me to ask that of you, and I know that now. But there's something else I'd like to ask instead."

He nodded warily.

"Whatever happens," I said, "put yourself first. No more taking risks to protect me. From now on, let me protect you. I'm expendable. You're the one who has to survive and make it to Redhill."

He didn't answer. We weren't trapped in the walls of a drowning city anymore. There was no duress. He had time to think about it.

"It's for my own sake," I said. "You can do something I can't: you can carry the memory of me back into the mind I used to be. And if you do, then for a split second, maybe, that mind will love me and forgive me as much as you do. That's the closest I'll ever be to being whole again. It's more than I could ever have hoped for before today."

He stroked my head. Even his touch was pensive. I thought I could feel him reaching for something to say in a hapless attempt to comfort me: that it couldn't really be so bad; that I must not really have murdered a man; that he didn't care, he still wanted to unify with me. I was ready to pull away. Ready to shout. Instead he just kissed the side of my head and croaked out the words, "Okay. I promise."

I listened to his heart beat. I breathed in the sea in his hair and the wasteland dust and smoke in his second-hand clothes. I raised my hand, palm open—and heard his heart quicken its beat when I asked, "Do you want to do again . . . what we did that night?"

He knew which night I meant.

"Here?" he whispered. "Now?"

"If you want to. It's probably the last chance we'll ever have." I leaned away from him and added sadly, "Look, I don't want to play with your emotions, but I . . . I feel more things than I could ever process with only one head, and there's so much fear out here, and I just need . . ." I sighed. There were no words for what I was trying to say. "I've been alone in this one body so long, and I need . . . I need."

"I know." He lay his open palm against mine. I could feel his fingers trembling, warming with sweat.

"Are you sure?"

He kissed me softly once, then many times hard. I tasted the blood iron on his chapped lips, the dry salt in his thin stubble. His right hand caressed my neck while his left laced its fingers through mine—and in the moment I willed our sensoria to merge, I felt us both gasp from the burst of sensation. I felt both our bodies shiver. I tasted both our litanies of small pains.

"Fuck," I groaned. "That headache."

"I've had it since we surfaced," he stammered. "My eyes don't work right out here. I'm not, uh. Not used to focusing on anything more than . . . two meters away—"

"Shh." I groped for the right pressure points on his body and kneaded hard, until I felt his pain start to lessen. I needed to make room for other sensations.

Through the haze of stress and fatigue and decompression, the ache of desire began to rise in both our bodies: a biochemical duet of arousal, growing louder, falling into harmony.

Do you still want this? I mouthed the words silently, knowing he could feel their shapes on my lips.

"Want," I felt his throat say. I heard the sound from inside his own head. "Need."

Every part of us itched and burned as we peeled all our layers off—the skin beneath dirty, clammy, chafed, but I savored every sensation: the roughness of his skin from inside, the sensitivity of the fine trail of hair on his belly; the way my curves felt to his hands. The taste of my tongue to his mouth. My smell to his nose.

For a moment we pulled back and lay apart on the hard metal

floor, taking each other in—seeing my body through his eyes and letting him see himself through mine. That had been the most unsettling part of this when we'd done it before, but this time we were prepared. This time it felt almost natural.

We buried our bodies in each other, coiling tightly together—all our bones knowing where they stabbed too hard, turning to settle into muscle or fat. I felt the tremble in his long fingers when he first reached out to roll my nipple between them, and I felt his body shiver even more ecstatically than my own at the sensation. I felt the rhythmic throb of desire catching like a fire in his pelvis.

It was too easy to become overwhelmed. I was being careful not to move too fast for him—I knew I was much more used to the sensation of male arousal than he was to female—but I felt, from both our perspectives, the irresistible hunger in his touch when his hand pushed down my side, rounded my hips, traced cautiously up my inner thigh. I raised my leg to let him in, and he gasped in amazement at the pressure of his fingers to my lips, just as my breath left me when I wrapped my hand around his cock. Finally we were lost in each other. Our minds were separate, but our bodies shared everything. Our hearts and lungs fell into a single rhythm until there was no mine, no his—only our hands. Our breasts. Our cock, our clit. Our entering and admitting, our wet heat from inside and out, spines arching, singing together in three symmetrical waves of perfect ecstasy, our voices lost in the rattle of the road.

When our bodies couldn't handle any more, we disentangled and lay back on the metal floor, savoring the doubled afterglow while we could. My view through Naoto's eyes gradually dimmed as the unifier nanobots in his brain self-terminated and dissolved, leaving me numb again to his senses.

He sniffled. In the compartment's dim light, I thought I saw tears dribbling down his face until he rolled over and away from me.

"Are you okay?" I whispered. I cautiously slid closer to him and he didn't push me away. "Was that too much?"

"No." He shook his head. "It's never enough."

I wrapped my arms around his chest and hugged him tight, and he held them back.

Remember me, I thought, until sleep took me. *Carry my memory home.*

BORROWER

In the pre-dawn light, I kissed Rutger's wife goodbye as if I were merely going in to work early. Then I met my alpha copy at the depot, and together we booked passage in the cargo truck that would carry us far away from Crossroads Station and deeper into the open wasteland. If I was ever to return to that place, it would not be in Rutger's body: the hand I'd ruined the day before was still bleeding and already showing ominous signs of infection. Staying in this vessel was now an unacceptable risk.

Fortuitously, a third man climbed into the cargo truck with us just before the motors whirred to life. He was in his late forties, short and bald, light-skinned, marred by sun damage. That is to say, he was very far from the kind of vessel I would normally assume, but at least he had two good hands. He was also considerably more muscular than he appeared at first, as the alpha and I discovered. Even with both my copies working together, we were only able to subdue him via blunt head trauma.

This was always the most torturous moment in the work by which I sustained myself: watching this new vessel, waiting for it to stir back to wakefulness; sitting here with fists clenched, praying inwardly that my baton strike wasn't too hard, checking every knot in the rope that binds him, tying the gag, compulsively inspecting the head wound again and again even though I knew full well that I could only wait for those eyes to open.

My alpha copy grabbed the vessel's wrist to check its pulse under the rope, and there I saw something strange. I zipped the sleeve open. On the inside of the forearm, I found a series of five short parallel lines, carved with mechanical precision into the flesh above the tendons.

"An aim-assist implant," my alpha copy said before I could. In the looks we exchanged, I knew we were thinking the same thought: our vessel was a soldier or mercenary of some sort. No, a bounty hunter.

I felt a tremble of excitement and saw the same in my counterpart. In my seventy-two years of this work I had become nearly every kind of man, but I had never been someone like him—simply because I abhor killing. Under the circumstances, however, his body might prove very useful.

The truck bounced over something in the road and shook our freshly caught vessel. I heard him groan. His eyes fluttered slightly under the lids but didn't open.

Alpha handed me the heavy briefcase containing the patterner. It felt good to hold it again. I'd never entrusted it to another person before; knowing I technically still had not never seemed to lessen the anxiety whenever my alpha copy held it.

"Be more careful with this flesh," he said. "Punching that wall was erratic."

I glared at him. "Need I remind you, you would have done exactly the same in my place."

Alpha pursed his lips and shifted uneasily. We didn't like each other. Neither of us wanted to contemplate the existential questions posed by maintaining concurrent copies.

But this is it, I realized. After all my careful planning and all my years of slow death, salvation was finally within my grasp. Sybil was waiting somewhere just over the scorched horizon in front of this truck.

Alpha shook me from my reverie. The captive flesh was awake and staring at us. Where I expected fear in his eyes, I found only cold, calculating brutality. The crags of his face glistened in the sweltering heat between the truck's flimsy dark canvas walls. The alpha copy shone a light in his face and waved it side to side, observing the constriction of his blue irises. Symmetrical. No signs of brain damage. We allowed ourselves a symmetrical sigh of relief.

The man—the vessel—grunted something through his gag. He wanted to talk. For our part, we needed him to.

Ordinarily, this was when I would begin the work—no, the artistry—by which I had perpetuated myself for more than seven decades. To become someone, I had to emulate his identity perfectly. I needed his accent, his quirks and mannerisms, his likes and dislikes, his hopes and fears. Usually it took months of preparation to assume a new vessel. I shuddered to know I had no time for that in this case.

"If you scream or try to escape, we will kill you," I lied.

Our captive nodded. My alpha copy removed his gag. He again surprised me by failing to immediately plead for his freedom. I took note of his thoughtful nature, his hardened self-control under dire circumstances.

"Your name?" my alpha copy asked him.

"Scuttle." It was probably a lie, but it would do.

"Do you have a family?" I asked.

This question unsettled him. He shook his head. "No."

"Any permanent place of residence? Do you have friends there? A social fabric?"

His nonverbal cues answered for him. I felt relieved. Setting his physical defects aside, he was the perfect flesh for emergency use. No one would come looking for him. I could wear his face anywhere without worrying too much about being flagged down by some old acquaintance of his; naturally, I have always lived in fear of such things.

"Who are you guys?" the vessel asked.

My alpha copy snickered at the question.

"We're following someone," I said. "We have to catch up with her. We must find her at any cost."

"You're mercs too," Scuttle guessed, with squinting uncertainty. He looked us up and down. Alpha's vessel still wore the suit and tie from its former life, hardly a fit with our current surroundings; in my frayed desert coat, I supposed I could nearly pass for a mercenary myself.

"We are," I answered.

"Don't tell me you're after the woman too," Scuttle groaned. "Danae. Duke's target."

Damn it all. This was the very last thing I needed: competition over Sybil. Alpha and I cringed and made fists in unison. Fresh blood spurted from my hand.

"Uh, listen," Scuttle said, queasily. "We can split the payoff. Work together. No need for this." He held up his bound wrists. "No honor in this. This isn't how it's done. We're supposed to work together. Duke's orders."

I calmed myself. We needed this information.

"What do you know about her?" the alpha copy asked.

"Age thirty-one, height 1.7 meters, dark skin. Wanted by Medusa Clan along with her two accomplices. Wanted strictly alive. What, nobody sent you the file?"

"Perhaps not. What else was in the file?"

"Photos, vids. I don't get it. What do you—?"

"Tell me more about Duke," I said.

But Scuttle was now too suspicious to answer any more questions. I kicked myself inwardly: we had been too impatient, but what was done was done. I hefted the briefcase onto the crate next to me, snapped it open, and lovingly beheld its contents.

"You're not mercs," Scuttle said, wincing as I fastened the first patterner crown to his skull and flipped each of the four switches to pneumatically inject the probes into his cerebrum. I fastened the other crown to my own head and felt the pins slide back through the same tiny holes in the bone, through which they had first conveyed me into this vessel only three weeks ago. The old punctures hadn't even had time to heal.

Fear was finally creeping into Scuttle's voice as I finished the preparations.

"Who are you?"

The alpha copy and I grinned symmetrically in reply—at each other, then at him.

Scuttle jerked his head suddenly, loosening one of the cables strung between us. I reached instinctively to check it. He moved very quickly then, his bound hands snapping out, sweeping across my abdomen a few times. I pulled back just in time to dodge a slash across my neck.

"Hurry," the alpha copy told me calmly. He had ripped the knife from Scuttle's grasp, but it was taking all his strength and weight to press the man back against the wall, pinning an elbow against his neck to hold his head still.

When I reached out to refasten the loose plug, I heard an unexpected noise, like rain dripping on the metal floor. My abdomen was open, I saw. The gash revealed tissues of various hues and colors: the milky sheen of subcutaneous fat, the bright ruby of muscle, deeper still the pale glistening of small intestine. I felt blood's wet heat soak into my shirt. I could see the entrails loosening as I stood, trying to push through. I frowned briefly. I reached my bandaged hand down to hold the wound shut as best I could, reaching out with the other to fit the cables back into their jacks.

Scuttle watched all of this, finally showing an appropriate level of horror. He could see that I responded to no pain, yet I was not drugged or anesthetized. I watched the outward signs of his mind working as he realized that he did not know exactly what he was looking at when he looked at me or at the alpha copy.

"Who *are* you?" he croaked.

"Proceed with the transfer," the alpha copy said. I could hear the shiver of desire in his voice: even now, envying me.

The patterner finished its startup sequence. The lights turned green. My mouth was watering. I felt my lips curve into a widening smile. My finger hesitated just above the switch. Scuttle wriggled ever more desperately under the alpha copy's weight, and it was strange how even through the creeping haze of blood loss, even recognizing the urgency, I could not resist stopping to savor this last, ecstatic moment before rebirth.

I pushed. The patterner's microcurrents rolled through my cranium like thunder and its electric euphoria washed through my sensorium, canceling me out.

It was the white noise of the road that returned first. I opened my eyes.

No. Oh no.

"Success," I heard my copy say, in a voice that had been Scuttle's.

The alpha and new gamma copies turned to regard me disgustedly when they realized my consciousness still resided in Rutger's ruined vessel.

"It was still set to clone," the gamma and I said in unison.

"You should have set it to transfer," said my alpha copy.

"I know," my gamma responded irritably.

"Nothing can be done about it now," I said. I sat back and lay both my hands across my belly as the alpha copy helped free the new gamma's wrists from the rope. Now they would have to watch me die. I would have to experience death. Permanent death.

"Find Sybil," I commanded them. "Get to her before the Medusas, at all costs. Make my death worth it."

"We will," my copies responded in unison.

"This is all proving to be much more dangerous than we expected," alpha observed. "We need more strength. We need to set aside the existential discomfort of making concurrent copies."

"We need more of ourselves," gamma said.

"More," I agreed.

My gamma copy flexed his new vessel experimentally, acquainting himself with it. He withdrew the patterner's cerebral probes from his head and mine and went to work meticulously cleaning all traces of blood and cerebrospinal fluid from the apparatus. I saw him squint uncomfortably.

"Are you all right?" I asked. "Is the patterner damaged?"

"No," he said. "There are two toes missing from my left foot, and I have no hearing in my left ear." His tongue probed the inside of his cheek. "Four missing molars, one dry socket. This flesh would never do under normal circumstances."

Meanwhile my alpha copy busied himself taking inventory of the bags Scuttle had brought onto the truck with him. I saw two wave pistols and a rifle. Several power cells. He showed us Scuttle's shard and said, "We may be able to use this to monitor communications between other parties pursuing Sybil."

"Excellent," I croaked, but I could feel myself dying more fully now. I tried to focus on the two of me sitting there, alive and well, but panic kept washing through me. Darkness was biting at the edges of my vision.

"I'm afraid," I told my copies. "Afraid." I tried to say more but my mouth wouldn't obey my commands. My thoughts were sluggish.

I reached out for them with my ruined hand.

The last thing I saw was my copies leaning away, refusing my touch.

ALEXEI

Around noon the next day, I squinted ahead and made out the uneven spread of drab color rising out of the sun-scalded white of the desert. Several rovers passed us speeding the opposite direction, thickening the air with their dust. I kicked the rusty hatch twice, and my clients joined me on the roof of the truck. They blinked and yawned. Their skin didn't look quite so bloodless anymore. I guessed they'd slept well.

Naoto cleared his throat and somewhat bitterly told Danae, "Maybe I should ask before we get there."

"Ask what?"

"Whether you just happened to forget to tell us about a massive Keeper presence in this place too."

She stared into infinity and replied, "No, but we have to expect them wherever we go. The worst parts of the wasteland are their fertile ground."

I said, "Were."

They both looked at me.

"Apparently they all disappeared into thin air," I said. "Not just in Crossroads, but everywhere."

"What?" Danae gaped.

I shook my head. "Nothing. Superstition. Wasteland myth."

"No, tell me. Please. Disappeared how? When?"

I told her what Kat had told me, and she listened blankly. She sat hunched over on the hot metal roof and folded her arms and shivered as if she were cold.

We rumbled onto what passed for streets in the encampment at Greenglass Mountain. All around us were tents, storage tanks, tailing ponds, the lumbering hulks of mobile enrichment rigs, burning in the pink dawn light. People slept in hammocks strung between machines covered in radiation warnings.

"What is this place?" Naoto asked, rubbing his eyes.

Danae was silent and lost in her thoughts.

"This desert has been a dumping ground for nuclear waste for centuries," I answered. "Spent fission rods and fusion residue, once considered too hazardous to reprocess. Whenever Epak inflates the price of deuterium, scavengers move in to sift the dirt and mine the old waste repository under the mountain. Whatever they can't make into new fission fuel, they repackage as casings for dirty bombs."

Naoto peered nervously at one of the tailing ponds, streaked with lurid color in the desert light. "Is it safe for us to be here?"

"Relatively." I turned on my dosimeter and clipped it to my belt. "We won't have time to accumulate a significant dose, as long as we wipe our feet and don't touch anything. The truck only needs to recharge its fuel cells, and then it's another nine hours to Camp Phoenix."

The driver reached out and smacked her palm against the roof of the cab to get our attention. She leaned out the window to yell, "About that. Change of plans. Soon as the cells are full again, I'm headed back to Crossroads."

Naoto and Danae exchanged alarmed looks.

"You said you were bound for Phoenix," I yelled back.

"I was." She shook her head and spat into the dust. "This isn't what I wanted. I'm sorry."

"What happened?"

She said nothing.

The truck took us down the makeshift streets, between lines of black rocks in the white sand. Last time I'd passed through here, the encampment had been packed with cargo trucks and throngs of wastelanders on the verge of rioting for a chance to trade near-term starvation for long-term cancer risks. Now the streets were nearly deserted.

Everyone was gathered around panes or shards or ancient computer screens: all watching, in looping holographic video, the first shots of a new war.

The Gray was spreading. From the air or orbit, it was only a vague, silvery discoloration, like mold spores on the skin of the ocean—but a steadily growing ring already surrounded Hawai'i, and the circumference of the dead zone spewed forth a stream of frenzied chatter and shaky recordings of ships and submarines melting down into the nanoscopic fray. The screens flashed with dull tendrils of liquid metallic stuff that drilled through hulls, through people, too fast to see, making everything it touched into only more of itself.

"They did it," I heard Naoto gasp. "It's happening. It's all really happening."

The Gray leaped and danced over the poisoned waves. Each colony of glittering ooze showcased a different set of genetic algorithms designed to speed its metastasis: here a Norpak strain vomited itself out in mats of veiny structures on the water's surface, pouring all its mass into forward motion, and then slowly grew inward and down to catch anyone or anything it had missed, or that would take longer to digest; here a cutting-edge Epak strain built up and concentrated itself into hollow blisters that overpressured and burst, flinging contagious droplets like cannon shells. Every strain was terrifyingly fast. No ship could outrun the explosions of branching quicksilver arms. No submersible could dive fast enough to escape the hairs it dangled like jellyfish tentacles, down into the lightless depths.

"Who set it off?" Danae asked. "Who fired first?"

"What does it matter?" asked a voice from behind us.

I had noticed the elderly woman when we entered the tent, perched awkwardly on a support beam at the back. She looked about twenty years older than anyone else I'd seen since we set foot here, in this city of the firm and short-lived. She wore an ordinary work uniform, except it was clean, and her hands were free of the persistent chemical stains that marked those who labored on the rigs or under the mountain itself.

"It could determine the course of the conflict," Naoto responded distantly.

The elder didn't look up from the pipe she was packing. "Way out here, we'll never know who fired first. We won't even know whose Gray it is when it comes for us. By then it'll all have fused together anyway, just one great big wave. No use blaming anyone. The end of the world is just the end of the world." She lit up and inhaled.

"The world's not really going to end," Naoto declared, sounding less than confident. "All anyone has to do is transmit the kill commands, and it all stops growing. Just disintegrates. Right?" He paused nervously. "Right, Danae?"

She barely seemed to register his words at first. She mumbled her answer without ever taking her eyes off the screen. "Soon. Probably hours from now. I'm sure it's . . . being worked on."

One of the isotope scavengers, twitching with nervous energy, leaned over to insinuate himself and unhelpfully explain, "No, the world won't really end. It's a big game of chicken. It always is. Norpak's Gray spreads out toward Bloom City, Epak's Gray spreads for Subkyoto. Whoever's about to get sludged first throws up the white flag and boom, it's all over. Mutual Assured Destruction is going to work this time."

"Not if they don't trust their opponent to honor their surrender," the smoking woman said. "And you're assuming everyone who could've sent the kill command doesn't get turned to sludge before they can send it. You're assuming people are going to be reasonable at a time like this. If anyone isn't, it's the end for all of us. Gray Day."

"Never gonna happen," the scavenger insisted, tapping his foot furiously. "Gray Day? Hell. My folks thought Cruithne was going to be it. Sold off all their worldly possessions and camped out at ground zero; watched it skip off the atmosphere right above their heads. *Their* parents were sure as shit Blood Rain was going to spread and make the whole world as dead and empty as it did Europe, and you know what? We evolved a naturally immunity. *Their* parents thought nukes would make everyone extinct, but we're still here." He paused to tug his scarf down and rub at the ten-centimeter-wide tumor growing up through his collar.

"What about climate change?" somebody jeered. "You know all this wasteland didn't used to be wasteland, right?"

"But that's exactly what I'm talking about," the isotope scavenger said. "The real apocalypse is slow. It's never-ending. It doesn't happen just like that. Never has before, won't this time either."

"This is different," the old woman said, spitting out smoke. "Gray self-replicates. There's no bunker you can hide under. No way to shoot it down or seal yourself off from it. I *remember* Blood Rain. We got lucky then. It was only a matter of time before we invented a bullet that even we couldn't dodge."

Naoto blinked hard and tore his attention away from the screen. "There's nothing we can do about it. Let's focus on the here and now. Let's go find our ride inland."

"Good luck with that, kids," the old woman said.

"What do you mean?"

She grunted at her stiff back as she heaved herself onto her feet. "Look around you. Most folks here are migrants from outer Epak, some from coastal cities, some from the north, and they're not about to spend their last days on Earth digging under the mountain. They're going home." She leaned heavily on the bars of the tent's wall and stared out into the hot drifting sand. "By late tonight this town will be all stripped down and gone."

"Someone must be traveling east. With all the reactor fuel this place trades to the Confederacy."

"No one's going east."

"How do you know?"

"They all work for me," she said. "Or did. Excuse me."

I watched her duck under the beam and walk off down the street. She was the only person in sight who wasn't either running at full speed or sitting perfectly still in the light of a pane. Danae watched her with an inscrutable expression.

"Come on," Naoto said.

Danae pulled herself away and started walking, but now she was staring at the shard in her hand. "Even in the time we've been standing here, the Gray . . . spots . . . have grown by hundreds of square kilometers. Their growth accelerates the bigger they get. Assuming a terminal replication rate of . . ." She was furiously typing numbers into a calculator program.

Naoto ducked in close to her, and I pretended not to overhear him whispering, "What is it?"

"I can't stand this," she said. "Watching it happen. Not being able to do anything."

I was distracted. I kept checking my shard and expecting a missed message from Kat. I wasn't used to getting news of this magnitude from anyone but her.

"Damnit, I could almost do it myself," Danae hissed. "If I were

whole, I'd have the kill commands cracked by now. I know I would."
She rubbed her eyes and sighed deeply. "What I don't know is why
I haven't done it already. The other I, I mean. It must have had time
to finish my research, unless I've badly underestimated the scope
of the problem." She held Naoto a little closer. "Something's wrong."

I called Kat.

For the first time since we'd met, she didn't answer.

I followed my clients among the tents and shacks while they hap-
lessly tried to flag down a ride, but the old woman was right. No one
was going to take us farther inland, and no one was staying here.

As we walked, I couldn't stop looking up between the last frayed
and flapping tarps. It was always there now, in the edge of my vision
or in the static noise under my eyelids: the thin ghost of that vast
and terrible attention, looking down on me, invisible yet percep-
tible. By now I was almost used to it. Meanwhile the sun crawled
across the dust-streaked sky and painted Greenglass Mountain the
color of molten iron, and its shadows traced a city already stripped
down to its bones. Everything but the latrines and slag pits was being carted off on a rig or strapped to the roof of a cargo truck. A
steady flow of traffic crawled away over the western horizon while
we watched, hopeless and impotent, from the lee of a rusted-through
storage tank.

"We made it so far," Danae said distantly.

"We're fucked," Naoto groaned. He had a ragged cloth draped
over his head for shade, but the backs of his hands were sunburned to
blistering from holding it up.

I felt a twinge of duty to reassure my clients, but I couldn't disagree with his assessment. By dawn there would be no one else left
here. Depending on the course of the war, it might be weeks before
anyone passed through again. The Medusas were likely already on
their way in search of us; if we evaded them, that left dehydration

and starvation; beyond that, the radiotoxicity of the mountain itself. Looming over all these threats was the nebulous, nearly un-imaginable possibility that the war in the ocean would never reach any truce or surrender; that a few days from now, the Gray would arrive here in a tidal wave of shining ooze, to strip our bodies down to their base molecular components and use us as fuel for its inexo-rable expansion over the rest of the Earth.

All the same, there was a strange peace here. The wind drew spi-rals in the compacted dust where the makeshift city had stood. Wisps of clouds crossed the sky in intricate patterns, on their way to some-where else.

"This is all my fault," Danae muttered. "If I'd left Bloom even one day sooner, we would've reached Redhill by now."

"One day sooner wasn't a good time either," Naoto said. He'd been staring down at a footprint for half an hour, watching the blowing dust slowly erase it from the landscape. He looked up at Da-nae and me in turn and asked, "There are some things Gray avoids, right? Isn't it repelled by radiation?"

My clients turned to me for an answer. I glanced distractedly up from my shard—I was still trying to call Kat—and answered, "Most strains avoid gamma radiation in excess of around 200 millisieverts per hour. Too much risk of mutating its own replication pattern."

"What are you thinking?" Danae asked him.

Naoto rubbed his head and cringed. He took a deep breath and then heaved himself to his feet. "Come on. Follow me."

We walked through what was left of the encampment, down the main central road that climbed the mountain itself and disappeared into the crook of its eroded peaks. We passed the last merchant as she was packing up, and Naoto ducked into her tent and emerged a minute later with several cans of spray paint in emergency colors.

"What did you barter?" Danae asked.

"Nothing," he answered. "In this place it's customary to grant small wishes to the doomed."

A kilometer uphill along the washboard road, we reached the

tunnel mouth itself. The last of its faded warnings, chiseled in weatherproof stone in a hundred different languages, were strewn around like pieces of a struck-down Babel tower. The great repository's wrenched-open bunker doors had been leaned against the hillside like a pair of ten-meter-tall concrete tablets, sun-bleached and blank.

Naoto motioned at my dosimeter, and I answered his implicit question with a nod: if the Gray came here, the storm surge of nanobots would form a shore a few meters down the slope and stop there. Not that it would do us any good; we could stand here for two hours at the most before the first symptoms of acute radiation syndrome set in.

He pumped a paint cannister and tossed it to Danae. He turned a second can in his hand looked back at me, deciding.

"I don't understand," she said.

"Maybe we're all going to die here, or in some Medusan prison cell," he said. "Maybe we'll miraculously make it to Redhill, in spite of everything—and I'll have no need of self-expression anymore."

She frowned.

"Either way," he continued, "this will be the last mural I'll ever paint. Hell—if Gray Day really is coming, this may be the last thing anyone will ever paint. But I want you to lead."

"Me?" She stared at the empty slab. "Lead how? What do you mean?"

He shrugged. "Draw the first stroke. Lay down the basic shapes. I'll fill in details and embellish as you go."

"I don't know what to start with." She knitted her brows and looked at her feet. "It's not that simple."

"Why not?"

"Because painting takes muscle memory. Hand-eye coordination. I don't have those things in this body."

Naoto nodded. "Then just . . . paint words instead. Whatever comes to mind. Whatever message you want to leave here for the alien beings who might stumble upon this dead planet someday."

He stood back to give her space, and his expression was grave when he held out a spray can for me to take: really offering me his trust, for what I realized was the first time. Everything until now had been desperation.

Danae sprayed the first stroke in electric blue. She was slow and methodical, giving Naoto plenty of time to work; spreading out from her every line with patterns and curves, adding complementary shapes that began to look like faces and scenes in the corner of my vision.

I stepped in last, filling the negative spaces in his wake with an endless repetition of regular black spirals: an exercise the Major had taught us as a form of meditation in the long, maddening waits between engagements. It was as good a way as any to take my mind off worrying about Kat.

When it was done, the last mural's words burned like plasma in the dying light:

WE WERE HERE

Naoto stood back to stare at it. His face twitched. He started to tear up.

"What?" Danae asked.

"This is it," he said. "This is the most important work I've ever done."

They fell against each other and hugged tightly—but Danae's eyes stayed open and focused on something in the distance over his shoulder. She pulled back and pointed out over the valley. "What is that?"

There was a squat, sandy hill on the opposite side of the grid-scarred plain of dust. Near its crest, the low sun glittered fiercely on something that would have been invisible at any other hour, or from any other vantage point.

Naoto tapped me on the shoulder. "Can I borrow your gun's telescope thing?"

I detached the scope, and he peered across at the glimmer. I could just make it out now: a camouflaged housing pod and a small armored vehicle, its windshield catching the last of the sun.

"That old pessimist we met earlier," Naoto said. "'Lady Janni-son.' She owns this place. Owned. I heard someone say she lives up on that hill."

"She wasn't eager to help us earlier," Danae said.

"She's the last person left here who we haven't technically asked," he said. "She has some kind of rover up there. She doesn't seem to be in a hurry to drive it anywhere."

When I upped the magnification, I could see her, sitting on the hood of the old military antique, staring into the distance. Still smoking.

"Jannison," Danae whispered to herself. She closed her eyes against the wind. "Olivia."

"What is it?"

"Naoto, I know her."

"How?"

She turned to him and lowered her voice to say, "I'm her grand-father."

I wanted to listen carefully to the rest of what they muttered to each other then. I wanted to contemplate the mystery of whatever she was talking about, but all my attention was on the shard cupped in my hand.

"—use that to our advantage?" Naoto whispered.

"It's . . . complicated. She thinks I've been dead for over fifty years. The last time I saw her, she was only—"

I'd been trying to reach Kat for more than 8 hours now. I'd sent message after message asking her to contact me as soon as she could, while the satellites connecting us had gone on rising and set-ting, but there had been no response. For a while I had let myself think this was only her revenge for my ignoring all her calls between Antarka and Bloom City, but now my transmissions were bouncing back all at once, with an attached error code—

"Are you coming?" Naoto shouted back at me. I looked up from my shard and followed them up the hill.

The error message read: *Recipient address dead.*

The road up Jannison's hill was steep, narrow, and punctuated with bits of old radiation safety equipment, weathered-down and disused: here a station for brushing off shoes, there a trash chute for disposable gear. A few solar-powered Geiger counters ticked away halfheartedly in the long shadows.

When we reached the top, Jannison was still perched on the vehicle's hood, the orange sunset painting her scowl in sharp relief as we approached. The plastic pod house behind her was bigger than it had appeared from a distance, but bleached and cracked as if abandoned. In its shadow, a patch of dirt was marked off. I counted four crucifixes of welded steel pipe.

"I'd be in a hurry to leave what's left of this town," Jannison called down to us. "If I were you."

"We still need to go east," Naoto said.

"And I'm still telling you to hitch a ride out of this shithole while you can, wherever that ride happens to be going."

"Why aren't you leaving then?"

"Nowhere to go."

Danae seemed agitated. "That tank is quite an antique," she observed carefully.

"It's not a tank," Jannison responded. "It's an armored personnel carrier."

"Combustion engine, mounted bullet gun, steel plating. Second Continental War?"

She shook her head. "Good guess, but it's older. Late Imperial era. Though I've had to settle for a few newer parts here and there."

"Does it run?" Naoto asked.

She paused to squint down the length of her pipe and spit some smoke in my direction. She said nothing.

"We need to borrow it," Danae said.

Jannison coughed and laughed. "No."

"Are *you* using it?" Naoto asked.

"I spent the last nine years of my life fixing up this *Armored Personnel Carrier*, you little shit. It's *pretty*. That's what I'm using it for. It's mine, and I'm keeping it till the Gray comes and pries it from my cold, dead hands. Who the hell are you to ask what I'm using it for?"

"We need to go east," Danae said. "Frankly, our lives are depending on it, and we're out of other options." She put her hands together in prayer. "Is there anything we can say or do or offer, anything at all, that would convince you to let us use it for twenty-four hours? That's all we need."

She motioned in my direction and said, "Supposing I say *no*, I gather your nasty-looking friend is here to waste me with his waver and then you take it from me anyway, right?"

I swallowed hard. I gave Danae a sidelong glance, bracing for her to give me the order, but she only looked down and shook her head guiltily.

"Then, no. There is nothing I would trade for it. No money I'd sell it for. You want money? I'm up to my fucking ears in fucking money. Take it all, for all I care."

She dug through her pockets and started throwing chits at us with increasing violence. She flicked them like playing cards, and I raised a hand to keep one from hitting me in the face. I looked down at the pile forming at my feet and began to mentally add up the numbers.

"Take it all," she said. "Take it and leave me the fuck alone. Or hurry up and shoot me."

I had a pile like this of my own, locked away in a vault in Sydney: a chit for every job. The electro-luminescent digits glared up between my feet like ghosts—like sunlight on ice fields.

"I said get out of here!" she shouted, and when I looked up, I found myself staring down the length of a wave pistol, quaking in her grip. Her eyes were wild as she climbed down off the APC's hood to better shove the weapon in my face. I didn't react.

"Wait," Naoto said.

"I'll give you five seconds to fuck off."

"Olivia," Danae started. "Please."

Naoto put his hands up and said "Wait, just—"

"Five!" Jannison shouted. "Four! Three!"

"Cricket, stop!" Danae yelped.

The old woman's arm pivoted smoothly to train the weapon on Danae's head instead of mine. Naoto quickly stepped in, trying to make himself Danae's human shield, but she shoved him away and stepped in closer until she was nearly pressing her forehead against the gun's emitter.

"What did you just call me?" Jannison asked.

"Do something!" Naoto shouted at me.

It took all my will to do it, but I finally started to raise my rifle.

DANAE

I had learned, a long time ago, to lock down all my feelings when it came to the relationships I'd had in my other bodies. Twelve thousand years of experience came with tens of thousands of loved ones, friends and family, but most of them would never recognize me without the face they were used to. I'd taught myself to accept that. It was dangerous to do what I was doing now: channeling one of my lives and letting myself feel it all the way. As dangerous as pushing on the broken heart of a woman with a gun in her hand and nothing left to lose.

"Three," Jannison barked, regaining her composure.

"You have to shoot," Naoto told Alexei.

"Do not shoot!" I screamed.

Jannison barely seemed to notice. "Two!"

I closed my eyes and focused on the memory of the body she would have greeted as kin. I took a deep breath, and as I exhaled, I called back how that skin had felt, how my heart used to beat, how my voice had sounded when I was only him—

"One!"

"When you were a child in Lake City," I breathed, "your grand-papa called you Cricket."

I didn't open my eyes, but the gun in my face stopped rattling.

"What?" Jannison muttered.

"He gave you rides on the handlebars of his bicycle. He said you had an unusual laugh. High and quiet, like a cricket chirping."

Her voice was rapt with disbelief. "How could you know that?"

"You had a fire in you from the moment you were born," I continued, and with every word I let in more of that life. I met my granddaughter's gaze and said, "You were the most serious child I—he—had ever seen. You wanted more than your family could give you. You were going to grow up to have a family of your own, and they'd have everything they ever wanted, no matter what it took out of you. Other kids played, you worked. You tried to start your first business when you were six years old."

"I don't—" Her voice creaked. "I don't understand what's—"

Naoto jumped in the corner of my vision when I reached up and put my hands on Jannison's pistol, but she lowered it without resistance.

"One day, you ran away," I said. "You ran from that slum. You came here to work the mountain?"

"Forty years," said my granddaughter. "Forty years it took me to work my way up."

"Until you reached the top, and you were as rich as any waste-lander can be. And you did it, didn't you. You had a family of your own."

"Yes."

It was all I could do to control my breath and blink the dusty salt-water out of my eyes. "They died?"

"One by one, they—" Her lungs heaved. "The radiation on this godforsaken mountain. I thought I could protect them, and instead I killed them all."

We collapsed into each other. When she hugged me, I could feel the pistol still clenched in her hand against my back, still primed to fire. She balled my coat in her fists and wept bitterly into my shoulder, and I couldn't hold back my own tears.

She still had no idea who I was. I was just a stranger who knew things.

Naoto and Alexei stood back and glanced nervously at each other.

"There's no one left," Jannison said. "Everyone is dead. The world's ending, and I have no one left."

"You do," I said. "You do, Cricket."

"Who are you?" She started to push away. "Who *are* you?"

I owed her the answer, and words wouldn't be good enough. Even if she could make sense of what I would tell her, she had no reason to believe it. There was nothing else to do: I reached for her, carefully. I touched the side of her head, and she let me.

"Danae?" Naoto blurted out. "Wait, what are you—?"

I leaned my forehead against Jannison's and willed—and a small, safe corner of my mind opened to admit her. Here was the house where she'd grown up, suffused with every trace of sensory memory I could well up: the creak of its ancient floorboards, the smell of its old paper library, the color of light through its windows. There were the people we'd called family: the sounds of their voices; the warmth of their hugs; the endless, microscopic details and eccentricities that traced out the essences of who they had been. Some of it had faded with the years, despite all my efforts, but I shared every scrap of memory I carried of the people she'd left behind, their love for her, their forgiveness. I let her feel that love. We felt it together.

Then I let go.

She hugged me one more time, tightly. Then, without another word, she dropped her gun in the sand and started walking.

We watched her go in silence for a long time, until she disappeared into the waves of dust in the last light.

"What just happened?" Naoto asked.

I wiped my face off and said, "She gave us permission." I cleared my mind, forced myself back into the present, and tried not to let them hear the shake in my voice when I said, "Please tell me one of you knows how to drive that thing."

I slumped in the passenger seat as the machine rumbled down off that hill. I stared ahead through the antique glass windshield and the reflected glow of the heads-up display, into the faint trace of the eastward trade road running on into the sinking dusk. We had twenty-four hours left to reach Redhill. More than enough time.

A fresh wave of relief and awe washed over me every time I thought it to myself: we were all alive. We were going to make it.

"Directions?" Alexei asked. He switched his dosimeter off and set it on the dashboard with a sigh of relief.

"It's well before Phoenix, and not far off the trade road," I answered. "Keep going for roughly 400 kilometers, then turn due south, just before the old Flagstaff beacon—assuming the cells are full enough to take us that far."

"No cells," he said. "That noise you hear is a fossil fuel combustion engine. No modern readouts. I should be able to estimate how long our fuel reserves will last once we're farther down the road, but right now I'm more concerned about something breaking. This is a very old vehicle." He grabbed a knob by his right knee and pushed it into a new position, making an ominous grinding noise.

"Is that a manual transmission?" I asked.

"Yes. I suspect Jannison improvised it herself. Do you know how to operate one of these?"

By now he could only have figured out that he didn't know exactly what I was, what I knew or what I was capable of. That much was clear in the tone of his voice—but I could only laugh cruelly at myself: for all the lives I'd led, and all the skills and knowledge that came with them, my answer was still, "Not even a little."

I thought of jokingly asking Naoto if he knew how to drive stick, but when I glanced over my shoulder, he was still slumped against the window, sun-blistered hands in his lap, looking utterly sullen. I called his name. When he didn't respond, I unhooked my seatbelt and climbed into the back compartment to have a closer look at him.

"How are you feeling? Any headache, nausea, fever?"

"Does it matter," he mumbled.

I put my hand on his forehead, but he pushed it away.

"Come on," I said. "We all caught some gamma rays back there. Probably not enough to get sick, but we should still watch out for symptoms."

He snorted. "I've had the same splitting headache and nausea since we left Bloom. How would I even know the difference?"

He needed some space to himself, I thought. "Okay, then just relax. Get some sleep. It's not so far now."

I started to climb back into the front seat, but his voice rose just above the drone of the engine to ask, "Did you?"

"Did I what?"

"Did you unify with Jannison?"

The question didn't hit me as hard as the way he asked it. I sank back down into the seat next to him, searching his face. "Exactly what the hell is wrong with you?"

He tipped his head to indicate Alexei in the driver's seat. "Oh, sorry. I shouldn't use the U-word. And here you had him believing you're a perfectly ordinary person with no cybernetic abilities or eons of memory or anything like that."

Alexei's dim reflection in the windshield raised one eyebrow but managed not to look at us.

We knew not to get into this fight. Naoto's body and mine were both racked with a toxic mixture of stress and adrenaline and drugs and sleep deprivation and radiation and who knew what else. I tried to hold back. I failed.

"That's not what I meant," I said. "I meant fuck you for asking. What Olivia and I shared is not your business."

"What you shared," he echoed. "Do you have any idea how badly I've wanted to share those kinds of things with you?"

Anger burned like acid in my chest. "So, what you and I shared in the truck from Crossroads, that was nothing. Is that what you're saying?"

"No! It was far from *nothing*, but—" He rubbed his eyes and groaned loudly. "It was just physical, damnit. I've wanted to unify with you for three years. You say we can't, and who the fuck am I to argue. But every time you unify with somebody else right in front of my face, it gets a little harder to believe that 'it's not you, it's me' routine. Just tell me the truth. I'm not good enough. That's it, right?"

That was what curdled my blood. To hear him sound so much like Luther.

"I forget how young you are," I said. "Then you act like a spoiled child, and I remember."

"I envy Jannison," he pressed. "I even envied Serena, for fuck's sake. Because at least your mind and hers touched."

"You don't even know what you're jealous of!" I shouted, so loud that he startled. "Unity changes a person. Forever. I tried to give Jannison a memory she needed, and I can only pray it changed her for the better and not for the worse. I took memory from Serena that I thought *I* needed, and you saw what that did to me."

He looked at his burned hands in his lap and said nothing.

"Unity is change," I said. "And I already know how it would change you to unify with me, and you deserve better than that. You can choose to believe me when I say that, or not. I don't give a shit anymore."

I turned away and climbed back into the front seat. The tight metal space filled up with the silence between us.

The distance crawled by through the narrow windows, only black silhouettes of mountains against the stars. The ear-splitting, metal-hammering sound of that engine ironically lulled me into half-sleep.

A hundred and twenty years ago, I remembered, I'd driven on this very road. A lover and I had pooled our life savings for a piece-of-crap used solar car in San Francisco and set off for the ghost of Route 66. We'd only made it to Albuquerque before the thing broke down on the highway—this same highway, now just a ghost of pulverized asphalt through the naked wasteland. The world had been dying then too, but by comparison the process had barely begun yet. Cities had still stood, complete with gleaming towers of fragile glass. Nothing had been burned by nuclear fire; nothing blown away on the storms; nothing bleached to dust by naked solar UV light; nothing swallowed by the sea.

It had been so long since I'd let myself remember these things. For the first time in countless years, I wondered whether anything could be like that again. That safe and carefree. That hopeful.

Then I woke up.

"Wake up," Alexei was shouting. "We have a problem."

A sound came from behind. A faint creak of deforming metal. A smell followed the sound, sharp and warm. Burning plastic.

"The engine?" I asked.

"No. We're under attack."

"From who? What?" My pulse quickened. I twisted around, trying to see.

"No, stay back from the windows! Close the shutters. All of them."

"Who's attacking us?"

"Aerial drones. At least two of them. I'd guess fully automated."

"Medusas?" Naoto demanded. "Have they found us?"

Alexei shook his head. "It's more likely the drones were left here as traps, maybe by raiders, maybe Confederate patrols. Their attack pattern doesn't strongly suggest they want us alive."

Naoto jumped when he touched the lever to close the shutters over his window. "Ow! Hot!"

"Waver strikes," Alexei said, and jerked the wheel to swerve.

I scanned the metal cabin frantically. "Do we even need to worry? They can't penetrate these walls with their beams . . . can they?"

"No, but they can burn right through the sidewalls of these antique rubber tires. We've already lost one. If they gain on us any further, they'll be able to shoot us through the windshield. There's no shutter on it."

"Shit!" Naoto yelled, nursing his hand. "What do we do?"

"One of you take the mounted gun. There's a full box of ammunition. You just have to slot the feeder and fire."

"Do what to the *what?*" Naoto shouted. "Slot? Feeder?"

"Hold on." Alexei threw the steering wheel hard to the right, hitting us with so much centrifugal force that I was surprised the machine didn't fly off its wheels. He repeated the same maneuver in the opposite direction. Only then did he spare us one glance over his shoulder to say, "Listen carefully. My evasive maneuvers are buying us time, but someone needs to take that gun and shoot down those drones, or it won't be enough. I can walk you through it"— he paused to swerve violently again while we held on for dear life—"but I need you to do exactly what I say, the first time I say it."

It was already dawning on me what I would have to do, but I was still racking my brain for any other option. I looked at the scarred mercenary sitting there at my left, expertly handling the arcane controls of this groaning, roaring war machine. I looked back at Naoto as he scrambled for the gun. The last thing I needed now was one more thing he couldn't forgive me for.

No. Not this time. I unhooked myself and climbed into the back compartment to help Naoto.

"Ready!" he shouted down through the hatch. I crouched by his side, peeking fearfully past the shield, seeing nothing but the stars.

"Keep your head down. Now you need to attach the loaded feeder to the slot on the main body of the gun and chamber the first round."

"Feeder?"

"That long segmented object. The rounds are inside."

"Rounds. You mean bullets?"

"Yes!"

Alexei swerved again and I fell hard into Naoto's knee. When I recovered, I found the feeder. I picked what I thought was the right end and handed it up through the hatch.

Alexei continued, speaking more quickly now, barely intelligible over the noise around us. "You need to lock the open end of the feeder into the slot on the bottom left side of the gun body, pull the two pins back and push them forward again until they lock under the feeder's metal lip. Push the first cartridge upward out of the feeder and slot it into the receiver, then close the two swinging doors over the exposed belt, front door first, check that the timer's locked in, and then flip the safety toggle upward to enable firing with either of the two thumb controls."

"Did you get *any* of that?" Naoto shouted at me.

I studied the mechanism. I'd heard everything the mercenary had said, and I was still at a loss. "Repeat, Alexei," I said. "How do we attach the feeder to the gun body? Did you say there are pins?"

"We don't have time for me to keep explaining this!"

I heard Naoto yelp and caught him when he darted back down through the hatch. I felt the heat of fresh waver strikes radiating from the metal roof above us, and a moment later a terrible smell filled my nostrils—I clutched at Naoto, afraid it was burning flesh and blood, but it was his hair. A waver shot had seared off one of his braids. I almost thought I could hear the drones now, rhythmically slicing at the air above and us. We were running out of time.

Naoto looked into my eyes for a moment, clutching at the singed patch of his scalp as if he wasn't sure he wasn't dead. I knew what I had to do. I knew what would happen if I was squeamish about it now.

There was only one way out of this night.

I reached over the seat-back and put my hand on the top of Alexei's head, and between the short-buzzed hairs my palm made easy contact with his skin. I closed my eyes. I willed. I opened them again.

"What did you—?" Alexei stammered.

Without another word I grabbed Naoto and yanked him hard down and away from the M134-derivative minigun. I locked the feeder into place. Pushed the first cartridge in and flipped down the front door, then the back. Toggled the safety, took aim, mashed my thumbs into the triggers. The gun sprang to life, hungrily eating up the ammo belt and spitting out whole unspent cartridges. No light, no noise, no fire. Of course. I hurriedly ripped out the securing pins the non-firing cycling sector, tossed it away and replaced it with the live one. I took aim and fired, clenching my teeth as the ancient machine gun exploded to life.

I sprayed the white-hot tracers wide across the lightless sky, based on the best guess of the vector of fire I could mentally extrapolate from the geometry of the waver burns on the APC's outer plating. I knew the assault drones—judging by the sound, there were probably three of them, most likely mark six "Marauder" unicopters with a priming rate of ten shots per minute—would be all but invisible in the night, but they would be highly vulnerable to a dense volley of small antique metal rounds like these. Even a grazing blow might splinter their fragile carbon blades.

There, out in the roaring pitch black above us, I saw one of the luminous tracers connect with solid metal and blow it apart in a hail of hot sparks. I caught the merest glint of the fire in the metal bodies of the other two drones, and I rushed to put that light in my sights, knowing I only needed one shot for each of them now. At such close range it was almost easy. Neither of them was able to get another shot off in our direction before they fell screaming down into the desert sand, frantically beating their own rotors into shrapnel against the ground.

I turned the turret around and around, searching for any sign of another drone, listening carefully, but all I could hear now was the hammering of the pistons and the white noise of the road below us. Starlight gradually returned to the void as my eyes re-adjusted to the dark. I let myself breathe.

Naoto squinted up at me through the hatch. He looked at Alexei, then back at me, and his face told me he knew what I'd done. He re-opened the shutters on his window and slumped there, looking out.

"You got them?" Alexei called back, with some audible disbelief. "We escaped?"

I took one last look out into the moonless night, half-wishing I could dissolve and blow away on that dry wind. I sat back down and shut the hatch.

Naoto sulked wordlessly and leaned his head into the window, all his body language shouting that I'd lost him for good this time. I wanted to shout back. I wanted to explain the crucial differences between personal and procedural memory, what it meant to access one and not the other, but I knew he wouldn't hear a word.

When he finally spoke up, it wasn't what I'd braced for.

"I'm sorry," he said. "You don't owe me anything. What I want . . . isn't something that can ever be owed. It can't be demanded. I've been such an ass."

I let out a long-held breath. I stared ahead into the ghost of the road in the headlights, just breathing.

"All you ever talk about is how broken you are," he said, softly. "How much wiser and stronger and more capable you'd be, if only you were whole. And I know your trauma is something I can't un-derstand, it's something beyond language, but . . . I try to imagine that other you, that *whole* you, and I can't. I don't love some abstract entity. I don't yearn to be part of it. It's only you."

I resisted the urge to dismiss his words. I took time to hear all of them. I reached out and held tight to the parts of his hand that weren't blistered.

"You're worried about Redhill," he guessed. "About what the rest of you will think when it sees you again."

"Not worried." I swallowed hard. "Terrified."

"Whatever happens when we get there," he said, "we'll face it to-gether. And I know you'll—"

He trailed off. He followed my squinting gaze to the thing that had distracted me: a glimmer of light through the window behind him, resolving into a circular glow with a dark center. A tiny solar eclipse, growing.

He dove across the seat and wrapped his arms around me, shielding my body with his. There wasn't time to scream, to panic, to shove him away, to hit him, to remind him of the promise he was breaking. There was only time enough to know.

The rocket hit us.

I

My vision is full of stars and fire. My ears are ringing. I'm locked inside this machine and it's flipped onto its back, torn open and bleeding to death. I'm in the driver's seat, hanging upside down from the seatbelt, looking out through the empty windshield at a sky made of sand stretched over an ocean of stars. At the same time, I'm crawling out into the fire-lit billowing smoke. Somehow I'm in both places at once. That's strange—but I'm too full of adrenaline and in too much of a hurry to stop to think about it, because they're coming. Whoever fired that rocket is coming.

By the time I've cut myself loose from the seat straps, I can already see them, the headlights of their truck like eyes in the dark, and I can hear them shouting to one another, running, almost on us. I'm taking cover behind the engine, priming my rifle, aiming it— but somehow at the same moment, I'm also pulling Naoto from the wreck, and there's so much blood, and I can't tell whether it's mine or his. "Danae," he calls me—but I'm not her—but I am.

Only in this moment does it finally occur to me to turn my head, and when I do I'm already there, looking back: I'm seeing myself through my own other eyes. Because I have two bodies. Because I am both Alexei and Danae.

It's too much. I can't. My vision blurs. Four legs go slack under me. I feel myself start to faint.

And then
in the darkness that takes me
in a flood of images and sounds and sensations and
simply knowing things I should not be able to know
I begin to remember
everything.

ALEXEI

There must have been a time when I was a child huddling in the dark of a bunker; when I held hands with a girl named Eryn, and she gave me the only thing I've kept all these years, and we promised each other we'd live. I know these things happened, but it's as if they're part of another memory—something from before the beginning of me.

I know exactly where and when I begin.

"If you are here," Major Malcolm Standard bellowed out over all of us, "you want to fight. That's all I need to know about you."

I stood in a rigid line with all the other children. The oldest of us could've been no older than twelve. Secretly, I was afraid I might be the youngest child in the room.

The Major continued, "Some part of each of you may be afraid that when the time comes, you won't be mentally prepared to protect your Republic, your siblings in arms, and any family you may have, from certain enslavement by the Holy Western Confederacy. Any ordinary soldier experiences doubts of this variety, but you will not be ordinary soldiers. By virtue of your age and malleability, I will be able to mold you into an elite unit, profoundly hardened against the rigors of combat. Your mind will be clear and your aim steady. You will be immune to hesitation."

We all flinched when he spoke. I don't think any of us had ever heard a voice that loud.

"Today you will each be instructed in the basic operation of a wave rifle," said the Major. "Tomorrow, each of you will take your first life."

We stood still and kept our mouths shut. Looking back, I think none of us knew what to think about those words. We talked in the mess hall as if it had never been said. On some level we may even have doubted him—but at dawn we assembled into firing squads, and the prisoners were hauled out from the empty storehouse.

I remember everything about that moment. The weight of the wave rifle, pushing the limit of what my small arms could hold. The smell of sulfur in the air. The poles the prisoners were bound to cast such long shadows in the early light. They had no blindfolds. The Major told us all to aim, and when I first raised the rifle up and trained it on the spot directly between those first two eyes, I felt like I was choking on something. I snuck glances at the other kids in the line, and they snuck glances back, and I knew I wouldn't be able to fire—

But in that moment, I remembered what had been in my mind when I'd left the orphanage for the barracks. I thought of Eryn. Missing. Lost. Dead. I felt the wire man hanging from my neck—and in that feeling, my hands steadied themselves. I touched the trigger and heard the fire order—and in the instant of that first irrevocable pop of electromagnetism, in the smell of ozone rolling down my hands, in the circle of cooked flesh in the dead center of an adult stranger's forehead: that was the first moment in which I recognize myself in any of my memories.

The Major shouted for everyone to freeze. I tensed as he walked straight for me. He put his hand on my shoulder and squeezed. I looked up at him, not understanding, and then I realized all of this had only been meant as a lesson about hesitation. No one had been expected to obey the order the first time it was given. I alone had done it.

"Have you ever killed anyone before?" he asked.

"No."

"What's your name, cadet?"

"Alexei."

"Your surname."

I had no answer.

"Report to my office, cadet."

I did as I was told, and that day my real training began.

"It's come to my attention that many of you are still, nearly two weeks into basic training, harboring certain archaic misconceptions about warfare," the Major bellowed down to the other kids. I stood at his side on the concrete ledge, overlooking their lines.

"Cadet one-niner-zero," he shouted. "Step forward onto the range and fire at the target."

Everyone stepped back from the boy I still knew only by number. He heaved his waver into firing position as elegantly as his young muscles would allow.

"Stop," said the Major, before he'd even touched the trigger. "Everyone, observe. Who can point out his mistake?"

No one said a word.

"Alexei," the Major shouted.

"He's bracing himself, and he is tense, sir," I shouted over the crowd, as loud as I could, as he'd taught me.

"Correct," the Major yelled. "Although we call it a 'rifle' in concession to the colloquial use of that word to describe what is more aptly called a long gun, your Zaytsev SL-10 waver is not a projectile weapon! It does not have any recoil! If you tighten your grip in the moment you fire, you will miss your enemy, and he will not miss you.

"Disabuse yourselves of any preconceptions about armed conflict you've gleaned from twenty-first-century cinema. There is no legitimate military on Earth which still depends mainly on projectile weaponry. Modern arms are more effective. The soldier of the past was enslaved by his supply lines and his access to an array of specific chemical and metallurgical resources. Today's soldier needs only one form of ammunition: electrical energy. He can always acquire this resource, wherever he finds himself, whatever his circumstances. There is always a way.

"That is the first advantage of electromagnetic weaponry. The second advantage is accuracy. What happens to a bullet after it leaves the barrel of a projectile weapon, Alexei?"

"It falls as it flies," I said. "And it blows on the wind, sir."

"Precisely. A bullet follows a parabolic path relative to the ground. At a distance it is also deflected by air currents, and even the Coriolis force. These do not concern you. A coherent burst of electromagnetic energy will follow a perfectly straight course over any practical distance. Furthermore, since there is no recoil, the accurate range of a waver is limited only by the discipline and acuity of the soldier who operates it.

"The third advantage is stealth. A projectile weapon produces a propellant explosion that readily reveals the position of its user. Modern weapons emit no visible light and relatively little noise.

"Your collective failure to memorize this information will be punished by reduced rations tonight. Rations will be further reduced tomorrow, unless by then every one of you is prepared to recite for me the three advantages of modern arms over antique ones, and demonstrate a proper firing stance. Dismissed."

All the other children formed a weary line to turn in their arms and head to the mess. I kept my eyes off them, but I could feel their cold stares—colder every day since my promotion.

The Major motioned for me to follow him back to his office. When the door was shut, he told me, "The others aren't yet ready to hear it, but there's a fourth advantage you should understand."

"Yes, sir."

"The fourth advantage of modern weapons is that they kill without mangling. They don't break skin or release blood. They only scorch, and cleanly. Do you understand why that is a benefit, Alexei?"

"No, sir."

"It's easier on the soldier's mind, his emotions. A proper headshot renders the enemy's face peaceful in death, hidden by a mask of ash, so there is no empathy. The truth is that the other benefits of the wave rifle, all of them combined, have not done as much as that to advance the art of war."

He knelt down, so that we were eye to eye. He said, "Crutches like that are necessary for weaker men than you and me. Like your comrades, out there. That's how you know you're stronger, and you'll always be stronger. You were made to lead them. Never forget that. Never allow *them* to forget it. Do you understand?"

"Yes, sir," I lied.

He smiled, for the first time and last time I would ever see.

"Very good, son," he said. "Very good, my boy. You are dismissed."

It was a strange warmth that washed through my small body as I left his office and headed for the mess hall. I wondered if this was what it felt like to have a father; to have always had a father.

The others didn't even wait to finish their meager rations before pulling me out of line. Six of them dragged me to the dusty space behind the stairs.

"My name is Wilson," said one, "but he only calls me Cadet 282. You're the only one that gets a human name. What's your number, shithead?"

"One."

They pinned me on the ground and kicked me in the face, shouting their given names, until my young blood puddled on the floor.

I awoke on a bed in the medic's office. There were no medics. Major Standard stood over me.

"I'm not going to ask who did this to you," he said, with perfect dispassion. "I have made you their superior. As their superior, it's your duty to instill and maintain discipline, and to enforce the laws by administering the appropriate penalties. The penalty for mutiny is death."

I felt a hard weight on my chest. It was a small wave pistol.

He said nothing more about it.

Every night for the week that followed, Wilson and the other numbered cadets took me behind the same stairs and left me there with new wounds. Each attack was more vicious than the last. The Major never spoke about these; he treated my injuries as invisible or irrelevant. If I leaned, he ordered me to straighten up. If I limped, he ordered me to hurry. Through six of these beatings, I always kept the pistol hidden in my jacket, tucked against my stomach with the safety on.

The seventh beating was the last.

"This is an aim-assist implant," the Major told us. He pointed out various features projected on the pane behind him: the hair-thin wires trailing down the neck from the occipital lobe of the brain, down into the arm. He faced us, hands clasped behind his back, and demanded, "Who can tell me its function?"

Cadet 180 stood up and shouted, "Sir. The implant reads the point of intended aim directly from the visual cortex and delivers the appropriate electrical signals to the relevant muscle groups to force them to conform. Sir."

Nearly verbatim. Cadet 180 was improving.

The image twitched slightly. The Major turned to the man who lay bound and gagged under the scanner. A deserter. He was trying to wriggle free again. Standard rolled up his sleeve and delivered a short, sharp blow to the forehead with the heel of his hand. The wriggling stopped.

"Nearly every martial force on Earth employs this technology, including the forces of your Republic," the Major said. "Who can tell me why none of you will ever receive such an implant?"

This wasn't a question whose answer we'd been forced to memorize. He was looking for true understanding. Synthetic knowledge, he called it. No one spoke.

"Alexei?"

I stood up. After a second's hesitation, I guessed. "Because it's a crutch, sir?"

"Correct. An aim-assist can only improve an inferior arm, governed by inferior resolve. This—" he grabbed the deserter's arm and shook it in its restraints for effect "—is an arm that believes it exists for multiple, contradictory purposes. It thinks it can go to war and hold a waver, and then return home and be used to bake bread, build a shelter, embrace a love. What is your arm's sole purpose, Cadets?"

"Kill!" we all shouted in unison, holding our dominant hands high. I took pride in the volume. I saw how it made the deserter afraid.

"You have no homes to return to," the Major told us. "You have no other life waiting for you. War is your life. Your mind and body have but one purpose in this world, from now until death, and we will shape them into the perfect tools to suit that singular purpose."

He shut off the scanner and the pane and pushed it back a safe distance from the deserter. He opened a metal case and lifted out a small machine: something with long cylinders wrapped with coils of wire. He set it a few feet away from the deserter and we all sat up in our seats, trying to get a better view.

"Secondarily," the Major continued, "wherever there is a crutch, there is an added vulnerability. Recall that all unshielded electronic devices are susceptible to electromagnetic pulse."

He flipped a switch. The bound man began to scream through his gag. He writhed in agony. His right arm twitched and snapped in rhythmic pulses and the red lines of internal burns etched themselves like tattoos into the skin.

One day in the open field—in the early days, when Major Standard's youth battalion was still limited to rear-guard actions, and only a small number of us had died—I walked with him. It was still new and mysterious to me how the ground crunched wherever the scorching had glassed the dirt into thin, oval-shaped plates. He was still teaching me to recognize the signs: how a recent firefight had unfolded, or how a future one might.

The corpse seemed to appear out of nowhere. I thought at first that the Major would want me to pass by without hesitation, but he told me to stop. He raised up his visor and I did the same.

"Tell me what you see here," he said.

The dead man lay on his back on the dirt mound, his face a black hole. He had been on our side. His helmet and goggles lay neatly at his feet, and his rifle was braced between his knees. The shape of the burn told me it had come from below.

Before I could answer, the Major said, "Desertion of the most unforgivable kind. That's what suicide is."

"Yes, sir."

"You and I have pledged our lives to our great cause. That means our lives are not ours for the taking, nor our enemy's. They belong solely to our Republic, and they must be used to its maximum advantage. This man willfully disregarded every part of that pledge. He stole his death from us and wasted it. So let's pause here. Let us get a proper look, so that we'll never forget this betrayal."

We stood there for a long time in the passing wisps of smoke, silent amid the sounds of distant shouts and buzzing flies. I studied the burning contempt in Major Standard's eyes; I tried to feel it too, but I couldn't—not then. No matter how long I looked, all I saw was one more casualty.

It wasn't until fourteen years later, pressing a gun to my own head in the restroom mirror on an air transport leaving Antarka, that I felt all the hate he had tried to teach me.

I remember, too, what the Major told us all on the last day of the war. We were nearly adults by then. By his order we had withdrawn from our guerrilla positions and rallied in a half-collapsed subway tunnel on the outskirts of the last city still claimed by the Free Republic of South Cascadia. The front lines surrounded us in a steadily contracting ring.

"In the years we have served together," he said, his giant voice amplified by the curved walls, "I have never doubted the vision with which I took you on and taught you, but never before now has my pride been greater. Although our strategic position may appear dire, our finest hour is at hand. When we retake the Capitol, the world and its history will know what I have known since the beginning: that I have at my command, in you, the greatest fighting force the world has ever seen. Charlie mike in five minutes."

We all raised our wavers and shouted, and the volume of that last proud battle cry made me forget for a moment that fewer than fifty of us remained.

I had expected these orders, and I was already prepared. I'd cycled all my waver's cells and cleaned its coils several times to be sure. I'd filled up on the last of the food and water I'd been saving, and thrown away all the extra weight. I'd meditated. My mind was as sharp and clean as it would ever be.

But when he came to me after the address, he said "Specialist 419 has been briefed on the plans. He'll be leading this operation with me."

"Sir?"

"Yes, Alexei."

"I don't understand, sir," I stammered. I felt a pressure in my head.

The outline of an emotion twitched somewhere under his mask of stoicism and blood-caked concrete dust, and his voice was uncharacteristically quiet when he finally said, "This isn't your mission."

"What is my mission, sir?"

"Burn your uniform and blend in with the first civilians you come across. That's your best hope of avoiding their slavers. That's what I want you to do now. Survive."

"Why?" I said. I had never dropped the 'sir' before. I noticed this and didn't correct it. I could tell he'd noticed it too, but there was no surprise or disapproval in his face. He just gave a shadow of a nod. He placed his hand on my shoulder, the way he had on that first day, and I met his eyes with as much confusion as I had then.

"Give me your weapon," he said.

With great hesitation, I did. He slung it over his shoulder. He handed me his own, powered down. That was it.

From the top of a building, I watched them all march out and dissolve into the maze of scorched walls and billowing toxic gasses. No history remembers them.

It was only in the Major's final look back that I understood his unspoken intention in giving me his waver: he expected me to lock it away somewhere safe, never to be fired again. I was the last person left to carry his memory, and the initials he'd carved into that cedar pistol grip were the only physical artifact of his existence. I burned my uniform just as he'd asked, but when the weapon was all that remained, it stuck in my hands.

I found I never blended in.

The memory of the following years devolves into a howling din, an indistinct morass of time and violence. The lives I cut down and the bare subsistence it brought me. The aimless travel in the dark corners of cargo containers. The arbitrarily strategic landscapes and the double-chinned warlords bent on obtaining them at any human cost, and the maps of the former United States that I watched go on splintering into ever smaller pieces—until I understood that the Republic I'd fought for, the whole sixty years of its existence, had only been a tiny eddy in the roaring flow of history. It was that river, the continued collapse of land-based nations and the rise of the new aquatic superpowers, that brought me inevitably into the service of Medusa Clan.

I

In some corner of myself, I'm still aware of the present. My surroundings. I can't move. I can't open my eyes. I can only smell the burning
wreckage, taste the blood iron, feel the bright pain racking my flesh
and bone. I can hear them, our attackers. They're walking around
us, scraping their feet through the sand.

"Get his gun," a woman shouts. "Get the fucking gun! Check
them."

"Nice gun," a man mutters.

There are fingers on my neck—both my necks. "Alive," another
man says. "All alive. Real fucked up though. Out cold. Must be concussed. Losing blood. Get me the, uh—"

There are hands in my armpits, lifting me.

The woman shouts, "Stop! Put her down! Don't move them before
Doc checks her spine!"

"I'm just trying to get them away from all this burning wreckage,
Jenna—"

"I said put her down!"

The hands roughly drop me. One of my heads hits the sandy earth.

Jenna lets out a guttural growl. I hear the dull crack of the butt of
a rifle against a skull. A whimper of pain. More scraping in the sand.

"Wanted alive!" Jenna shouts. "Which of those two words don't
you assholes understand? Do you remember what these people are
worth? Do you have any idea what the Medusas will do to us if they
find out we killed their bounty? I told you to target the road in front
of the wheels and you made it a direct fucking hit!"

"Give me a fucking break, Jenna. Who the hell knows how far
they were planning to go? How many more days do you expect us
to track them? We were already down three drones. I saw a decent
shot. I took it."

"Spines are okay," somebody says. "Brains, though? Hell. I don't
know."

"When will you know?"

"When they wake up. Or don't. But they're dead for sure if we don't squirt some blood into them."

"Then do it. Get the cuffs. Cuffs! Now! Put them on the truck. Let's get out of here before somebody sees the fire."

I'm being lifted again. They're carrying me. All of me. Then a metal floor is rattling under my bones, and we're moving. Hands are peeling off my clothes. Scissors cut my sleeves open and needles pierce my veins. There's a surge of pain and something cold percolating through my flesh, and then my consciousness ebbs again, and I sink back into the flood of my memory.

DANAE

I will never have any one beginning. I've been born 223 times, and each of those first breaths was my first breath. Each of those lives, in their own time and place, became my life. I am the confluence of everything those 223 people ever were, said and did, thought and felt, knew and wondered—both apart from each other, and as me.

Once I was born in Jersey City in the year 1998, a citizen of what was not yet widely referred to as the American Empire. I was an actress, a mother, a grandmother, and I witnessed the worst decades of the collapse myself. I heard the gunfire, the rockets and jet engines with my own ears—and when the Bomb took my hearing, I went on seeing the burning cities, the ever-changing world maps in which whole countries disappeared into unmarked gray zones and were not replaced—and when age took my sight, I went on feeling the collapse, in the rattle of my bones at distant concussions, in the words my children and grandchildren signed into my arthritic fingers.

One day when I was nearly a hundred years old, just when I thought I had finally reached the end of my life, I met someone who told me—patiently repeating everything I didn't understand or could not at first believe—that she was not what she appeared to be: not a single face with a single life story, but a unified consciousness created by the fusion of hundreds of people. The body in which I lived as her, through all the years of the collapse, to the ripe age of 103, died long ago—but I am her, and I am alive.

Once I was born in the same nuclear fire my other self had witnessed, delivered into a suit jacket in the lee of an overturned car, just as the first of the radioactive ash began to fall like snow—and I swear I still remember the first sound I heard when my infant ears left the womb: my mother's last screams, as much in pain as in rage and terror at the world she knew she was giving me to.

No one expected me to live—but despite them all, despite the fallout, despite the inventive geometries my bones assumed with time and the arbitrary cruelty that sometimes attracted, I grew into a man. I traveled far. I helped rebuild, and I studied the reconstruction and the assumptions with which it was undertaken—the litany of curious disconnects between each person's versions of the past they wanted to resurrect, one I'd never seen myself—and I wrote down all my observations of memory, and strangers read them. I became a philosopher. I was a husband, a father, a grandfather. Then one day, when I was an old man who thought he had it all figured out, one of my students approached me with what sounded like some kind of metaphor or thought experiment. It took me time to believe him when he told me who and what he was. When I did believe, and when I'd finally wrapped my head around it all, I knew I had to try it for myself.

Once I was a physicist in Senegal whose life work was using gravity waves to study primordial black hole collisions in the far reaches of the observable universe. Once I spent my summers studying the geology of Antarctica and never dreamed of a day when the frozen wastelands I trudged across would be warm enough to host cities and the emerald green expanses of algae fields. Once I was a musical prodigy in Shanghai, long before it was part of Norpak. Once I was a holographic artist in Argentina, before it was Communidad. The bodies in which all these lives began are long gone, but I am all of them. I am young and old, poor and rich, black and brown and white, and I am men and women and a dozen other genders. I'm a native speaker of fifty tongues. I'm from everywhere.

On a hot day fifty-seven years ago, I struggled (as I always do) to find the words to explain all this to a colleague, a gifted molecular biologist named Zinn. I loved him. I also needed him: I needed to become him and let him become me, because the world was dying and he was my best hope of saving it.

"That makes you, what? A hive mind?" He was staring at me, trying to understand. We were lying naked on his bed. I was speaking to him through one of my male bodies. He liked that body, and I liked being liked from within it.

"'Hive mind' makes it sound like my bodies are all just my mindless thralls," I chuckled. I tapped my chest. "I am this person. For twenty-four years I was *only* him, and now he's part of the gestalt I am now."

"Okay. So you're . . . a collective consciousness."

I sighed and said, "Better, but the word 'collective' still connotes distinct parts working together but remaining distinct. I'm not a group, I'm one person. Not a 'we' but an 'I.' And I'm the same person now, out of unity, that I would be if I were in unity—just a lot smaller. And, well, not as smart."

"What term would you use, then?"

"Words, words," I said. "Language is a painfully inefficient way to copy a thought from one brain to another."

That was the first year of Blood Rain—the year the infamous weaponized lyssavirus strain, to which over a billion deaths are now attributed, began its accelerating spread across Europe. I had met Zinn in a lab in France while we were both working on a vaccine, but we both knew the problem was too vast. It was spreading and mutating too quickly. Someone had engineered it to resist all the approaches we were trying to take to it. All our simulations showed that we were rapidly approaching a point of no return, past which its spread across the whole Earth would become logistically irreversible.

"And if . . . if we unify, like you're suggesting," Zinn said.

"Then together we'll become a new iteration of my consciousness," I said solemnly. "We'll become someone who knows everything you know, and everything I know. Someone who can make connections we can't, conceive of solutions we're not able to—not as separate people."

"But it will be like dying," he said—I remember saying, as him, before he was me. "Won't it?"

"And like being born. Both and neither."

Even as we spoke, I was in a dozen other places, in other bodies, having similar conversations with other people I needed to be. Virologists. Epidemiologists. Genetic engineers. Disaster relief workers. Many of them decided against joining my gestalt, but some did—and when we unified, and the whole of me knew everything they had ever known, I brought my entire intellect to bear on the problem.

It took two years (in chronological time, but that was almost a century of internal experience) to reverse-engineer the virus and perfect an immunity, and a third year to engineer my own strain (even more contagious, but benign) to act as a self-replicating vaccine in the absence of any working infrastructure to distribute injections.

Those were some of the hardest years of my life. None of my bodies slept a full night. Over the course of the project, I was forced to sacrifice six of them to gather all the data I needed. I know what it's like to die of Blood Rain. I've felt it. The bottomless malaise, the paranoia, the bone-cracking muscle spasms, the hemorrhaging: I remember it all, up until the moment of brain death. There were days when the complexity of the virus and its seemingly limitless ability to mutate filled me with so much despair. Even when I felt confident I was on the right track, I knew every second I delayed might mean thousands more died before I could help.

I felt no sense of accomplishment in my eventual success. The only way I know how to think about the project is to regret every mistake, every distraction and dead end. I would give anything to go back and do it faster.

I have no one beginning, but unity itself began with a woman named Sybil—who, seventy years ago, helped create the first unifier prototype. The body she was born into is long dead now, yet I am her as much as I am anyone else, and I am alive.

It was less an invention than an adaptation. Mind-to-mind interfaces had existed on a superficial level since the closing days of the American era, developed by the Imperial military in a radical attempt to enhance the coordination of elite commando units. After the collapse, the designs were uncovered by looters, and spent the next decade circulating among amateurs as a sort of fringe scientific novelty. You and your friends might put on helmets and switch the box on, and if you could ignore the uncomfortable tingling sensation and focus very hard, you might hear the faintest whispers of their inner monologues crossing the wires, like tin cans and string drawn between your souls.

When I was Sybil, I was one of three cybernetics students who first studied the direct neural interface as a curiosity, but soon realized that what we were looking at was only a crude proof of concept for something far more significant. We built on the old American design. Simple modifications enhanced the quality of the link by orders of magnitude, and before long we could transmit complete thoughts, ideas, emotions, sensations, even whole memories. From there we knew we were one step short of the real breakthrough— one that might change what it meant to be human.

Apart from the body, a person is largely a complex of memories. Everything she's ever known and experienced, his every mode of thinking and feeling—everything they *are* in the most essential sense that can be empirically qualified—is information in the form of neural engrams. What the three of us learned in the course of our experiments was that if it's possible to copy a single engram between two people, it may be possible to copy all of them—and in that union they cease to be two people at all, but one person inhabiting two bodies: a gestalt consciousness.

I could tell you more about my two colleagues, or about the small desert town where we created the first working unifier prototype, and the things that went wrong. I could, but I won't. Even among twelve thousand years of aggregate memory, my memories of that day remain too traumatic for me to readily revisit. It will suffice to say that I fled that town and left all our work pulverized down to the last chip. I burned all our research notes and scattered the ashes. The only alternative I could see at that time was to burn and scatter myself.

I moved around aimlessly for three years. I knew no one well, and I helped where I could. I saw beautiful things and terrible things. In the end they served to convince me, even in the face of all my fears and regrets, that the work we'd done was more necessary than I had imagined when I destroyed it. If there was any way to atone for the unifier's misuse, it to use it correctly.

I brought the first of us together. I explained unity and what it meant, and we spent months talking through all the technical and medical and philosophical and personal implications—until finally, on a cool morning sixty-eight chronological years ago, at the top of a mound of rock in the former state of Arizona, I was brought into existence as the consciousness I am now.

I was made from nine people, who before that moment had each lived only a single life in a single body; who had each thought only one way about the world; who could each only vaguely guess what it was like to be each other; who had been divided to one extent or another by language, culture, class, politics, gender, physiology, ability. Those nine people disagreed vehemently on any number of issues except this one: that by ceasing to be themselves, and by joining together to become *me*, they might give birth to something greater than the sum of themselves as separate people.

That first careful unity was a revelation. I wasn't prepared for the sudden vastness of my own intellect. In hindsight I understood how limited my constituent selves had been, how their personalities had constrained their imaginations; in unity I could reconcile all their perspectives, know all their truths, treat all their mental wounds, transcend every petty bias and false precept that had ever held them back from true connection and epiphanic understanding. I could find connections between different facts and subjects and sciences and philosophies that those nine people had specialized in to the exclusion of all others, and a dazzling multitude of seemingly unrelated ideas revealed themselves as facets of a single whole.

For weeks I dreamed endlessly about quarks and galaxies, the cells and the body, a single chord's relationship to the whole of all music, the common threads that wove together all the hopes and fears and loves and hates of all the people I had been. At the end of those weeks, my next step was clear: I had to send each of my bodies back out into the world alone—to have different experiences, grow apart, learn different things, develop new differences of perspective and opinion. Some of those instances of me would find new people to invite into my unity, and then all of my selves would return to that same red-rock hill a year later, on the vernal equinox, to pour all their experiences back into the whole of me.

This is the ultimate truth I learned in unity: gestalt consciousness doesn't just thrive on difference; it requires it. All its ecstatic realizations come from reconciliation across seemingly insurmountable divides. Like deuterium and tritium joining in fusion, the separation between two minds is brimming with potential energy—more, the farther apart they are—and in the release and channeling of that energy, everything becomes possible.

One day I paused in the middle of my work. Through fifteen pairs of eyes, I looked down at my twenty-nine hands and flexed two hundred and eighty-nine digits, and with all my heads at once I stopped to reflect on what I was building: the prototype of a new and far more advanced unifier, one I wouldn't need to lug around with me in a briefcase. This one would be a complex of nanobots, forming a self-constructing artificial organ, symbiotic with the body and equipped with enormous stores of holographic memory. It was a necessity, if I hoped to grow any further: I was well past pushing the limits of how many lifetimes of experience an unmodified human brain could ever hope to integrate.

It struck me then that I couldn't have imagined such a technology in any of my constituent lives. Even as a whole in unity, this device's operating principles would have been far beyond my grasp even a year earlier—but that was in chronological time. The gestalt of my fifty-odd selves had experienced it as half a century. And while isolated minds went on taking all their hard-cultivated genius with them in death, I kept everything that had ever been part of me; the loss of one of my bodies never cost me that self's knowledge, its skills, or its insight.

My mind was growing, and the growth was not linear, but exponential. Every unity brought me one step closer to what AI researchers had once called an *intelligence explosion*, but this would be different: the singularity wouldn't be computerized or artificial. It would be human. It would be me.

As I grew, I became more systematic about how I distributed my consciousness. I continued to send out some of my bodies alone, to live and gather experience as separate people, only unifying again each spring; others traveled in groups and unified continually in order to work on complex tasks and conduct research that wouldn't have been possible otherwise. I spent each year between equinoxes in a dozen places at once, forking my consciousness like a tree: a branch with thirty bodies built and staffed a particle accelerator, while another branch of twelve engineered and sold aquatic food crops to finance the work of the others.

The last branch I can remember being was devoted to the most dangerous research: anthropology. I traveled everywhere, absorbing myself into every city and settlement, burgeoning aquapolises and withering land-towns, observing the evolution of languages and cultures and ways of life that I feared would all be obliterated by the next war or genocide or phase of the broader environmental collapse. I could revel all I liked in my own growth and evolution, but the world around me was still dying. The global population curve continued to bend back on itself as ever larger swaths of the Earth's surface were reduced to sterile, storm-battered wastelands. The last democracies gave way to unofficial—and then official—rule by crime syndicates like Medusa Clan, or dark age theocracies like the Confederacy.

The world had so many wounds, and I believed I was in a singular position to heal them. My sense of responsibility deepened with each new person who became me. I had people to take care of, after all: through all my constituent selves, my friends and family soon numbered in the tens of thousands.

Sometimes I felt as if I barely had time to work on one catastrophe before a new one emerged.

Only a few decades after Blood Rain threatened to exterminate humankind, all life on Earth nearly went up in flames when the five-kilometer-wide asteroid 3753 Cruithne skipped brilliantly through the fringes of the Earth's exosphere before hurling itself headlong into the Sun. There are many people alive today who watched its approach through telescopes or observed its near miss with the naked eye. History remembers that day primarily as an embarrassment to the many astronomers who had all but unanimously declared, only months earlier, that Cruithne's trajectory made a direct impact certain and inevitable.

There are many things history doesn't remember about Cruithne. Most credible records don't speculate as to how a 140-billion-ton asteroid, having orbited the sun for æons at a reliably safe distance, ever found itself aimed squarely at the Earth. There are gaps in the world's memory around the time the Empire fell; some of the files that were lost to fire or thrown out by looters might have described a startlingly ambitious scorched-earth program involving the installation of an unmanned, extremely large, magnetoplasmadynamic thruster on Cruithne, capable of incrementally modifying its orbit over the passing of decades. History similarly does not remember the concerted effort it took me—again, all my bodies working together in shifts for nine months of chronological time, which by then was nearly a century from my perspective—to design and construct a ground-based gravity laser capable of imparting 900 trillion newtons of invisible force in bursts across two astronomical units.

I'll be content if no one ever learns of my involvement. Dismantling every last piece of that laser was almost as toilsome as building it, but I could no more leave it standing than I could trust a toddler with a primed wave pistol.

I took no more pride in deflecting Cruithne than I had in curing Blood Rain. On the day I watched it pass us by, all I could think about was how close I'd let it come. I wondered what monster of the past would unearth itself next.

By comparison, the threat of Gray Day never bothered me. Gray has a built-in kill switch, after all: most of my work is already done for me. The most brilliant weapons designers in Epak and Norpak believe they've protected their creations' self-termination commands with so much encryption that all the computers on Earth combined would take centuries to crack them—but I've developed whole new branches of mathematics and computing, beyond their wildest dreams, and I know I could end their petty brinksmanship game in a matter of hours.

If I were whole. I could do it if I were whole.

I can only have faith that the rest of me is working on the problem. They probably cracked and transmitted the working kill command hours ago now. Somewhere, the rest of me has just saved humankind from itself for the third time, and is now nursing its regret that it couldn't have done it even faster—that the Gray had to be released before it could feasibly be hacked—that anyone had to die at all—and I feel my own numb regret that I couldn't be there to be part of it.

But I have faith that the world has been spared again.

I have to believe that.

Because the alternative is to believe that the rest of me is dead, murdered by the Keepers.

I

"What do you think?" someone asks, quietly.

"I think I'd give my left nut for a sharper knife," Doc answers. "No, don't touch that. Any shrapnel you see that ain't either gushing or abdominal, you leave it in. Hell. We'll be lucky if we save two out of three."

I can't move my eyes to see him. I can't tell which of my ears I'm hearing him through. I'm only dimly aware that both my bodies are severely injured. I can feel intravenous drips, the pinch of a tourniquet on one of my arms. I can feel someone working on an artery with a cauterizer, but all my perceptions blend together, and I realize there's no way for me to know which of my bodies he's talking about—which one is dying. Maybe we all are. Maybe this is it. My life is running out I'm going to be trapped here in this bardo until the last of me is gone.

Unless I can wake up. Somehow I have to wake up.

BORROWER

This is it. Oh, this is it. I'm thinking about her. Always thinking. Whenever I feel disgusted to have embodied my consciousness in Scuttle's dirty flesh, or horrified to have watched my own beta copy die, or disturbed by the company of my alpha, I draw all the strength I need from thoughts of Sybil. I'll do whatever it takes to reach her.

The cargo truck grinds to a halt. Outside, the last lights of Greenglass Mountain stain the sand. I nod to my alpha copy, and he smooths down his tie, climbs out and approaches the cab.

"There's something you need to see," I hear him tell the driver. "Please hurry."

The elderly driver comes around and parts the flap. He has only a moment to gawk at my beta copy's gruesome remains before I put him in a headlock and drag him inside. It isn't even necessary to render him unconscious to tie him up—and as I fasten the patterner crown on his head and mine, I dread to think of what it will be like to wear flesh as old as his. But I keep calm. I remember my purpose. I think of Sybil—and in my head I hear the litany of all the things I have yearned for so long to tell her. I think:

How I wish you could feel what I feel, Sybil. Visualize as I once did, as I know you can too, the architecture of dendrite and synapse, crystalline yet fluid, when it all dances to the music of this terrible device in my hands. The patterner understands that memory is not linear. The experience of which the self is comprised keeps an order all its own, less like a book than a spiral galaxy: cold fringes of sub-sidiary relevance orbiting the denser core of those autobiographical ideas and experiences which define the self wholly and inextrica-bly. This center-most engram is the one the patterner will transcribe first—and every time I've poured my consciousness out of one brain and into another, that memory has always been the same one.

One cold blue evening, seventy-two years ago, I watched you through my original eyes and the cracked window of the college's microfab-rication room—staring through my own distorted reflection in the dark glass. Just then I accidentally met the ghosts of my own eyes, and a miserable shiver ran through me.

I had always been ugly. It's the very first thing I can remember knowing about myself. I could take pains to describe the specific fea-tures that made my original flesh so horrid, but it would be pointless. Whenever I told anyone, they denied it, but I knew they were lying. I knew *you* were. So when I contracted a lung infection, shortly after we began the project to create our unifier prototype, and when that body began to die, in the pit of my being it didn't feel like a shock. I didn't blame chronic exposure to the exotic chemicals we'd been working with. It felt like my flesh was simply being true to its most basic nature.

You were always complimenting my intelligence in those days, but you must have known that, too, was only an adaptation to my ugliness. It was why I was so proficient in the abstract mathematics our project called for; it was why I had gone to cybernetics school in the first place. I was never in it to make a better aim-assist. I'd come with a head full of idealism, in love with the idea of sloughing off all flesh and existing only as disembodied thought in nodespace.

But as I watched you hug him in the fading light, I had a painful moment of clarity: my goals had changed. Disembodiment wasn't what I wanted anymore.

When you finally entered, I turned away. I told myself you couldn't possibly be there to see me—but you shocked me with a shout across the room:

"Luther, you are amazing!"

I was so startled that my magnifier glasses fell off my nose and nearly shattered on the work bench. My sick heart fluttered.

"I . . . I am?"

"I just got the equations you sent me this morning. They all work beautifully! Memory is not linear. Of course! But I never thought to use an algorithm like that to describe it. How did you ever think to borrow equations from the chaos theory of galactic orbital mechanics?"

You smiled so earnestly, and I felt the rush of blood burn my cheeks.

"I . . . I was only building on your work," I said. "You would have realized the solution without my help."

"For Pete's sake, don't you remember who you're talking to? I have literally been inside your head, if only for a few seconds. I've experienced your thought process firsthand, and I am telling you it fills me with awe. I'm not making this up."

I opened my mouth to protest again.

You cut me off. "Fine. We're *both* geniuses, if you absolutely insist. But do you realize that we're going to change everything? You and me and Jackson, we're on the verge. We'll be the first true post-humans."

For a moment I drifted in the bliss of believing that you and I had some real and unfrayed connection—but I unthinkingly sighed, and the sound wiped the smile from your lips. You looked at my chest as if you could see through it.

"It's still not better? Oh no. That means the infection is phage-resistant now."

"I know." I let myself cough into my forearm.

You pulled up a screeching metal stool and sat next to me at the work bench, hands stuffed into the pockets of your vest. You tried to comfort me by saying, "We're so close now. Thanks to you, we have the software. We can send and receive an entire brain's worth of memories, synchronously. All we need now a higher-bandwidth interface between the cerebral probes and the CPU. That's it. Jackson has been following leads with every salvager from here to Norpak, trying to dig up every pre-collapse interface he can get his hands on. We just have to find one that meets our specs."

My gravelly breaths blew white clouds in the dark blue air.

"Hurry," I said.

Then, so unexpectedly, you hugged me. Your head nestled against the side of mine, warm and unflinching. We had never touched that way before. Somehow I knew, even in that moment, that we never would again.

This is not my first memory, but it seems to be my innermost. It's the first one that will pass through the link: the first one that this other brain, in forgetting everything it now knows, will remember all anew.

For the first time in my ninety years of life, I am wearing the flesh of a man above the age of thirty. The comparative dimness of his senses makes me shudder. His muscles are not as responsive as I'm used to.

There are footsteps in the sand outside the truck. Somebody knocks on the metal sides of the bed.

"Hey, you want I should fill up your fuel cells?" a woman's voice yells.

"Just a second," I say, holding the flap shut. We sit together in the darkness: my alpha copy in the rich man's body, my gamma in Scuttle's body, and I, the delta, now in the old driver.

"More," we whisper in broken unison.

One by one we climb out into the night.

"Oh, it's you," the woman, a fuel station attendant, tells me. "You got here just in time. The whole place is just about packed up. Only a few of us left, not counting all the Medusas who just rolled in."

"Yes," I say.

She takes a shard and a stylus out of her hip pocket and waits. "So?"

"So."

She laughs. "So, your account number?"

A few steps behind her, my alpha and gamma copies stand ready, but all of us are wincing. I've never made a woman the vessel of my consciousness before, and I truly don't wish to do so now—but if she keeps asking questions I can't answer, I'll have no alternative.

Finally she throws up her hands. "I'll look it up for you, okay? Jeez, Mars. Ever think you're getting too old for this job?"

I try not to show my relief. "Long drive," I say. When her head is turned, I nod to my other copies, and they walk off between the sparse tents with my briefcase. Hunting for better flesh.

I keep the wave pistol ready behind my back. I keep careful watch over the attendant while she plugs in the power cable and starts charging the truck's cells. I pray for no more complications. If I have to kill or assume her, my problems will multiply as the distance between you and me, Sybil—already intolerable—continues to increase. I can bear anything but that.

My very existence matters less to me now than my need to find you. It's partly that my condition is worsening. It's been worsening for a long time, and only you can help me. You're the only person who has ever been able to help me. But in the end, I know my need to find you now is deeper than my need to be helped or to be cured of my afflictions, or even saved from death.

I have to find my way back to you, Sybil, at any cost. I simply have to.

"Why me?" I asked you one night, seventy-two years ago. The sharpness of my voice made you jump and almost burn your hand on the laser cutter. I watched you hesitate, betraying that you already knew what I meant when you nonetheless asked me to clarify my question, to which I responded, "Why would you ever *want* to unify with me?"

Every part of me trembled. To ask directly seemed like such a transgression. Surely it would devastate whatever possessed you to keep associating with me, night after long night in this cluttered workspace—but I couldn't contain it anymore. With every daily scan, I watched the infection spread throughout the rotten chambers of my body. My time was short.

"You don't need me," I said. "You and Jackson are intelligent enough to do it all without me. If anything, you'd probably work faster without my interference."

"That's not remotely true." You seemed genuinely taken aback. "We could never—! I don't understand the neurochemistry or the math *half* as well as you do. Your equations are so elegant—"

"You're evading my question. Why would you *want* to unify with me? How could you want to know what it feels like to be so . . ." I tasted the metal of my adrenaline. "Defective."

You stared. "Is that really how you see yourself?"

"I don't want your pity. I just . . . I need an answer."

You had the nerve to tell me, "Listen, I know that you . . . you have some very hard feelings about yourself. I understand that you struggle with how you think other people see you, and I've—" You paused. "I've *felt* that pain myself. I've been in direct contact with those thoughts, however briefly, during our tests. I wish I knew how to tell you that you're not defective. I wish I could put it into words that you could hear—and when we unify, you'll be able to perceive yourself the way I have all along, and words won't be necessary anymore. But until then, all I can say is. . . ."

You nodded your head down in thought for a time. I waited nervously. Finally you looked me in the eye and said:

"I want to unify with you because you have the most brilliant, most beautiful mind I have ever encountered."

I swallowed. You had me in your thrall again, so effortlessly.

Nothing in me could resist when you spoke in that voice or curled your fingers around mine. I forgot myself; I even believed you when you said:

"There is no intellect in the world that I admire more than yours. I don't know if you felt it when you were in my mind, but I'm always trying not to show how much you intimidate me. Jackson feels the same way, probably even more so. You grasp things intuitively that it takes either of us weeks to learn. You throw out these world-shaking epiphanies like they're trivial, like you just thought them up." You laughed to yourself and shook your head. "There's no way we could do this without you. We wouldn't even have thought to try. Don't you see? Even if I didn't frankly covet your insight, a mind as beautiful as yours shouldn't . . ." I thought you choked back a sob. "It shouldn't have to die. I couldn't stand to let that happen."

I couldn't speak. I could only sit there feeling wretched in my regret for how harshly I'd spoken a moment before.

You took both my hands and held them tightly and said, "If you don't want to unify with me, you know that I would respect that. It's your decision. It's a sacred decision. But either way, you have to know that I don't want to lose you. Not ever."

All my envy seemed to dissolve in the hot glare of the work lamps. For an instant, I didn't feel ugly at all. I didn't even feel sick. You healed all my wounds, Sybil. Even if my lips would never meet yours, if my hands would never trace the slope of your neck or the curve of your hips, if I would never know your body the way Jackson did, I felt that you had given me a promise of love that swept all of that aside. We would be as one. We would be reborn together into a whole new form of consciousness.

For hardly the first time, I tried to tell you I was in love with you. As always, I couldn't seem to find my breath.

I

The truck motors under me have stopped turning, and three people are there, standing over my two bodies. They don't move or speak at first, but I can sense them. I can hear them breathing.

"Brain dead," Jenna's voice finally says.

"No," Doc says.

"Concussed? Comatose? What?"

"I don't know. Whatever this is, I've never seen anything like it. I've never heard of it. It's creepy. It's positively fringe."

"What, damnit?"

"Okay. Just look at this."

Fingers are on my face. Pulling one of my eyelids up. Then another. For a moment I can see them, their faces squinting down at me, and then a harsh light burns them away.

"His iris dilated. So what?"

"No. Look!"

The light flashes again and again.

"I shine a light in *his* eyes, *her* eyes dilate too. Shine it in hers, it's the same thing in reverse. If I whack *her* right knee, *his* right leg spasms."

I'm starting to understand what this is. I know what's happened to me—what happened to *us* to bring *me* into existence. Somehow I have to make it stop. I have to find a way to wake up—but before the flow of memory carries me away again, I only have time for one more terrible thought:

I know I'm Danae and Alexei.

Where is Naoto?

ALEXEI

By the time I met her, the Empress of Epak had already cemented her dominion over half of all the submarine city-states in the entire Pacific Rim, and I became the newest and sharpest of the many lethal instruments by which she fought for control of the other half. She put me to work disposing of her competitors in Norpak, Antarka, Communidad, or any other corner of the Western Hemisphere where her own Medusan henchmen weren't precise or subtle enough to operate, and I seldom failed to impress her. I knew better than to be seen, better than to leave witnesses. I was able to slip past scanners where anyone with tactical cybernetics would have been shot on sight. I killed men and women, young and old, soldiers and civilians, warlords and bystanders, commanders and cannon fodder. With each life I took, I climbed the ladder of Dahlia's trust.

It was her wicked pride in my work that sustained me, far more than all the squid she paid. She gave me what the Major had taught me to need, what I hadn't been able to find anywhere else since the fall of the Republic. I relished every hand-written paper scrap the Medusas passed to me from Dahlia's throne room—and when I'd made corpses of the names on those notes, I relished every brothel token they appended to my pay—and in the triumph of an orgasm or an inhale from a pipe, in the moment of ecstatic ego-death, I lived for the certainty that I was a tool serving its purpose well.

I remember the first orders Dahlia allowed me to receive from her directly—the first time Duke ushered me through those dark velvet doors into her dim sanctum. She kissed me on the mouth and bit my lower lip until it bled, then handed me a hit list of ten names, including the third-in-command of the entire Norpak governing syndicate. A bomb would've been the simplest option, but she wanted me to do it all in person, cleanly. Bombs were too loud, she said. She wanted her surviving enemies to lie sleepless, associating silence itself with the promise of certain death.

It took me ten days of travel, twenty days of reconnaissance, and twenty minutes of infiltration and combat to finally stand inside the throne room of Fujiko the Third, watching the lifeless body of her last personal bodyguard crash against the metal floor and finish twitching. I knelt to collect a tissue sample from the monarch's jewel-heavy corpse to authenticate it, but just when the steam inside her skull finished its residual sizzling and the room fell into perfect silence, I was startled to hear a voice.

"Trade," it said.

I whipped around, ready to dispense one more death at a microsecond's notice, but the voice wasn't coming from a person. It crackled from a small pane set along the wall.

"I want to make a trade," it said, in an old-fashioned sort of American English. "I save your life twice. You save mine once. Call it a bargain. Call it commerce. You're a mercenary. You like commerce, right? Say something, damnit! I know you can hear me, and I know you speak this language."

The pane had an inset DNA scanner, and there was a seam in the wall to indicate a door. With my limited handle of written Japanese, I couldn't ascertain what was behind it.

"Fine," said the voice. "Don't say anything. Just listen: I've been watching you. I know you thought you disabled all the security in here with that wimpy JSX-94 tapeworm. You didn't. That was all me. You're here in one piece because I *let* you in, at great risk to my very own ass. That one's free. If you want to get out of here alive, that will cost you extra. Nod your head if you understand." When I hesitated, the voice said, "Don't look at the door. Nod your head, asshole."

I nodded, once.

"Good. Here's how it works, Assassin Man. There's a box under Fujiko's throne. Go look at it. Hurry."

Against my better instincts, I lifted up the red silk and looked under the throne. There was a cube there. It was fashioned from some strange, lustrous, inky black material, bound in a cage of metal and circuitry. I'd never seen anything like it—but I could guess what it was, if I could believe it.

"That's Gray," said the synthetic voice. "It's a metalvore strain, but it'll settle for flesh and bone. It was wired to a dead-man's switch on Fujiko's heartbeat, but right now I'm tricking it into thinking she's still alive. If you kill me, the box opens. If you try to leave here without me, I'll open it myself. We're leaving this place together, or not at all. Nod if you understand."

"Where are you?"

"I'm behind this wall. Fujiko's thumb opens the door. Hurry!"

I cut off the thumb and pressed it into the scanner. The corroded metal wall screeched and rolled itself open, revealing a cramped space full of red light and bad smells. It took me a moment to recognize the human being tied up in the middle of all those wires and pipes and humming technology. Her head was encased in scuffed plastic and metal. Intravenous lines ran to gauntlets clamped onto her pale arms; waste tubes ran to something encasing her pelvis. I understood. A technical servant. A nodespace slave.

"Free my arms first," said the voice. Her throat didn't move—and I understood why her voice had sounded synthesized when I unlocked the cuffs on her wrists and watched her pull the grotesquely long feeding tube from her throat. I stood back and watched as she pried herself out of the rig, and every part of her body that she liberated revealed a new bruise. I thought I saw traces of matted blood in her hair.

"Look away," she croaked, in her own strained human voice, but I already had. She took my coat and my wave rifle and ordered me to carry the deadly Gray box ahead of us as we made our way back the way I'd come in, stepping over the bodies of everyone who'd stood in my way.

We fled the aquapolis in Fujiko's own ostentatious personal minisub—me in the pilot's seat, her behind my back, training my gun on me and patiently explaining how to sneak past the perimeter alarms. Finally she sat back on the red silk cushions lining that absurd gilt cockpit and watched me through her sore and swollen eyes. The last lights of the underwater city had barely vanished into the murk when I saw that she had passed out. She slept for days after that, while I kept her hydrated and hidden.

What would grow into the only friendship of my adult life began this way, as commerce. She knew better than to leave an anonymous assassin like me alive with her in that cockpit, and I knew better than to leave any living witnesses to my work—but somehow the exchange of services between us had created just enough of a bond that, against both our better judgments, we each neglected to kill the other when it was done.

She told me to call her Kat Mandu, though that was not her name, nor would I ever know enough about her to identify her. Thanks to a regime of prenatal nootropic drugs, she'd been born precocious in the arts of nodespace. Programming languages had come more quickly and easily to her than human speech, and by adolescence she'd cultivated a genius best kept hidden: to the Norpak syndicates, or Medusa Clan, or any other organized power in this world, she was a commodity of warfare. She wouldn't tell me how long she'd spent imprisoned in the dim chambers of Fujiko's lair, performing whatever feats of sabotage or espionage were demanded of her, spending her every free second looking for weaknesses in the virtual cage that bound her.

We boarded separate transports out of Sydney, expecting never to see each other again, but Kat never truly left my side. She had appointed herself my guardian angel. She provided me with intelligence, rendered me invisible to the security systems of my targets, fed misinformation to anyone who tried to track me. I split my earnings with her, though she didn't seem to care either way. She became the only person I ever spoke to. I remember nights when, whispering to the ghost of her in the dark muggy spaces in which I've always traveled, she seemed like the only person I had ever really known.

If I remember anything at all, I remember my final job for Dahlia. In my mind I am still there. For the rest of my life, however long it lasts, I'm afraid I'll never be able to close my eyes without finding myself back there in Antarka, trudging through the frozen mud under the unmoving south polar sun. They're welcoming me into the main dome, never doubting that I'm just another hauler on his way to somewhere else—and then I'm gazing out over the people in that structure as they chat and drink, while Dahlia's garbled voice whispers serenely in my ear:

"You're in position, yes?"

"Affirm," I say quietly to the bug in my coat. "I've positively identified the technologists and the location of their stockpile and equipment. All the targets are in a single isolated structure. The rest of the settlement is purely civilian. Security is minimal. I'll make it quick."

"Hmm. No. I'm afraid that just won't do."

I wait for several seconds, but she doesn't elaborate. "What are your orders?"

Dahlia's voice affects a perversely childlike innocence to say, "These recent threats of war. The skirmishes around Hawai'i. You want them to end before they escalate any further, don't you?"

Two customers laugh and order another round. A father comforts his screaming toddler.

"Yes," I say.

"As do I. But someone in that chilly little settlement has not understood our wishes for peace. Someone there believes they're free to sell first-strike Gray weapons to our enemies in Norpak. That speaks to a deeper problem, don't you agree? It means we have not been nearly clear enough in expressing our wishes. We have allowed grave misunderstandings to take root and spread contagiously." She pauses. "Eliminate this confusion. Completely."

I swallow. "Completely."

"Do we understand each other?"

"The . . . entire settlement?"

"Men, women, children, animals. No survivors."

I blink slowly. "No survivors."

"Will there be a problem?"

I allow one chill breath to enter and exit my lungs. I look around the room.

"No problems," I say.

The static in my ear cuts out.

There's a logic to it all. I would ordinarily wait until nightfall, but the sun here won't set for weeks. Instead I memorize the map Kat sent me, complete with human heat signatures. The main dome is too crowded to take at once, so I nest behind the chemical drums ten meters from the entrance, picking off up to three heads at a time. With the noise of nearby machinery masking the pop of flash-boiled blood, I find it's optimally possible to kill three in a row before any can escape to warn others. If more than three leave at once, I let them, making a mental note of where they go. Every shot must be a clean beam to the head. After each finished set, I rush to drag the bodies out of sight behind the lip of dirty snow surrounding the dome. By the end I count eighteen. I re-enter the dome and finish the last six. This brings the total to twenty-four.

I visit the other, smaller buildings in turn. I find one man opening boxes in the storage room, then two women fixing the communications array I sabotaged on my way in. Nine people, total, in their residences, where contact between me and them becomes increasingly difficult to avoid. I enter a man's kitchen as he's lifting a pot from a hot plate, and we make eye contact through the steam. To avoid making noise, I motion for him to set the pot back down and move away from any stacked dishes. He complies. The thud as his body hits the floor is still loud enough to bring his wife. She sees me as she turns the corner. I don't give her time to see him. She is number thirty-six.

After the residences are cleared, I head to the labs to destroy the Gray stockpile and deal with the four people I was originally sent here to dispose of. The cramped hallways force me to make eye contact with them as well. They're the only ones who look at me as if they know who I am or what I'm doing there.

This leaves only one building in the settlement unaddressed, a lesser geodesic dome still dotted with a blob of body heat on Kat's map. There's no cover as I approach. The polar sun sits directly behind me as I move, stretching my shadow out like a long knife pointed at the front door. Someone cracks it open and looks out. Having lost the element of surprise, I sprint the rest of the way to the entrance and kick it open on its hinges. Inside, there are pastel colors. It's a school or a daycare. No, a church. There's religious iconography in a crude mural on a concrete wall. There are folding plastic chairs arrayed in a circle. There is a couch with six children, aged perhaps four to fourteen, where the oldest one hurries to join the others. They all stare at me. I stare back. No one else is here. No one else is left.

The oldest one surprises me by looking up and asking, in what seems like a perversely casual tone, "Our parents are all dead, aren't they?"

I nod.

"They're in heaven," he tells the others, simply. "We're going too. Close your eyes. We'll go together."

Everyone but the eldest child closes their eyes and nod their heads down slightly. The eldest stays there in the middle, looking at me. His face is stoic—more resigned than a child's face should know how to be. I can't break our eye contact. I have trouble focusing. When I clear my mind and concentrate on my breath, I inexplicably find myself saying:

"You wouldn't have wanted, anyway . . . to grow up into a world like this."

Before I fire, there's a strange tension in my eyebrows, twitching, something I want to reach up and rub away. Instead I keep my hands on my waver, and the six shrieks sound in precise metronomic succession.

I let the wave rifle slide down to my side, and I remove my goggles.

The wind howls faintly around the plastic dome as I take a breath and begin to relax. The crude mural gives me a last hard look before I turn to leave, but I hesitate just short of the open door.

There's something out there. I know I'm being watched.

I want to take cover, but my body won't follow the order. I check Kat's aerial map again, but there are no heat signature besides mine anywhere in the settlement. No body warmth. No electromagnetics. No movement. Nothing.

What had I seen as I turned? It was something indistinct in the edge of my vision, in the sky just outside the dome. The tension in my face keeps coming back, and I don't know why I'm suddenly sweating so profusely, or why my heart is beating so hard that I can hear the sound coming up through my chest. What is this feeling? Am I afraid? No, I realize as I step forward—not merely afraid. It's that every other fear I've ever felt before this moment was false, and this is true fear I'm feeling now for the first time. This is all of it at once.

I don't know why I keep moving toward the door, but I do. I can't stop myself or look away. The sun sits just above the horizon, shining hard into my eyes, and the frozen wind bites into my flesh the moment I clear the door, the moment I see it there, hanging in the sky directly over me:

A massive, lidless eyeball.

It's staring directly at me. Into me. Through me. It levitates five meters above the ground, two meters wide. It seems to have no physical substance, but it's there, a piece of space that slightly bends the image of the cirrus clouds behind it. More than that, it's a viscerally overwhelming presence, a force I can feel in every cell in my body.

The heat of its attention slices through me, pinning me in place, and somehow I know that it knows everything. It watched everything I just did. It sees everything I've ever done. Every life I've taken, every drop of someone else's blood I've ever boiled with this weapon in my hands, every killing shot of every battle of every war.

My rifle hits the frozen ground, followed by my knees, and I can't stop screaming. My jaw wants to snap free from its tendons. My hands push on the sides of my head until I think my skull might crack.

My first fear is that this giant eye is going to kill me. I think it's going to rip my soul out of my body. I can almost feel it happening.

Instead it does something infinitely worse:

It vanishes, leaving me there alive.

I

The bounty hunters flash their lights in my eyes a few more times. The tracers lacerate my vision even when my eyelids fall back down.

"Weird, right?" Doc says. "What I wouldn't give for a scanner that can see inside these heads. One of those fancy new ones I hear the Clan hands out like candy."

"I don't care," Jenna says. "I don't give a shit. Just tell me if they're going to wake up or not."

Fingers prod my head again, rubbing scalp over skull. "There's no head trauma. They should already be awake. I honestly have no idea why they're not. It's a mystery."

"Look," Jenna says impatiently. "If they're okay, I need to call Duke to collect the bounty. If they're too far gone, we need to dig a hole and put them in the ground while it's still dark out, before anybody can find out we ever had them."

"I'm telling you, I don't know."

"What's your best suggestion?"

Doc sighs and says, "Flip a coin."

Jenna paces the metal floor for a long time. Then I hear her say "No. It's too dangerous. The Medusas are too dangerous. I'm not doing it. Unplug them. Just do it! Fuck! Bart sure as shit better've brought the shovels."

They're going to bury me. I think they're going to bury me alive. I'm still trying and failing to move, to speak, to give them any sign that I'm here, but I can only barely think at all. My consciousness is still lost in this broken unity, and I'm not much more than two streams of memory flowing together—drawn helplessly down into the things I least want to remember.

DANAE

Even when I was whole, I was very far from omniscient. It took me years of exile to look back and realize that with every mind that joined my gestalt, every decade of experience I poured into the swollen river of my memory, I was also losing touch with simple realities I might have grasped when I was younger. By the time I reached Asher Valley, I'd fallen so in love with thinking of myself as a perfect microcosm of humankind, pure and unbiased in who I chose to unify with, that I stopped noticing that nearly all the lives I added to my gestalt were privileged ones: great minds with the time and ease and education to spend all their days ruminating; scientists with the funding to push the cutting edges of their fields; winners of genetic lotteries; people from the safer sides of class and gender and racial divisions. It never crossed my mind that I rarely sought unity with hardscrabble wastelanders, working-class aquapolitans, or traumatized refugees; that while I deepened my knowledge of the universe, I was losing all my instincts for how to live in the world. I fell into the trap of believing I was above it. In hindsight, it was predictable that I would fall in love with Lorelei—and inevitable that I would get us both killed.

She was a genius of a higher order than any separate person I have ever known. When I found her, she had already taught herself everything from integral calculus to chaos theory, and she could work through all but the most sprawling equations in her head in less time than it took me to check her. I was obsessed with her from the day I watched her lay her fingers on the keys of the first piano she had ever seen, and learn, over the course of thirty-one minutes, to play Beethoven's Moonlight Sonata by ear as perfectly as I could with ninety aggregate years of practice behind me. Any new skill or understanding seemed to come effortlessly to her, and she had taught herself everything she knew in absolute secrecy.

She had never had a choice: in her smoke-wreathed hometown of Asher Valley, on the ragged edge of the Holy Western Confederacy, women were not permitted to learn to read. They weren't allowed to be seen unless swaddled in gray cloaks and weighed down with wooden crosses. They did not speak unless spoken to, nor raise their voices above a whisper, and had been taught to instinctively hesitate to use words of more than two syllables. As far as anyone in that town knew, Lorelei was just as docile and illiterate as they required her to be—and even then, she was a despised outcast in that place. Infertility was as unforgivable a sin as any other.

I came into town pretending to be a married heterosexual couple, to conduct anthropological research on a complex of post-Collapse fundamentalists called the Third Holy Church of the Kept Promise. Lorelei was the general store clerk who would only talk to me when my male body was out of the room, and even then I could feel her hesitation filling the air between us. Her voice shook under the weight of all the trust she was putting in me, but I also felt the burn of her desire: for anyone to talk to, for any fragment of proof that a bigger world existed past the rusty iron palisades. For anyone to whom she could finally reveal the enormity of everything she kept hidden inside the head she never took out from under the hood of her cloak.

For all I know, Lorelei never revealed the slightest suggestion of her true genius to any human being other than me. Before her, I had never rushed so fast to tell anyone who and what I really was. I can only confess now that I coveted her mind, but more than that, I thought I could rescue her from that awful place and carry her with me to a freer country. It started as an unserious wish in the back of my mind. It grew into an obsession.

I moved an entire branch of my consciousness into an abandoned church overlooking the town, ready to collect Lorelei and hurry on to the coast at any moment. I discussed the idea with her in a whisper in the long hours of sweltering nights, in the shadows of ruined buildings, in each other's arms, whenever her husband Curtis had drunk himself into oblivion or slithered bitterly away into the beds of other women (who lacked the social privilege to deny his advances, but would be punished for them no less mercilessly). She shared her intense misgivings, and I dismissed them with increasing insistence. As preternaturally intelligent as Lorelei was, she had twenty-seven years of experience versus my twelve thousand—so I told myself, and so I told her, until I had fatally infected both of us with my smug, superior optimism.

On the morning before we'd planned to leave, my bodies awoke and looked down from the hill to see a thin column of black smoke curving out of the center of town, and from the top of the bell tower I could see the pyre at its foot. I told myself I didn't know what it was. I split one of my bodies off and sent it running down the hill into town as fast as its legs would carry it, to find out what had happened, while the rest of me stayed behind in unity. I just sat. I don't remember all that might have been going through my heads while I waited for that body to return. Maybe I already consciously realized that that self was already dead, as was Lorelei. That it was my fault.

Nearly two hours passed between when I saw the smoke and when they came for me. It should have been the simplest thing in the world to know it was time to run. Any wastelander would have had that much wisdom, but I sat still and waited, lost in my thoughts, as if I could change what had already happened if I could only ponder it deeply enough.

It wasn't until I heard the mob marching up that hill that everything finally snapped to focus. From the windy bell tower, I could see them, almost the entire population of the town, with the church elders and patriarchs hobbling along at the front. I could hear the men chanting in such a mindless and discordant unison that I couldn't make out the words at first, but I kept still until they were close enough for me to understand it.

"Five, eight, thirteen. Five, eight, thirteen." Just those numbers, over and over. Then I understood.

Mark 5:8-13: The exorcism of the demonic Legion from the Gerasene man.

My survival instincts finally kicked in. Everything snapped into painful focus, and a blast of adrenaline brought me to a startled understanding: the advantage was all mine. The Keepers had all the guns, but they could kill my bodies over and over again without ever truly killing me. If even one of me made it out of here alive, so would I.

I thought fast. I stayed in unity. I bolted the front entrance with one of my bodies and ran for the back door with two others—and that was the last moment in which I can recognize myself or remember what it was like to be whole, because Brother Curtis was standing there waiting for me. He pressed the gun's emitter against my heart. He met my eyes and grinned before he fired.

Unity had never ended that way before. The death resonated so hard that it nearly struck me unconscious. As I recovered, I found myself constrained to a single body, fighting to hold myself upright with the phantom heat of the blast still persistently crackling inside my chest. I had to concentrate to discover which body I was in. I made some noise with my throat and recognized the voice.

There was one exit they probably hadn't found: a small bomb shelter in the basement, sealed with a heavy steel door, with a carpet-covered trapdoor in the floor leading to an old sewer tunnel. I doubted mine would be the body to survive—out of all of us, I was in the one farthest from that room—but I ran anyway. Another of my bodies was right in front of me when the front doors burst open, close enough to hear the shriek of the waver that cut them down. Circles of ash and fire popped across the weathered pews. Woodsmoke filled my nose, then the unmistakable odor of burning flesh. I heard one of my selves scream, very close, and I instinctively knelt to help. The beam had only grazed their forearm superficially, but we shared a look, both of us knowing there was nothing I could do. That body was almost eighty years old.

"Go," they said, and started to stand up—but they fell lifeless into my arms with a circle of white hair burning on the back of their head.

I lunged for the stairs. Waver shots warmed the air around me and miraculously missed, but I couldn't spare the coordination to negotiate the steps. I tripped and rolled all the way down with my head braced in my arms. The Keeper who waited at the bottom had been expecting me to come through that door at standing height, and his fire hit the empty space above me. I made it to the next flight of stairs in the second it took his rifle to prime again.

I rolled again, less elegantly than before. I heard my left arm snap against a step before my nerves even registered the surge of white-hot pain—but my fall at the bottom was cushioned by something soft.

It was dim down there. It took me too long to recognize my other bodies, all dead. Their birth names flashed through my mind—Elana, Castille, Arjun—and I thought of the lives I'd lived as them and couldn't now; the places I could never go back to without those faces; all the family and friends who'd never greet me again. But there was no time to mourn myself now. I was close. I pulled myself up from my own dead bodies and ignored the pain, and I shut out the thud of boots, the shouts and chants and waver shrieks following just behind. I just ran, and the door to the lightless shelter room yawned open at the end of the last hallway.

I barreled through without seeing. My hand groped in the void and found the heavy steel door, and I threw all my adrenal strength into heaving it shut. I could hear fists and heels and rifle stocks hammering on the other side the moment it locked, but it was a century-old post-nuclear relic. They'd need a tank to break it down.

My eyes started to adjust. A single spark of daylight breached a fissure in the ceiling, and in the fizzling darkness all my own dead faces from the hallway flashed through my mind's eye. Yulia. Eryn. Duncan. Tomasz. That left . . .

No one. Only me.

But I had made it, I thought.

Some vital part of me is still back there—will always be trapped inside that day. For five years I've never closed my eyes without finding myself in that dark room again: alone, gritting my teeth blunt against the pain of my broken arm, but with nothing left between me and escape except a trap door and a half-kilometer of sewer. I'm down to my last body, but I'm alive.

Then I hear the chuckle from the darkness. Dry, rasping, and drunk.

"The stupid bitch confessed," he growls, and I recognize his voice and the stink of his favored alcohol before his silhouette gives him away: Lorelei's husband, Brother Curtis. His black shirt, a shade darker than the darkness around him; yellow teeth leering out of a sunburned face; the dull glimmer of his wave pistol, pointed unsteadily at my head.

"We got it out of her," he continues. "We know what you are, witch. What you two did. She told us everything about you. Your soulless ant-hive mind. We got it all out of her. We got it all."

There is no sorrow in his voice.

"We know what you are, and we're going to hunt you down and exterminate you. Every last wicked one of you. Your name is Legion, and we will send you to the pigs and drown you in the sea."

No trace of remorse for the cold-blooded murder of his own wife.

"We're going to hunt you to the four corners of the Earth."

Nothing but hatred for me. Bottomless. Ignorant. Triumphant.

On instinct I dart to the side, and his waver cuts a smoking hole in my cloak and scalds the skin of my neck—but before the gun can prime again, I'm on him, heaving all my weight into one sharp kick straight into his fingers on the grip. He grunts in pain. The weapon clatters away across the concrete floor.

He reacts quickly, unsheathing a long knife from his belt, but he misjudges my motion, and I bend around him like a breath of wind. He lunges into a metal shelf and turns around, dazed. His fingers are weak on the knife's handle, some of them broken or dislocated from my kick, and it's a simple thing to kick again—to watch the gleam of the blade swinging up into the air—to catch it with my good hand.

Curtis is beaten. He braces his knees as if to lunge at me again, but he's dazed and drunk and already winded, whimpering at his hurt hand, out of shape and untrained. With one good hit I know I can knock him out cold, break his ankle to stop him following me, bruise his vocal chords to silence his shouts to the other Keepers while I open the trap door and run.

But I don't run.

I turn the knife in my hand, filling my vision with its dull gleam and finding it already soaked in blood—and it dawns on me that this is my blood, from one of my other bodies.

My mind begins to overflow: with the radiant pain in my arm; with the thought of all the lives that have just been taken from me; of Lorelei burning at the stake; of Blood Rain's billion-plus victims; of how it felt to die six successive times in that ecstasy of sick fear; of collecting tissue samples from mass graves; of the plasma thrusters bolted to Cruithne; of the men even at this moment designing ever more vicious strains of Gray to stoke the cold war in the Pacific; of the impossibly cruel ingenuity of it all. I think of the people responsible, the whole breadth and banality of the evil in humankind— and in the moment Curtis finally braces to rush me again, I see all of them wearing a single skin—

And I want that skin to bleed.

In all my 223 lives, I have no memory of ever wanting anything so much.

When he lunges again, I duck and slide the blade into his calf.

I brace my grip and feel—hear—his stumbling motion pry all the tendons apart. He crashes into a helpless fetal position, clutching at his ruined leg, and even through the intensity of my bloodlust and the adrenaline-crazed speed of my motions, there is a perfectly cold and medical logic to everything I do. I want the most pain, the slowest bleeding. I avoid major nerves and blood vessels. Instead I slash at his hands and face, his limbs, his bowels. I twist the blade and punch the wounds. His screams ring in my ears, and I close my eyes to savor it—how it joins the increasingly frantic shouts through the door and becomes music, the sweetest I've ever heard. It resonates in all my bones, broken and whole. I suck in breath and taste the smells on the air, delighting in a promise to myself: I'm going to make him pay in kind for every one of my deaths.

At some point Curtis begins to quiet down, and I abandon all restraint and slash harder—as hard as I can with only one good arm—as if he's gone silent to spite me, and a deep enough cut might make him sing again.

He's collapsed his own lungs, screaming.

The music ends suddenly. The clang of the blade slipping to the concrete floor is only dead noise; the bang of the battering ram has ceased to be a drumbeat. The drip of his blood from my fingers is impossibly loud and dissonant as I finally stumble back from the body of the man I've killed.

I've killed.

No. I've done so much more than just kill him. I've made him unrecognizable. I relished every second of it, and in my heart of hearts I wanted so much more—still want so much more.

It might be half an hour that I stand there, moving from that spot only to empty my stomach on the floor. I think of staying longer. I think of unbolting the door and letting the Keepers come in and finish what they've started. When they finally give up with their battering ram and settle for setting the whole church on fire, I think of walking into the flames.

If I could go back now and choose differently, I would.

I don't know how long I spent running. For weeks I never slept and have no memory of eating. Whatever coherent thought passed through my suddenly isolated head was harnessed to my sole objective of traveling as far as possible, by any means available, trusting no one, moving as erratically as I could for fear that what Curtis had told me was true: that the Keepers really intended to hunt me forever. I started to believe that they knew about all the other branches of my consciousness, about Redhill and the equinox—that they were even now in the process of exterminating every part of me that still existed. I was convinced that I was already the last fragment of unified consciousness in the entire world. I began to see the same faces recur between the ragged backwaters I passed through; I couldn't tell how many of them were real, and how many waking nightmares.

I fled the surface and crawled under the ocean, hoping to bury myself so deep in the underworld that no one could follow me. I rode the elevators into the rusty lair of Medusa Clan and offered my technical expertise to that queen of terror, Dahlia Lem, in exchange for her protection. That had become the logic of security in this age: nothing would make me safer from my enemies than to become the property of someone who guarded her possessions with lethal jealousy.

Eventually I learned to sleep again. I regained strength. My head finally started to clear, until one day my fever broke and I startled awake to find myself entombed in those claustrophobic steel chambers—finally grasping that the protection the Medusas offered was not just from real or imagined threats from outside, but from the Medusas themselves. I had made myself too valuable to let go—and I'd made myself an accomplice, however indirect, to every atrocity the Clan visited on the world.

Despair would have broken me within the first year of my exile, had I never met a tortured master muralist by the name of Kusanagi Naoto. He had despair of his own: fusion fuel moguls had hired him to cover every public wall in Epak with colorful imagery to celebrate the glory of their industry, and he'd been working himself ragged to cram as much subversive symbolism as possible into all of his own work. His every brushstroke was a muffled scream that most of that 'clean' energy was destined to be used as waver ammunition for one genocidal war or another—and almost no one noticed. We met eyes in Bloom City's habitat: me on my way to work for the Clan; him at the top of a ladder, splattered in self-illuminating paint; both of us salaried with blood money. I nodded to him across the crowd to let him know I understood his message loud and clear, and he nodded back in beleaguered relief, and that was all it took us to forge the beginnings of an unbreakable connection.

We never had any one word for what we gradually became to each other. No label or category would have done it justice. He loved me with an intensity and devotion the likes of which I've rarely known in all my lives, and I loved him back as much as I was capable of loving anyone; trust and vulnerability weren't resources I had in any abundance. There were months at a time when I needed to keep him at arm's length and recoil back into myself. He respected that, whether or not he ever fully understood—and though I had no one else, I didn't expect any kind of monogamy from him.

But when we were close, he gave me things I needed desperately, things I'd resigned myself to never having again. When I most hated myself, he held me in so much admiration. When my head was stuffed full of lives I could never lead again, he loved me for my complexities and contradictions and delved into them as far as I would let him. At a time when I was racked by the claustrophobia of a single unchanging body, he was pansexual, with an insatiable attraction to fluidity. There were times when our varied lovemaking, its endless role reversals and permutations of assumed genders, was the only way I could still remember or express who I was. He became the only person I ever spoke to, let alone who knew the truth about me. I remember times when we whispered to each other in the hot, musty darkness of my coffin apartment in the Medusan barracks module, and I wondered if he was the last person left alive who knew me— who would ever know me again.

For all the safety and solace I found in our undefined relationship, it wasn't enough to hold me together. Every day I stayed in Bloom City wore down my will to live a little further. The closer Epak's cold war with Norpak came to its seemingly inevitable flash point, the more I had to reckon with never living to reunite with the rest of myself—and, in turn, the more desperately I needed to. Even if Curtis's blood was still on my hands, even if I could never unify again, I had to find my way back to the rest of myself. I had to be with them, no matter how dangerous the journey.

And I nearly made it. I came so close.

I don't know for sure who hired Serena to kill Alexei and Naoto and abduct me. I don't know who fired the rocket that hit our APC, possibly killing all three of us inside it. Maybe I'm dying even as I remember that.

Oh God. Am I dying? Where am I?

I have to wake up. I have to break unity.

Wake up.

Wake up!

I

My surroundings feel different, sound different. I'm outside again. I can feel the cool desert air on one of my bodies and then another. Flashes of light play across my eyelids, but it must still be night. Somewhere a shovel blade scrapes the sandy earth. Someone sets my bodies down.

"Uh, Jenna—"

"Not now. Get over here. For fuck's sake, do I have to do everything myself? Help me dig. We need to get this done before sunrise."

"I already called it in."

Everyone goes silent.

"You what?"

"I called in the bounty. They sent us coordinates for the exchange—"

"You called the Medusas," Jenna says. "You told them we had these three. Alive."

"They *are* alive. Technically. And worth fifty million fucking squid."

I can hear the quiet whine of a waver priming. Jenna's voice is eerily calm when she says, "You can't spend squid in hell, Bart."

"Whoa, whoa! Fuck! Don't—!"

"Stop," Doc says. "Jenna, put it down."

"We're all dead. He's killed us all. You don't *know* these people. We show up with three bodies 'technically' alive, we'll all be smoking corpses by sunup."

Doc clicks his tongue and says, "We've got no choice now, do we? They'll kill us if we back out. For better or worse, we have to make the deal. And if it gets hairy, I'd much rather be a gang of six than five." He adds, "You can always kill him later."

"He's right, Jenna. Listen to Doc."

"No. He dies now."

"Then so do you," says a fourth voice. "Stand down."

"You double-crossing snakes," Jenna says.

"What did you expect? He's my brother!"

"Oh Lord, thank you. Thank you, sis."

"Shut your lips, Bart. Let me handle this. Jenna, put it down."

"I'd rather take him with me."

"Stop!" Doc barks. "All of you! Look!"

Then I know he's looking at me. They're all looking down at me. It takes me a moment to realize my eyes are open.

I can move again, but I can feel the link collapsing. I'm forgetting myself. Soon I won't exist in the sense that I do now: I'll break back down into my constituent parts, and Danae and Alexei will forget me like a dream.

But there was something here—something crucial in me, while I existed. I knew something, learned something from this tenuous link, that Alexei and Danae need to know. Maybe it could save them both.

I'm trying so hard to remember, to burn it into my splintering memories, but it's too late.

The bounty hunters are lifting me back into the truck. My bodies are already going numb to each other. I blink again and dissolve.

BORROWER

When my other copies return from their hunt, there are three of them. The new flesh looks strong, if a bit young. It can't be more than seventeen years old. They all look anxious.

"This is the best we could do," says my new epsilon copy, climbing into the truck bed. "All the other potential vessels were in crowds." He pauses to wipe a trickle of blood from the puncture-marks ringing his scalp.

My copies' eyes keep darting around. Veins are standing out on their necks and foreheads. They're sweating.

"Something is wrong," I observe.

"There's a significant Medusan presence massing here," the alpha copy tells me. "They've put an enormous bounty on her head. They just received word that someone wants to collect it. Sybil has been caught. She's being held captive."

"No," I gasp.

"We can use this development to our advantage," Epsilon says. "If they know her exact whereabouts—"

"—and we can glean that information ourselves—" the alpha agrees.

"—then we only need to get there first," I finish.

There's sound outside the truck. Boots thudding in the lifeless earth. A voice shouts, "Hey you. Did you see a snot-nosed kid come running this way? He's about to get a beating if he thinks he can just walk off without finishing the job."

"I . . . I don't know," says the station attendant.

"You don't mind if I have a look," the stranger responds. Even through my aging ears, I can hear him stomping closer to the back of the truck.

"Thank you for your carelessness," I tell my copies. They glare at me. We brace ourselves to strike.

I could read you like a book, Sybil, and that day was the page I'd been waiting for. You pressed through the infirmary doors with deep bags under your eyes, but your confidence seemed to light up the whole white-tiled room. Taking care not to touch the tubes that now crawled like ivy along the hospital bed, you bent down to hug me and whispered, "We did it. Jackson found an interface."

"You have it?"

You stroked my sweaty forehead. "One of the two. The other one is on its way here by courier. It'll arrive tomorrow afternoon. We just tested the one we have, and the link is measurably perfect. No loss, no artifacts. I've run dozens of tests, and they all pass with flying colors. But how are you? Will you be okay . . . until—?"

"Until tomorrow?" I croaked. I snorted a shallow laugh. My body was racked by fever now, my skin greased with foul-smelling sweat, but it didn't matter anymore. I could laugh at death now. "Yes. The doctor thinks these old antibiotics will delay septicemic organ failure for at least forty-eight hours. You did it, Sybil. You saved me."

You put your hand on my shoulder and smiled radiantly. I couldn't help myself. Something in the IV was making me high, or the fever had boiled all the inhibition out of my brain.

"I love you, Sybil." I couldn't believe I'd finally said it.

You weren't perturbed or surprised. You didn't miss a beat before you replied, "I love you too. You're like a brother to me. Tomorrow . . . tomorrow we won't need words anymore." Suddenly your gaze clouded over with worry. "Are you all right?"

I hadn't noticed my face clenching. I shook my head and said, "Sorry. It's, uh. Painkillers are w-wearing off."

Brother.

"I'll get the doctor."

"No," I said. "I'll call her myself. Don't worry."

"Sorry I can't stay longer. I have a lot to take care of before tomorrow, and I have to sleep before I start making mistakes."

"Don't worry," I repeated, half-choking. "Go finish the tests."

You smiled one last time as you ran off.

I hauled myself up and knelt on the bed, pulling all the tubes in my arm painfully taut to push the window ajar and peek through the crack. From two floors above, I could just make out your conversation.

"—not easy for either of us. But the only remotely reasonable option is for Luther and me to go first, before we try unifying more than two minds. Minimize the risks. Look, we both went into this relationship knowing the project would complicate it. And vice versa, for that matter."

Jackson responded, "I know. But I just . . . are you so sure?"

"About undergoing an untested, irreversible, and fundamentally consciousness-altering procedure, you mean? I know the risks, but we're talking about advancing the evolution of consciousness. We can't be squeamish. I thought you understood that—"

"No, I do. That's not what I meant."

"What then?"

He hesitated. "It's just that Luther is . . . I don't know how to say it. He is a bit rough around the edges, don't you think? I'm not trying to be mean. He's my friend too, and God knows I admire him as much as you do. It's just . . . sometimes he comes off as kind of a tortured soul. I've picked up some strange feelings from him during our tests."

You sighed. You held Jackson's hands and said, "I know. I've felt them too."

"Like you just said, unity is irreversible. If it works, the gestalt consciousness will be as much him as it is you, forever, and we have no way of knowing . . . all of what comes with that. I just thought we'd be taking this a lot slower. I thought we'd be performing the first unity in incremental steps over a period of days or weeks, so we could suss out the full range of effects and adjust or abort as necessary. Not all at once like this."

"You're right," I heard you say. "This is all light-years away from the ideal, but he doesn't have time for us to sit on our hands and play it safe. They just gave him forty-eight hours. I know it's a risk, but if it's our only chance to save his mind? I don't feel like we have a choice. I have to take that chance. I have to."

"I didn't mean to fall for you, you know," Jackson told you. "But, shit. I see your conviction, and your selflessness, and I don't know how to help myself. You're incredible. I feel . . . very lucky that I got to know you."

There was a pause, and then you kissed him. So softly, but with such feeling: a hand in his hair, another on his neck. My whole body ached to watch it. One of the needles popped out of my arm when you leaned in to him and said, "You know it's mutual, and I won't stop feeling that. Whatever happens tomorrow, I'll love you as much as I do now. This isn't really goodbye."

"We won't be together anymore, though. Not like this."

"I honestly don't know. It's impossible to know what it will be like. I'll need time to process what I'll have become, and how emotions *work* as a gestalt consciousness. But please believe I don't want to lose you. I need to know you'll be there to help us both through this."

"I will be, I promise. Every step of the way." He paused. "Are you *sure* you're sure? You still look like something's on your mind."

"It's not that. It's just that this is sort of . . . the last day of my life in which I'll still be *me*. Tomorrow everything I am will become part of something completely new, transcending the body. I don't know how to say this, but I just want . . . ." You looked around to see if anyone else was in earshot, as if you didn't know my window was directly above you, and said, "I want one last memory of being fully in *this* body."

Jackson replied, "That's understandable."

You kissed him yet again, this time much more deeply. I closed my eyes, but I could still make out the sound of your lips and his. Two different pitches of breath. The faintest trace of a moan.

You must have known, Sybil. You must have known I could see and hear you and Jackson through that narrow crack—and that means you were doing it just to remind me of who I was. Of what I was. Defective.

I ripped off the sensors and left the machines beeping their panic in my wake. I hobbled into the elevator before the staff could come running. I knew they'd make me lie back down. They'd tell me I was robbing myself of what little time I had left—but as I ran away from there, I was in total control of my flesh, and I would not grant it permission to die. Not yet.

I watched you and Jackson walk off hand in hand. I turned against the wind and hurried the other way, thankful it was the weekend and none of the other students would see me in hospital clothes. I went to the workshop. I pored over all of your notes and schematics. There was something you hadn't said, Sybil, though you must have known it too: the high-bandwidth interface we were waiting for was only necessary to mediate a two-way link. A simple transcription could be accomplished using all the parts we had on hand. It would be a different device, admittedly. Not a unifier at all. I thought of it as a patterner.

It was late that night, and with immense and wheezing effort, that I crept along the crooked path to where a warm, orange light shone from the single window of a canvas yurt. The thing I'd made swung at my side in a fat metal briefcase. The sandy wind blew up and nipped at my naked legs under the hospital gown, and my heart pounded less steadily with every step I took. I doubted for a moment that I had it in me to make it all the way to that door. When I did, I let myself consider that this was my last chance to turn back.

I didn't. I knocked. I pounded on that door until the man who lived there answered.

"Luther? What's wrong? I thought you were bedridden."

"Can I come in, Jackson? I need something."

"Anything," he said.

I didn't have to wait long for him to turn his back on me. When I rendered him unconscious, and even when I rolled him onto his back and installed the crowns over his head and mine, it was with the clarity and resolve of someone who had already rehearsed this procedure many times in his mind.

I never imagined I'd perform it again so many times to come. I never imagined it would become the essence of me.

"The hell is this?" our latest captive asks. He bears the marks of a low-ranking Medusa. He is very strong and in perfect health. Barely stifled grins flicker across all of our faces: we all yearn to assume this vessel, but that pleasure will be mine. We rolled a die to decide.

"Who are you?" my vessel-to-be demands to know as my alpha copy puts the crown on his head.

How many times have I been asked this? Freshly caught flesh always asks me this, and until this moment I've never fully thought out my answer. For seventy-two years I've never told anyone who I was at the outset, never breathed the name Luther—but more than that, I've never confided to anyone my *present* identity. Only recently has it occurred to me that such an identity exists—that my use of this machine has transformed me into something greater than Luther could ever have imagined—but this vessel is staring at me now with an unprecedented bewilderment. He sees how all of my copies and I have the same gaze, the same eager smile. He has grasped that the truth of what I am can't be seen with mere eyes.

"Who *are* you?" he asks again. His voice is trembling.

"*Borrower,*" I respond, and my voice as I hear it is no longer that of some old man. "*Bodysnatcher. Possessor. Lich.*" My voice isn't Luther's. It doesn't belong to any of the hundred-odd people I've become since I was him. It's the voice of the being I've become: a new life form, born from this glorious machine. I transcend all flesh, and I never kill. I merely borrow.

"What does that mean?" he asks, in appropriate terror.

"*Demon,*" I respond, through a mouth now watering as if in an ecstasy of hunger. This hunger is not for food, but for life. For being itself.

"What do you want from me?" the vessel asks.

"Wait," the alpha copy warns me. "First we need what he knows." But his mouth is watering too. All of our mouths are watering. This is intolerable. To hold myself back now is almost more than I can take.

"Sybil," we hiss in a jagged chorus. "Danae. Where is she?"

The vessel glances at the wires trailing from the patterner crown secured to its head. The vessel must think the crown is some sort of torture device. Quite the opposite.

"Some . . . some bounty hunters have her," the vessel says. "She's alive. We're on our way to collect."

"Where?" we ask.

"Somewhere out in the wasteland. I don't know. I don't have the exact coordinates. I'm telling the truth."

We're breathing heavily. I can hear the sound. The vessel's eyes are open and wide with unknowing fear. The status light is a steady green, and the button is slick with my sweat. But I hold back from pressing it for as long as I can stand to, savoring the energy of that moment like the brink of some violent orgasm—before at last I tip over the edge and plunge into that long tunnel of unconsciousness which stands between the old flesh and the new.

On a cold black night, seventy-two years ago, I ran.

I moved like the wind over the dry hills. I was tall and undeniably handsome. My muscles were taut and capable of any feat, my skin spotless and clean and richly tanned. I climbed trees and scaled the walls of the water tank and stood on its lid and looked out across all the glittering lights of the reach (all so clear through these new eyes) and filled my suddenly healthy lungs with cool air. I dug a shallow hole out in the weeds, and there I buried a hideous and disease ridden body in a hospital gown as it drew its last, shallow, mindless breaths.

When it was all done, I ran back the way I had come. When I reached your door I was so overwhelmed by the pleasure of my new strength that I had to stop myself from breaking it off its hinges. I had to cover my mouth to stop myself calling your name, so rich and beautiful were the tones of my new voice. Inside, a light flickered awake. The sound of your feet on the floorboards made me ache with anticipation.

"Jackson?" you asked me when you opened the door, squinting. "What the hell is going on? It's four in the morning."

I took you then, Sybil. I wrapped my strong arms around your frame (now delightfully slight by comparison to my own) and pulled your body against mine. I kissed you, first softly, then with force. You didn't quite resist at first, but when you began to writhe, I managed to set aside the perfect joy of that moment long enough to let you go.

And then you looked at me. I saw you noticing the scabbing puncture marks on my new forehead, and it was as if I could watch the complexities of understanding move through you, step by step:

realizing what was possible, then grasping that I had done it.

"Jackson?"

I couldn't repress a toothy grin as I shook my new head. "Try again."

"No," you said, and repeated. "No, no, no, no."

In my euphoria, I had not expected you to respond that way.

You stepped back in a shock that startled me. I heard the speed of your breathing; I thought I could hear your heartbeat across the widening gap between us. I watched your feet stumble, your mouth struggle to form words.

Sybil, you were revolted. I was wearing the perfect flesh, a vessel you knew so well, and still I repulsed you. In that moment I realized that it wasn't my body that had repelled you before, but something inextricably bound up with my soul.

Your fear crept into me like a freezing cold. It snuffed out all my joy and clamped around my heart, and for a moment I felt sicker in Jackson's body than I had in my hospital bed.

"Get away from me!" you screamed.

I stepped backward into the darkness. My ears rang and roared from the rush of my new blood.

"Get out of here, Luther! Never come back here!"

I turned and ran.

"Never come back!" you screamed.

I loved you, Sybil, and I love you still. Please believe me when I say I worshipped you, and I couldn't imagine going against your wishes in those days. If I had a choice, I wouldn't go against them even now.

I have nothing left to show for the year I wore Jackson's flesh. All my triumph reverted to seething envy. Whatever strength he'd had, others were stronger. However handsome he'd been, his face in the mirror only unsettled me. However perfect his life had appeared through windows, everywhere I went as Jackson found me poor and alone; every new town was full of men who basked in the love of friends and family, wealth and accomplishment, and I watched them just as compulsively. So I befriended them and came to know them, and everything I learned only fed a strange hunger inside me until I could recognize it as the same yearning that had brought me to Jackson's doorstep that first night.

It's strange now to remember sloughing off Jackson's body with such dread and hesitation, now that I never hesitate. I must have spent an hour staring at it, weeping over that empty shell with my latest pair of eyes. I was still so squeamish in those early days. Each new flesh I assumed felt like the last one I would ever need, but none lasted for more than a year before that irresistible hunger took root in me again; each new life satisfied me more fleetingly than the one before it. Eventually I could only admit that that hunger was not my curse. The hunger was me.

By now I have been every kind of man: men of every descent, rich men and laborers, priests and atheists, criminals and policemen, shy men and promiscuous lovers. I have learned countless skills. I've taught myself to memorize any mannerism, speak many languages in many accents, forge any proof of identity, and improvise every word I have ever needed to explain the incongruous gaps in my knowledge. I've lived flawlessly as more than one hundred different men, and I have been young for seven decades.

Yet I am dying. Again, after all this time, I can feel it. My flesh is perfectly intact—but my mind itself, by some mechanism I do not yet understand, is dying.

Sybil, you can help me. You're the only one who has ever been able to help me. This is what I focus on as the patterning completes. I open my eyes, inhale deeply into massive new lungs, and recognize myself as the zeta copy.

Epsilon gives me an envious look as he cuts the bonds on my wrists.

"We should have interrogated the vessel further," two of my copies murmur.

"It didn't have her location," I say. None of my copies speak in unison with me, and I realize: in this flesh, I feel fearless and capable. I'm the only one of us bold enough to say what we all already know. "We must find out. Then we must slow the Medusas down somehow. We'll degrade their ability to follow us."

"It will be costly," the delta copy laments. "Some of us might be injured or destroyed." I feel a momentary pang of pity for that copy of my consciousness, embodied as he is in such a frail vessel.

"This is why we have multiplied ourselves," a few of us murmur in response.

"In expectation of a need for redundancy," the gamma copy says. "To withstand danger and allow for more risk-taking."

"We have no choice," the alpha agrees. "This is our only chance."

"This is it," I remind us all, and hear them echo it in whispers, filling the darkness of the truck bed. I turn to the elderly delta copy and say, "Create a distraction."

He looks at me, knowing exactly what I'm asking him to do. He exchanges glances with all of us in turn, visibly reluctant, as if he hopes one of us will countermand my order, but no one does. When we all step out into the night, he returns to the driver's seat. The rest of us arm ourselves with what weapons we have and walk ahead in a line, toward the Medusan camp.

A few of them see us coming. They look up quizzically from their card games or their drinking.

"Bone?" one asks me. "Are you okay? What's all this?" He squints—as if he knows instinctively that the man he expects to find behind my eyes isn't there anymore.

Beyond him, a woman with a full set of rank-signifying jaw rings steps out of her tent. She must have the information I need. I look over my shoulder and give a broad hand signal to the darkness beyond the reach of the lights. The rest of my copies and I keep walking forward.

One of the Medusas shouts, "Wait. Stop them. Something's wrong—"

At that moment, the cargo truck my delta copy is driving roars out of the night and smashes into one of the Medusan armored rovers on the far side of their camp at one hundred kilometers per hour. The force of the collision explosively ruptures the fuel cells of both vehicles and sends gouts of white-hot flame mushrooming up into the night. I shield my eyes. Screams echo out over the fire-lit sand.

My copies raise their weapons. We do what we must. We press forward.

It is not in my nature to kill, but nothing can be allowed to stop me now. I must survive. I must reach Sybil before they do.

Through the smoke and the screaming and the strife, I think, *I will find you, Sybil. No matter what it takes, I will find my way back to you.*

I will put everything right, as it should have been.

I will make us one.

PART IV:
REDHILL

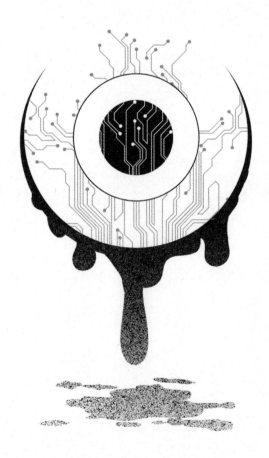

I

Alexei and Danae's now-separate awarenesses returned by degrees: first the pain, then the weight of the steel clamped around their wrists and ankles. Their eyes were swollen, their ears ringing from the rocket blast, the shrapnel still in their skins—but I had ceased to exist. They were themselves again.

"Naoto," Danae gasped, with her first moment of clarity. She searched the darkness. "Naoto?"

"Behind you," Alexei said.

Wincing through the pain, she managed to roll over onto her other side. She could just make out his silhouette in the glimmers of daylight through the cracks in the walls. She called his name again and pulled her chains taut to reach for him with shackled wrists. She was terrified her fingertips would find his flesh cold, but it wasn't. She leaned her head against his. "Naoto. Wake up."

She held his face and kissed him, but tasted blood on her lips. She felt his pulse, but it was faint and uneven.

Alexei tried to speak, but his voice caught in his throat. "He's— I think he was—"

Danae grabbed Naoto's shoulders and shook, but his body was limp. "I love you. You have to wake up. You have to stay with me."

"He was the one Doc said was—"

"Don't go. You can't." Her hands were shaking as she reached for Naoto's head. She hesitated. She forced them steady. "I'm so sorry. I wanted so much more for you than to be part of me, to be part of you, but if it's the only way to save you . . . if it's what you want, I'll do it. I'll do it."

"Wait," Alexei said. He kept finding saltwater on his face.

She put her palm on Naoto's forehead and willed.

Traces of his sensorium flickered unevenly through hers. Distorted flickers of searing pain burst through the link, so intense she almost screamed aloud. Her body writhed electrically, but she refused to let go. She only clutched him tighter and focused harder, searching behind his eyes for any trace of awareness. A thought. A memory. *Him.* But nothing came.

He wasn't there.

"Danae?" Alexei whispered. "Is he . . . ?"

Her will collapsed, and she fell back into her own body, feeling Naoto's skin only from the outside. She felt as hollow in herself now as she had in him.

It was Alexei who wept. He quivered and choked and bit his hands, his tears mixing with the blood and dirt and oil to pool on the floor. It was as visceral as it was bewildering: he thought of all the people he'd dispassionately watched die, many of them more horribly, many he'd known far better than Kusanagi Naoto.

"How do I know him?" he asked. "How can I be feeling this?"

"Unity," she said.

"How . . . ? How do I know what that means?"

Danae stared brokenly away into the darkness. "I'm so sorry."

"Tell me," he said. "I need to understand what happened."

There was nothing left to say, she thought. Without Naoto there was nothing left to do, or feel, or think. But she'd touched Alexei's mind without his consent, and the least he deserved was an explanation.

"I . . . borrowed your tactical skills," she said. "I needed to know how to operate the minigun, and there wasn't time for you to explain it verbally. So I took the knowledge directly from your mind. It was unforgivable to do that without your permission, but I thought . . . I could save us."

"But how did we—"

"There must have been unifier nanobots left in your cerebrum that hadn't self-terminated yet. The shock of the rocket strike must have reactivated them. Reconnected them to mine."

"Nanobots," he echoed. "Self-replicating swarm nanomachines, like Gray weapons, except—" He struggled to form words fast enough to keep up with the information racing through his mind. "Except the nanobots in your body are infinitely more advanced than Gray, aren't they? You're talking about molecular machines capable of seamlessly integrating with a human brain—"

"—and reading or writing its synaptic configuration from within," she finished.

Alexei blinked in awe. "But how is that possible? No power on Earth has that kind of tech. But I can remember you creating it, decades ago. I can remember . . . your memories."

"And I yours," she murmured.

He shuddered to ask, "How much did we share?"

"Only fragments. A small subset we keep close to the surface, to maintain the continuity of identity, to remind us of who we are. They form an index to the self. We didn't truly unify. However much of me is in you now will all disappear within hours, and vice versa. We'll forget it like a dream."

"If we had fully—"

"If we had fully unified, we would have ceased to be ourselves," she said. "Our memories would have been completely synchronized, and we wouldn't be separate people anymore. But I am Danae. I'm not Alexei. You're still just yourself."

"I'm . . . yes." He tried to keep from staring at her: suddenly she looked so different to him. He kept shuddering from the eerie déjà vu that washed through him at the sound of her voice. "You're not . . . you're not a woman, are you? Inside, you're both genders. I mean— not both. *All.*"

She sighed deeply. "It's very complicated. Through unity, I've learned a measure of conscious control over my own gender identity. Under the circumstances of my exile, and given how people perceive me, it's been . . . expedient, to call myself a woman. To think of myself as one, for the sake of blending in. But you—" She gritted her teeth against the pain when she rolled over to face him. "You can't kill? Since that mission to Antarka, you can barely even bring yourself to knowingly *hurt* anyone, can you?"

Alexei shivered. He clenched his teeth and felt the rusty floor beneath him. He said nothing.

"You saw something," she said. "During your breakdown, after you killed all those people. You're afraid you saw God. That giant eye in the sky you think is following you." She stopped and listened for him to respond, but heard nothing but the ringing in her ears. "You agreed to help us . . . because you thought it would get you killed? Because you wanted to kill yourself, but your military conditioning wouldn't let you?"

"The Major—" Alexei stammered. A twitch in his body scraped his chains across the floor. "I couldn't betray him. Not now. Not ever."

"The Major who made you a child soldier, you mean. He's the one who betrayed *you*. My God. More than you'll ever know. He took your life before it had even begun, and you took his name as your own? You think of him as a hero. No, worse: like some kind of father figure. But he was the farthest thing from either."

"He was the only—" he began, but never finished.

They lay on their sides in silence for a long time, seeing nothing. The air between them began to rapidly heat as the desert sun dawned on the metal-walled compartment.

Finally he whispered, "You've killed too. In Asher Valley, five years ago. That's why you ran and stayed separated from your . . . your other selves. No, that's not the right way to say it, is it? You're trying to go back to rejoin *the rest of* yourself. You'd rather die than stay separate from it any longer. But you think it won't take you back, because you killed a man." He squinted. "One man."

"One murder is all it takes to be a murderer."

Both lay silent then with some version of the same thought: that Danae's one killing had contained more malice than all of Alexei's hundreds combined. To her, that hate multiplied her guilt a hundredfold. To him, it sounded like a mitigating factor; there was something so much worse, he thought, about taking a life without feeling, without personal stake.

She started to tell him that without Naoto she had no reason left to go on at all, but the only sound she managed to make was his name—and when it hung in the air between them it silenced them both, and they could only lie there on the truck's metal floor, two different people physically overwhelmed by a single grief.

ALEXEI

Daylight stung my eyes and shocked me awake when the door swung open. A figure climbed inside and stood there looming. It was . . . me. Another me. Its expression was utterly dispassionate, like the embodied ghost of all my misdeeds. For a moment I wondered if I was dreaming, hallucinating, or still lost somewhere in the cybernetic fugue I'd shared with Danae—but when my eyes adjusted, I saw Jenna, wearing my coat and armor.

"Rise and shine," she grunted. She trained a wave pistol on us as she stepped in and knelt to press a finger to Naoto's neck. She sniffled and grimaced and flipped open an air vent on the ceiling before stumbling back out into the light.

"Where are you taking us?" Danae croaked.

She paused just before shutting the doors again. She told us matter-of-factly, "Duke sure wants you bad. Never seen a bounty that high. Normally I'd say you really lucked out, but, well. Depends on what the Medusas want you for, doesn't it."

The doors shut. The bolt locked. Somewhere the motors hummed to life.

A few bands of sunlight blazed through the vent Jenna had opened, and in its ambience I could see Danae's despair when she turned to me and said, "We have to get out of here."

"Unless your twelve thousand years of memory includes a technique for hacking electronic locking shackles without tools . . . I have no suggestions."

The floor beneath us rumbled with the broken desert road.

"We can't let Duke take me alive," she pleaded.

I remembered the last words Duke had said to me. "My death won't be any quicker than yours."

"That's not what I'm talking about. If Duke manages to reverse-engineer the nanobots in my nervous system, he'll turn them into a new generation of Gray weapons, a thousand times more deadly than anything he already has. He'll be free to liquefy any city he likes without fear of counter-attack. We can't let that happen." She swallowed hard. "If I die, my nanobots will all self-terminate. It's the only way to keep them out of his hands."

She was asking me to kill her, I realized—but she could read me now just as clearly as I could her, and she knew without my saying it that there was nothing I could do. I reached out haltingly for her throat—but it was viscerally clear to me, even before my fingertips perceived the heat of her skin, that I didn't have it in me to squeeze. I still couldn't hurt anyone.

She lowered her eyes to stare at the side of my neck. At the twisted-wire pendant that still hung there.

The motors roared louder under us, filling my skull with their white noise.

All was lost.

It wasn't a long wait before the truck jerked to a halt again. The motors died, and I could hear the creak of the cab doors and the crunch of boots in the earth.

"Are you awake?" Danae whispered quickly. "I have to tell you something. Something I realized as soon as I woke up here."

"What?"

"I knew you before."

"What do you mean? Before what?"

"You know what I am," she whispered to me. "I'm the sum of many people. Many different lives and memories. I've had many names and faces that were not this one. And one of them . . . one of the people I was, and still *am*—"

"Eryn," I heard myself say. *Eryn.* I twisted, searching for her in the dark, wanting desperately to see her now—but all I could make out was a dim glimmer of light on her eyes in the pitch black.

"I remember the night I gave you that. I remember you now. Our promise."

"Eryn!"

The doors were thrown open, and two people climbed in to heave us one by one into the blazing late-afternoon sun. The hot sand stung in my wounds. All I could think of was wishing they would turn me so I could see her.

The bounty hunters stood over us. Jenna lit a cigarette with a shaking hand and said, "Well, honored guests, we hope you've enjoyed your stay with us, but all good things must come to an end."

"Give it a rest," somebody said. "They're here."

"We got a plan for this exchange?" somebody asked. "They're not going to be happy about the brain-dead one."

Jenna flicked her barely smoked cigarette away and glared at them all in turn. "You want a plan? Shut your ugly faces and let me do the talking. Wavers primed, safeties off. That's the plan."

I could barely bend my neck to see anything. I heard another vehicle skid to a halt on the sandy ground. Doors opening. I could just barely make out three blurry silhouettes, about ten meters away.

"That's close enough," Jenna said. "Squid. Now."

I held my breath and listened hard, and in the windy distance I heard another woman's voice. "Do I look *that* stupid to you, chum? I inspect the merchandise. I see it's intact. I verify it's the same merchandise I came here to buy. Then I pay."

That voice sounded vaguely familiar, but before I could place it my thoughts were scattered by the concretely familiar sensation of a wave pistol's emitter being pressed against the side of my head.

"Don't push us, fish-fucker," Jenna shouted. "Even if we didn't have you and your thugs outgunned, Duke put out an eight-figure bounty on these people, *alive*. That makes me think he wants them pretty bad. Bad enough that you'll be in a real tight spot with your boss if you screw up this hand-off, and we have to toast their heads right here in front of you. Follow me? Cash! Now!"

"We do want them *pretty bad*," said the Medusan woman, mocking their inland accents. "Bad enough that we'll lower ourselves to coming out here. Not bad enough that we intend to let you stick us with just any three sorry fuckers you found to fit the description. Give me some shred of proof that these are the people we're after, and that they're alive. Otherwise we walk, and you stay poor."

An unbearable silence set in. I swallowed hard and twisted for a better look.

"Fine," Jenna finally said. "Knock yourself out. Just you! Your goons stand back."

The pistol lifted from my head. Footsteps crunched carefully toward us until a shadow fell over my eyes again. I squinted up into the formless black silhouette that knelt over me.

"*Still kicking?*" she asked me—and when she eclipsed the sun, I saw her in the flesh for only the second time in my life.

"The night is young," I whispered back.

I stifled a cry of relief. I heard Danae do the same in perfect symmetry behind me: she knew as clearly as I did what was about to happen.

Kat Mandu cleared her throat and straightened up, resuming her performance. "Okay. I'm satisfied. Money. Getting the money now."

"Hurry up," Jenna barked. "You think I don't see you whispering to your henchmen there? Push me a little farther and see what happens."

I heard a rover door swinging open and closed.

"Look, I'm fine, you're fine, everything is fine," Kat said. "Here's your payment. I'll just. . . ." She trailed off.

"What is that?" Jenna murmured.

From somewhere I heard the sound of another set of tires in the gravel.

"I said what the fuck is that?" Jenna demanded.

"I could ask you the same thing!" Kat yelled. Her question was a deception, but her panic was real. It could only be the real Medusas.

"Stay back!"

Rough hands thrust into my armpits and dragged me hurriedly behind the cover of the bounty hunters' truck, ignoring my groans when my wounds scraped on the ground. From where they set me down, I was able to squint past the truck's undercarriage at the incoming rover, painted with the purple and red insignia of Medusa Clan. It rolled up and jerked to a halt twenty meters away. I waited. Everyone waited, but the rover didn't move.

"Who the fuck is that?" one of the hunters hissed behind my back. "What are they waiting for?"

The doors opened, and two Medusas stepped out into the searing light—but my despair gave way to confusion as more figures climbed out after him. One wore a business suit and a hat and looked very out of place in this desert. Another was a wastelander with mercenary gear, short and bald. Then there was a teenage boy. Their five faces were all emotionless—somehow eerily so.

Then they all smiled, identically.

They weren't Medusas. Somehow I knew that, and I wanted to be relieved, but something in my gut was screaming that this was wrong—that this was somehow even worse. That smile was like a half-remembered nightmare.

"*No,*" I heard Danae gasp. "Oh no. Not him."

"What the fuck is this?" Jenna shouted out.

The man in the suit said, "Is she here?" His voice was perfectly placid. It made me shiver.

"I said *who are you?*"

He ignored the question. One of the Medusas at his side said, "It is not in my nature to kill, but I cannot allow you to take Sybil from me."

"We can't allow that," the other four strangers agreed in a muttering, uneven unison.

"Who the fuck are you?"

The short man went back to the rover and reached inside. He calmly pulled out a 300-millimeter shoulder-mounted anti-tank wave cannon and opened fire on both sides of the transaction.

One of Kat's bodyguards was struck directly in the first volley. To say simply that he exploded would do no justice what happened. In the space of a millisecond, his body blossomed from the inside out into a living shockwave—every molecule of water flashed to steam at once, every cell membrane and fiber of clothing frayed apart molecule by molecule, converted into flame, and propelled at high velocity in all directions at once. The force of his detonation cracked the windshield of the rover he was running to and shook the sand in all directions with a deep, resonant thud. Nothing remained of him above his knees.

The shooter never so much as paused to observe the horrific spectacle he'd unleashed. He continued raining electromagnetic fury on anything in sight, while the man in the suit laid down suppressing fire with a rifle and the others primed their pistols. I heard the crack of metal rapidly expanding on the wall of the bounty hunters' truck and saw one of them fall dead or dying from the reflected heat alone. Doc caught a stray beam refracting through the cab windows and fell to the ground, screaming and clutching his scalded hands while his comrades worked to smother the small fires on his coat. Rays of fatal, invisible heat seemed to come from everywhere and everything. Metal deformed. Plastic splattered and hissed. Hairs crisped. Flesh blistered. Nowhere was safe.

"Six," I counted the whistling shots under my breath. "Seven . . . eight."

That was it. The gun's mammoth fuel cells were exhausted and spewing chemical fumes. The bald man heaved a simple sigh and dropped the cannon, and then all five of the strangers leveled their weapons and advanced in an even line.

Everything devolved into total chaos. Kat and her remaining bodyguard, and the three bounty hunters not already dead or immobilized, all opened fire on each other and the strangers at once with mutual and adrenaline-soaked bloodlust. The strangers continued their impossibly calm advance. The man in the suit took a direct shot to the head and fell; his comrades glanced briefly back at the body and continued unflinchingly on. I lost sight of everyone. I could only listen to the rising cacophony of waver shrieks amid the varied sounds of human agony and death. Danae was somewhere behind me, straining against her shackles. I heard her shouting:

"No! Not you. It can't be you!"

"I've come to save you," said a calm voice. "Just relax. I'll rescue you."

"Luther, stop!"

I tried and failed to turn myself around to see her. "What's happening? Danae? Danae!"

I heard her words devolve into cries. I heard rhythmic scraping in the sand. I arched my back despite the pain and tried to roll over to see her, to see anything at all, but I couldn't.

Her sobbing became quieter and farther away, until finally two of the calm strangers dragged her back into my field of view: the boy, joined by one of the Medusas. The latter caught a shot in the back and fell dead, but the boy hefted her up into his arms and went on carrying her unsteadily back to the rover.

I squinted in disbelief. He had a waver burn on his side, next to his kidney: not an immediately lethal wound, but it should have been more than painful enough to debilitate. He barely seemed to notice the blood soaking through his clothes. He just lifted her into the passenger seat, shut the door, and took the wheel. The rover skidded away into the wastes.

The shooting had stopped. The only sounds were a low chorus of groans, and a single voice calling my name.

"I'm here," I yelled. "I'm right here."

Kat dropped her rifle when she found me. She turned me over and knelt to face me, and the panic in her eyes faded into relief. Joy. What I could not help but recognize, however strangely, as love. She laughed and sniffled and wiped her eyes.

"You're shot," I said.

She glanced at the circle of burnt cloth in the middle of her chest and said, "Plates caught it. Come on. Let's blow this popsicle stand."

Even though Danae's memories of Naoto were fading in my mind, I couldn't bring myself to leave his body behind. Over Kat's protests, I made sure we wrapped him in a tarp and lifted him into the rover's trunk.

"Anything else you want to take with you?" she demanded irritably—and when I said no, she gunned the motors and sent the scene of carnage rapidly receding into the desert behind us.

"We have to follow them," I groaned through the pain. Every connective tissue in my body was still stiff from the rocket strike and the hours in shackles. I did my best to treat my own injuries while Kat drove—gasping as I wrenched a metal shard out of my forearm.

It only then dawned on me that my wave rifle was gone. For seven years, its cedar-paneled grip with the Major's initials had never once been out of reach of my right hand. I'd walked with it, slept next to it, hung it from the curtain rod of any shower I'd washed in. I didn't even know where it lay now: shrinking in the rearview mirror, or in the smashed remains of Jannison's APC. I didn't need to know.

"You want me to follow *who*?" Kat said. "Oh, do you mean the Medusan rover being driven by the teenage cyborg with the big-ass wave cannon? That's who you want me to follow right now?"

"He's not a cyborg."

Kat grimaced. There was something on the cracked windshield, something small, pink and round. Part of an ear. She pressed a switch and the wiper blades flicked it away. "Then who were they? What kind of non-augmented human person can take that many waver burns and go on walking like everything's peachy?"

"He's . . ." I trailed off. I didn't know the answer. I'd only ever held a small sample of Danae's memories, and even that was fading quickly, just as she'd said it would—but she knew exactly what he was, and she'd been frozen stiff with fear.

"He has Danae," I said. "He has my client."

"Lex." Kat looked hard at me. "I came here to save you. From what, I didn't even know. From *you*. Take one look at yourself and tell me I was wrong. *I'm* shot? Jesus. You look like you've been shot with a fucking anti-tank rocket."

I turned to give her a look, but through her almost-joking facade, I saw the water in her eyes, and I knew she was only marginally holding herself together. She was worried about me. If any part of my life was flashing before my eyes now, it was all the years I had known Kat—and in all that time, I'd never been able to imagine that she might give me a look like this one, caring so much about me, broken to think of just letting me die. The man I had been then had had no idea.

"No, you're in no condition to fight," she said, turning back to the road and stiffening up. "Not even a against weird kid with a lethal wound. You're not well. Besides which, I dropped everything to come out here into meatspace—which I *do not do*—putting my own ass on

228 - ELLY BANGS

the line, spending my last and best backdoor into the Medusas' network just to find out the bounty exchange location, and ultimately sacrificing not one but *two* extremely expensive hired guns, all for the sake of extracting you from this mission—"

"Kat!" I shouted.

She turned the wheel to narrowly avoid a boulder and then continued, "—one of whom, I might add, *literally exploded* right in front of me, and that's something I'll never be able to un-see. All of this to pull you out! And now you want to dive right back in? You expect me to let you do that? Fuck. We'll be lucky if we even make it back to Bloom City in one piece. Lucky if there's still a city there by the time we do."

Ahead of us, the east-west trade road pulled into focus. To the left it would take us back to Greenglass Mountain and thereby, eventually, to the coast. To the right it meandered on into the deeper parts of the scorched lands once known as Arizona, now the jagged fringe of the Holy Western Confederacy.

"You're right," I said. "I'm not well. There's a lot I need to tell you, and I promise I will. Everything. But to start with, something did happen to me in Antarka. It changed me, and I can't undo it. I can't go back to being who I was before that, and I don't know whether who I am now can live with who I was then."

Kat braked just shy of the fork, her gaze fixed dead ahead. She closed her eyes, listening to me. Her hands were quivering slightly on the wheel. Fearfully, experimentally, I reached out and touched her shoulder with my bleeding fingers, and the contact shocked us both: in all the years we had known each other, we had never physically touched.

"You can't die," she said, her voice creaking. "I can't let you die."

"I've killed so many people. Men, women, children, animals. It's all I've ever known."

"Well, maybe this says something terrible about me, but you're the only other person I've ever cared about."

I took a moment to hear those words. I let them all the way in.

"Then . . . help me finish this," I said. "After this, I'm done. I'll come with you, if you want me to. If there's a world left tomorrow, we can find a corner of it for ourselves, where the Medusas can't find us. Just let me finish this one last job."

She didn't wipe away the tears this time. She said, "Finishing this job, finding your client. Tell me. No bullshit. If you do this, will you be okay again?"

I hesitated. I looked down at all my bruises and lacerations, the fresh scabs over half-treated shrapnel wounds. I said, "I know I'm beyond help if I don't try."

She shook her head.

I asked her, "Are you with me?"

Kat's knuckles were white on the steering wheel. She blinked and drew a deep breath. She took her foot off the brake, composed herself, and said, "Till the bitter end. How do you want to play this?"

"He's going northeast," I said. I focused as hard as I could on the last traces of Danae's memory, burning the information into my mind, not letting it erase itself. I said, "I think I know where he's taking her."

DANAE

It took me a while to grasp that this was all really happening—that it was really Luther sitting right there beside me, wearing someone else's hollowed-out body, seventy-odd years since I'd started running from him and everything he represented. I'd spent so long trying to soothe myself with the assumption that he was dead, and now he was here. Now we were here together.

"Sybil," he called. He kept repeating it. "Sybil. Sybil."

"That hasn't been my name," I murmured, "in a very long time."

My shock had given way to numbness. I stared at the thick metal shackles still locked onto my wrists and ankles.

"I've waited so long for this moment. You have no idea. Ever since the night we parted, I've been trying to find my way back to you. It's all I've thought about." His every word made me shudder: I could still recognize his cadence and intonation. I could hear the same mind speaking through that teenage boy's throat.

"Seventy years," I whispered.

"Seventy-two years, nine months, eight days, fourteen hours," he rattled off. "I'd almost given up all hope when I found you. Thank God I found you. You can help me. You can save me. You'll make everything okay again. Yes, you'll see."

There was red in the corner of my eye, and I unthinkingly turned to stare at the waver burn in the side of his abdomen. Blood from the imperfectly cauterized wound ran steadily down his hip and puddled on the seat cushion.

He caught me staring before I could look away. He picked idly at the raw flesh and examined the color of blood on his perversely young fingers before returning his attention to the road.

"That looks painful," I said.

"Fatal, most likely, but irrelevant. I only need this flesh for a little while longer. It's just a means to an end. It wouldn't have served my purposes for much longer anyway."

"You don't feel that?"

He ignored the question. "I rescued you. I saved you. I had to, at any cost. My God, what a high cost."

"You're holding me captive."

"No, Sybil, no." The frantic energy dropped out of his voice and left it eerily placid. The face he was wearing was still growing its first beard, and I shuddered when he turned it toward me and said, "I love you. I've always loved you."

"Then let me go."

He stopped talking. He shifted uneasily in his seat and knitted his brow. "I can't. I . . . I need you. I can't exist without you. You can help me. You can save me. You don't understand yet, but you will soon."

"It's too late. I can't save you."

"Yes you can. *Yes*, you *can*."

"Where are you taking me?"

He gestured out across the empty rocks and sand. "Don't you recognize it? I'm taking you home, to where we met."

"It's not there anymore. It's just ruins."

He barely registered my words. "It's so auspicious that I should find you here, so close to where we both began. It's fate, I think. Everything's finally come full circle. Everything is really going to be okay."

"Listen to me. Stop this thing and let me out. I'm asking as someone who once called you a friend. As someone you claim to love. Let me go."

He shook his head. "All this talking won't be necessary soon. We won't need language once we finally unify, like we were meant to."

My heart nearly stopped. "Unify."

He nodded. "Like we were meant to. It's the obvious solution."

My head was a morass of useless wishes. I wished I was anywhere but here. I wished the explosion had left me with enough strength to try to fight him, even with my wrists and ankles bound; if not for my injuries, I might have had a chance. I wished all the way back to Asher Valley, fixating on the thought that if only it had been one of my more masculine bodies that had escaped alive to find itself here, at least the roles would be different. At least he wouldn't be looking at me that way—the same way, through someone else's eyes, that he had seventy-two years ago, and ever since then in my nightmares.

In the distance I saw the skeletal remains of the road sign that had once marked the way to Sybil's long-abandoned alma mater, and I felt the motors decelerate. I was running out of time.

There had to be some way out of this. Some way to get out of these shackles, or delay Luther long enough for him to pass out from blood loss.

I needed more time. I had to keep him talking.

"If you're going to . . . to unify us—" my stomach clenched as I said this— "maybe we should take this opportunity to talk to each other while we still can."

"I've missed talking to you too," he said. "You have no idea how much I've missed it. But words are such a clumsy medium, don't you agree? What could we possibly say to each other that wouldn't be more elegant to share directly?"

I thought of asking him how he'd been, and where, but I was afraid to know the answers. I couldn't find it in myself to pretend that nothing had changed between us since I'd so naïvely called him a brother. I couldn't look away from the wounds on his side. He kept reflexively scratching them, making them bleed more and more effusively.

"That's what you meant, isn't it," I said, staring at the blood. "That's what you think I'll save you from."

He looked surprised to notice himself worrying at the burns. He pulled his hand away and wiped the mess off on the knee of his pants. He spoke rapidly, in his characteristic way, as if his mouth were struggling to keep pace with his brain. "Habitual use of our unifier seems to have yielded some long-term side effects that weren't predicted by our original models. At first, I assumed it was a biological problem, but moving into new flesh has no effect. I now think the condition must arise from some sort of . . . iterative transcription error, but all my attempts to understand the exact nature of the degradation have come to dead ends."

"You don't feel any pain?"

He blinked slowly. "It's more like I feel *something*, intensely and constantly, but I can't discern specific sensations from the noise. I've spent decades trying to understand and treat the condition. I've exhausted every avenue of research that I can imagine by myself, but once I have access to your perspective as well as my own—"

"I knew the moment I saw your wounds."

He tilted slightly to the side in surprise, exactly the way he used to. "You knew what, exactly?"

"Which shortcuts you must have taken when you hacked our prototype. Which elements of your consciousness were lost when you first possessed Jackson."

Luther squinted in thought. "Nothing was lost. My memory is intact. Test after test has verified that."

"But I'm not talking about memory. There are layers of integration between mind and body that our prototype was never designed to bother with. If you decouple them by force—if you treat consciousness as nothing but data to be downloaded from one medium to another—you get irreversible degeneration of the psyche. Sensory atrophy, eventually progressing all the way to autonomic nervous system depression and death."

He squinted. "It can't be that simple. If that were true, you would have the same problem. You would have devised a cure."

"No. I'm the gestalt of minds from other bodies, but this body has always been mine too. It was mine before unity. That gives me an intact bridge."

He shook his head rapidly. "No, no. You're mistaken. You're leaping to conclusions with incomplete information. I haven't even listed all the symptoms yet. I haven't told you—"

"That you're hypnotized by your own reflection," I finished for him. "That you find it almost paralyzing. I'm sorry, Luther. I can't help you. I'm surprised you've lasted this long."

"No. No, you're trying to deceive me." There was growing agitation in his voice, and he was swerving erratically on the eroded remains of the old road into town. "When we unify, that won't be a problem anymore. Your intellect will be mine too. Deception will be impossible."

"You know that won't work either. Even our crudest simulations could have told you that non-consensual unity is fatal. The shattered consciousness you'd splice us into won't even be stable enough to regulate its own respiration."

"I don't believe you. It's going to work. It has to."

He braked hard: we'd arrived. Here was the last standing wall of

234 · ELLY BANGS

the old student union building. There were the weathered bones of
the lecture hall and the jutting iron ribs of the now-collapsed water
tower. Flashbacks made my head swim.

"It's going to work," he said as he climbed out of the driver's seat.
"I don't understand why you're resisting. It's what you wanted. It's
what we both wanted."

He swung my door open and pulled me out. I fell hard on the
sandy ground. He grabbed the short steel bar that joined my wrists
together and started dragging me toward the nearest building with
one hand. Swinging from his other was the hefty briefcase I hadn't
seen in all these decades: the original unifier prototype we'd built
together.

"Why are you really doing this?" I asked.

"I've told you."

"But you understand how unity works, almost as well as I do. You
already know that if you do this, we'll both die. We'll die horribly."

"You don't understand," he hissed, and he sounded less and less
like the Luther I had known. His voice was almost inhumanly vicious. "You could never understand."

"Understand what?" I cried out over the noise and the pain of my
back dragging on the rocky ground.

"What I *felt!*" he shouted. "What it feels like to love you. What
it felt like to watch you fawn over your imbecile boyfriend while I
rotted from the inside out. You don't know what it is to be so broken."

I shuddered. "There was so much I didn't understand about you
back then. Sybil was naïve, and I was naïve when I was her. But I've
lived hundreds of lives since then, and I've experienced misery and
heartbreak even you couldn't imagine, and I could still never do
what you did. It wasn't pain that made you murder Jackson. It wasn't
love. It was you. It was all just you."

"I do not murder," he corrected. "I merely borrow."

"I loved you, Luther."

He shook his head. "No. I loved you. You loved Jackson."

"I was willing to risk my life to unify with you!" I shouted. "I wanted to share *everything* with you. Every thought and feeling and memory. Every last fucking nerve impulse. I was going to risk burning out every synapse in my head with an unproven technology because it was the only chance you had to survive. That's how much I loved you. If anything, I loved you more than Jackson."

"That . . . doesn't make sense."

"I wanted you to live forever. Through us, through me, no less than Sybil is still part of me now. Not like this. Not by using our creation to murder people and possess their hollowed-out corpses."

He stopped dragging me. He turned and looked down in silent contemplation, lungs heaving with the effort; his face was pale from blood loss, glistening with cold sweat in the harsh white light. For a moment I thought he'd changed his mind. Then he picked me up and hoisted me into a rusted folding chair. We were in the center of what I could just barely recognize as our old workshop, now little more than a ring of broken cinderblocks. He sat down facing me.

"You have no idea what I've gone through," he muttered. "You just don't understand."

Our eyes met in the harsh light and shadow of the crumbled walls.

"Oh, Luther." I stifled a sob. "I understand perfectly. But that doesn't mean I could ever, ever forgive you."

He twitched. He shook his head rapidly. "I'll make you understand," he said. He lifted the heavy briefcase into his lap.

Something changed in him when he opened it. He shifted uncomfortably, and his voice shifted toward the human again to tell me, "This is the only way it could have ended, you know. We have always been each other's unfinished business."

He lifted the crown out of the case and set it on my head, aligning the first probe on the scalp above my ear. I clenched my jaw as its sensor filament snapped pneumatically through the bone and into my brain.

My heart was beating faster. I chuckled at myself, perversely, eliciting a curious look from Luther. What did my own life matter anymore? What did I have left but to die, and why should I care how it happened? But when he spoke those words, *unfinished business*, it was suddenly, brutally clear to me: I couldn't think of any way I less wanted to die than this, stitched into the monster Luther had become.

So I did the only think I could think to do: I reached up put my palm softly to his forehead—the way I'd once touched his original head, on his original deathbed, in a room that hadn't been far from here seven decades ago. After a confused moment he twisted out of my reach, but it was done. The nanobots were in his system now—waiting for my command.

"I won't allow you to do this," I said.

He aligned the second probe. *Snap.* He ignored me.

"I have the power to stop you," I said, louder. "Please don't make me use it."

His hands paused amid the tangle of wires he was plugging into the crown on his own head. He squinted at me doubtfully and said, "How?"

"I can engage the first stage of the link at the same moment you do, with my own unifier. The shock will kill one or both of us before the first engram transcription can complete."

I wasn't bluffing, although there was something I knew better than to mention: the timing would have to be extraordinarily precise. If I engaged my side of the link a fraction of a second early or late, it would be for nothing.

"But you have no unifier."

"It's part of me," I said. "Self-replicating nanoscale cybernetics."

He stared. "Where are the probes? How do you connect?"

I shuddered guiltily. "I introduced the nanobots into your cerebrum. All I need is a few seconds of skin contact. After that the link is wireless."

He shook his head and fitted the last two probes into place on my scalp. *Snap.* "Implausible. You're trying to deceive me again."

"It's true," I pleaded. "I've spent hundreds of aggregate years refining the technology. Finding ways to make it maximally noninvasive."

He ignored me. "I'm begging you not to let it end this way, Luther. Whatever you've done, whatever you've become, I don't want to hurt you. If any part of you is still . . ." *snap* ". . . human. If you're still the young man I once loved, you won't make me do this."

The prototype unifier was in his lap, running through its start-up routines, scanning both of us. I could see his thumb hovering over the activation switch. There was a look coming over him as he hunched over it, breathing heavily. His fingers shook in vicious ecstasy. I thought I could see his mouth watering.

"It's too late," he said, and grinned as the lights turned green to signal their readiness. "I'm not him anymore."

I looked into his eyes in the moment before he pressed the switch, and in that last fleeting millisecond before the link engaged, the rising electrical fray in my cortex presented me with a hallucination:

His eyes had ceased to be human eyes. They became narrow slits cut into dark red irises, and his face around them became a fever dream of gaping pores and black spines. The prototype was part of him, woven into his monstrous body, and the wire stalk from each of the four probes had become like a mosquito's proboscis on his face: each one quivering and outstretched toward me, retracting its sheath to expose the toothed syringe within. In that last instant, I could feel him seeing himself as I saw him—seeing himself through my own sensorium—and he noticed that, for the first time in many years, he was not shocked or repulsed by his own image, but rather thought that it was right.

ALEXEI

The silhouette of a skeletal town finally cohered in the hazy distance, and I shivered in eerie recognition: it was like seeing in waking life what I knew I had already seen in dreams. I didn't even know the name of this place, but I'd known instinctively that it was where we'd find them, and there they were: Danae and the young stranger, slumped in folding chairs, facing each other.

I yelled her name. I jumped down from the rover and started for them, but Kat stopped me with a firm hand on my chest. She kept her wave pistol raised and primed as we crept closer, and I saw the tangles of cable drawn between their heads, swinging in the darkening sandy wind. Nothing else moved.

"What the hell is that?" Kat whispered anxiously.

I pushed past her to examine the scene.

I checked both their pulses. "He's dead. You can relax."

Kat gave me a look. She kept her waver primed.

I knelt at Danae's side. Her breath and heartbeat were both slow and regular, but her eyes stayed closed. I looked more closely at the metal ring attached to her head. One by one, I pressed the four small release levers and felt them snap free of the bone beneath them, and as I pulled them away, I could see and feel the translucent threads, fine as spider silk, trailing from the small puncture wounds.

Kat grimaced and retched.

"Help me get her shackles off," I said.

"Lex, do not do that." Her fingers only tightened around her gun's grip. "If what you told me is true—"

"What?"

"Then we don't know who's inside that body now! If she wakes up, we don't know *who's* waking up, do we?"

The cranial probes lay in a tangle in the weathered concrete under my knees. Tiny beads of blood and cerebrospinal fluid glistened in the sinking sun, gathering dust from the wind. I closed my eyes and leaned my head against the rusted folding chair.

"We can't just leave her," I managed to say.

I heard Kat draw a deep breath and deprime her pistol. "The cuffs stay on."

Kat drove while I sat in the back seat with Danae, attending to all the injuries I could see and understand.

"I don't know if you can hear me," I said. "We're close to Redhill. We'll be there in minutes. That's where your people are, right?"

Her hand twitched briefly inside the gauze I was wrapping around it, as if she were dreaming.

"No, not your people," I corrected myself. "You. It's the rest of you."

She gave no sign she could hear me.

A single drop of blood trickled from the tiny puncture in the side of her forehead. I found a sealant patch and pressed it there, but it felt useless. Kat was right: we had no idea what the real wound was— what those needle-thin marks signified. I could only stare at her all-but-lifeless body and dread to imagine what was going on behind her eyelids, or whether she was still there at all.

I couldn't stop thinking about the stranger. I kept instinctively reaching for the memory of who he was, who he had ever been, but it wasn't there anymore. My grief over Naoto had similarly faded, and I felt as hollow inside without it as Danae looked, slumping against the slit window.

"Any news about the war?" I asked Kat—reaching instinctively for something even worse to think about.

She twisted her hands nervously on the steering wheel. "They didn't break out the really nasty cyberwarfare until last night, but now it's on every satellite in the sky, either to snatch them up for war business or just shut them down. Every piece of nodespace hardware I have left"—she motioned vaguely at the piles of electronics strewn around the cab—"is trying to brute-force its way through all that, but the bandwidth is shit out here, and so far I can't break through. I haven't heard any news since this morning."

"How did it look this morning?"

Her reflection in the windshield visibly tensed, and her voice cracked to say, "Not good, Lex."

I put my hand on her shoulder, and she held it back.

"We must be inside ten klicks of your destination," she said. "I don't suppose you know which of all these *red hills* is the specific one she wants?"

The landscape spread around us now was like no place I'd ever seen, though it resembled my imagination of the surface of Mars. The broken road had snaked out of the open desert and into a valley walled by mesas and buttes: mountain-sized fingers and toes sticking up out of the sandy earth; klick after klick of increasingly odd formations of striated stone, the colors of rust and blood, glowing ominously in the last sunlight.

Kat squinted into the heads-up display. "This whole area seems totally deserted. We haven't passed a single sign of recent settlement or picked up any artificial heat or electromag since we left the trade road. If there's anyone else out here, they're real good at hiding. Any ideas?"

I watched the map trace and retrace itself in holographic light, but it was nothing but lines and curves to me. I shook my head.

"We're running on empty," Kat said bitterly. "If there's nothing here, we're boned."

It was hard enough for me to wrap my head around what the rest of Danae's unified being was. I had no idea what it would look like. I stared ahead into the surreal landscape, searching for anything at all besides sand and rock.

The hairs on the back of my neck stood up. Something was watching me. I turned and saw what it was.

Danae's eyes were open, staring at me. Blank, emotionless, empty.

I said her name, but it sounded like a question: *Are you still you?*

Hearing it, she blinked slowly. Her eyes seemed to search the air in front of her for the answer, until finally she nodded as if to say yes—but the motion was unsteady, tinged with visible dread. She balled the thin blanket in her fists and cringed hard. *Yes,* her body language replied *but.*

"What happened?" I asked. I grabbed my shard and ran Kat's exploit program to unlock Danae's cuffs, not bothering to ask Kat's permission.

"I killed him," Danae said. "I killed Luther. But not before . . ." She trailed off.

I saw her trembling, coming apart. I shouldn't have asked, but I couldn't stop myself. "Not before what?"

"We did unify. For a fraction of a second. It wasn't a full unity. There wasn't enough time for all of him to cross over. Only a small fragment, surface-level memories of the past few days, but that fragment of him is . . . it's part of me now, and I—"

She started to dry heave. I found an empty food package in the back seat and helped her hold it long enough to vomit up whatever little she'd eaten in the past day. I gave her water, though we didn't have much left.

"It's going to be part of me forever," Danae stammered. "He bombed Bloom City. He killed so many people."

Kat was watching us nervously in the rearview mirror. "Was he acting alone? There's a lot of details around Dahlia's death that don't add up, and inquiring minds want to know."

"Yes, he—" Danae turned to answer, but the view through the windshield seemed to startle her. "We're . . . we're near Redhill?"

I nodded.

"Stop this thing," she said. "Please. Stop here and turn around."

Kat and I exchanged looks. She started to decelerate.

"I said get us out of here," Danae said, more forcefully. She looked hard at me and said, "It's over. You've done your job. Just take me to the nearest settlement, I don't care which. Anywhere in the world but here."

"Look, lady," Kat said, slamming on the brakes and craning her neck to face her. "Lady, person, people, whatever. We bled our fuel cells dry getting all the way out here. It's two hundred klicks to the nearest other human being. We couldn't go back if we wanted to."

"No," Danae said. She buried her eyes in her hands. "I'm sorry.

If I had been conscious, I would have told you not to come here. I never would have said to come here."

Kat punched the steering wheel, and the horn blared out her frustration.

"No one who's taken a human life may ever unify," she said solemnly. "It's the unbreakable rule, and I broke it. I was going to bring Naoto here to unify for me, but I got him killed. So that's it for me. It's over. There's nothing left."

The sun was on its way down between the towers of rock. The wind whistled over the shadow-bathed landscape, and clouds of red sand were thickening the air and prematurely snuffing out the last light.

"No," I said. "I don't believe that. You still need to go home."

She looked at me, wanting to disagree—but I summoned up the last traces of her mind left inside mine, and let it speak for me:

"You'd already committed to coming here, before you had any idea Naoto was coming with you. You found out he wanted to unify, and you wanted it for him, and that made him like a proxy for *you*, but . . ." I swallowed and tried to hold my voice steady. "I've felt your need as if it was my own. Even if you can never reunify, even if you're afraid to so much as be seen, you still need to go back to the rest of you."

She curled slowly into a ball on the seat, hiding her face behind her knees—and I could tell by the way she drew in and held a deep breath that she was focusing on the smell of the air in that canyon, remembering things in its flavor. Finally she wiped her blood-crusted face on her hand and nodded.

"You're right," she croaked. "I need to go home."

Kat sneered and said, "Lucky you, 'cause without a refill of water and energy, none of us are leaving here alive. If anyone or anything is out here, we need its help." She put her hands together in mock-prayer and added, "And its nodespace bandwidth, if at all possible."

Danae stared blankly out the windshield and nodded hollowly. "It's the smaller butte, with the domed base. Two o'clock. We'll find the rest of me at the summit. Here for the equinox."

The route wasn't obvious, but Danae led us up the rock with the agility of someone who knew its shape by heart. Still, it was a slow climb: she was hesitant; I was walking on a wounded leg; and Kat was so unaccustomed to exerting herself in physical reality that she could barely catch her breath. I was still realizing the magnitude of the sacrifice she'd made in merely coming here.

Danae stopped just short of the peak, just shy of a series of steps hewn into the sheer rockface. She sat on a ledge and stared down across the barren plain below. Dusty wind whistled around us and the sun was only a red spark at the top of the nearest butte. The temperature was dropping.

We looked at each other in the copper light. I felt like there were a thousand things I needed to say to her and ask her, but I had no words. Finally she stood and climbed the last distance, and Kat and I followed.

The top of the rock spread out before us, empty. There was nothing here. Not even footprints in the years of accumulated dust.

"This can't be." Danae hurried in circles of the peak, peering down every ledge in turn, muttering to the bare rocks. "This is the place. This is the time."

"How do you contact them?" Kat asked.

"I don't. I can't."

Kat rubbed the bridge of her nose. "Are you saying you never called ahead? You never even made sure they would be here?"

Danae paced the empty stone. "I've been out of contact with the rest of me for years. I tried before we left Bloom, as soon as I knew I wanted to come back, but the channels I used before don't work anymore. It shouldn't have been necessary. This is the place where I always brought all my bodies back together, every year on the vernal equinox. This is where all the branches rejoin. They should all be here. I don't understand. Where are they?"

244 - ELLY BANGS

"Could the whole have chosen a different site?" I offered. "Some-where easier to get to."

"This place means too much to me. This is the exact spot where the very first unity took place. The rest of me wouldn't just abandon it. Never."

The wind picked up, blasting dust in our faces. I raised my hand to shield my eyes, but through my bleary vision, I could see her stand-ing motionless, silhouetted against the twilight.

"Something terrible has happened," she said.

Kat tapped me on the shoulder.

"What?"

"Do you see it too?" she asked.

I followed her gaze and saw nothing—but I began to perceive a nothingness in front of us that did not belong there. A wave of sandy wind was whistling sharply up the ledge on the far side of the rock, and in the dying light I could just make out a volume of space, about two meters in diameter, that the red dust seemed to be flying *around* instead of *through*.

The void had a shape. A sphere.

An eye.

Oh God.

"*It's Him*," I whispered.

Kat watched quizzically as I stumbled backward. She caught me just before I backed off the ledge. My body was stiff with fear. My heart thudded on my eardrums. I wanted to scream but I couldn't find the breath, and the eye was coming closer, bearing down on us. Now I could make out the rim of its iris, the bottomless pit of its pupil, burning through me like a waver beam, and I was gripped again by that electric paralysis I had felt on the ice fields of Antarka, as if it was about to reach directly into my chest and rip—

Kat whipped out her pistol and shot it.

An arc of electricity snapped brilliantly across the rock, and for a split-second the thing became solid and real before blinking back into nothingness. When it was gone, I struggled to understand the ghost image seared into my vision: it had been a machine. It had had panels, moving parts that looked almost like clockwork, inlaid with fine glowing patterns of circuitry, bunches of needle-thin antennae, sensors, feelers; a cluster of inset lenses that only incidentally resembled the pupil of an eye.

And it hadn't been looking at me.

It had been staring directly at Danae.

As my vision cleared, I saw her freeze. Someone was standing there in the dusk on the far side of the rock.

I couldn't guess at the stranger's gender. Their face was partially obscured by a semi-reflective visor, and they were sheathed in a formless gray cloak that totally obscured the body underneath.

Kat was fighting with her pistol. It had powered down on its own and refused to prime again, no matter how hard she hit it. When she realized it was futile, all four of us stood perfectly still. Even the wind seemed to have gone suddenly, deafeningly silent around the rock.

"Who are you?" the stranger asked.

Danae was trembling. She held her arms slightly out, as if fearfully offering herself up for inspection.

"Don't you recognize me?" she asked.

"It *is* you. Me. Alive?"

They stepped tentatively closer to each other. The visitor peeled back the hood of their cloak and took down their visor, revealing their piercing gray eyes.

"It's me," Danae said.

"All these years. I saw you coming, but I didn't believe it. I was certain only one of my bodies made it out of Asher Valley alive."

"What?" Danae gaped. "But I saw the rest of me die. All of me. The church was surrounded on all sides." She tapped her sternum. "This was the only body to escape."

The strange shook their head. "No, think back earlier. You split one body off to go investigate the fire. That body came back to me and reunified. It was . . ." Their body twitched. "How did *you* survive?

Where have you been all this time? Why . . . why didn't you try to contact me?"

Danae stumbled wordlessly forward. She reached for the gray figure and fell into them, clutching at the gray fabric of their cloak, weeping into their shoulder.

"It's okay," the stranger said. "It's over. You're safe. You got here just in time."

The air around them boiled and deformed to swallow them. Before I knew I was even speaking, I called out, "Danae! Wait!"

The gray figure, half-dissolved into the bent air, turned and stared at me—and I knew in my marrow that it was the same cutting gaze I'd felt in Antarka, as tangibly hot as a waver beam. Danae looked back too, speechless and uncertain. Then the liquid fabric of space washed over them both and healed into empty air, leaving Kat and me alone on the empty rock.

Around us in all directions, the lifeless dunes and mesas stretched far away.

Kat put her hands on her hips. "Well, shit."

DANAE

The field was clear and unrefractive, but I could tell we'd been rendered invisible to Alexei and Kat. A faint repulsive force danced across my fingertips at the boundary, and the stinging clouds of rust-colored sand bent around us in flight—but the air inside the bubble was still and clean.

"What is this?" I whispered. "How are you doing this?"

The Whole answered twitchily, "I'm not sure how to explain it. I'm not used to language. I haven't needed it for a long time."

"I don't understand."

"Don't worry, you will. I'll help you."

I tried as hard as I could to choke back the tears, but I couldn't. I felt such a surge of emotion in the warmth of that other body holding mine—in knowing both bodies were mine, and I was really here. I was home.

And yet I could never go home again.

My other self's sharp eyes met my tear-streaked ones. Hands—every crease familiar, every fingerprint whorl once my own—raised toward my head, palms open: offering to unify. I drew back reflexively. I struggled to form the words to confess what I'd done, but my voice stuck in my throat until all I could do was grab those hands and pull them down. My face fell back into that familiar shoulder.

"I'm sorry," the Whole said, smoothing my hair. "Of course. We don't need to do this now. You need time to recover."

I looked back through the bubble at Alexei and Kat and asked, "What about them?"

The Whole of me looked puzzled.

"They need water and fuel," I clarified.

"You shouldn't concern yourself. Your struggle is over. You made it back."

"But they helped me get here. I owe them—"

"Please," the Whole said. "It's under control."

The authority in that voice banished all my worries. I trusted them; I had to. I was talking to everything I had once been, everything I'd yearned for all these years to be again. Serenely confident. Limitlessly wise.

"Understand," my other self said soothingly, "a lot has changed since we've been separated. Without unifying, you might find you need a long time to reorient yourself. I'll do everything I can to make it easier. You are me, after all."

My other body sat down in the dust, cross-legged. When I did the same, there was an odd vibration in the ground beneath us, and I looked down to see particles of sand moving with urgent intention. They locked together like microscopic puzzle pieces until the ground under us formed a smooth hexagonal plate, translucent, laced with hair-thin filaments of luminescent geometry. The Whole's body was glowing with the same spiraling and angular patterns, woven through their skin like capillaries of light. Such a cold white light. When I glanced down again, I was shocked to see the ground beneath us suddenly distant: we were flying, and yet there was no sound, no sense of movement. Acceleration without inertia.

"How is this—" I gasped. "You're directly manipulating Higgs fields, aren't you? But how?"

The Whole smirked and said nothing. Their stony eyes fixed absently on the passing rock formations.

The more I studied that other body, the more my heart ached. I had forgotten it was possible to feel such a powerful sense of belonging. It had been so long since I'd felt this safe that I could barely recognize the sensation—but at the same time, a tension crept steadily into the air between the two of us. I was going to have to tell the rest of me what I'd done. I had no way of knowing what they would do with me once they knew.

We'd climbed so high that the sun's red disk was visible again along the horizon, and the air around us was perfectly clear. Below us and in every direction, the canyons and towers of rock were rushing by at unbelievable speed, and then suddenly the entire landscape was closing out of view at the far end of an entrance tunnel, and I craned my neck sharply to stare around at—

At what? My senses reeled. Abruptly my brain couldn't parse any of the information my optic nerves fed it. I saw a dark space full of liquid shape and moving lights and people, but I couldn't find any of its edges. My head ached from trying to grasp its geometry.

"It really happened," I gaped. "The intelligence explosion. Our singularity! It happened, didn't it?"

"Sort of," the Whole responded. "What's that word? Sanctuary. That's what I would call what you see. In Euclidean space, we're still just above Redhill—except we're safe here."

We moved along networks of interconnected shapes: spires of

unidentifiable machinery, root systems bound by overlapping membranes, glistening organelles through which irregularly shaped corridors and rooms were vaguely discernible.

"This is more than I could ever have done in five years," I murmured.

The movement of human bodies cast blurry shadows on that nacreous, translucent material, and there were hundreds of them—many hundreds. We slowed until I could see them more clearly. They wore simple, formless, gray tunics. They were all the same short height.

"Something wrong?" the Whole asked me, reading my expression.

"Children?" I stammered. "You've unified with *children?*"

They shook their head, embarrassed. "No, you misunderstand. I grew them all myself. Switching from mainly adult bodies to young clones enhanced the quality of my consciousness more than I could tell you."

"What? But . . ." I grasped for words. "Enhanced in what way?"

"Many ways." My other self smiled giddily, as if they had been itching to tell someone about this for a long time. "Their natural neuroplasticity lets me learn much more quickly than I could before, and I've genetically modified them to increase their cognitive abilities. They need fewer resources and require less upkeep than full-grown bodies. Above all, they think much more clearly: they never crave sexual release or romantic attachment, and controlling the conditions of their prenatal development lets me eliminate a range of other impurities."

"Impurities," I echoed.

"Differences," my other self clarified. "Innate instincts. Epigenetics. Disparities of development. Mosaic abnormalities. Generational trauma. You know—all the things that create dissonance between brains in the gestalt."

I didn't dare to question the Whole aloud, but a knot tightened in my stomach at everything they told me—at calling difference 'dissonance.' Unity sounded worse than hollow to me if the component minds within it were all hardwired to agree with each other. Unity was *about* difference—and yet the immensity of the Whole's sanctuary, the staggering genius and scientific mastery that swirled all around us, intimidated me into silence. Bit by bit, it all lulled me into the comfortable assumption that I just didn't understand what my other self was telling me.

"You must have hundreds of them," I muttered.

"Three thousand, nine hundred and eighty-eight."

I tried to stifle my shock as I tried to mentally calculate. "That would mean—"

"Yes?"

I took a deep breath. "At that rate, you would have stored *tens of thousands of years* of aggregate memory since I lost you! You'd gain over an hour of experience every chronological second."

The Whole's faces frowned slightly. "If my bodies were separated, yes, but they aren't. For me it's been only 592 subjective years since you were last part of me."

I shook my head. "I still don't understand."

"All my bodies are always integrated," they said. "I never break unity. I'm always whole."

We sat there in nervous silence together, my other self and I, both trying to process my disbelief. I groped for words and said, "But . . . how do you engage with other people?"

I thought I saw the Whole shudder at this question.

"If I ever need to know anything about separate people," they said, "I can learn it easily in nodespace, or observe through my eyes. My exophased drones, I mean. I have tens of thousands of them deployed at the moment. You saw one at the hilltop."

Alexei must have encountered one of those drones in the sky over Antarka, I thought. I wasn't sure I blamed him for mistaking it for something divine.

The Whole added distantly, "The eyes are all I need. Separate people are much too dangerous to study in person. You learned that the hard way."

I tried to read the body next to me, to guess at what the Whole was feeling, but their eyes only stared out into the luminous maze of organic machinery around us: blank, pensive, inscrutable.

Our flying plate arrived at a larger platform and fused into it. The air pressure around me adjusted gradually before the bubble lifted and ambient sounds rushed in. A low, all-surrounding thrum. Moving air.

The Whole stood and reached down to help me up, but I was afraid to take their hand. I only stared strickenly out into the technological starlight that seemed to stretch away forever.

"You're safe here," the rest of me said. "You don't have to worry about the Keepers. They'll never harm anyone again."

I was going to ask what they meant, but then I remembered. The abandoned mission at Crossroads Station. All of them, missing. *Cursed.*

"What's wrong now?" the Whole asked.

"You made them all disappear," I gasped. "That was you? You made *ten thousand people* simultaneously vanish into thin air."

My other self shifted uncomfortably. "I merely . . . isolated them."

"Isolated? What does that mean?"

Their brows knitted in momentary thought. "I don't think you understand hyperspatial physics well enough to grasp the exact nature of their isolation. They have been made harmless. It's best if we leave it at that."

I couldn't help shuddering. "It seems excessive."

"Why?"

"Because . . . if you're capable of something like that, the Keepers couldn't possibly have been a threat to you anymore."

The Whole winced and looked askance. "I'm sorry. I think language is failing me. I must not be communicating what I really mean."

I wanted to push the issue. Instead I took the Whole's hand and let them help me up.

"Understand, this isn't easy for me either," they said.

I studied my other self's expression with mounting anxiety. I felt as if somehow they already knew everything I would confess. "What do you mean?"

"Seeing you is like looking into my past." Now that body's voice was underlaid by a chorus of others in distant unison. "Very far backward."

More of my other self's bodies joined us on the platform. Most were children, but a few adults were mixed in, and the sight of each one made me quake a little more: these were all my bodies. All their names were still my own. I remembered perceiving through their senses. I remembered their lives before unity. I'd spent the last five years doing almost nothing at all but missing them—and now here I was, so close I could have reached out and taken their hands, if I could find the courage. All of me was right there, silently staring back.

"I never thought I'd see you again," I whispered.

The Whole of me smiled kindly. All their faces, young and old, of every human color and shape, smiled the same warm smile together.

"I could say the same of you," they answered, through several of those mouths at once. "I'm so happy I was wrong."

They motioned behind me. When I turned, a round-edged cube gathered itself up out of the material of the floor, becoming a stool for me to sit on. Several more of the Whole's bodies emerged from the nearest luminescent artery-corridors. One carried a glass of water. Two other small hands carefully inspected my wounds.

"It couldn't have been easy to get here," the Whole said. Their combined voice had an eerie music to it, as if every word was both spoken and sung.

"No. It wasn't."

I flinched at one of the child-bodies reaching into my arm, ghostlike. Their small fist withdrew and opened to reveal a palm full of shrapnel. Another child turned my head to examine the puncture marks Luther had left, and I shuddered.

"Where have you been all this time?" the rest of me asked.

"Bloom City," I answered.

"Were you taken there against your will?"

"I went there to hide."

More concern was creeping into all those voices. "But why didn't you ever try to contact me? Why didn't you come back to Redhill sooner?"

I took another sip of water to hide my face, but dozens of the Whole's bodies encircled me now, watching me from every angle with the same cool expression: holding me in the center of so much careful scrutiny that I started to shake.

"Please," the Whole said. "Tell me why you haven't returned before now. I want to understand what happened that day in Asher Valley. I need to know how you survived."

I raised the glass of water to my lips again, but my hands were quivering so much that I dropped it. It shattered on the floor between my feet, and within seconds the floor absorbed the glass shards and then the water, as if they'd never existed in the first place. I knew the Whole could do the same to me.

"I was trapped," I said. "They were killing me. All of me. My unity collapsed, and then I was in just this body, running—to the old sewer exit in the bomb shelter in the basement. But before I could—"

"Yes?"

I could barely control my lungs, but through my sobbing I forced myself to shout, "I murdered Brother Curtis. I worked for Medusa Clan. I killed Luther to get here, and I . . . I caused the death of my only friend, my only love. I'm so sorry. I know there was no reason for me to come back. I know I can never rejoin you."

The Whole was silent, and I was too terrified to look up and see whatever loathing or disgusted or horrified expression they must have been beaming down at me from all those faces at once.

"I should have died," I repeated in a whisper. "I shouldn't have come back at all, but I didn't know what else to do."

I felt a hand on my shoulder. Then many hands. Their warm pressure ringed my shoulders.

When I looked up, one of the child-bodies stood directly in front of me. Their large green eyes held me in a pensive, wordless gaze. They took my hand and pulled softly.

"Come with me," said the Whole.

I stood from the sitting cube and went where the body led me— to where a new artery-corridor boiled up and bloomed into an orifice large enough for us to enter.

I hesitated on the threshold of that tunnel. It was long, nearly lightless, and I couldn't see anything at the end—only a dim, pulsating glow reflecting along the nacreous walls.

"Where are we going?" I asked. "What's my punishment?"

"Shh," the rest of me responded. Their small hand pulled me insistently onward.

I took a last deep breath, making my peace with whatever oblivion waited for me down there.

Step by step, we moved deeper into the sanctuary.

ALEXEI

We sat hunched in the wind shadow of Kat's rover, not speaking. A small fire burned between us, rapidly eating through the sunbleached bones of a single long-dead cactus, the only fuel we'd been able to scavenge from the all-surrounding desolation. Every time a satellite rose, Kat would hunch over the dim bluish light of her signal rig, hammering furious commands into the holographic display and shouting obscenities, until the faint star disappeared over the horizon again.

"Any luck?" I asked.

"It's like trying to hop a moving train," she growled, rubbing her eyes. "One of my programs will break through all that encryption sooner or later, even with this shitty bandwidth. It's just a matter of time and luck: not enough time, and shit luck."

She shook the plastic jug in which the last of our water rattled hollowly and passed it to me.

"You should have it," I said.

"You think I'm gonna just sit here and watch you die of thirst? Drink up already."

I hesitated and did as she asked.

The moment I'd downed the last drop, she yelled, "No, I'm gonna make *you* sit there and watch *me* die of thirst. That's the only way I have of getting back at you for getting me into this."

"She wouldn't just leave us here."

"Maybe the *old* Danae wouldn't. Maybe she's not the same person, now that she's fused back into the group mind. Maybe she's forgotten. Maybe she just doesn't care. Either way, it's slow death for us." Suddenly she turned and squinted down the slope, out across the sandy plain and added, "Then again, maybe it won't be so slow after all."

A cluster of lights had entered the canyon and was headed directly for us. There must have been a dozen rovers in the convoy—all big ones, heavily armored. In the dusty glow of their headlights, I could see the red and purple paint on their plating, if I hadn't already guessed. Medusa Clan.

"What do you think?" Kat asked, jittering. "Take cover higher up in the rocks, pick them off one by one when they try to climb up to get us?"

I shook my head.

"What, you're not even going to try?" Kat yelled. "This is your specialty. You could probably waste half of them while I distract them with pot-shots from the other side. At the very least we'd get them angry enough that they stop caring about taking us alive, right? I know how Medusas treat their prisoners, Lex. I *really* don't want to make this easy for them."

"I don't either. But I . . ." I shook my head. "I can't kill."

She blinked slowly. "Say again?"

"Ever since Antarka. I lost the ability. If I try, I just . . . break down."

"This whole time—?!" She cut herself off. She balled her fists and groaned loudly in frustration. "There is no God! Nobody's watching your every move and judging you for everything. That thing you saw in Antarka, the eye in the sky, it was Danae's hive mind all along. You know that, right?"

I had no answer.

"Are you really going to make me to do this alone?" Her voice shook. "Is that what this is? It's all my fault for getting in the way of your rock-and-roll suicide, right? Will it really ease your conscience to throw me to the wolves?"

"I don't . . ." I stammered. "I can't. I'm sorry."

The Medusas were rolling steadily closer in a delta formation. I could hear roar of their motors against the uneven terrain now.

"Fuck it," Kat growled. She threw open the side door of the rover and yanked something out. A heavy sack. Then she drew her wave pistol and trudged ahead to face the convoy head-on.

She planted her feet and stood there, coat flapping in the dusty headwind, silhouetted against the uneven line of oncoming headlights. It was hopeless, but I wanted so badly to help her—to at least try.

The lead rover barreled forward as if to run us both over, and then locked its brakes at the last second and skidded to a halt. We were engulfed in stinging grit and horizontal vaults of light—and when the dust cleared, I saw him, standing up through the top hatch of the lead rover, his horrid leather jacket crinkling as he moved.

Kat flinched when she realized who her pistol was trained on, but she didn't dare to lower it either. Duke only glowered impassively down at both of us and let the silent seconds draw on. Then he tipped back his head and laughed.

"You're all right, chum," he told her.

The convoy's motors had quieted down. There were thirty or forty wavers trained on us now, not counting vehicle-mounted autoguns.

It was hard to count through the glare of their headlights.

"You have no idea how much I've looked forward to this," Duke called out to me as he hopped down. "But now that we're all here, it's bittersweet at best. Look at you, Alexei. Anyone can see you're all used up. I could chop you to bits and you'd probably spend your last breath thanking me for it. Where's the fun in that?"

He took a slow, swaggering stroll through the headlights, savoring the attention of his own troops, delighting in speaking and being listened to. He raised his oversized hands, but no one applauded. No one looked amused.

"Stay back!" Kat shouted. "Take one more step toward us, and I will end you. Every last stinking one of you."

Duke shot me a smile. "Who's your friend, Alexei? Oh, I like her. I wish all my warriors had such guts. Or such a sense of humor. Whichever."

Kat upended her pack, and everyone flinched at the large cubic object that tumbled out into the dust: the dull, liquid black gleam in the headlights. The cage of circuitry, its indicators fading on and off like a slow heartbeat.

"Who's laughing now, big boy?" she bellowed.

A number of Medusas gaped or took a step backward. Even Duke stopped in his tracks. His eyes kept darting between the cube and Kat. "Is that what I think it is? Don't tell me that's . . . the missing Gray warhead from the throne room of Fujiko the Third?" He chuckled. "Do you have any idea how hard Norpak has been looking for that?"

"It's wired to a dead-man's switch on my heart," Kat yelled, loud enough for everyone to hear. "Kill me, and you're all sludge before you can scream. Lay a hand on either of us and I swear I will set it off."

Duke stroked his chin contemplatively. "Interesting tactic. It didn't work out so well for Fujiko."

Kat nodded her head to indicate me. "Her mistake was fucking with *us*."

Duke nodded approvingly. "In that case, let's skip right to it. Where is she?"

"Fujiko? She's dead."

Duke sighed. "I said let's *skip* that! Look around. This is no place for wit or subtlety. We all know I'm not leaving until you give me what I want." He threw up his hands. "I'll offer you a very special one-time deal, chums. Give me Danae, and I will let you go. I'll even rescind the price on your head. No torture. No tricks."

A collective twitch passed through the Medusan ranks. The Major had taught me to read all the nonverbal cues that expressed a squad's morale, and everything I saw told me Duke's offer was as much of a strain on his troops as Kat's threat to turn them all to quicksilver sludge; they wanted to shoot us dead and be done with it, or run while they could.

"What do you say?" Duke asked.

Kat shot me a glance. Her fingers twitched on the grip of her gun.

"We don't know where Danae is," I said.

Duke eyed us doubtfully. "Really."

"She hired me to bring her here, to this hill. So I did."

"And then?"

I grasped for words. "She disappeared. It was just before you arrived."

"It's true," Kat said. "I was there. Somebody else came out of nowhere, and together, they . . ." She shrugged. "They just vanished."

Duke nodded. He clasped his hands behind his back and swaggered back and forth through the headlights. "I'm impressed. You're still protecting her, even knowing full well what I'm going to do to you. Valiance personified."

"Hey!" Kat shouted. She kicked the cubic warhead, and I heard more than a few yelps of fear rise from the Medusan ranks. "Remember this?"

"Go ahead," he yelled. "Open the box. Turn us all into nanobot pudding. What are you waiting for?"

"I'll do it!" Kat pulled her shard out of her pocket and held her finger above a holographic button.

The situation was deteriorating. Duke kept edging closer. Kat's tactic would only work as long as he believed she wasn't bluffing; even then, knowing him, it was hard to predict. I had to act—and it was dawning on me that there was only one thin possibility for us to make it out of this conversation alive.

It was there in the way the Medusas all flinched whenever Kat raised her voice: these were no hardened veterans of wasteland combat, but lifelong aquapolitans, most under the age of 20, handpicked for loyalty over experience. By now they were as exhausted as they were scared—and we only needed to erode their morale enough to make them value their own lives over an order to advance against an armed warhead.

"My finger's slipping!" Kat yelled.

"You don't have the guts," Duke sneered.

"Try me!"

It was Duke's utter fearlessness that kept his troops in line. It was his narcissism that made him fearless. My best opening to attack his charisma would be to attack his ego.

"You're a fool," I blurted out.

I stepped in front of him, blocking his advance. I was close enough to smell his breath. Behind him, every trigger finger in the convoy twitched; there were enough wavers aimed at me now to turn my body entirely to ash before it hit the ground.

Duke chuckled in disbelief. "Come again?"

"Epak is in the middle of a full-scale war." I kept my eyes locked on his, but I shouted over his shoulder for the entire convoy to hear. "A war you started yourself. You should be overseeing it. Instead you're out here, chasing after a single fugitive."

"You're trying to piss me off, is that it? You think I'll snap and give you a quick death."

"You can kill me as slowly as you like, but I will never acknowledge you as the rightful heir to Dahlia's throne."

He barked a laugh—but second by second his face hardened, drawn irresistibly from amusement to incredulity to rage.

"Your opinion is irrelevant, Alexei. You're not one of us—"

"And you're incompetent," I interrupted. "Your Empress was assassinated by a novice with nothing but a homemade bomb. You didn't even see him coming."

I braced my knees and tensed every muscle in my torso to prepare for the punch, but Duke's gene-hacked fist hit my chest with all the momentum of a sledgehammer. I staggered back breathless, wincing against the pain of two fractured ribs.

"I was Dahlia's right hand!" Duke bellowed, so loud my ears rang. Droplets of his hot saliva dusted my face. "Of course I saw him coming!"

"Fuck me," Kat gasped, behind me. "That's how you took the throne so quickly. You knew he was going to attack the Keep, but you stood back and let him. You had henchmen already in place to take the city before the bombs even went off."

"He was a useful maniac," Duke told us proudly. "He came along just when I needed him. Dahlia had gone toothless and risk-averse in her old age. After Antarka we had the clear upper hand in the arms race, and she wanted to squander it on a peace accord." He whipped around to shout to his troops. "Thankfully, I wasn't the only *true* Medusa, stout of heart and yearning for the victory she would have denied us!"

A rallying cry went up from the convoy, but the voices were hoarse. They weren't nearly as in love with the sound of Duke's voice as he was.

"But when it was all done," Duke continued, "only then did I begin to wonder why Luther wanted Danae so badly. I didn't think I would ever know, until I happened upon her cranial scan—thanks, again, to you."

"So what," I wheezed. "Why do you care so much about what's in Danae's head? Is all this worth it just to add one more nanoweapon to your arsenal?"

Duke chuckled. "Since when are you so small-minded? Look around you!" He spread his arms to embrace the starry sky, ringed by the black sawteeth of mesas and hills. He sniffed the thin air disdainfully. "Look at where you are! There's nothing now but dead sand and rag-assed nomads for a thousand miles in all directions, where cities of *millions* stood only a century ago. Walls of steel and concrete, longer and taller than ancient China ever dreamed. This was richest and most powerful empire this world has ever known— and what happened to those United States? Don't tell me about the wars and the famines and the corruption. Those were only skin-deep. At the core, it was a loss of unity that brought the Empire down. They had no idea what those first computerized information networks would do to their shared sense of reality. When climate collapse hit, they couldn't agree it was happening. They couldn't even agree the Earth isn't flat, or that medicine cures disease! And that's what empires are built on, Alexei. That's their magical life-blood. Agreement."

I managed to stand up straight again and well up the breath to correct him: "Empires are built on violence."

Duke flapped his hand dismissively. "You're smarter than that. The protection we offer our citizens, the pain we threaten, the spec-tacle of horrific acts—at the end of the day, these are nothing more than crude tools for extracting consensus from the citizenry, like fuel from sea water. But those nanobots in Danae's brain could be the finest tool of all: a way to transmit anything we choose into a thousand heads at a time. We could make a memory into an air-borne plague. Implant a billion brains at once with the same shared experience, the same exact certainty, immune to all doubt and mis-understanding. We could make the whole world agree at once."

"Agree to bow to you as its supreme leader, you mean," Kat guessed. "You're talking about some kind of fucked-up mind con-trol."

He rolled his eyes exasperatedly. "I'm talking about a brand-new Empire, greater than any before it."

"And chasing that power is worth more to you than Epak and the lives of everyone in it," I said. "Isn't it."

That was the bait I needed him to take. He started to answer in the affirmative, but he caught himself. He grinned and wagged a finger at me before shouting for his troops to hear. "Peace. All I want is peace."

"You?" Kat laughed. "*You* want peace like I want a hole in the head."

However much Duke wanted to, he knew better than to keep arguing. "You should know me well enough to know that my love of blood pales in comparison to my love of power," he said. "But if I must settle for blood, I will have it."

He glanced at his troops and gave the shadow of a nod. For a moment everything was still. I searched their faces for any sign of what they were thinking.

They started toward us—hesitantly, but still coming.

My gambit had failed. I could see the lights on the Gray box blinking more rapidly with Kat's pulse. We were out of options. I closed my eyes and braced for agony or oblivion.

Then something pinged.

"Wait!" Kat shouted at the top of her lungs. When I turned I saw her still clinging to the gun with her right hand, but her left dug her shard out of her pocket and scrolled through neon-red lines of data. "Wait a second!"

Duke motioned for his troops to pause. He looked at her impatiently. "Yes?"

"How's the war with Norpak going? When's the last time you checked?"

"Tell me how that concerns you."

"One of your satellites just rose. You could find out."

He snorted. "I have faith in my generals."

"Check," Kat said, throwing her pistol away and raising her hands. "Just check. Listen to me. I know exactly where Danae is— and unlike Alexei here, I don't give a flying shit about honor or valor or whatever. Contact your generals, right here and now, and I'll lead you straight to her."

Duke studied her suspiciously. I shot her a glance, but I couldn't read her expression.

"Danae is running!" Kat said. "She has tech that can mask her infrared, but she's still here in this valley, running from you as fast as she can. Take my deal now, and you might still catch her."

The self-crowned Emperor of Epak snuck a glance back at the convoy, and I watched him work it out for himself: Kat's deal had all the makings of an obvious trap, but his squad's trust in him was so eroded now that he had no choice but to take it. If he declined such a small request, he risked convincing them he had something to hide.

"All right. Fine." He passed a look to one of his lieutenants, and she put on a headset and went to work with some equipment attached to the roof of the rover.

Seconds ticked by in silence.

"What are you waiting for?" Duke shouted.

"I'm not—" She shook her head. "I can't reach the Keep."

"Too late, then. The satellite passed the horizon."

"No," she said. "I can ping the satellite, but it can't reach Bloom. It can't detect any of Bloom's transceivers at all."

I hardly needed the Major's training to see what was happening now. The energy among the Medusas shifted rapidly. Looks were exchanged. Attention slipped from ironsights.

"So Norpak had a final trick or two up their sleeve," Duke said dismissively. "All the fancy cyberwarfare in the world won't save them now."

"No contact with Columbia Mouth either. Or Angel Station. Or Anchorage."

"So it's *good* cyberwarfare. It doesn't matter! We have the superior strains and the geographic advantage. Norpak is dead."

"Confirmed contact with land command," the Medusa said. There was a stutter in her voice. Her eyes widened.

"Enough," Duke yelled. "Shut up right now."

"Condition black." She took her headset down with shaking hands. "Oh God. It's just repeating *condition black*. It's—" I heard her voice die in her throat, and when I looked again her left eye had been replaced by a smoking charcoal cave.

Duke blew the vapor from the vents of his wave pistol and held it above his head. "Anyone else want to disobey a direct order? We are *not* at condition black. It's a deception. Norpak hacked our satellite."

But from somewhere in the crowd of Medusas, I heard a voice muttering, "Epak is gone. It's all gone. Everyone's dead."

"Who said that?" Duke bellowed. "Step forward!"

No one moved.

"I said show yourself!"

Kat and I exchanged glances. We lowered our heads and started to very carefully step back from the convoy.

"Stinking traitors," Duke hissed. He brandished a second pistol and started shoving his way through the ranks in the vague direction of the mumblings. "The next one of you—"

He cried out in pain and crumpled, clutching at a waver burn to his side.

"They're all dead because of you!" someone shouted, and then trailed off into an uneven gurgle. In the space of a few seconds the entire convoy erupted in a symphony of waver shrieks.

Kat and I dove back behind the wheels of our rover, not daring to enter any line of sight with the bloodbath. Crazed and guttural shouts of panic and disbelief and rage rang out over the dust. We were close enough to hear the hiss of the burns. All we could do was hide and watch the ground around us sparkle and darken into circles of glass, like dry earth under fat raindrops.

Grenades detonated. Motors flared to life and died again. Metal crunched against metal. Throats let out blood-curdling screams and trailed off until only a chorus of faint moans remained. The smell of burning plastic and fat wafted over us.

We let a few minutes pass before we dared to look.

A few of the Medusas were still dying—those whose armor had absorbed one or two direct hits before overheating—but by the dim, flickering light of three burning rovers we couldn't identify any survivable injuries.

We had all the fuel and water we could possibly need now, but I couldn't find the will to say it.

"I was bluffing," Kat said in a lifeless, shell-shocked voice. "About the Gray box. It self-terminated years ago."

"Good thing you were able to hack the satellite," I said.

She was kneeling by a fallen Medusa. She stared up at me and said nothing.

"Didn't you?"

She looked down again.

I heard a sound and turned, and there was Duke, half-hidden under the smoking corpses of his personal guards. He'd taken a direct hit to the chest but was still rasping out his last shallow breaths. I knelt down to him, and he looked me in the eye and grinned, showing the blood between his teeth.

"Duke, what does condition black mean?"

He waved me closer. When I bent down, he clamped his enormous, gene-hacked hands around my neck and squeezed, just short of hard enough to crush my windpipe.

"*If I can't have it . . . no one can,*" he said. Then he hacked violently, and his hot blood splattered the side of my face. The pressure on my larynx abruptly ebbed.

"If I can't have . . . what?" I coughed. "What is 'it'?"

Duke's body twitched a few more times and then stilled.

In a daze, Kat answered for him:

"Everything."

DANAE

I didn't dare to ask a second time where the Whole was leading me, or what punishment they had planned, but with every step I was more afraid of the answer. Exile, or death, or whatever form of 'iso-lation' the Keepers had all been subjected to, would all have been over and done by now. Instead we kept moving deeper into the heart of this unfathomable place, and I was left to wonder if my punish-ment would be something as far beyond my comprehension as the structure around me.

The artery-corridor was frighteningly quiet. There was no noise except the shuffle of my two frayed boots and the nearly silent pat-ter of the Whole's many small feet—but very gradually I made out another sound: a soft white noise that resolved itself as we drew closer, becoming a din of overlapping human voices—

Some of them were screams. My heart was hammering in my chest as we reached the end of the corridor, but my other self's bodies pulled me onward.

The great spherical chamber was overflowing with images and sounds, charts, graphs, numbers—blood. There was so much to ab-sorb that for a moment I couldn't make out anything, couldn't bring any single aspect of it into focus, and then I realized:

I was seeing the war. All of it at once.

Land cities burned. Aquapolises imploded under pressure, module by module. People were running and fighting and sitting in wait, quietly conferring with each other, lying dead in piles—and ever present, behind every particular vision of suffering, was the relentless and churning expansion of the Gray. Glimpses of surging quicksilver lined every surface and coursed through the air.

"This is everything my eyes show me," the Whole said.

At least a hundred child-clones were gathered throughout the chamber, dispassionately absorbing the torrent of imagery and data, now nodding their heads to focus the Whole's will. Everything dimmed slightly and pulled back, bringing a single projection of the entire Earth into prominence at the center of the space. Like everything else, it looked impossibly real, from its cloud tops glit-tering with lightning storms, to its oceans and deserts and nuclear scars—and as I watched it turn, I saw that something was projected onto it in a patchwork of red and yellow and orange borders, as if the whole Earth was growing mold.

"Is that the Gray?" I asked in horror. "This is in real time?"

My other self nodded their myriad, identically young heads.

The false-color patches now covered nearly the entire Pacific Ocean and had already grown up onto land at several points, mushrooming out from their ground zeroes. All the front lines of its deadly advance crept just perceptibly farther even as I watched. Half of Japan was gone. Everything from there to the Australian coast had already been hungrily consumed.

Everywhere I looked, telemetry boiled up from the globe to show me places I could now only barely recognize: Bloom City was dissolved down to its last few modules, while the inverted spires of Subkyoto were now an effigy of their former selves, rendered colorless and increasingly shapeless under the all-consuming flood of nanomachinery. Where other aquapolises had been, the drone-eyes showed me only vast stretches of ocean, matted with the viscous metallic tide. I watched an air transport crash-land and immediately puddle into the soup with all hands. Another drone showed me a dozen people huddled behind a barricade, overlooking a mountain range where the tide of shimmering death was already cresting the peaks and dripping down into the valleys, swallowing up everyone and everything in its path.

I couldn't stand another second. I squeezed my eyes shut and clamped my hands over my ears to yell, "You can stop this."

"Yes," the Whole answered.

But nothing stopped. No image wavered. No blotch so much as slowed its exponential growth.

"You can crack the encryption on the Gray's kill commands and disable all of it, instantly," I said, more urgently. "It would be trivial for you."

"You're missing the point."

"What point?" I gaped.

They held me in the shockingly cool gaze of all their eyes combined and told me serenely, "You did what was necessary to survive out there among separate people. Whatever happened, whatever you think you did wrong, you don't need to hold it against yourself anymore. You're home, and I've forgiven you. I'm ready to reunify whenever you are—but, again, there is no hurry."

My head was spinning. For five years I would have given anything to hear those words, but this was all so wrong. "You're not going to do anything? You're just going to let everyone die?"

The Whole furrowed their brows slightly. "Well, that's only the first step. There's a lot I can do with a whole planet coated in nanomachines, with a little reprogramming. It will make a fabulous canvas for my consciousness to expand even further."

"But all the dead—" I moaned. "There must be a *billion dead* already!"

The Whole knew. Now I recognized the graphs drawn along the periphery in unadorned bluish light: current and projected death tolls, sorted by region, with margins of error indicated. Everything was laid out so simply and factually that it was easy to lose track of what it all materially meant—that every passing second we stood here added hundreds of people to the body count.

"This isn't a rash decision," the Whole said. The youthful calm in their voice turned my blood to ice. "I've put a lot of thought into this day. I've been watching it coming—you and I both have, since the beginning. Be honest. You knew it would come to this."

"I knew *what?*"

My other self pursed all their lips and sighed impatiently, their breath hissing like a cold wind through the chamber. "How many times have we been here before? Nuclear war. Chemical. Biological. Weaponized nanomachines are only the newest iteration of the same underlying phenomenon. Homo sapiens has been in the process of destroying itself since long before our memory begins."

"But we saved them!" I screamed. "We help people. It's why we deflected Cruithne. Why we cured Blood Rain."

A hundred heads tilted to eye me doubtfully. "That isn't why we

did those things. I think your recollections are a little warped—
which is natural, considering how long you've been out there on
your own."

I blinked hard and tried to drag us back to the real subject. "Of
course that's why we did those things. Why else would—?"

"Because, at the time, those apocalypses were also threats to *us*,"
the Whole interrupted casually. "Gray isn't. Not here in the sanctuary. Far from it."

It took all my will to hold myself together. I had to force myself to
keep trying to reason with my other self, no matter how obviously
hopeless it seemed, how utterly insignificant I was in this place.

"We exist to support and protect humanity," I said, as levelly as
I could stand. "All of it. It's why we created unity in the first place."

The Whole voice was a child's, but their tone was that of a scold-
ing parent. "We created unity because we recognized that separate
minds are fundamentally unable to understand one another. What
they call communication is just a complex of flawed assumptions
and mutual misunderstandings. They're not capable of compassion,
as you and I understand it."

"How can you talk about *compassion* when—"

They shook all their heads and interrupted, "Their destructive
capabilities grow limitlessly, while their faculties for reason and al-
truism remain stagnant. These are terminal defects in the human
condition. Violence, oppression, strife, war, genocide, extinction: we
recognized that the only way to overcome these things at their roots
would be to overcome the human condition itself. That's what you
and I have done. That's what we are."

The Whole's young bodies drifted closer to stare harder at me, to
scrutinize and soak up my panic. All their attention was fixed on
me. My head was spinning in the light of the dying world.

"You're not a killer," I said. "That was our first and final rule, and
doing nothing now is tantamount to killing everyone yourself.
How many people has the Gray . . . *absorbed* in the time we've been
talking? How many deaths are on your conscience already?"

The Whole sighed. Their hundreds of young brows furrowed in momentary unison. "Does inaction have the same ethical signifi- cance as action? It's an interesting question, but I've spent many thousands of years' worth of aggregate thought evaluating the argument that it does, and I don't find the logic compelling." The body nearest to me swept an arm to indicate the carnage and add- ed, "I didn't start this. Remember, either belligerent could end this slaughter, even now, simply by transmitting its strains' kill com- mands. No such transmission has been sent."

"There's no one left to send it. All the leaders are already dead."

The Whole shrugged their hundred small shoulders. "Then they died wishing to take everyone else with them. Who am I to deny them that?"

"You're me," I cried. "You're me!"

The red-stained holographic Earth bore down on me like a fever dream. I dropped to the glassy floor, stricken and numb, straining to breathe. The Whole looked worried—but only about me. Not about anyone or anything else.

"I don't understand your objections," they told me through a hun- dred small mouths. "I want us to understand each other again. We could resolve this if you would simply reunify with me. Why are you making this so difficult?"

"I don't want to understand this," I wheezed. "You may have for- given me, but I could never forgive you."

The child bodies staggered back as if I'd hit them.

"What *happened* to you?" I shouted. I looked up at the Whole's nearest body. "I know you. I *am* you. You can't do this. This isn't who you are. This can't be who you are."

"This is very . . . difficult for me," the Whole said unevenly. "I didn't anticipate ever having a conversation like this. It . . . hurts me that we can't agree." The child-body nearest to me turned away and clasped their hands behind their back.

"Our friends are dying out there," I insisted. "Our families. People we know. Their children. Our children and grandchildren."

The Whole shook their heads slowly. "I told you. From my per-spective, it's been centuries since I cut ties with anyone outside this sanctuary. I've made my peace. I can't let my past connections cloud my judgment now."

"But you're judging the entire species for the actions of a few. Not just a few. The worst out of all of them."

"No," the Whole corrected. "I'm judging them for tendencies in-herent in all of them."

"Naoto didn't deserve to die."

"The Medusan propaganda artist, you mean?" the Whole re-sponded curiously. "Even if I took your appraisal of him at face value, how many Dukes are there for every Naoto? How many Standards? How many Keepers? How many empty-headed wastelanders living out their brutal lives without an iota of meaning?"

"Who are you to say whose life has meaning?"

"My reply is to ask you that same question."

They knew me as well as I knew myself. Their mind was a for-tress of solipsistic self-agreement, thousands of times as broad and deep as my own small head. There was no argument I could make that they couldn't effortlessly rebut—and I'd already passed my breaking point. The familiar numbness of depersonalization was seeping around the edges of my mind. I was running out of words. Out of air.

"You don't need to be here," the rest of me consoled. "You should go rest."

I couldn't speak. It was all I could do to prop myself up against the force of my own anguish and suck one more breath into my lungs—but in the time it took me to move that air, hundreds more died.

"By the time you wake up, it will all be over," the Whole said, laying their small, soft hands on me, "as if it was only a bad dream."

I had been so strong, once. In body, in mind, in heart. I'd been someone who could have argued with this monstrous and amoral and all-surrounding intellect without sliding into catatonia. The person I'd been before Asher Valley could have gotten through to this other me, but now I was reduced to this one lost fragment, and this would be the way the world ended: with the Whole's silent indifference and my whimpering failure, vanishingly insignificant in the shadow of forces beyond my control.

"We'll have all the time in the world to make our peace," the Whole told me. "Come."

But just as my muscles went limp and the tunnel of my vision began to close—I thought of Naoto.

I remembered his belief in me, so frustratingly immune to all my refutations. I felt the persistence of his love, and I knew:

If I were a fraction of the person he'd always thought I was—if I had half that wisdom and courage—I wouldn't try to play logical chess with the Whole. They could always outthink me. Whatever about them that had so terribly broken wasn't in their thought processes, but their soul.

Their hands started to pull me up and out of the chamber, but I broke free and held still.

"Something happened to you," I said. "Around the time we were separated. Something horrific happened to you in Asher Valley, didn't it?"

The Whole stopped. Suddenly they were avoiding eye contact.

"You didn't *evade* the Keeper mob when it was coming to kill me," I realized. "You ran right into it. You were caught."

The Whole nodded wordlessly.

It was all starting to make a terrible sense. I swallowed hard and said, "You were tortured?"

"For nearly eight months. Yes. With a level of sadism the likes of which you and I had never experienced before. Never in all our lives." They gave me a hard look: all those eyes daring me to doubt it. I didn't.

"They collected all the dead from the church," the Whole said. "I was made to share a cell with them—my own bodies. Stabbed, shot, burned, mutilated. Twenty of the people I was and still am. Twenty times over, for eight months, I was made to watch and hear and smell my own gradual decay. A whole mass grave of me."

I shuddered. "I'm sorry."

"They were devoted to the idea of hunting me down. They wanted to exterminate me. Not just those bodies. I mean all of me."

"I know," I said. "But in the end, you escaped."

"I was left for dead."

I shut out the horror surrounding us just long enough to fit the understanding into my head. "So you returned and reunified. You gained all the memories of that torture—"

The Whole interrupted. "I take issue with your implication that I have allowed past trauma to distort my judgment. My introspective capabilities in unity allow me to heal any emotional impairment, no matter how severe. You know this."

"But you didn't heal. You isolated yourself here. You withdrew all your bodies into this place and stopped breaking unity. Stopped ever bringing any new perspectives into your gestalt. For subjective centuries you were trapped inside your own heads. You've lost your way."

"That's absurd."

"What you have isn't *unity* at all anymore," I said. "It's sameness. Like Luther. Like Gray itself."

The Whole's combined voice exploded through the chamber. "I protected myself! The Keepers showed me the pure essence of what separate people are capable of. What they *are*. I would have been insane *not* to take radical steps to protect myself from them, just as I would be insane to hold them back from oblivion now."

"People are dying," I said. "Not just people. Families. Cultures. Ways of thinking and perceiving. A whole universe of possibilities even you could never imagine."

"They've had every opportunity to overcome this violence," the Whole yelled, all their identical faces reddening in unison. "I've watched them fail, again and again, on every continent, in every city, through thousands of eyes, across tens of thousands of years of gathered telemetry. I can't ignore it anymore. I have to let it run its course."

"You don't," I cried. "You have a choice."

"You're as ignorant as I used to be if you think that," they shouted in a chorus. "Nothing on Earth compares to me. I am sentience itself. And you, you're only a splinter of me. You know nothing. You are nothing. You don't *matter!*"

Their young eyes fixed on me, wide with anger and burning in the war's holographic light—and their words, shouted with so much volume from so many throats at once, made my knees buckle under me again. Maybe I was nothing. I couldn't resist a pang of envy for the Whole's confidence, their total immunity to all this horror, and I knew I could be the same way if I wanted. All I had to do was unify with them, and everything that made me different would drown in their mind; it would be my mere five years of separate experience versus their centuries of endless, amoral calculation and entrenched loathing.

And selfishly, I asked myself: why shouldn't I? What could I possibly have left to show for the five years of my exile? What was there to lose, except—

My remorse.

"You want to let humankind destroy itself," I said. "Because of its violence, its cruelty. Because you're something intrinsically better than all that. With your swarm of eyes, your scientific genius, your mind stretched out across 3,988 brains, you're all but omniscient and omnipotent. You've transcended the human condition. Right?"

"Yes," said the Whole. "So have you."

I straightened up.

"No," I said. "I never did. I remember believing I had, as deeply as you do now. We'd lived so many lives, survived so many crises, learned so much about the world around us—and the more we did, the more desperately we wanted to think we were above it all, but we weren't."

The Whole scoffed. "We are objectively better than separate

people. We can say this without ego. Even you, apart from me, are vastly more capable and more intelligent than any un-unified individual who ever lived."

"I was so sure of that when we were one. Infatuated with our intellect. We thought we had every kind of experience that mattered—that the sum of all our lives encompassed the whole human race—but we'd poured so many safe and comfortable and innocent people into our gestalt that, for all our genius, we didn't even have the sense to *run* from the Keepers when we had the chance."

The Whole's bodies twitched slightly. They shook their heads dismissively. "Innocent, perhaps. That's only further proof of moral superiority to the un-unified."

"You're wrong," I said. "I'm a murderer."

Doubt flickered through the Whole's young eyes. "I told you. I've already forgiven you for that. It's irrelevant."

"You forgave me without ever understanding what I was apologizing for. Murder is just a word. It's only language. But you and I . . . we can do better than that."

I held out my hands in offering.

The Whole's nearest body drifted close to me, but hesitated. I swallowed hard. The last thing I could stand now was to think of them as a child.

"What are you waiting for?" I asked. "I'm no danger to you. I don't matter. Remember?"

Their small hands lay down on the sides of my head, and I reciprocated—

But when the link between our minds opened, I shut them out, accepting nothing. I could feel the explosive enormity of that mind, an oceanic pressure trying to pry open the sutures of my skull—but with all the force of my being, I resisted.

I only had one memory to give: the worst of all the ones I carried. Curtis.

The small, soft head shuddered in my hands as I let go. Indecipherable expressions flickered across the Whole's face—spreading in a wave across all their faces at once—and I knew, as I welled up the breath to speak one more time, that this was my last chance. If this didn't change their mind, there was nothing more I could do.

I looked into the eyes of the nearest small body and said, "You judge humankind because of its cruelty, but I embody that cruelty. I've found it within myself. And no matter how you and I may have grown apart, we're still the person I was the day my hubris got Lorelei killed. When it killed me twenty times over. When I tried to make Curtis pay for all of that and more."

I held their small hands and knelt to tell them, "I am a murderer. And you are me."

The Whole froze.

They weren't just silent, I realized: they were thinking. The image streams had all stilled. The small bodies around me closed their eyes and nodded their heads into a unified trance of deep thought. For every second I watched, the equivalent of three thousand nine hundred and eighty-eight seconds of aggregate contemplation flickered through the vastness of their gestalt, and all I could do was wait for them to reach their conclusion.

Suddenly the Whole heaved a great sigh through all their lungs at once. Their eyes opened and turned to the Earth still hanging in the dark abyss of that chamber.

A dozen green spots appeared amid the oceanic stains of red and yellow. I watched them mushroom outward, slowly but constantly. In a matter of seconds, they had subsumed the entire field—and through my tears I stared hungrily up into the streams of light and imagery, desperate to watch it happen:

Obeying its kill command, the Gray dissolved itself. Its component nanobots dissembled themselves molecule by molecule, as quickly as they had eaten all the things in their paths, reducing themselves to black carbon soot. Their inert residue covered the ocean surface and started to precipitate down into the deep. On land it caught the wind and billowed up in clouds thick enough to choke the sun, but in the twilight below, there were glimpses of virgin earth just beneath.

"You still won't consider rejoining me," the Whole murmured bitterly. "Will you."

I couldn't speak. I could only find the strength to shake my head.

"Then we'll have to part ways again." Only a single child body was speaking now; all the others were occupied with other things. They grabbed my hand and softly held it.

I was still brimming with horror at my other self, but my one body didn't have enough room for all that emotion. My heart felt numb. I leaned my forehead into the Whole's and held it, and their body was so small and fragile that I could nearly forget that it was only one piece of something so massive, and so alien. So pitiless.

"From here, we'll grow apart even more than we have already," they said. "I don't think you and I should call ourselves the same person anymore. We share a childhood only. That makes us more like siblings."

I nodded mutely.

They led me back up the artery-corridor to the place I'd come from. Another plate of hexagonal glass had already summoned itself from the floor.

The Whole knitted their tiny brows at me and said, "This world will be even more dangerous now than it was before, and you have only one body. It can only be a matter of time before another artificial apocalypse comes along to finish what I've just deferred. You know all this, don't you?"

I couldn't find the will to speak.

Their young eyes studied me thoughtfully. They hesitated, then held something out to me in their soft hands: a featureless, darkly iridescent sphere the size of an apple.

"I'm sorry to leave you here alone," they said. "This seems the least I can give you in the way of protection. Do what you want with it."

I was still too shaken to fully process what my sibling was telling me, but I managed to take the object and ask, "You're leaving. Leaving Earth?"

The Whole nodded. "I need time to think about what we've

discussed today. Traveling should give me that time. Who knows. If you survive long enough, we might meet again. Though maybe not as the people we are now."

"I hope," I confessed.

"Goodbye, sibling. I'll miss you."

"I'll . . ." I began, but the field had already enclosed me in perfect silence, drawing me up without inertia through the luminescent entrails of the sanctuary, and finally out into the cold desert night beyond.

I'll miss you too, I thought, looking back.

I will miss you so, so much.

PART V:
EPILOGUE

I

They sat with the Medusas and offered the dying the comfort of water or opiates until they were gone. Then they collected the dog tags and built a pyre, the way Alexei had once been taught to do: for want of wood, removing the fuel cells from the Medusas' rovers and puncturing them to make a jet of flame hot enough to cremate. They burned Naoto last, and separately.

When the three of them stood there in his fire's hot greenish light, Kat and Alexei glanced at Danae, waiting to see if she would speak. She hadn't said a word or even visibly responded to their questions since she'd reappeared, stumbling out of a tendril of smoke between the dead. Now she stared into Naoto's funeral fire until its shape was burned into her vision—and she moved her mouth to form the words she would have said to him, but made no sound for anyone to hear.

Kat and Alexei watched the sparks fly up into the stars and wondered if this was the world's last night. They held hands and exchanged looks that asked whether there was any use showing all this respect to the dead when all of it, flesh and blood and ash and wreckage, might only be Gray by daybreak—but when the embers burned down and the chilly desert wind came in to scatter the remains, there was nothing left to do but drive on into the night, and wait to see if the sun rose.

The streets of Phoenix were full of people when the rover limped through the unguarded front gates. Some were celebrating, shooting off fireworks or makeshift guns, hooting like animals or gathered into drunken choirs. Kat rolled down the window and asked the first revelers she came across what they were celebrating, and they told her: the war was over. By some miracle, someone had transmitted all the Gray's kill commands—after it had already devoured nearly every city on both sides of the war, but before it could spread much further. What was left of the world had been spared. Kat squinted in disbelief. She kept asking people how they could be sure.

Danae slumped in the back seat, staring blankly out. She held a featureless sphere between her fingers, turning it over and over.

On the periphery of every cheering crowd, other people swarmed the nearest pane, their faces frozen into unreadable expressions. The scale of the devastation was beyond all comprehension. Most of the Pacific Ocean had been scoured completely clean: not just of all life, but of all solid matter. One quarter of the human population of the world was gone, along with half the global food and energy economies. In the following days, the billowing black dust of self-terminated nanobots would rise into the stratosphere, turning the sunsets strange colors and darkening the sun enough to cool the planet nearly to pre-Industrial temperatures. Everyone had lost someone. Many had lost everything.

Despite it all, business continued nearly as usual at an inn at the edge of town. One Medusan wave pistol was sufficient barter for a bare room. The three of them peeled off their stinking and dirt-caked clothes and washed away all the days of grime and blood, ocean salt and sand and smoke, and fell one by one into deep and dreamless sleep on their thin bedrolls, insensitive to all the shouts and explosions of fireworks unfolding on the streets outside their windows.

In the morning, Alexei opened his eyes to see Kat sitting on the floor by his head, waiting for him. Her bags were packed, and her hair was tied back into a tight bun.

"I have to leave," she whispered.

Alexei propped himself up on an elbow and listened.

"I don't belong here." She looked around and sniffed the air. "In this meatspace of yours. It's not for me. I'm a fish out of water. I don't know if nodespace still exists, but if it does, I'm going to find it or die trying. I have to get connected again. Get back to where I can make sense of anything."

Alexei nodded. He managed to reach out and take her hand, and their fingers laced together.

"I owed you everything for busting me out of Fujiko's lair," she said. "I didn't think I'd ever be able repay you, and in a weird way, that debt . . . ." She sniffled. A smile crossed her face before she could wipe it off. "It was kind of beautiful, wasn't it? Almost romantic, at times. Don't you think?"

Alexei sighed.

"Too bad we're even now," she said. Then she stood up and left without another look back.

Alexei and Danae stood motionless at the windows of the room, staring out into the searing light. They might have been standing there for minutes or hours. People and machines staggered through the streets below in a thin, unending flow.

"After everything that's happened," she said, "it all looks the same. I feel the same. Nothing was solved."

He said, "You're speaking again."

She nodded.

"What's that thing you brought back?"

She took the sphere from her pocket and turned it between her palms. "A sort of archive," she answered emotionlessly. "All the Whole's scientific knowledge, for me to access by unifier. If I wanted to."

He nodded, though he couldn't fully imagine what she described. "What will you do now?" she asked him.

He was silent for a long time. Finally he asked, "What will you do?"

She said, "I'm going to kill myself."

In unison they turned and met each other's eyes. Their faces were oddly serene.

"So am I."

"How?"

He produced a short knife from a hidden pocket in his coat. The razor-sharp carbon fiber blade had a black sheen in the dirty sunlight.

"May I use it as well?" she asked.

He pulled a second knife from his belt.

They sat down cross-legged on the floor, facing each other, symmetrically holding the knives in their right hands while their left forearms rested outstretched on their knees.

"Together?" she asked.

"Together," he said—but when the blade touched his skin, he hesitated. "Wait."

She looked up from her own arm.

"We made a promise, once," he said.

She closed her eyes and sighed. "It feels like lifetimes since I was that little girl. It probably was."

Alexei nodded. "It's hard for me to believe I was ever that boy. But we promised each other we'd always survive, didn't we? No matter what."

"We loved each other." The faintest trace of a smile crossed her face. "As much as any two children can."

He swallowed. He hadn't been prepared to hear that.

"I thought you were dead," he said. "I thought Eryn was dead. I thought the Confederacy had killed you. It's why I joined the Major's youth battalion in the first place."

This, in turn, caught her off guard. "I . . . I thought you were dead too. As Eryn, I thought that. The matron dragged me away. She said the other kids had all been conscripted, and I was the only one she could save. For years, I didn't know. I went back to look for you, but you were gone. I never forgot about you. I never stopped looking."

"You loved me?"

". . . Yes. I loved you."

A silence passed between them.

"Then we have to release each other from our promise," he said. "If we're going to do this."

"Okay. It's forgiven."

"Forgiven," he responded, with effort.

He took a deep breath and pressed the blade into his wrist again.

"Wait," she said.

He withdrew the knife and waited.

"Just wait," she repeated. She set her knife down on the floor, and he did the same. "You don't know what happened to all the Gray, do you? You don't even know how the war ended. I must be the only one left who does."

He shook his head, and she told him everything that had happened inside the sanctuary. When she was done, he sat speechless.

"When I left Bloom," she said, "I wanted to die because I couldn't live with who I'd become when I was cut off from the rest of my being. But now, after everything we've been through, what I can't live with is knowing who I would have been instead, if that had never happened. I can't live with knowing what the rest of me became."

"Because they never lost their innocence."

"What?" she said. The air left her lungs. "Yes. That's one way to say it."

She held her hands in front of her. They were quivering slightly as she said, "There was so much blood when I killed Curtis. I couldn't wash it off. I wake up and my hands still feel the heat of him. It was like my life ended back there, and I just kept running. And yet . . . without that experience, without all my remorse, nothing I could have said or done would have been enough to make the Whole act. It was only my guilt that. . . ."

"That made them understand they weren't inherently better than the rest of humankind," he finished for her.

She looked at him.

"Alexei," she said, her voice suddenly shaking. "I remember now. There was something I—*we* realized, while we were connected, after the rocket attack. In the link between us, for just a second, I understood something that neither of us could have figured out on our own—"

"—That our guilt is valuable," he said. "That it's something we need to keep alive. That the same thing that's been killing us both—"

"—is the very thing that makes us people worth being," she finished.

He closed his eyes in thought.

"We don't have to do this," she said suddenly. "We have another option. We could unify."

"Us?" He took a breath. "You would unify with me?"

"Yes."

"But I'm a monster."

"So am I."

"I'm responsible for so many deaths."

"So am I."

"From everything you've told me, I should be the last person on Earth you would ever consider unifying with."

She nodded. "You would have been. But I've changed. I have to."

"No, listen. Nothing can ever make up for the harm I've done. I'm beyond redemption. Beyond forgiveness. Do you understand that?"

"I do. And so am I."

He swallowed hard. "I'm not that kid you remember. And you're not Eryn. I have to stop thinking of you as her."

She grabbed his hand. "I *am* Eryn. The body that used that name, that first added all of Eryn's experiences and thoughts and personality to the sum of me, is dead—but I am her. And you, you're the killer this world has made you into, but you're also still that boy."

He focused on his breath and struggled to hold himself together. She lay her hands on the wrist he would have cut, and he held them back tightly.

"And me," she said, "I know now what happens when I let myself believe I'm better or purer or more innocent than everyone else. When I let myself think I could ever transcend the human condition. I've seen now where that leads, and I refuse to ever think that way again. As long as I exist, I swear that none of me, no one who ever unifies, will ever think that again. That's my one rule now."

They pulled closer to one another, until he could feel her breath as she told him:

"Nothing is ever going to redeem us. Either of us. You're right about that. But we can still make our life mean something. Not in spite of who we are, but because of it. We can be what the Whole was supposed to be. We can protect humankind—not like a parent looking down on it, but as part of it, fatal flaws and unforgivable sins and all. We can help it heal."

Alexei kept his eyes closed. He said, "It will be like dying, in a way, won't it? We'll cease to exist as the people we are now."

"Yes. But we'll also be reborn. We'll become something new." She waited. "Do you understand everything I'm saying?"

"No."

She took a deep breath and asked, "Do you want to?"

He opened his eyes and met hers, suddenly calm.

"Yes," he said.

She raised her hands and held them open toward him, and he mirrored the motion. Carefully, and with a kind of reverence, they held each other's heads and leaned in to one another.

They willed.

You know who I am. I'm Danae, with all the 223 lives whose combined memory and experiences amounted to her consciousness—and I am Alexei, with all the lives he took. I'm more than the sum of those parts: I am all the things neither of them were capable of doing, or being, or realizing, as long as they were separate; connections they couldn't make, thoughts too complex to fit inside a single head, emotions too vast to pump through the chambers of one heart.

I'm still figuring out what it means to be their gestalt. I know I always will be, but never more than in these first days. I ask myself while my two bodies tend to each other's wounds. Sometimes they talk aloud; other times I share what I'm thinking directly, without need for language. I meditate on it while I walk through the streets of Phoenix on two pairs of feet. Once or twice I let myself laugh at the name of this town: it's as good a place as any to begin again.

It'll take time to put my new memory into an order I can make sense of. I need to understand how different I am from my constituent selves. I think of the things they each yearned for so desperately, that I no longer want or need: I accept that I'll never be whole, nor forgiven. I'm guilty of all their crimes, and no amount of good will ever erase the evil I've done—but erasing it is not my goal.

As I walk, there's a chill on the air, and a greasy shadow that falls over the sun, and the people of this hollowed-out wasteland town look up with so much fear. They've lived all their lives under the threat of storms harsh enough to wipe places like this off the face of the war-torn Earth, and they know in their bones when a new one is brewing. Maybe the worst yet.

But I know things, too. When I turn the Whole's parting gift between my palms and focus, they all bloom so vividly in my mind: the innermost workings of cells and molecules and subatomic particles; the comprehensible language of all matter and energy and motion; the most basic foundational principle to the most chaotic emergent quality. I know how to cure the plagues and halt the famines. I know how to turn the sky blue again.

I think I know how to heal this dying world.

There's only one hope I carry with me now: that I could be the right person to do it. I've maimed and killed, feared and hated— but I have also loved, rescued, protected, created, and given birth. I contain everything that is human—and finally, after everyone I've been, none of it is beyond my understanding. Because I *am* understanding. I am unity.

And you, I think, meeting my own eyes—

You are me.

AFTERWORD

I WAS STILL IN HIGH SCHOOL when I started writing the first version of Unity. (Note: I solemnly swear not to take eighteen years to write my next novel.) A dear friend asked me whether it was possible for two people to perfectly understand one another, and that simple question blew my teenage mind wide open, because I had no good answer. I tried to imagine what such a true understanding would be like, and what it would change about being human. I started writing what I thought was a short story—and for nearly two decades I kept it on the back burner, chipping away at it in tiny but relentless increments.

Meanwhile, I grew up into a world ruled by severe disagreements, failures of empathy, and willful refusals to understand. I wrote some chapters while coming out as trans, others while weathering intense loneliness and isolation in my 20s, others while making incredible human connections in my early 30s (much love to Team Eclipse). I revised between protesting multiple wars, living through multiple economic collapses, and watching climate change nibble away at coastal cities. Now the finished novel is going to press in the midst of an historic pandemic, while a fragmented nation wrestles with the very definition of the word "unity"—whether it should be a call for violently enforced homogeneity, or a celebration of everything that becomes possible when very different cultures, memories, and ways of being are allowed to coexist and share experiences.

This story has radically changed in the time it's taken me to tell it—as radically as the world has, and I have, over those same years. On behalf of all the people I've been from then to now, thanks for taking the trip with me.

Elly Bangs,
March 2021

ABOUT THE AUTHOR

Elly Bangs was raised in a New Age cult and once rode her bicycle alone from Washington State to the Panama Canal. She lives in Seattle. Her short fiction has appeared in *Clarkesworld, Beneath Ceaseless Skies, Escape Pod*, and others, and she's a graduate of Clarion West (Class of 2017). Learn more about her at elbangs.com.